IN A WORLD OF SHADOW

Ashok reappeared crouched in the kindling tree's boughs, his insubstantial form a hovering storm cloud, his cloak fanned over the branches like a veil. The remaining hounds surrounded the tree, leaping straight into the air, their fangs shredding bark and needles.

ONE CITY IS A BEACON IN THE NIGHT

Ashok waited. In his form, he felt nothing—not his wounds, not the bone scales of the armor pressed against his chest, or the branches caressing his face with needles. He longed to feel them. With the pain gone he was an empty shell, adrift on the barren plain. He waited impatiently to get back in the battle while the hounds tore apart the tree.

AND ONLY ONE MAN CAN SAVE IT

Slowly, it seemed to Ashok—when only a few breaths had passed—he felt his flesh solidify on his bones. His weight pressed down on the kindling branches—creaking, straining, but they held him. The needle branches opened small wounds on his cheeks. The pain in his shoulder and bent leg had reached a peak. Then dizziness engulfed him, and Ashok knew the fight was almost over. His body had reached its limits at last. Soon the pain would give way to oblivion.

But he would enjoy every breath he had left.

IF FIRST, HE CAN SAVE HIMSELF

Ashok grabbed the branches. He unwrapped and needles.

"Time to eat, pups,"

UNBROKEN CHAIN

Throughout the Shadowfell, live the strange shadar-kai, a people of shadow who live only as long as they can find sensations in their gray and fading lives—people like Ashok, a chainfighter. But in the city of Ikemmu are those who have learned to use their fierce need for adrenalin and danger to better their city and their civilization.

Also by

JALEIGH JOHNSON

UNBROKEN CHAIN

JALEIGH JOHNSON

UNBROKEN CHAIN

©2010 Wizards of the Coast LLC

All characters in this book are fictitious. Any resemblance to actual persons, living or dead, is purely coincidental.

This book is protected under the copyright laws of the United States of America. Any reproduction or unauthorized use of the material or artwork contained herein is prohibited without the express written permission of Wizards of the Coast LLC.

Published by Wizards of the Coast LLC

FORGOTTEN REALMS, WIZARDS OF THE COAST, and their respective logos are trademarks of Wizards of the Coast LLC in the U.S.A. and other countries.

Printed in the U.S.A.

Cover art by Cos Koniotis

First Printing: July 2010

9 8 7 6 5 4 3 2 1

ISBN: 978-0-7869-5626-5
ISBN: 978-0-7869-5760-6 (e-book)
620-24745000-001-EN

U.S., CANADA, ASIA, PACIFIC, & LATIN AMERICA	EUROPEAN HEADQUARTERS
Wizards of the Coast LLC	Hasbro UK Ltd
P.O. Box 707	Caswell Way
Renton, WA 98057-0707	Newport, Gwent NP9 0YH
+1-800-324-6496	GREAT BRITAIN
	Save this address for your records.

Visit our web site at www.wizards.com

Welcome to Faerûn, a land of magic and intrigue, brutal violence and divine compassion, where gods have ascended and died, and mighty heroes have risen to fight terrifying monsters. Here, millennia of warfare and conquest have shaped dozens of unique cultures, raised and leveled shining kingdoms and tyrannical empires alike, and left long forgotten, horror-infested ruins in their wake.

A LAND OF MAGIC

When the goddess of magic was murdered, a magical plague of blue fire—the Spellplague—swept across the face of Faerûn, killing some, mutilating many, and imbuing a rare few with amazing supernatural abilities. The Spellplague forever changed the nature of magic itself, and seeded the land with hidden wonders and bloodcurdling monstrosities.

A LAND OF DARKNESS

The threats Faerûn faces are legion. Armies of undead mass in Thay under the brilliant but mad lich king Szass Tam. Treacherous dark elves plot in the Underdark in the service of their cruel and fickle goddess, Lolth. The Abolethic Sovereignty, a terrifying hive of inhuman slave masters, floats above the Sea of Fallen Stars, spreading chaos and destruction. And the Empire of Netheril, armed with magic of unimaginable power, prowls Faerûn in flying fortresses, sowing discord to their own incalculable ends.

A LAND OF HEROES

But Faerûn is not without hope. Heroes have emerged to fight the growing tide of darkness. Battle-scarred rangers bring their notched blades to bear against marauding hordes of orcs. Lowly street rats match wits with demons for the fate of cities. Inscrutable tiefling warlocks unite with fierce elf warriors to rain fire and steel upon monstrous enemies. And valiant servants of merciful gods forever struggle against the darkness.

A LAND OF
UNTOLD ADVENTURE

DEDICATION

To Tim, for being the best part of every day,
and to my mom and dad, for always being there
to help me get through the rough spots.

ACKNOWLEDGMENTS

Many thanks must go to my editor, Erin Evans,
for believing in the possibility of Ashok, and to my
brother, Jeff, for long car rides spent discussing
shadar-kai culture. Their patience and insight
helped this book come alive.

I will speak of shadow. The known world, Toril, has its mirrors and doorways—some that shroud the way to another realm entirely, a dark landscape where the souls of the living and the dead entwine. We call this realm the Shadowfell. It exists alongside our world, embraces it, a dim reflection and a passage all the dead must take to their eternal rest or ruin. But I want to speak of the living, of the beings that breathe, think, and feel within the nightmare realm. How can anything exist in a world of shadow? That was the question that haunted me, the reason I stepped through the Veil.

—Tatigan Carrlock, Collected Observations of Ikemmu, The Year of the Ageless One (1479 DR)

CHAPTER ONE

18 Nightal, The Year of the Ageless One (1479 DR)

The shadow hounds chased Ashok across the plain to the base of the Aloran Tor.

In the lee of the towering mountain grew a solitary tree, a gnarled mass of trunk and trident fork branches covered in black needles that were sharp to the touch and could cut if raked over tender skin. It cast a discomfiting shadow. Ashok's people, the shadar-kai, called it a kindling tree, for its wood was only good to burn.

The Aloran Tor, always a thumbprint of distance on his longest journeys. The plain yawned wide and hazy for miles, a colorless patchwork of scrub grass and cracked soil. Overhead, clouds hung oppressively low in the sky.

In the perpetual half-light of the Shadowfell, there was no day and no night, only a long stretch of sameness broken by dust storms or stinging rain.

He'd walked through both, and the hounds had followed.

Ashok clutched a dagger in his left hand and a spiked chain in his right. He used the former to draw a rough circle around the kindling tree. The eroded soil parted easily for his blade.

When he was done he pressed two fingers into the oozing bite wound in his thigh. Pain ran slick knots up his spine, and Ashok shuddered with pleasure. The pain sharpened him. He was aware of everything, every sound in the private wilderness: the wind, his heartbeat and ragged breathing, the wing rush of a raven landing in the tree.

Ashok looked up at the bird. Its attention was fixed on the blood coating his fingers. Blood was the brightest color for miles. Ashok smiled.

"Not yet," he said.

He put a knee to the plain. "For your feast, pups," he said, tracing the circle in blood. "Take this blood, but come no farther."

Still crouched, Ashok gazed across the plain to the west. Amid the howling winds he detected another sound, one he'd been waiting for: the baying of hounds. They'd run their prey to ground at last.

Four immense shadow mastiffs charged the Tor, their bodies drawing in what little light suffused the Shadowfell, until all Ashok could see were the creatures' eyes—metallic silver points buried in rolls of obsidian flesh.

"Come ahead!" Fierce, defiant laughter exploded in Ashok's throat. He pounded his chest with his fists and sprang to his feet. His wound was on fire. He reveled in the pain and the blood oozing down his leg.

So alive . . .

Ashok sheathed his dagger and whipped the chain above his head, launching one end into the kindling tree. The shadow raven cried out in deep-throated alarm and took flight. The chain's spikes looped around a thick branch and caught. Ashok held the other end of the chain and braced his good leg against the tree trunk.

Two of the hounds vanished as they reached Ashok's bloody perimeter. The others pressed their drooling muzzles into the ground, their teeth bared and craving, starved for Ashok's blood. The distraction bought Ashok a few breaths more to live.

The other two hounds reappeared in a shadowy vortex directly in front of Ashok. Their muscled hindquarters tensed, and the creatures sprang at him. Ashok used the tree trunk to push off and swung on the chain. His momentum carried him past the first hound and into the second. The force of impact was like kicking a stone wall.

Ashok let go of the chain and fell on top of the hound. Snapping teeth clipped his chin and neck, barely missing the tender veins. Ashok rolled with the beast, over and over, until he could grab his dagger from its sheath. He buried the curved blade in the hound's neck.

Howling, the hound teleported several feet away to die, leaving Ashok with a bloody dagger and the second hound bearing down on him.

The beast hit him in the back and drove Ashok flat to his stomach, his face pressed into the dirt. He could smell the gamey hound and his own blood from the circle. The hound bit him in the shoulder, its fangs tearing through clothing and armor and flesh. Ashok felt the pain explode down his arm. His vision went white around the edges, and his left arm was suddenly numb.

He forced his body into a crouch, spilling the beast off his back before it could tear his arm off. The other two hounds shook off their blood frenzy and charged.

Ashok lunged to his feet and vanished.

He reappeared crouched in the kindling tree's boughs, his insubstantial form a hovering storm cloud, his cloak fanned over the branches like a veil. The remaining hounds surrounded the tree, leaping straight into the air, their fangs shredding bark and needles.

Ashok waited. In his weightless form, he felt nothing—not his wounds, not the bone scales of the armor pressed against his chest, or the branches caressing his face with needles. He longed to feel them. With the pain gone he was an empty shell, adrift on the barren plain. He waited impatiently to get back in the battle while the hounds tore apart the tree.

Slowly, it seemed to Ashok—when only a few breaths had passed—he felt his flesh solidify on his bones. His weight pressed down on the kindling branches—creaking, straining, but they held him. The needle branches opened small wounds on his cheeks. The pain in his shoulder and bent leg had reached a peak. Then dizziness engulfed him, and Ashok knew the fight was almost over. His body had reached its limits at last. Soon the pain would give way to oblivion.

But he would enjoy every breath he had left.

Ashok grabbed the dangling chain still buried in the branches. He unwrapped the other end, jerking it free of bark and needles.

"Time to eat, pups," he said, and jumped.

Uwan nodded to the guard as he passed and entered into the temple. It was lit only by a row of candelabra behind the altar. He saw Natan kneeling before the massive sword of Tempus carved into the concave wall; its blade absorbed the candles' glow and sank the light into the shadows.

The vestments of Tempus hung loose and shapeless on the thin body of the cleric. His head was shaved, and behind his ear was a small tattoo of a bird's wing. Uwan knew that beneath the vestments, a much larger tattoo of a sword stretched from Natan's shoulder blades to the small of his back. Uwan's back bore a similar marking. He noticed with dismay how Natan's gray flesh looked sickly even in the candles' glow. The cleric's cheekbones and the lines of his jaw were sharply defined.

"How long has he been here?" Uwan asked the guard.

"Since the Pendron bell, my Lord," the guard said. He stayed at rigid attention, with his eyes fixed unflinchingly on Uwan.

"I see." replied Uwan. "Stand outside the door, if you would."

When the guard had left, Uwan crossed the room in a straight line toward Natan. There were no benches in the temple to impede movement—services were conducted with the crowd standing, their collective gazes focused on Tempus's sword.

Uwan stopped a few feet away from his friend. "Have you slept?" he asked.

Natan raised his bald head stiffly. He shifted to look at Uwan but stayed on his knees. "I was dreaming about hounds," he said. His eyes were black like Uwan's own.

Uwan nodded. "I hear them too sometimes." he replied. "The echoes from the caverns—"

"No," Natan said. "My Lord, I saw something."

Uwan felt a surge of excitement in his blood. "Tempus has spoken to you?" he exclaimed.

"At last," Natan replied.

A soft breeze stirred the candle flames. Uwan told himself it was the natural air currents moving through the tower, but the sword carving glowed in the sudden movement of the candles' light.

My Lord, I feel you, Uwan thought as he swallowed. "What was the vision?" he asked.

"A person, my Lord," Natan said, "a shadar-kai, but not of this city."

"You're certain?"

"He has never touched Ikemmu's soil."

Uwan nodded. "One of Tempus's agents, then," he said. "What of him?"

"An ephemeral image," Natan said. "Not enough to tell whom he serves."

"What is your feeling—fair or foul?" Uwan asked.

"I don't know. My Lord, I urge you to be cautious," Natan said as he rose up on his knees with his head bowed to lay his hand on

Uwan's gauntlet. Uwan got on his own knees, impatient with such gestures.

"My Lord!" Natan exclaimed.

"Tell me," Uwan hissed as he clutched the cleric's thin shoulders. He was strong; his arms were thick and encased in shadowmail and a greatsword was strapped to his side. His white hair hung past his shoulders, the strands so thin and pale as to be colorless against his gray skin.

Natan's eyes lost focus as he recalled his vision. "The baying of hounds," he said, "I saw shadow ravens wheeling high above an open plain. They looked down on a circle of flame, my Lord. This shadar-kai was standing in the fire. He held the flames in his hands, wielded them like a weapon."

"A sword," Uwan said. "The sword of Tempus. He is sent by our god, Natan. He must be."

"My Lord, there is more," Natan said. "The fire . . . It was the city. Ikemmu was burning. There is danger here."

"From what threat?" Uwan demanded. Who would *dare?* he thought. "The drow or the surface world?"

"Tempus would not tell me."

"No, of course he wouldn't," Uwan said. Defending the city was his task. "Anything else?"

"No, my Lord," Natan said. Sorrow deepened the hollows of his face. It pained Uwan to see his friend in such a state.

"Natan, you must take hope from this vision," Uwan said. His heart beat rapidly, though he tried to assert control. It was difficult for Uwan to contain his emotions when his god spoke to him, as He did through Natan. "Don't you see? This is the sign we have been waiting for. This shadar-kai will bring the blessing we have sought. I am sure of it."

"I do have hope, my Lord. But still I beg you be wary," Natan said. "We know nothing of this shadar-kai. If he comes here, he comes from the Shadowfell."

"You mean that he will not be like us," Uwan said, nodding. "I understand you. We will take precautions."

"Not only that, my Lord," Natan said. "Remember, when this shadar-kai comes, he will bring the fire. I have seen it."

"Perhaps," Uwan said. "Perhaps not. Trust Tempus, Natan. He will not lead us astray. Now, tell me this shadar-kai's face—draw it if you must. I'll send out patrols before Exeden chimes. We'll find him."

"Yes, my Lord," Natan answered.

"Blessed be Tempus's sword," Uwan said, touching his chest.

Natan mirrored the gesture. "Blessed be us all," he replied.

The shadar-kai patrol traveled across the plain of the Shadowfell above for a day and a night before they came upon the Aloran Tor and the kindling tree. Four shadow hound corpses lay sprawled beneath the needle branches like rotting fruit. Among them lay the body of a young shadar-kai man.

Cree moved swiftly from hound to hound, prodding with his katars to make certain they were all dead. Had he been his brother, Skagi, he would simply have chopped off their heads with his falchion. Blunt, Cree thought, and unnecessary.

When the patrol had secured the area, Cree sheathed his weapons. "Is he dead?" Cree asked Skagi, who was kneeling next to the prone shadar-kai.

Skagi bent over and looked for the rise and fall of the shadar-kai's breath. "He breathes," Skagi said, his gaze roving over the bites covering the shadar-kai's body. "I don't know how, but he lives."

Cree came up beside him. "That's him," he said. "See the scars on his neck? Three claw marks under the jaw, and part of the left earlobe missing too, exactly like Uwan said."

Skagi nodded. His muscular arms were relaxed at his sides, but his hands never strayed far from his falchion. He went bare-chested to show off a field of dark green tattoos covering the left half of his body like a shroud. He wore black breeches and unlike Cree, his head was shaved. His lower lip was slightly deformed from a dagger slash, the flesh crooked and jutting as if he had something lodged in his teeth.

"He's been out on the plain for days," Skagi said. "No telling how long he's been unconscious."

The shadar-kai's lips were cracked, and his face was swollen and chapped by the vicious winds. Thick braids of long gray hair were blood-matted. Cree thought the man looked about Skagi's age, not yet cresting his twenty-fifth winter.

Skagi picked up the shadar-kai's chain lying beside him. "He carries a reaping weapon. Looks like he cut the hounds up fine with it."

"Where do you think he came from?" Cree asked.

"Not our concern," Skagi said. "Make a litter," he added, instructing the rest of the patrol, and pointing at Cree. "Help me clog this bleeding. Our only job now is to get him back to Ikemmu alive. Uwan can deal with him."

"The Watching Blade sees all," Cree agreed, and they set to work.

CHAPTER TWO

Awareness returned slowly to Ashok's mind. With his eyes closed, he thought he was still lying on the open plain, but everything about his body felt wrong. His chest rose and fell without impediment—the hound no longer held him down with its putrid weight—and there was no fire in his breath, no pain eating up his lungs.

He spread his fingers against the ground and felt softness, cloth brushing against his bare skin. He had almost forgotten what "soft" felt like.

Not the earth then, or tree needles, but something else entirely, something he'd never felt before. Ashok's thoughts drifted—was it death? His flesh in the mouths of the hounds? But there was no pain.

Peace numbed his mind and threatened to carry him off to unwaking sleep. His soul was a separate entity from his body, towed on a string carried by the bloodthirsty raven.

The raven waiting in the kindling tree . . . A drifting soul . . .

Not yet.

Ashok lurched awake and sat upright. His head swam as his spirit slammed back into the corporeal and tried to hold on. Shivering violently at the displacement, the weight and weightlessness, he dragged in breath after breath, his hands clawing for the dagger on his belt. It wasn't there.

Wildly, Ashok felt around for something sharp, anything that would cut. His skin went numb, first at the fingertips, then up his arms. Everything was soft, blunt edges, nothing that could hurt him.

"Not yet!" Air hissed through clenched teeth, with a whimper like that of a dying animal.

Ashok put his hand to his mouth, his teeth finding the soft flesh of his inner wrist. Biting down, he sighed in light-headed triumph when the skin broke and pain shot up his arm. Blood filled his mouth, making him gag, but Ashok didn't care. As soon as the pain took over, the numbness went away, and focus returned.

Not yet. He wasn't going to fade. Not yet.

When he'd taken in enough of the pain, Ashok dropped his arm and spat a bloodstain on the stone floor. Wiping his mouth, he tried to get his bearings.

He was in a narrow chamber, lit faintly by lanterns fastened halfway up the walls. His vision adjusted to the low light, and he could perfectly see the line of beds that filled the chamber. A few were occupied with sleeping forms, including the bed next to his, but the majority sat empty.

Ashok looked down at himself. A thin blanket covered the lower half of his body. The cloth and the bedding underneath him were the softness he'd felt. He'd been stripped to the waist, and his weapons were gone. He didn't even have his boots.

The wounds in his thigh and shoulder had been bandaged and treated with herbs. Ashok could smell them when he touched the wrappings, and he felt a slight heat. He touched his forehead and realized he was sweating, yet the chamber was cold. The bites were infected.

Whoever brought him here had taken pains to treat him, and had probably saved his life. His captors obviously didn't intend to kill him.

Not yet.

Ashok slipped from his bed and moved around the room, thankful for his bare feet in that he stepped, without sound, right up to the other beds. The sleeping occupants were bandaged as carefully as he was, and none of them had any weapons to hand.

All were shadar-kai.

He'd been captured by another enclave. Ashok cursed his ill fortune at not having bled to death sooner out on the plain. The only reason he was still alive was to provide information. His captors would torture him, to start. And when he refused to break, they would bring a wizard in to tear open his mind and take from it every bit of information on the strength of his enclave, its numbers and resources. He had to find a way out or a quick death before that happened.

The chamber had only one door. Ashok went to it and put his ear against the wood. He heard muffled voices, at least three.

"Three guards," Ashok murmured. He tapped the door in soundless contemplation. "Any chance you have my weapons, faceless friends? Or can I borrow your own to kill you?"

Behind him, Ashok heard a gasp. He spun, his hand going for a chain that no longer hung at his hip.

The shadar-kai in the bed next to his was sitting up, half hanging over the side of the bed. He clutched the frame, his body jerking in spasms, one leg held at an unnatural angle, as if he wanted nothing more than to shed the appendage. He'd been wounded in the thigh, like Ashok, and the wound had reopened, filling the bandage with blood and sickly yellow pus.

"Help . . . me," he whispered.

Ashok glanced at the door. The voices were still speaking, but he couldn't make out the words.

"I ask you!" The shadar-kai's voice rang against the walls. Outside the door, the voices fell silent.

Ashok backed quickly away from the door and went to the shadar-kai. He pushed the man back onto the bed. "Be quiet," he hissed. He didn't want the guards to investigate the noise. They would see he was awake, and the interrogation would begin. He needed more time.

"Who . . . are you?" the man said. His glazed obsidian eyes searched Ashok's face, but Ashok could see his concentration fading in and out. Only the pain kept him conscious.

Only the pain, always the pain.

"I'm the one you begged for aid," Ashok said. He touched the edge of the man's wound, probing skin that was on fire. "Your leg is rotting. You need a prayer, or you're going to die."

"Only She . . . can help . . . me," the man said, his teeth chattering. "Lady Beshaba! Hear me!" he called.

Ashok kneeled by the bed and grabbed the back of the man's head, pressing his other hand against his mouth to form a vice. "If you don't stay quiet, you won't draw your next breath. Do you believe me?"

Dazed as he was, the man nodded. A hint of fear worked its way through the fever pain.

"I'm going to uncover your mouth," Ashok said, "and you're going to answer my questions. Convince me you're telling the truth, and I'll let you live. Understood?"

Another nod.

Ashok removed his hand from the man's mouth but kept a grip on his skull. "Are we still in the Shadowfell?" he asked.

"The Shadowdark," the man replied.

"Near the Aloran Tor?"

Confusion. "I don't know what that is."

Ashok jerked the man's sweat damp hair. "You're lying. The black mountain—a yawning maw pointed to the west."

"Y-Yes," the man said. "We call it Dark Crest."

"Who is 'we'?" Ashok said. "Where is this place?"

"Ikemmu," the man said as his shoulders jerked. His mouth twisted in a smile that stretched uglily over his teeth. Ashok thought he was on the edge of delirium. "You're in . . . Ikemmu," the man said. "The Watching Blade . . . sees all."

He raised his hand and swiped the air as if reaching for something. Ashok followed the fevered gesture and saw, above the lanterns, an enormous sword carved into the wall. He hadn't noticed the sword at first, but looking upon it fully, the weapon seemed to fairly swallow the room with its presence. It drew in the shadows and light, forcing Ashok's eye to focus on it wherever he stood in the room. Everything else diminished in its presence.

The wall around the carving had been bricked in faint red and shaped to form a shield beneath the sword. The brick and the lantern glow combined lit the whole scene afire. A strange, disturbed sensation crawled along Ashok's spine. He had an errant thought: the sleeping shadar-kai weren't alone in the room. They never had been. Someone else was there watching, waiting.

Ashok shook off the feeling. The man's delirium was starting to affect him. He was wasting time.

"How big is this place?" he demanded. "How many guards?"

The man tried to speak, but his teeth were clamped so tightly together that gurgles and foam were all that came out. The shadar-kai's eyes rolled up in his head, and his body jerked in violent spasms that rocked the bed. Ashok could barely hold him.

The door opened. Before Ashok could react, a slender, bald shadar-kai entered the room and walked briskly over to them. He wore a black tabard embroidered with a smaller rendering of the carving on the wall. Ashok went into a defensive crouch, but the cleric ignored him and took the spasming man by the shoulders. The wounded shadar-kai stared past him, his eyes eaten up with the sword on the wall.

"Arnare, do you hear me?" the shadar-kai said. "Arnare, we're losing you. You must reconsider your decision. You must let me heal you."

The man tried to jerk free, but he had no strength. "She will come."

Impatience ticked the cleric's face. "We've sent for the Beshaban clerics once a bell for the past day. They've not responded. By the time they come it may be too late."

The man's head lolled to the side, as if he couldn't support its weight. "Then that . . . is my fate. Beshaba's hand. No . . . other." With a surge of strength, the man shoved the cleric away. "*None.*"

Ashok watched the exchange in wary silence. He knew he should have run, or attacked the cleric while he was distracted, but confusion rendered him immobile. Why did the cleric waste time speaking to the man? he wondered. He should have healed or killed him instantly.

Sighing, the cleric let the fevered man sink back on the bed. He pulled the blanket up over his shivering body.

"A waste," the cleric murmured. His gaze rested on Ashok. "You're awake. Are you in pain?"

The cleric took a step toward him. Ashok bared his teeth and lunged at him.

"Back," the cleric said calmly, raising a hand.

A massive weight slammed Ashok in the chest, driving him back against the wall. Dazed, he slid to the floor. When he looked up, the cleric continued to approach. Weaponless, Ashok put his hands up in front of him.

"What have you done to yourself?" the cleric demanded. He pointed at Ashok's bleeding wrist, the crescent-shaped bite wound.

Ashok ignored the question. "Who are you?" he said as his blood dripped onto the floor.

The cleric clasped his arms behind his back, but Ashok wasn't appeased by the gesture. He stayed in a crouch, an animal cornered. *I'll take your eyes first*, his stance promised.

"I am a servant of Tempus," the cleric said. "You were brought to His temple because your wounds were life-threatening. I bandaged and treated them with herbs, but you still need healing. I was waiting for you to awaken so I could ask your permission."

"My permission?" said Ashok, a snarl building in his throat. "You ask a slave's permission before you put the knife to him?"

"You're mistaken," the cleric said. "There are no slaves here, no torturers."

"Aren't I a prisoner?"

The cleric shook his head. "Perhaps someday you will see how we treat our prisoners," he said. "No, you are here at the behest of Uwan, Lord of Ikemmu, Watching Blade who guides us all."

Ashok felt his gaze inadvertently drawn to the sword carved on the wall.

The cleric followed his look. "Tempus's hand," he said. "Will you allow Him to heal you, through me? I swear no harm will come to you."

No harm. Ashok knew better. The magic would bore into his brain, expose his enclave's secrets. No, he couldn't let that happen.

Ashok turned to the wall. He would bash his head on the stones. One quick impact was all it would take.

"No!" the cleric cried, too late.

Ashok slammed his head into the wall. He collapsed on the floor, his vision hazy. The cleric moved above him, but his face seemed very far away. His lips were moving; Ashok could barely make out the words.

"Forgive me, but I cannot let you die. Father of Battle, touch your warrior," the cleric chanted. "Give him the strength to fight anew and the wisdom to see the folly in harming this most perfect vessel. Tempus, bless us both."

The cleric fell silent. He had one hand on his chest and the other on Ashok's head. A serene quiet overtook his visage, as if he were waiting patiently for someone to whisper a secret in his ear.

Between one breath and the next, Ashok felt the sharp pain in his head and wrist subside to a dull ache, and then his vision slowly cleared.

When Ashok looked at him in confusion, the cleric said, "Now do you believe that I will not harm you?"

Cautiously, Ashok rose to his feet. He sat on the edge of his bed and stripped the bandages from his thigh and shoulder. He wiped away the herb concoctions and saw that the wounds were healed.

"You need more sleep," the cleric said. "To replenish your strength. My name is Natan. What may I call you?"

Ashok hesitated, then gave his name.

The cleric nodded. "Where do you come from, Ashok?" he asked.

So the interrogation begins, Ashok thought. He stayed silent, watching carefully as the cleric wadded up the soiled bandages and straightened the blankets on Ashok's bed. Briefly, he went to check the fevered man, and his face creased in disappointment.

"He won't last to Pendron," Natan said. "Blood-thirsty Beshabans." He threw the bandages on the floor in disgust. "Fight your *enemy*—never neglect your own."

A feeling like hot iron swam in Ashok's chest. He stared at the dying man, whose entire body lay rigid, as if he were already a stiffening corpse.

"Just do it," Ashok said. "He's helpless. He won't fight you."

The cleric looked at him in mild surprise, then shook his head. "That is not His way. A warrior has the right to choose his own death."

Ashok turned away. The chamber door stood slightly ajar, beckoning.

Natan saw where he was looking. "Do you come from the empire, Ashok? Is that where you will run?"

"No," Ashok said. "I'll run far across the plain until the Aloran Tor is a black hillock in the distance, and the Mire River runs dry. I'll hide in the kindling forests and bury my trail in the trees. You'll die in the wilderness trying to follow me."

Natan sighed and raised his hands in surrender. "As you wish. Though the path to the surface is not an easy one. Stay here at least until the next bell chimes. By then you'll be rested enough to travel."

The cleric moved from bed to bed as he spoke, checking the other wounded. He lingered next to one, his hand on an older shadar-kai's chest. After a few breaths, he shook his head.

"Another waste," he said, "a prayer unanswered."

Natan went to the door. "Bring a litter in here," he called out to someone. "This one is gone."

Ashok tensed when two more shadar-kai clerics entered the room, but they paid no attention to him. Between them, they placed the limp body on the litter and carried it solemnly out of the room.

Natan watched them go and turned to Ashok. "We have not harmed you. Don't waste your life. Rest here, and then we'll talk more."

"Do I have a choice?" Ashok said.

The cleric looked at him for a long time in silence. "No," he said finally, and left the room.

Natan locked the sickroom door behind him, though he sensed it was a futile gesture. If Ashok wanted to, he could tear the door off its hinges.

The clerics set the litter with its burden on the floor.

"Well, my lord?" Natan asked. "Do you believe he is a friend or a foe?"

The body on the litter opened its eyes and sat up. Uwan stripped the fake bandages off his arms. "A rough beginning," he admitted. "But I still believe the will of Tempus brought him here. He will serve Ikemmu."

"Or doom it to the fire," Natan said. "He believes we are the enemy."

"Not surprising," Uwan said. "You were right. He comes from the Shadowfell." He looked at Natan. "We can't let him leave the city."

"Keeping him here might be difficult, my Lord," Natan said. "He gave his name, but he will answer no questions. It is only a matter of time before he attempts to escape."

"He was practically feral when he awoke," Uwan said. His face turned thoughtful. "I lay in that bed because I wanted to get an impression of him, unfettered by any outside influence. I haven't seen that reaction in a long time. I'd forgotten the desperation, the lack of control, how it transforms and imprisons a body."

"Like a hound himself," Natan said. He hesitated then added, "But it seemed that he showed pity for Arnare in his fever."

"At last, something to thank the Beshabans for," Uwan said. He picked up his discarded armor and donned the shadowmail vest. "We have to earn his trust by giving him ours. When he wakes next, give him food and let him leave the tower."

"Alone?" Natan said tightly.

"I'll send Skagi and Cree to watch over him," Uwan said. He belted his greatsword at his waist and threw the black cloak of rank over his shoulders. Tempus's sword cut the fabric down the middle in silver embroidery, the blade a phantom of the weapon at his belt.

"What if he tries to escape?" Natan said.

"I fully expect he will." Uwan smiled. "It promises to be an interesting day."

CHAPTER
THREE

Ashok descended a spiral stone staircase. His prison was a tall tower. At the bottom of the stairs there was a guarded door. A shadar-kai woman in plate armor with a helm and hood covering most of her features stood at attention beside the exit.

Ashok hesitated, his hands aching for his chain and dagger. The familiar weights were absent, held by Natan and the rest of his captors, but they'd given his bone scale armor and shirt back to him, along with his boots and cloak.

Natan had told him he was free to leave the tower. Did the cleric truly expect him to believe that they were going to let him walk freely out of his prison into the open air? His captors were playing with him, giving him a taste of freedom before they tightened his chains.

He would make them regret their foolishness.

Cautiously, Ashok approached the door. The guard stepped aside and opened the door for him herself. Momentarily stunned, Ashok recovered quickly and darted outside. The guard shut the door behind him. He stood alone in an unfamiliar courtyard, at the brink of a city for which he had only a name.

His black eyes transitioned without effort from the light of the tower to the lantern-lit expanse of an underground cavern. Roughly twenty feet ahead of him were the remnants of a stone dwelling.

Two of its walls had collapsed, leaving a small space and plenty of shadows to conceal him. Ashok ran to the dwelling and crouched among the ruined stones.

From his hiding space he beheld a crescent-shaped guard wall in the distance, a thirty foot high stone barrier that abutted steep walls to the north and south. Shadows grew from the guard wall and moved—teleporting from one end to the other like ghosts.

He counted sixty guards, though it was impossible to get an accurate number from such a distance. He knew of only one other shadar-kai enclave that occupied such a defensible position in the Shadowfell.

Ashok reached inside his armor. Long ago, when he'd assembled the pieces of bone, he'd attached an extra strip of leather to the inside of the breast to form a pouch. Too small to hold a weapon, he used it instead to conceal secrets, anything he didn't want his brothers to find. Now he removed a strip of soiled bandage he'd taken from the sickroom. Natan had left the cloth wadded up on the floor. He crouched and picked up a piece of blackened slate from the ground.

Clutching the slate in his hand, he slid his finger along the sharp edge. It opened a small wound that brought a familiar, welcome sense of focus. It was not enough pain to set his heart racing or cause a surge in his veins, but even the small wound was a pleasure. He smeared blood between his thumb and forefinger, and used the latter to ink the number of guards and the height of the wall onto the bandage.

If he could somehow lay his hands on parchment and true ink, he would be able to draw a map of the city. When he managed to escape, he could determine how far the city lay from his own lands, and how far down. The information would be useful to his enclave when determining how much of a threat Ikemmu posed. Once they had all the necessary intelligence, his people would gather, and together they would strike at Ikemmu with all the strength they possessed. Annihilating an enclave of Ikemmu's size would be a triumph such as Ashok's people had never known.

It would bring them back to life again.

He slid the bandage back into the pouch and cautiously ventured out of hiding. The guard wall embraced hundreds of the low, blocky stone buildings like the one in which he stood, some of which had been hollowed out or collapsed by fire. Others had been repaired and were now occupied. Smoke curled from chimneys askew, and torchlight brightened the narrow avenues between structures.

The torches made Ashok pause. With their light it was brighter down here than on the plains of the Shadowfell, where the shadar-kai were most at home. There should be no need of torches.

He saw figures moving between some of the dwellings. Ashok backed into the shadows and crouched down to observe them. A dozen or so were shadar-kai. Small figures moved beside them—dark ones, Ashok thought. The diminutive humanoids had ratlike faces and moved in quick, furtive spurts. They scuttled along behind the shadar-kai, watching for threats from the shadows and from each other. They dressed in black and carried long, curved daggers with black hilts. Some wore scimitars at their belts.

But not all of the figures Ashok beheld were small. He fixed his attention on the other creatures that moved in the torch light.

Warm-skinned, some dark and others light, they possessed strange eyes that were several colors at once in a face. They wore long beards, or none, and their flesh was smooth. Ashok tasted their scent on a sudden draft that blew down through the open end of the cavern— skin and hair redolent of wood smoke, food and sweat. But it was an odd, effusive smell—not the reek of a being native to shadow.

The shadar-kai walked among the strange ones with weapons sheathed, but many did not make eye contact with the warm-skinned beings.

Ashok remembered the lessons his father had taught him, about his own heritage and the races that existed in the world alongside the Shadowfell.

A world he'd never seen.

"Human, dwarf, tiefling . . . ." Ashok whispered the names he could remember as his vision tried to adjust to their appearance. His prison was growing stranger and stranger.

As Ashok watched the different races mixing together, he slowly grew aware of the rest of the city. The shadows and torch light grudgingly resolved themselves into movement, voices, and life. Ashok turned at the sound of falling water, and as he moved from shadow to shadow, coming around the side of the prison tower, his world turned with him and became something very different from all he had experienced before.

Ashok looked up. His vision blurred in the smoke-filled draft, and when it cleared he could take in the truth.

Not one, but four immense obsidian towers scaled the western canyon wall, their tops nearly scraping the immense roof of the city.

The towers rose over a hundred feet and looked from his small vantage to be almost as wide. Ashok could not begin to guess their true girth, or take in the scores of lights shining through open archways up and down the structures. The light-filled portals begged entry into the various tower levels, but Ashok saw the guards standing at each doorway. Their masked, armored forms clutched barbed spears hung with black and red banners—Tempus's sword and a crimson shield. They spiraled up the towers, snapping in the constant breeze.

"Gods," Ashok said, and he laughed out loud in spite of himself. He stepped out of the shadows, spread his arms, and bowed deeply from the waist. "Magnificent!" he cried.

When he could think again, he considered the numbers in his

head. He'd descended a spiral stair ten feet, no more, in the tower he'd just left. There had been a handful of clerics and wounded on that level, and he'd counted six doors leading to others rooms that might have been filled with shadar-kai. And those were just in the towers. More structures filled the landscape around them.

Ashok's mind whirled as he considered the numbers. As many as ten thousand, he calculated, maybe more, but not many less. There was no knowing.

"So this is Ikemmu," he said. "City of towers."

He'd forgotten the sound of falling water. The tower in Ashok's shadow was backed by a massive waterfall that slicked down the cavern wall, darkening the stones and ending in a large basin. The figures of dark ones, as well as the warm-skinned races, flitted about with jugs, collecting water and chattering at each other in the shadar-kai tongue.

Overcome by the grandeur of the city, Ashok put aside his instinct to hide, walked up to the water, and kneeled. The others cleared a path for him and kept their gazes averted. Ashok cupped his hands in the water. He raised the liquid to his lips and drank. It tasted glorious.

Out of the corner of his eye, he saw a shadow slide onto the water. Ashok sliced the basin's surface with the flat of his palm, sending water up in sheets. Squeals and shrieks sounded the dark ones' retreat, but the shadow dodged to the side. Ashok spun and kicked, but the figure that had approached jumped out of the way, and there came movement to Ashok's left.

With no other ready defense, Ashok vaulted the basin and stood to his thighs in the cold water, the stone lip a barrier between himself and two male shadar-kai warriors. The warrior on his left was armed with katars, while the one on the right held an elegant falchion. Hanging from his belt was Ashok's chain and dagger.

"You're a skittish one, aren't you?" the man holding his weapons said, not waiting for an answer. "We're not here to ambush you."

"Just as well," Ashok said. "I'd have killed you if you were." Water flowed past his thighs, its chill biting into his legs and cooling his tensed muscles. "What do you want?"

Amusement played across the shadar-kai's gray features. "We've come to show you the city," said the one with his weapons. He took Ashok's chain off his belt and tossed it at him. Ashok caught the hand guard at one end; the other hit the water, sending wet spikes into the air. His dagger was held out toward him by the curved blade.

Ashok stepped out of the basin, took the weapon by the hilt, and sheathed it. "Are you the leader here?" he said, his eyes taking in the belly of the canyon and the teeming city.

"Not by long ranks. I'm Skagi," the man said. He nodded at his partner. "My brother, Cree."

The other shadar-kai nodded at Ashok and grinned. He was smaller than his brother but quicker, Ashok thought, and silent in his black leather armor. It was Skagi's shadow Ashok had seen first. By the time he'd detected Cree, the man might have had a katar blade in his throat.

Ashok cursed himself. Too slow, fool. Your soul is on the block for the taking. You're letting the city impress you too much.

Ashok wound the chain and hooked it on his belt. "Why return these to me?" he asked.

"Orders," Cree said. "We're to escort you around the city. Anywhere you want to go."

"Except the gate," Ashok said.

"You don't like our hospitality?" Skagi asked. "We saved your life. It was our patrol that found you on the plain."

"I've never seen a lone warrior take on an entire pack of shadow hounds," Cree spoke up. "How did you do it?"

"Cree," Skagi said.

Cree laughed. "My brother wants to pretend he's not curious, but he aches to know as much as I do," he said. "How did you do it?"

"They were going to kill me," Ashok said. "No matter what I did, no matter how I attacked. Once I'd swallowed that, everything after was just good sport."

"For you or for the hounds?" Skagi asked.

Ashok shrugged. "Both," he replied.

The brothers were silent. Skagi watched him appraisingly. Ashok saw he had dark green tattoos covering the left side of his body. The symbols looked like chains and spikes woven together in a complex pattern. Ashok couldn't imagine how long it must have taken to complete the tattoo. In contrast, Cree had only two symbols that Ashok could see: curved blades above each of his temples.

Capable warriors, Ashok thought. More captors sent to watch over him. Maybe he could use them to his advantage.

Ashok turned and faced the guard wall. "Will you take me there?" he asked.

Skagi and Cree exchanged a glance. "You're mad if you think you can escape," Skagi said.

"Who says I'm not mad?" Ashok replied. He removed the chain from his belt and held it ready at his side.

"Go on, Skagi, he's testing you," Cree said. He slapped his brother on the shoulder, but Skagi wasn't paying attention. He was still watching Ashok.

A breath passed, then another, and finally the tension broke. Whatever Skagi had been considering, he'd obviously made his decision, for he grinned and relaxed. "Fine then, if you want a look. Uwan said we were to take you anywhere in the city you wanted to go."

"Uwan," Ashok said, after they'd started off. "He's your leader?"

"For almost as long as we've been alive," Cree said. He pointed to the south, to the fourth tower rising against the canyon wall. Enclosed by an iron fence, the tower was carved up by doorways and guards, the same as the others, but in between them were carvings of Tempus's sword. There were other pictures too: engravings of humanoid beings—not shadar-kai, Ashok thought, but maybe one of the other races he'd seen roaming the city. Vast wings sprouted from the backs of many of them. Even the ones that were barren suggested flight in some form or another, by the positioning of the carvings.

Ashok's gaze drifted up to near the tower's top. Here there was a carved image of a single eye. Outlined in white, it stared down at the fenced tower yard and out over the city.

It was not a large drawing, nor was it as absorbing as the sword carving he'd seen on the wall of the sickroom. Looking at it, Ashok thought it was out of place, hovering above the city, watching, waiting for something to happen.

"Is that where Uwan dwells?" Ashok asked, pointing to the tower and its unblinking eye.

"Most of the time he's below in the training yard," Skagi said. "That's Tower Athanon," he added, pointing to the fenced obsidian. He turned and looked to the tower where Ashok had awoken. "Tower Makthar, the temple home," he continued. "And in the middle, Tower Pyton and Hevalor, the trade houses."

Ashok repeated the names and functions of each tower in his head. The warriors were young, like him, but too eager, too trusting. In his own enclave, they would have been killed long before for these weaknesses.

They reached the outer wall. Guard posts had been set up at various points at the base of the wall and on it. Ashok counted slowly, keeping track of the shadar-kai moving along the wall.

"Convinced?" Cree asked, breaking Ashok's concentration.

"Of the might of Ikemmu? Yes," Ashok answered honestly.

"Caravan inbound!"

The shout came from the south. It was picked up by the other guards and carried the length of the wall.

Cree turned his attention from Ashok. "How far?" he called up to the nearest guard.

"Won't be long," came the reply. "They're moving fast."

"Ready the gate!" came a voice.

Ashok, Cree, and Skagi turned to see a woman standing at the center of the wall near the gate. Her head was shaved, and a tattoo like raking claws covered the back of her bare skull. She wore gray robes with black sleeves and gazed out over the wall, her black eyes unfocused.

"That's the Sworn of the wall," Cree said, pointing to the woman. "Neimal the witch. She holds the flame. No one enters the city without her leave."

"Is she watching the caravan?" Ashok asked.

"It's eating up the last dirt before the portal down to the city," Skagi said. "We open it and the gate ahead of their coming, so the wagons won't stall outside."

"Makes the beasts anxious," Cree said.

"Horses?" Ashok said with a snort. "They should be better trained."

Skagi laughed. Cree shook his head. "You'll see," he said.

They waited at the base of the wall. Ashok looked up. The wall was thirty feet high, just as he'd judged. A pair of spike-studded wooden doors and an iron portcullis comprised the gate. Ten guards with longbows on the wall surrounded the entrance, and five more stood on the ground, directing foot traffic off the main path into the city. From their side of the city, Ashok could see how badly damaged most of the stone dwellings were.

"There was a fire here," Ashok said.

The buildings, even those that had been repaired, were little more than hovels propped up against the greater towers. Ashok noted the dark scars where fire had touched the towers, though that damage was not nearly as severe as that where the flames had raked the lower city.

"It happened before our time," Skagi said.

"Before you were born?" Ashok asked.

"Before any of us," Skagi said.

"Caravan approaching!" called another voice.

It was the Sworn's voice that rang out over the wall. The woman raised her arms. In her left hand she held a black-hilted longsword. She made a gesture with her right hand, and the blade burst into purple flame.

"A warning?" Ashok asked.

"To any who would threaten the caravan or the city while the portal is open," Cree said. "It's under the witch's protection now."

Ashok watched the portcullis go up and the doors slowly begin to open. Beyond them, a rutted path ran for a hundred feet or so and abruptly ended at a cavern wall. A raised stone arch was set into the wall, and on the keystone was the carved sword of Tempus, its blade pointed down toward the ground.

The witch's sword flashed, and the stone arch glowed in answer. As they watched, a line of horse-drawn wagons rumbled through the active portal and approached the city. Their drivers shouted greetings to the guards on the wall.

Ashok's heartbeat sped up. Though it was suicide to make a run for the gate, his body trembled with the need to act. He'd been contained too long. The time to escape was while the witch was watching the caravan, when all their attention was focused on that portal.

"And no one is watching the wall," he said.

The brothers turned as one, but Ashok whipped his chain above his head and vanished, his wild laugh echoing in the air.

He teleported to the top of the wall, reappearing in his wraith form, half walking, half flying. The wall was eight feet thick at its widest point, just before the gate. Beyond lay the portal to the Shadowfell and freedom.

For a breath, Ashok's ghostly presence went unnoticed by the guards, whose attention was fixed on the caravan.

As substance returned to his flesh, Ashok began to run along the wall. He glanced over his shoulder and saw Cree and Skagi appear simultaneously behind him. The hunt was on, and he reveled in the danger.

"Alarm, alarm!" Skagi cried. "The wall is breached!"

Instantly, the warriors on the wall fell into formation, a single line of impenetrable shadows facing Ashok that were bow and spearmen, sword bearers and scouts, led by the bald witch with the flaming sword. She turned with a furious expression to see who had dared breach her line.

The witch's gaze fell on Ashok. Her lips pulled back over her teeth in a wicked smile as she pointed the flaming sword at him. He thought he could feel the arcane heat.

"Take him," she said, a command that carried up and down the line.

The warriors nearest Ashok surrounded him in a half circle, giving him no room to run except back into the city. Ashok struck out with his chain, tangling it with a warrior's blade. He jerked the man forward and punched him in the face. The warrior went down on his knees, exposed, but Ashok had no interest in killing him. He was focused on the hole the man had left behind. Other warriors tried to close the gap, but Ashok freed his chain and whipped again—two quick attacks that slashed across armor, ringing sparks and distracting them just enough for Ashok to plunge through the gap.

He had nowhere to go but the open air.

Behind him, one of the warriors grabbed the loose end of his chain, intending to snap him back, Ashok thought, like an animal on a tether. He dropped his end of the chain, drew his curved dagger, and jumped. He teleported in midair, aiming for the caravan and its horses.

Ashok landed beside one of the wagons. He had only a few breaths before his wraith form solidified. At that point, he could expect arrows to rain down from the wall and pin his corpse to the ground. If he could get to a horse first, use it as cover, or find a hostage . . .

A scream tore through the air. The sound, at once deep and shrill, the scream of a dying warrior, pierced the veil that held Ashok's spirit form. His ears rang, and a wave of terror rolled across him. The cry froze Ashok, scattering his thoughts like ashes.

He pivoted to stare at an iron cage tied to the lead wagon. Behind the bars a black, equine shape towered over him, its hooves striking bronze sparks against the metal. But there were no shoes on the beast to make the fire. Its flame came from within.

The nightmare swiveled its head in the confined space to stare at Ashok through slitted, crimson lights—eyes that had no whites, no room for emotion. But its presence, the aura of terror that bled from the creature conveyed enough. Steam clouds rose from its nostrils, and within the dark cage, fire ran up thick strands of mane, turning them to gold, the horse hair swallowed by embers.

Ashok, caught by the crimson-eyed menace, didn't realize that his form had solidified. He raised his hands, his fingers flexing, when he realized the truth. He looked up at the wall. The shadar-kai archers had their bows trained on him, as he'd expected. But they didn't fire.

The witch was among them, coldly furious, but she held a hand in the air, staying the attack.

Skagi and Cree appeared in front of him. Insubstantial, they caged him with the nightmare at his back. Ashok backed up a step and halted, aware of the nightmare's presence like a blade out of reach. Steam kissed the tender flesh between his shoulder blades.

"You won't kill me," he said to their spirit forms. He could hardly believe it himself as he looked up at the line of death on the wall, the witch with her flaming sword and barely contained wrath, ready to send the fire down and smite him. He thrilled to the moment, how close he'd driven them to the kill, and his heart pounded with exhilaration. "You've been ordered not to kill me—by Uwan," he realized. "Why?"

The wraiths became flesh, and Skagi raised his falchion. "You don't know what you're doing, little Blite. Come with us now, if you don't want—"

"It to hurt?" Ashok said as he opened his arms and stared down the warriors. "Come ahead. Come ahead!"

Cree was on him from the side. Ashok dodged the first katar and looked for the second, but it wasn't in Cree's hand. Ashok twisted, trying to find an opening to get around the man, but Skagi darted in from the left and grabbed him by the throat. With his empty hand, Cree got him by the right forearm. Together they drove him back against the cage bars.

Iron bit into Ashok's flesh, sending numbing waves down his spine. His skull sang with pain, and cloying ash filled his nostrils. The nightmare whinnied its terrible shriek again, but Skagi and Cree did nothing more than wince. Ashok let his knees buckle as the dark horse reared, striking its hooves against the cage bars inches from Ashok's head.

"No you don't," Skagi said, not loosening his grip. "It'll take more screams than that to break you, I'll bet any sum."

Cree grabbed Ashok's shoulder, and with Skagi's hand still at his throat they turned him to face the nightmare.

Blood crusted its withers, and the fetlocks kicked up ash when the creature stamped its feet. Forced to face the menace, Ashok clicked his tongue, as he might to a riding horse.

"Well met, slave," he said, his lips cracking in the dry, hot air. "They caught you too, eh?"

Steam hissed, making his eyes water. Sound rumbled in the nightmare's chest. It paced forward, bones clanging against iron, and Ashok was lost in the crimson radiance of its eyes. The light fed the fires in its mane, burning but never destroying.

"He should be unconscious by now," Skagi said. His voice was barely audible for the roaring in Ashok's ears. He fought the palpable terror emanating from the nightmare's body.

It is an unreasoning fear, he told himself. It doesn't come from you. Don't let it infect the flesh . . .

Straining against the hand at his throat, Ashok threw his weight backward into Skagi's body. Caught by surprise, the man stumbled. Ashok jerked his neck free and sucked in air, but the respite didn't stop the roaring. The nightmare filled every corner of his vision. He couldn't find his feet to run.

There was a sharp rap on the back of his skull—a katar hilt, Ashok thought: the young one was too fast. Ashok fell on his side on the hard ground. He looked up, a sliding glance filled with shadar-kai warriors, Neimal the witch, and the nightmare watching the scene from its cage.

So close. He'd been so close to freedom, only to have it snatched away by that creature. He knew of the nightmares, had heard them screaming on the Shadowfell plain. He had even seen one running down its prey from a distance. But nothing had prepared him for the feeling of hopelessness and terror.

Ikemmu. City of towers. Beacon in the Shadowdark. Home of nightmares. What was this place? he thought, as he slid towards unconsciousness.

The nightmare's crimson eyes were the last thing he saw.

CHAPTER
FOUR

IN THE DREAM, HE SLEPT ON THE GROUND NEXT TO THE DREGS OF a fire and breathed the leftover greasy stink of cooked game. They weren't supposed to light fires so deep in the caves, because the ventilation was poor. Ashok knew he'd be punished for it, but his muscles, weak from fighting, had craved the fresh meat to nourish him.

Ashok opened his eyes in the dark. He heard footsteps coming down the passage.

Which one was coming?

Ashok sat up, the dying embers illuminating his body. There was no armor to don—he wore the bone scales in his sleep. He kept his chain wrapped around his hand, and his dagger rested nearby.

All ready.

Which one would come?

He had no idea how much time had passed since he'd first gone to sleep, but his body felt stretched thin, un-rested. That was how they intended it, of course, his unknown enemy. The odds were better if Ashok was distracted by fatigue.

Keep sleep elusive, his father had told him. *Attrition will win you a battle, and a higher place in the enclave.*

But Ashok had eaten the meat. His foe had eaten none.

He heard the footsteps distinctly—a heavy tread and a bulky form filled the tunnel. Lakesh.

"I'm here, brother," Ashok said. His voice echoed down the tunnel. "Would you speak with me?"

"I would," Lakesh said, "with steel. I'd rather you'd not woken at all."

"Then turn and go back to your bed," Ashok said. Hope danced like a spider through his chest. "Speak with me in the morning, and use words."

"I can't do that."

Ashok released a breath and tightened his chain. His brother stepped into the chamber.

Big. Slow. A waste of flesh.

Instead of a hand, his brother held out a sword. Fever-bright eyes, trembling hands—Ashok recognized all the signs. His brother was ready to move up in the hierarchy, to replace Ashok as their father's favorite.

"I need this, brother. I'm the eldest."

Ashok stood. With the smoky fire between them, his brother's body seemed a mirage in the flickering light.

"I need this," Lakesh repeated.

Ashok understood that need all too well. The need to earn a higher place in the enclave, the need to please their father, all wrapped up in the constant need to keep their souls from fading.

They were slipping away faster as the years passed. Soon no amount of infighting would keep them anchored to the world. Would the shadows consume them, or would they destroy each other first?

"Come ahead," Ashok said.

Ashok awoke on the wrong side of Ikemmu's wall, lying in the middle of a rutted road. Distantly, he heard caravan wheels rattling, but it might have been the gusting wind. All sounds were watery echoes while the nightmare's scream rang in his ears.

Skagi and Cree stood over him. Ikemmu's four towers formed a backdrop like bars. Remembering Lakesh, and expecting an attack from the warriors, Ashok went for his weapons—gone again—and tried to spring to his feet. A wave of dizziness assaulted him, and he stumbled.

"Easy!" Skagi barked.

Cree reached toward Ashok. Viciously, Ashok batted his hand away. He came up to his knees, prepared to fight from the ground if he had to.

Cree stepped back and raised his hands. "We're not going to attack you," he said.

Breathing hard, Ashok tried to regain his balance. The warriors watched him; Cree looked ready to grab him if he fell again.

Why would they help him up? An image of Lakesh coming for his death while he slept went through Ashok's mind. Surely it was a trick to slip a katar between his ribs. But the warriors could have done that at any time while he lay unconscious.

Ashok managed to get to his feet, and Skagi again held his weapons out to him.

"You'll live," he said. "Sometimes the nightmare's screams make a body dizzy if he's not used to them."

Ashok took his weapons. It took him a breath to orient himself from the dark cave to the open spaces of the city. The dream had been so vivid that the wide expanse put him on edge. He was vulnerable out here in the open.

When Ashok felt steady enough, he turned to Cree and Skagi. "Why didn't you kill me?" he asked. He remembered the burning sword and the line of guards. The witch had wanted to kill him. He'd seen her barely controlled fury. "What do you want from me?"

"That's not for us to say," Cree said.

Ashok clenched his fists in frustration. He almost wished they would attack him, torture him. Those things he understood. But to be held and not harmed, free and not free—it made no sense to him.

"Where is the nightmare?" he asked. The echo of its scream was still in his head, and provided a momentary distraction.

"They'll take it to the pens for the Camborrs to break," Skagi said, "though Olra may be taking on more than she can handle this time."

"You train nightmares?" Ashok said, and a wave of excitement threaded though his muscles.

"We train anything we can break," Skagi said. "If you'd left any alive, we'd have taken your hound friends."

"But only those who've got the rank of Camborr—that was the name of the shadar-kai who first started taming the beasts—know how to train them without being ripped to pieces," Cree said.

"Is that what you are?" Ashok asked. "Camborrs?"

Cree shook his head. "We only just entered Tempus's service. We're warriors in training. Someday we'll serve the city in His name."

"And Uwan is your leader," Ashok said. He looked over the stone buildings to Tower Athanon in the distance. "I want to see him."

Ashok knew he would be denied, even expected the warriors to laugh at the request. So he was shocked when Skagi said, "Good—he wants to see you. He knew you'd try to escape. But you got us in the piss and bitter with Neimal for letting you run amok on the wall, so thanks for that. I wouldn't be surprised if she tries to burn you down when you're not looking." Scowling, Skagi drew his falchion and pointed to the tower. "Let's go," he said.

The warriors fell in behind him. Ashok noticed Skagi kept his blade in his hand and Cree's palms rested on his katars' hilts. But

Ashok had no intention of running again.

As they walked, Ashok was aware of the eyes that gazed out from the stone dwellings: shadar-kai, dark ones, and the startling other races that walked with them. Ashok kept his body tense in case of an attack.

When they approached the fence around Tower Athanon, Ashok saw weapon racks leaned against the bars. A hundred or more shadar-kai milled around a training yard, sparring or talking in groups.

Skagi pulled open the gate at the same time Ashok heard the tolling of a massive bell in the distance. He turned and saw the bells at the top of Tower Makthar, half hidden between four stone spikes, a black crown that speared the shadows of the cavern ceiling.

"The Trimmer bell," Cree explained when Ashok stared at the bell in confusion. "You were unconscious a while."

"What purpose does it serve?" Ashok asked.

"The bell?" Cree said, looking surprised. "Time. It's second bell. We mark six intervals of the day. How do you mark time where you come from?"

Ashok didn't reply. He thought of his chamber deep in the caves of the enclave. He had never marked time, not formally; he functioned according to the needs of his body. When he was hungry, he ate. When he was tired, he slept—when he wasn't defending himself from being killed in his sleep. His father and the other leaders of his enclave decided when patrols and hunting parties went out. Maybe they had marked the passage of time in some way, but he saw no purpose to it himself.

Hearing the bell, the shadar-kai in the yard formed up in ten lines facing the tower. With shoulders perfectly aligned, they stared straight ahead, unmoving, until the bell stopped tolling.

"Over here," Cree said as he and Skagi led Ashok to a section of fence off to the side of the formation.

A doorway at the base of the tower opened, and a shadar-kai man stepped out.

"There he is," Cree said, his tone reverent. "Uwan."

Unhelmed, Uwan had long, silken white hair and wore a suit of shadowmail and a black cloak. At his hip rode a greatsword. He looked not much older than the shadar-kai who stood at attention before him, yet he had an air of calm that the others did not possess.

The shadar-kai reached maturity at various ages, according to their temperaments. The wildest offspring, those unable to focus, might reach thirty winters with their minds not fully developed. Others who were able to better channel their manic tendencies might be fully matured at twenty. Uwan was obviously a case of the latter.

The leader stopped in front of the lines. Above his head, the unblinking white eye shone down on the scene.

"Welcome, my new recruits," he said, his voice carrying over the crowd of shadar-kai men and women. "You are here this day because you all share a common desire." He paused, his gaze roving over the gathered throng. Briefly, his eyes passed over Ashok but did not linger. "Do you know what you all have in common?" Uwan asked.

Silence from the gathering.

"None of you?" Uwan asked. With his hand resting on his greatsword's hilt, he paced up and down the lines. He stopped in front of a young man. "You," he said. "Tell me why you have come here."

The young one gazed up at Uwan, wide-eyed and stuck. The intensity of his leader's gaze numbed him silent.

"Speak!" Uwan cried. "Or if you will not—" With both hands he grasped the man's shirt and ripped the fabric away. The shirt fell in torn halves around the shadar-kai's waist.

The man's pale gray skin shone dully in the half-light. Glistening weevil scars traced crooked lines horizontally and vertically across his back. His bare arms were cut and scarred as well, and from elbow to wrist his skin was mottled by bruises.

Uwan stood back and spread his arms. "This is why you're here, recruits," he said.

With all eyes in the crowd upon him, the young man instinctively grabbed for his ruined shirt to cover himself. Uwan grasped his wrists.

"Don't hide yourself. You are shadar-kai!" He raised the man's arms above their heads. With their hands joined, Uwan stared into the young one's eyes. "The battles we have fought leave many scars," he said. "Never be ashamed of these marks you bear, for they are wrought by the deadliest foe the shadar-kai have ever known." He dropped his hands to the man's shoulders. "Tell me, warrior, who inflicted these wounds?"

The man met Uwan's unwavering stare. His chin rose. "I did, Lord Uwan," he replied.

Uwan nodded and stepped back. He gazed out over the crowd, but he had them. Nothing else existed except their leader. "Just so," Uwan said. "To be shadar-kai is to be at war with our very selves! Is it fate that damns us so? The gods? No.

"Our sires and dams were Shadovar. You know their names. They of the empire of Netheril—humans who lived so long in the plane of shadow that their offspring were born of shadowstuff. Our bodies are the vessel, but they are poor sanctuaries, friends, mistake me not. These fleshly constructs cannot hope to contain the shadows that are part of us and that would scatter to the winds were we not vigilant in restraining their flight."

Drawing a dagger from his belt, Uwan raised his forearm and put the blade against his bare flesh. "This is what you all have in common, and why you have come here today. This war you fight with yourselves every waking moment of your lives.

"To be shadar-kai is to *need*. Every base instinct, every

opportunity for stimulation seized." He pressed his blade, and a thread of blood ran down his arm. "We crave the pain, anything to heighten our awareness, to bind our souls to this form, while the siren song of the shadow seeks to draw us to oblivion. She sings to us constantly, and our souls hear her. If we grow complacent, friends, we greet our doom."

A cry of agreement came from somewhere in the crowd and was picked up along the line of warriors until they all shouted in assent.

"Do not despair, friends!" Uwan said, holding up a hand for silence. "Today marks a new beginning in your battle. You are no longer alone in this struggle. I will walk the path with you, but even that will not be enough."

Cries of protest rose from the crowd. Uwan held up his hands again. "No, friends, listen, listen!" he called. "I too, hear the cry from the shadows. I too, seek the pain, but the blood I shed is in service to a greater master than me." Uwan pounded his fists against his chest. "This vessel I pledge to Tempus!"

"Tempus!" A deafening swell of noise burst from the assembly. The warriors pounded their own chests and stamped the ground. Ashok thought that had they possessed weapons, they would have struck the air with blades in praise to the warrior god.

Beside him, Cree and Skagi took up the cry. The training yard was alive; the iron fence trembled with the force of shadar-kai devotion. Only Ashok remained silent, but he was not unaffected by the assault.

His heart pounded at the raw power and devotion of the assembled warriors. Ashok could not remember a time when he had been so stimulated and had not been in pain. With his speech, Uwan had every one of the warriors in his thrall. To the shadar-kai, he might have been Tempus embodied.

"In this place," Uwan said, when the crowd had settled enough for voices to be heard again, "you will train to fight, but you will also learn discipline, trust, and service." He took off his cloak, went to the scarred man, and threw the cloak around his bare shoulders. The young one looked up at his leader in awe. Uwan smiled at him.

"Your first duty is to protect your city," Uwan said to the warriors. "You are new recruits, but if you take well the lessons of your teachers, you will rise in the ranks. Some of you may become Camborr, the breakers of beasts; or Guardian, the soldiery that protects our city. You may choose to become teachers yourselves. Some of you may even become my Sworn."

"What are the Sworn?" Ashok asked Cree.

"His most trusted advisors," Cree explained in a low voice. "The Watching Blade has a council of advisors, representatives from the trade houses and the other races that dwell here. But the Sworn, like Neimal, are his military advisors."

"Is that what you aspire to be?" Ashok asked.

"It's what *everyone* aspires to be," Skagi said.

"Remember this, as you begin your training," Uwan said. "Only those who prove themselves worthy will bear the mark of Tempus. Fight well—against your foes and against yourselves—and you will be rewarded. Your bodies now belong to me. Use them in service to Ikemmu, and I will mark you with Tempus's sword." He held up his bloody arm. "Put not the dagger to your flesh, lest you be made weak. Weakness will not serve this city. Weakness will not serve us."

Uwan drew his sword from its scabbard. The blade glinted silver and black in the half-light. He raised it high.

"May Tempus drive out the weakness from our bodies and silence the siren's call! Our lives are now His, and with our deaths we go not to the shadowed oblivion, but to His side to fight forevermore."

"*Tempus!*"

The cry shook the air. Ashok looked up to see a colony of bats take flight from the tower, wheeling to escape the divine storm. The warriors cried their god's name and Uwan's, and before the storm passed, Uwan sheathed his sword and walked back inside the tower.

Ashok found he'd been holding his breath, one hand clutching the iron fence. He let go the air and iron. Skagi was watching him.

"Do you still want to meet him?" he asked. His tone tried for amusement, but his face glowed with the same fervor Ashok felt coursing in his blood.

With an effort, Ashok cleared his head. Despite his excitement, he knew his situation had not changed. He was a prisoner, and if they were truly going to take him to see Uwan, the leader of the enclave, he had to be ready to act. He would find out what his captors wanted from him, or he would die. Since it appeared he could not escape, there could be no other outcome.

"Take me," Ashok said.

CHAPTER
FIVE

WHEN THEY GOT INSIDE TOWER ATHANON, ALL ASHOK SAW WERE shadar-kai warriors. He recognized many of them from the training yard. They stood in groups, talking, arguing, sometimes wrestling their disagreements out on the floor, but Ashok got the impression it was done half in competition, half in jest. There was no violence to their movements, and nobody drew a weapon.

It stunned him that so many shadar-kai would gather in one space, where a knife might find someone's back so easily. In the caves of his enclave, the narrow tunnels provided a buffer that kept large groups from forming. There was always a wall to put your back against, and Ashok had learned to use the tunnels to his advantage.

While they walked up a spiral stair, Ashok counted ten levels of recruits and their living quarters. The next four were a series of heavy doors guarded by helmed and plate-armored shadar-kai. They were obviously not new recruits. Skagi said they were all Guardians: soldiers in charge of the city's defenses.

The top level of the tower had only one room off it, and the door was unguarded.

Skagi knocked twice upon it, then went back to where Cree waited on the stairs. "We'll be waiting below," he told Ashok.

"You're not coming with me?" Ashok asked, surprised again. "No guards?"

"That's the way Uwan wants things," Skagi said. "Get on with it."

When they'd gone, Ashok stood before the door. He considered taking out his chain but decided against it. Hundreds, perhaps thousands of shadar-kai stood between him and anything he could do to Uwan with the weapon.

Ashok pushed open the door and entered a lamp-lit chamber. A long, rectangular oak table surrounded by ten chairs dominated the room, and on the wall behind hung a framed portrait of a vast landscape.

As he walked to the table, Ashok's eyes were drawn to the painting's details. He'd never seen anything so lifelike in a picture. The inky shadows peeled back to reveal an overhead view of Ikemmu, its four towers prominent against the lighter canyon wall. The waterfall was there, and Ashok saw that the two towers in the middle, Pyton and Hevalor, were connected by stone bridges with curved tusks instead of rails at the edges. He'd not noticed the bridges on the real towers, they blended so well with the surrounding landscape.

"Do you like it?" said a voice.

Ashok hadn't heard the door open at the far side of the room. He tensed, but it was Uwan who came through, followed by the cleric, Natan. Uwan was again adorned in his cloak and armor. His greatsword lay on the table before a high-backed chair of polished wood. He looked over Ashok's shoulder at the painting, seemingly unconcerned that Ashok stood between him and his weapon.

"It was a gift," Uwan said, when Ashok didn't reply to his question.

Still Ashok remained silent. He wasn't sure what Uwan expected him to say.

Natan stood to one side of the room. He did not acknowledge Ashok's presence. His gaze was drawn to the painting too. His thin shoulders were stooped, and he seemed very weary, almost on the verge of collapse. Ashok was surprised. The cleric had shown no such weakness in the sickroom.

"I apologize for not welcoming you properly in the training yard," Uwan said. "But Skagi and Cree tell me you're not interested in seeing our city."

"Your city is a cage," Ashok said flatly.

Uwan shook his head. "You are not a prisoner, Ashok. You can come and go as you like."

"But I can't leave the city."

"I'm afraid not."

Uwan seemed amused, though his expression did not change. Ashok sighed. He was tired of such games. "What do you want from me?" he asked.

"A few answers," Uwan said. He glanced at Natan. Something passed between the leader and the cleric. Ashok had no idea what it was, but the cleric did not look happy. Uwan frowned and turned his attention back to Ashok. "Where do you come from, Ashok?" he asked. "You were far from any enclave when my patrol found you, but you seem too undisciplined to be fleeing the empire. You're a skilled warrior—that much was clear from the shadow hound corpses. Neimal, however much she wants your head, respects what you did at the wall today. You weren't afraid to take on her entire force. For whom do you fight, Ashok?"

"For myself," Ashok said. Let Uwan think he was a wanderer, with no enclave.

"No one holds your loyalty?" Uwan asked. "What of Tempus?"

Ashok saw Natan tense when Uwan mentioned the god's name. "My Lord, is this wise?" the cleric asked. "He is not—"

"Natan," Uwan said quietly, and the cleric immediately fell silent. "Well, Ashok?"

"Tempus?" Ashok replied. He thought the question was strange, but it was one he could answer honestly, giving nothing of himself away. "I'm not Tempus's servant," he said, meeting Uwan's gaze levelly.

Slowly, Uwan nodded. "I see. Well, if you won't tell me where you come from or anything else about yourself, I see little reason to trust you with my own motives for bringing you here. So, at this impasse, here are the facts. I've saved your life. I expect repayment for my trouble."

"In what form?" Ashok asked. He nodded to the portrait. "I have no coin to offer a city like this."

"I don't need your coin," Uwan said. "All I ask is that you remain in the city for a time."

"Forgive me, my Lord," Natan said as he took a step forward. "Please consider what you're saying. He can't be trusted to roam free."

Uwan didn't answer the cleric. "I could lock you in a cell, it's true, but that would be a gross waste of talent," he said. "Train with us, Ashok. You are skilled, but there are many things you could yet learn from us."

"*Learn* from you?" Ashok said, laughing. "Listen to your friend. I'm not of this city, and that makes me your enemy. Why would you want to make your enemy stronger?"

"We're not enemies, Ashok. That is the first thing I hope you'll learn during your time among us," Uwan said. "In any case, you could not join the ranked soldiers, not without first swearing fealty to Tempus." Uwan lifted his sword from the table. "None may rise in the military ranks without giving that oath. But you may dwell among us, as my guest."

"For how long?" Ashok asked.

Uwan offered an enigmatic smile. "Until I have a sign as to your worth," he said. "What is your choice, warrior? Dwell in a prison cell until your soul drifts away, or live among us and learn all you can?"

"There is no choice," Ashok said, "as you know. I accept."

"We are agreed, then," Uwan said as he held out his hand. Ashok did not take it.

After, Uwan gave instructions to Skagi and Cree about where Ashok was to stay, then he left the three of them and went back inside his chamber to Natan. "You continue to question my judgment," he said when he was alone with the cleric.

Natan bowed his head. "Forgive me, my Lord," he said again. "But you heard him yourself. He does not come to us at Tempus's behest. If that is so, my vision says he brings danger."

"Or it could mean that Tempus works unseen in him," Uwan said.

"My Lord, it is very easy to see things as we wish them to be, rather than as they truly are," Natan said.

"You're right," Uwan replied. His gaze strayed to the portrait, its unrelenting detail of the city, every shadow, every flaw. "We rarely see things as they truly are. Absent is our reminder of this."

"But not lost," Natan said.

"Did I choose the right course," Uwan said, succumbing to the uncertainty, "keeping him here? Perhaps I should have told him about your vision."

"He is not . . ." the cleric faltered. "I can't find the words. He is not whole. The times I've seen him, he seems always on the verge of fading. Even if he is not an enemy, he can't help us in his current state."

Uwan laughed softly. "So I'm to remake him?" he asked.

"Or send him away," Natan said. "Perhaps he cannot be saved."

"He has no regard for Tempus. I saw it in his eyes," Uwan said. "I could have cut him down for it."

"But you didn't," Natan said.

"No," Uwan replied. "I believe it is Tempus's will that he remain here. So I will do what I can."

Skagi and Cree led Ashok down the tower steps to the barracks levels. Smells of leather, steel, sweat, and smoke filled the air, reminding Ashok briefly of home.

They've given me up for dead by now, he thought.

Skagi stopped before a door on the second level. "This is home," he said.

Inside, a pair of lanterns had been turned down low. Six bunks were chained and bolted atop each other against two walls. Two of these bunks were occupied by shadar-kai men.

Ashok recognized one of them: the scarred man from the training yard.

"What have you brought us, Skagi?" the other man said. "Something to amuse, I hope."

He was tall when he stood, but slender, and he moved with slow grace. Black hair fell in a tightly bound horsetail down his back. He came to stand before Ashok, his gaze speculative.

"He's our guest," Skagi said dryly. "Ashok, this is Chanoch"—he pointed to the scarred man—"and Vedoran. You'll share space with all of us while you're here."

Ashok nodded to them both. Chanoch, the scarred one, had dark, unruly spikes of hair jutting out all over his head. Up close, Ashok could see his cheeks had been scored as if by claw marks. Ashok guessed by the size and the spacing that the wounds had been self-inflicted when he was a child. The scars and mass of hair gave the young man a chaotic, unfettered appearance. When he came across the room to greet Ashok he moved in jerky strides, like a young animal just learning to walk.

"Are you all in training?" Ashok said.

"All but Vedoran," Skagi said. "He's a sellsword. He's only squatting with us."

Cree chuckled. Vedoran made a rude gesture in Skagi's direction. "Officially, I belong to a trading consortium from Pyton," Vedoran said. He had a deep, rhythmic voice. "But I train within the military ranks in order to"—his lips curled in a mixture of amusement and disdain—"improve myself."

"Arrogant bastard already knows he can best any of us in this room," Skagi said.

Vedoran glanced at Ashok. "Perhaps not anymore," he replied.

Ashok said nothing. He went to one of the bunks and sat on the edge with his back to the wall.

After a breath of uncomfortable silence, Skagi spoke. "You wanted amusement, Vedoran," he said. "What did you have in mind?"

Vedoran was still watching Ashok curiously. He shrugged and turned his attention to Skagi. "I have business in Pyton at the next bell," he replied. "Time enough for a drink after. What say you?"

"Not without me," Cree said, and Chanoch was quick to agree.

All eyes turned to Ashok. Vedoran raised a brow, his eyes lit with challenge. "Coming, stranger?" he asked.

Ashok stayed where he was. His pale brow furrowed in consternation. "There are four of you," he said.

"Well, he can count," Chanoch said, and the others laughed.

Somewhere in the back of his mind, Ashok heard his brothers' voices.

Come with us, Ashok.

Yes, come. We're tossing the dice. We'll show you how to play, little one.

Ashok remembered smiles, outstretched hands like bait. Young as he was, he had known better than to bite. His brothers never sought amusements together, never made themselves vulnerable to one another, lest someone take the opportunity to rise in the ranks with their father.

"Let him be," Skagi said, when Ashok only stared at them. "There's no forcing him."

"Look at him. He looks like a lost pup," Chanoch whispered to Cree, as they turned away. Only Vedoran didn't move.

"We could show him the Span," Vedoran said. "He's new to the city. I'm sure he'd find it interesting."

"Speak, silent one," Skagi said. "Are you afraid of a challenge?"

"Am I afraid?" Ashok echoed the words, and the memories flew apart, his brothers' voices faded. Skagi, the arrogant man singling him out—that he understood. They were challenging him, looking for weaknesses. He was back in familiar territory. "No, I'm not afraid," he said. "Let's go."

Rhudk stood with his shadar-kai brothers on the dusty Shadowfell plain, watching the horizon for signs of life. Behind him lay a steep, rock-filled valley, which protected the caves of his enclave.

His black shirt was soaked in blood. With his right hand Rhudk clutched a gut wound that was slowly eating away at him. He had only a little time left.

It didn't matter. The wind was on his face, the battle was won, and even dying, Rhudk had never felt so alive.

When he was satisfied that no other enemies approached the caves, he turned his attention to the body at his feet.

His father's corpse was stretched out on the ground, burned

almost beyond recognition. Exposed skull bones and teeth, and a few wisps of hair were all that remained of the face of one of the great leaders of their enclave.

Other corpses lay strewn about the plain, dead where they had fallen. Magic had killed them all. The witch had struck from afar, before their superior numbers could overwhelm the patrol. They had lost more warriors than they should have, but at least they had prisoners to show for it. His brothers would begin interrogating them as soon as they tied up all the loose ends out on the plain.

"Has there been word from our brother Ashok?" Rhudk asked his brothers.

They answered that there had not been. Ashok, his father's favorite, was either dead or fled from the enclave. One of the others would take their father's place. Had Rhudk not been dying, it would have been him. He was the strongest. Had he not been injured, he could have taken on any challenger. They all knew it.

They circled like ravens, waiting for him to die. There was no need for them to take action to help the process along. Killing him in his weakened state would not stimulate them, would not set their hearts racing or bring the fevered light to their eyes. If killing him would not bring them those sensations, it was not worth the effort.

Rhudk smiled and tasted blood in his mouth. His own heart was racing, and the surge in his blood was beyond pleasure. It was almost worth it, trading power for his slow death, a suffering that kept his soul so tightly anchored to his body that he felt immortal.

Their enclave had been too long sequestered in the caves. The longer they stayed in the dark, the faster they were fading. Fighting amongst themselves no longer brought enough pleasure to sustain them. Battles such as this were what they craved. They'd traded their souls for a defensible home.

But there was nothing Rhudk could do about that.

"The patrol," he said. It was growing difficult to speak. Rhudk breathed through blood. "Find out where they came from. Start with the witch."

His brothers said they would. Rhudk sent them away to tend to the enclave and lay down on the ground amid the corpses. Staring up at the gray sky, he wondered which one of his brothers would emerge the strongest. He had always thought it would be Ashok. Ashok was the most intelligent and cunning among them. Rhudk was disappointed that the hounds had taken him; he hoped Ashok had given them a good chase. He wished his brother a good death, and closed his eyes to let the wind caress his face.

CHAPTER
SIX

Ashok thought he had seen wondrous sights enough in Ikemmu, but when they approached Tower Pyton, he had new cause to gape at his surroundings. The scent got him first.

"Brace yourself," Skagi said, laughing when he saw Ashok's wide-eyed countenance. "It's a drug the first time."

And it was. Pyton, Hevalor, and everything on the ground between the towers made up the trading district, and it was a teeming mass of many races, more than Ashok had seen near the wall. His curiosity overcame him, and he pointed and asked Cree to tell him their names. The group laughed at his ignorance, but Ashok didn't care. He wanted names to put to all the strange faces, and he remembered each one as Cree spoke.

At the base of the towers, an open-air market had been set up among the stone buildings. Wagons loaded down with every imaginable good were parked in front of the buildings, and human, halfling, and dwarven merchants hawked food: carts full of strange fruit, the colors so vivid they hurt Ashok's eyes. He'd never seen colors like that. Steaming meat on spits whirled past him clutched in dwarven fists. The stout men and women pushed the savories at the group. Skagi tossed them coin, and the group each took a haunch of boar.

Ashok bit into the meat and felt the juices slide down his chin. He was used to meat that had been long preserved in stores, hard biscuits, and water from a silt stream deep in the underground. The flavors of the hot, spiced boar assaulted his tongue and made him light-headed. He was shocked to feel his heartbeat speed up slightly. The intense spices stimulated not just his tongue, but his whole body, the way a wound sharpened him. He could hardly believe what he was feeling.

And it wasn't just the food. There were wagons filled with tools for building, fire-making, and weapon repair. Finely tailored clothing hung from iron bars suspended between the shops, breezes making crimson skirts billow like enflamed clouds. Ashok reached out in wonder to touch the fabric.

"Wipe the grease off before you touch!" a voice said as a hand slapped his hand away.

Ashok looked up at a tawny-skinned human man with flushed cheeks and thick brown sideburns. His eyes—brown and white and black—were hypnotic to Ashok with their circles of color.

"Eh, what are you lookin' at?" the merchant demanded.

"Your eyes," Ashok said.

"My eyes?" the merchant repeated, looking Ashok over curiously. "Haven't seen you before. What's your rank?"

"I don't have one," Ashok said.

"Nice armor you got though," the merchant said, passing his hand over the bone scales, poking and prodding. Ashok resisted the urge to snap the human's wrist. "Good color, the charcoal and white," the merchant continued. "Not white, though, more tooth-shaded. Bit muddled crimson too—I got a good eye for color. 'S not one of mine. Where'd you buy it?"

"I made it," Ashok said.

"Made it!" the merchant said, laughing loudly. His breath reeked of strong herbs and liquor. "A fine jester you are too. No, truly, where'd you get it?"

Ashok didn't reply. He started to turn away.

The merchant clamped a hand on his shoulder.

Ashok dropped his meat, pivoted, and batted the merchant's hand aside. He drew his dagger with his left hand, brandishing the weapon between his body and the human's.

"Ashok," Skagi said, appearing suddenly beside them. "Gaina, what's going on here?"

Cree, Chanoch, and Vedoran trailed behind Skagi. The merchant had broken into a sweat when he saw Ashok's drawn dagger.

"I was just askin' where he got the goods," the merchant said, pointing to Ashok's armor. "Said he made it—"

"And you called him a liar," Skagi said. "I heard you."

"Well he didn't hafta pull the blade on me," Gaina grumbled. "How'd you make it then?" he said to Ashok.

"From a boneclaw corpse," Ashok said flatly. "An undead. I killed it, skinned it, and re-fitted the bones."

For a breath, the merchant didn't speak. He opened his mouth, closed it, and rubbed his jaw. "Now I know you're jestin'. You're havin' fun at me. You can't make a suit of pretties; can't do nothin' for yourselves."

Cree flicked his nail playfully against Ashok's brandished dagger blade. "Except use one of these—can you say as much, Gaina?"

The merchant glared at Cree. "Fine, then. But tell your friend not to be touchin' the goods 'less he got cleaner hands," Gaina said.

"Now you're calling us dirty?" Skagi said, spreading his hands under the merchant's nose. "These turn your stomach?" He took some silver coins from his neck pouch. "What about now, Gaina? How about when they're silver, or when they bleed to make you safe as you squat in your bed at night—they aren't clean enough for you?"

The merchant shoved Skagi's hands away and sneered. "Don't smell that good either. Have your fun, then. But these hands"—he raised his thick fingers, beringed with silver and platinum bands—"hold the needles you're too good to touch. You don't mind wearin' the frippery, do you? But you won't stoop to makin' it with those cut-up digits. You remember that next time you come at me with the grease on your hands."

Vedoran cleared his throat.

Skagi looked up when the graceful shadar-kai stepped forward. "Our apologies," Vedoran said to the merchant. "Ashok, put the dagger away. Skagi, we have business," he said pointedly.

Skagi sniffed. He turned away and let Vedoran lead him on through the crowds.

Ashok fell into step behind them, listening. "If I'd known you were looking for a fight I wouldn't have asked you to come," he heard Vedoran whisper to Skagi.

Skagi, walking easily, shrugged. "Don't know what you mean. Gaina and I are old friends. It's not a good day unless we go about cutting each other down." His eyes narrowed. "He's a fat coward who's made a fortune in this market, and everyone up the avenue knows it. He needs to be reminded every so often who brings his food to the table."

Ashok felt a hand fall on his shoulder. The impulse to lash out, to cut with the dagger still in his hand was almost overwhelming, but then he saw Cree fall into step beside him. The young one moved like a ghost.

He must know he could kill me, Ashok thought. All he needs is an instant of distraction. Why doesn't he try? Why don't any of them take advantage?

Cree slapped him on the back. "A boneclaw?" he said.

"Yes?" Ashok said uncertainly.

Cree shook his head and grinned. "Outstanding," he said. "You'll tell me the tale someday."

Ashok could only nod. "What was that about?" he asked, changing the subject. "Between Skagi and the human?"

"Don't worry about it," Cree said, waving a hand vaguely. "It's just . . . the way things are. Everyone has a role to play to make the city work, but some people's roles are more important than others."

"And the human's role is to clothe you?" Ashok said.

"Not just him," Cree said. "All the merchants have their place in the trade district. They keep the coin flowing in and out of the city, but none of them would have a safe place to do business if the shadar-kai weren't here to protect Ikemmu from outside threats."

They walked on through the crowd and up into Tower Pyton. Ashok noticed that the farther they climbed up the winding stair through the tower, the less he saw of the other races. The upper levels were dominated by shadar-kai, and they were dressed in finery equal to that hanging from Gaina's wagon, and greater.

There were shops in the tower: weapon dealers and brewers, wine makers and jewelers. They passed levels with locked, heavily guarded doors. The shadar-kai who came out of those mysterious rooms carried padlocked boxes, often inscribed with faintly glowing runes.

Ashok passed a slender, hooded figure carrying an iron-shod staff with shadowy tentacles winding up the shaft. As they passed each other, almost touching, Ashok breathed in and smelled sulfur. He looked up into the face of the tiefling, and she smiled at him. The shadow fingers reached up from the staff and plucked at her hood. She swirled the staff in her hand, and they quieted. Then she was by him, and he was forced to keep walking up the stairs.

Vedoran halted them on a crowded level with many doors, open as those on the previous levels had not been. The doors gave the room an airy feel and revealed many open portals cut into stone down the hallways. They looked out on the city and the Shadowdark in every direction. Ashok went to one while Vedoran approached a shadar-kai seated at a long table across the room.

Guards stood at the portals holding their weapons and the red and black banners Ashok had seen from below. They stood on narrow ledges jutting out from the tower, watching the city below while strong winds threatened to pluck them off their perches. None of them seemed afraid to fall.

Ashok went back into the main chamber to look around. The room was finely appointed and centered about the table, which was heaped in food and wine. Soft-cushioned furniture was everywhere, and several shadar-kai lounged on them, drinking wine and eating off platters.

A man took a handful of wrinkled fruit Ashok didn't recognize off a plate and fed it piece by piece to the woman sitting across from him. Across the room, another man stood on his toes, blindfolded, his arms tied in front of him, while a woman drew a dagger blade lightly across his bare back and buttocks. The blade looked so sharp that if the man so much as twitched he would be sliced open.

All the shadar-kai were nude, with the exception of the man Vedoran was speaking to, who wore a pair of breeches and a sword tied with a sash to his waist.

Ashok turned slowly about the room, unable to credit his eyes with what he saw. The nakedness shocked him, although the shadar-kai were not over-burdened by modesty. Rather it was the complete lack of defense that disturbed Ashok. The men and women wore no armor, and he saw no weapons—save the woman's dagger—ready to hand in case an encounter turned into an attack. The utter trust of the communal atmosphere staggered him.

There were other doors off the chamber—ones that did not lead to the open air but to more private spaces. Those curtained off rooms held other couples. Ashok watched their nude outlines through the thin curtains and could hear them speaking in low, intimate tones to each other.

"That's Vedoran's master," Cree said, breaking into Ashok's thoughts. He pointed to the man seated at the table. "Karthan—good warrior, fair trader. They're not bad for Blites."

"Blites?" Ashok said. "Skagi called me that before."

For a breath Cree seemed taken aback. "That's right," he said. "I'd forgotten. But it's nothing to you, is it? I'm talking about the sellswords. But don't let any of them hear you call them Blites— they'll make you pay for it."

"Why are they called that?" Ashok asked.

"Blites don't worship Tempus," Cree said. "That's why Vedoran's only 'guesting' with us. He can't hold rank, can't serve the city in any official way."

"I don't understand," Ashok said. "Your leader claimed you would be rewarded for fighting for Ikemmu."

"That's true," Cree said. "And the sellswords are paid well for their work. But Uwan wants something greater for Ikemmu's military. He thinks the defenders of the city should be united by a strong god, and who better to understand the inner battles of the shadar-kai than the warrior god?"

Vedoran and the man finished speaking. Vedoran bowed and came over to them. A man came through one of the curtained doorways and nodded when he saw Cree. Cree grinned and went to greet the man. The two of them spoke for a breath or two, then Cree followed the man behind the curtain.

"We may as well go on," Vedoran said. "They've already found their amusements."

Ashok saw that Skagi and Chanoch had found partners, too, and were so engrossed in their own conversations, it was as if Ashok and Vedoran didn't exist.

"What of you?" Ashok asked.

Vedoran shrugged. "I seek other enjoyments," he said, his eyes glinting. "And I promised to show you the Span."

Curious, Ashok nodded to the stair. "Lead on," he said.

"Not that way," Vedoran said. "We'll take the shorter route."

He led them past the curtained doorways—Ashok caught hints of scented oils in the fabrics—and turned down one of the short corridors ending in an open archway. Vedoran nodded to the guard that stood at the entry and walked out on the ledge.

At a hundred feet up, the wind whipped their cloaks. Ashok walked to the edge of the ledge and looked down. He could see the market, the people, and the colors swirling together like a spilled stew. They stood adjacent to the canyon wall, a jagged slope that curved above them, blocking out most of the light. Somewhere behind them unseen, the waterfall spilled behind Tower Makthar. The wind carried the damp across the space into their faces. Twin lanterns hung from poles near the archway, and the light reflecting off the cavern wall cast eldritch shadows all around them. But for the wind, there was silence.

For a long breath, neither of them spoke. Ashok stood at the edge of the abyss, an observer, a part of the throng below and yet removed from them.

"You feel in control now, don't you?" Vedoran said from behind him.

Ashok glanced back at the shadar-kai. Beyond him, the guard stood silent, watching them.

Vedoran followed his gaze. He lowered his voice. "Ask him to step back into the tower," he said.

Confused, Ashok said nothing. He thought the man was playing with him, but the shadar-kai's face was an unreadable mask. He stared past Ashok into the abyss, waiting.

Was it another challenge? Ashok wondered. He took a step toward the guard and nodded in greeting. The guard returned the gesture.

"Would you leave us for a time?" he asked, in a tone of respect.

Without speaking, the guard turned and went back inside the tower.

Alone on the ledge, Vedoran motioned Ashok to join him at the edge. "Well done," he said.

"Why didn't you ask him?" Ashok said.

"Because he knows I'm a Blite," Vedoran said. A lazy smile spread across his face, but his eyes were hard. "He believes his god Tempus is better than any other, and that makes him think he's better than me. Knowing that, I'll be damned if I'm going to ask him for any favors. But he doesn't know what your rank is yet, so I thought I could use you to my advantage. I was right. It feels good though, doesn't it?"

"What?" asked Ashok.

"Being in control again," replied Vedoran, He stood with the toes of his boots over the ledge, dipped his head back, and closed his eyes. "Ironic, isn't it?" he said. "That to feel this centered, you have to stand on the edge of falling."

His body swayed from side to side. Watching him, Ashok's palms began to sweat. The vicarious fear beat a pulse in his blood. Vedoran seemed completely in control and at ease, yet he must know that Ashok could step forward in a breath and push him from the ledge. Ashok's breath quickened. He stepped up to the ledge beside Vedoran, tipping his head forward instead of back. He didn't close his eyes but stared down the canyon, the water beads brushing his face.

If he listened closely, he could hear the soft babble of voices drifting up on the wind. By the time they reached his ears they were too insubstantial to be words, but the murmur itself was rhythmic and soothing. The vibration hummed against his skin.

"Is this the Span?" Ashok asked.

"The bridges," Vedoran said, "between Pyton and Hevalor. There are three of them. The highest is ten feet below us."

Ashok looked, and he remembered the portrait in Uwan's chamber. But he didn't see the bridges.

"They were built of the same material as the tower, but altered to blend in with the canyon wall," Vedoran said.

"If enemies penetrated one tower," Ashok said, "they wouldn't have immediate access to the other."

"Precisely," Vedoran said. "We often teleport from level to level via these archways, but the towers are too far apart to teleport between them."

Everything about the city had been planned for defense, Ashok thought. Besieging Ikemmu would be a nightmare for any attacking force.

"Are you ready?" Vedoran asked.

Ashok looked at him. "For what?" he replied, though he thought he knew.

Instead of answering, Vedoran stepped off the ledge. He dropped, his black cloak billowing behind him, and landed in a crouch ten feet below Ashok. He stood, turned, and looked up at Ashok with that same lazy smile. He walked forward a few steps, seemingly treading on air.

Ashok's heart beat furiously against his breastbone. His legs quivered, aching for the jump. He took a moment to enjoy the sensations: the vertigo, the heat in his blood, the tense muscles poised for that instant of gratification when he stepped off the edge.

Live or die—it was all up to him.

Ashok opened his arms, caught the wind, and jumped.

The towers sped past him, impossibly fast. The slope of the canyon wall leveled out to a sheer surface, sucking away the darkness and lantern shadows like a spell. He could see the bridges rushing up to meet him, Vedoran's form coming closer.

It was over far too quickly. Ashok's boots hit stone, and he fell into a crouch to absorb the impact. Dust and rock scattered in his wake, the debris falling into space. With his arms spread, Ashok found balance on the edge of nothingness. Invisible hands held him up; one step backward or forward, and he was gone. But that breath in between was a century. That space was the only space that existed for him.

He looked up and met Vedoran's half-crazed eyes. Ashok smiled. He couldn't help it.

Vedoran laughed. The emotion seemed to steal his breath. His chest rose and fell as if he'd been running for miles. "You . . . You're alive, after all," Vedoran said. "I thought you were made of stone."

Ashok sat down, his legs straddling the bridge. He put his hands on the curved stone tusks rising up around him. The bridge was so narrow. Navigating it with any kind of burden would be an adventure in itself.

Vedoran seemed to read his thoughts. "Only the shadar-kai use these paths," he said. "The other races are afraid."

"Has anyone ever fallen?" Ashok asked.

"Yes," Vedoran said.

Ashok nodded. He lay on his back on the bridge, his arms outstretched in the constant wind. The force of the upswells was almost enough to bear their weight. He stared up at the cavern's ceiling. Between the distant stalactites were shadows even the city's lights couldn't chase away, making him think of the tiefling woman with the staff.

"This city . . ." He didn't know how to say it.

In Ashok's peripheral vision, Vedoran sat with an arm across his knee, the other propped behind him, holding his weight.

"Say it," he said.

"Is it yours?" Ashok asked. "It feels . . . old. Did the shadar-kai build it?"

"No one knows who built it," Vedoran said. "The lore I've heard claims the shadar-kai who settled the city were led here by their gods—Tempus, as you can imagine. You've seen the carvings on the towers."

"The winged folk," Ashok said.

"The clerics say they're Angels of Battle, Tempus's emissaries," Vedoran said.

Ashok caught a tone in Vedoran's voice, something like the vocal shadow of his lazy smile. "You don't believe them," he said.

"Skagi calls me arrogant," Vedoran said. "And so I am. But I'm not so full of hubris that I think any god would prepare a city just for my folk." He nodded at the buildings below. "I've seen the black scars. Someone burned the angels—if that's what they were—out of their city. Probably it was the Spellplague, but we'll never know."

The Spellplague. Ashok knew it only in stories: the Blue Fire that had raged across the mirror world of Faerûn, its tendrils reaching even to the Shadowfell. A force powerful enough to rip apart entire cities—he could well imagine such a thing to have scarred Ikemmu. But to consume an entire people . . . Ashok shuddered at the thought of extinction through the blue flame.

Above Ashok, a shadow fell from the clouds, spread dark wings, and descended toward the bridge.

Ashok and Vedoran came to their feet at almost the same instant, weapons in their hands. Vedoran pointed. "Cloaker," he said, as the thing angled toward them.

"Are you sure?" Ashok said.

"Oh yes," Vedoran said. "The witches say that the cloakers were here when the shadar-kai first came to Ikemmu. They called it *Sphur Upra*, the Gloaming Home. If you want to know how the city came to be, ask a cloaker." Vedoran chuckled darkly. "If you can keep it from killing you."

Ashok braced his feet so he wouldn't succumb to the vertigo of standing on the near-invisible bridge. He twirled his chain, waiting to see if the cloaker would attack.

It drifted down like its namesake, bone claws curled at the edges of the false fabric. Ashok kept the chain moving, swinging it above their heads and in front of his body. Still the thing floated, falling at a leisurely pace, coasting on the air currents.

"It's going to pass," Vedoran said.

"No it's not," Ashok said, and just in that breath, the cloaker tucked into itself. In the sudden absence of wind, it plummeted straight at them.

"Duck," Ashok said, and released one end of the chain. It sailed over Vedoran's head and snapped taut inches from the cloaker's flesh.

Quickly, Ashok jerked the chain back and grabbed the other handgrip out of the air. Vedoran took out a small belt dagger, threw it, and missed. The cloaker angled out of reach beneath the bridge.

"Which way is it coming up?" Ashok demanded.

"I don't know. Stop looking down," Vedoran told him. "You'll get dizzy."

He was right. Ashok swayed on his feet. He stepped back and felt his heel go off the edge. Jerking in a breath, he righted himself. So close to the edge, but he kept his balance. He was in control. Ashok's heart raced in exhilaration.

The cloaker appeared again from the opposite side of the bridge, spread its wings, and covered Vedoran like a curtain. To his great credit, the shadar-kai didn't struggle. Such an action would have certainly sent him off the bridge. Instead, he dropped to his knees, then to his stomach, pinning the cloaker under his weight. Surprised by the move, the creature came loose, its flesh folds hanging over the side of the bridge.

Vedoran skidded back, his boots kicking the thing away as it tried to grab for him. The cloaker folded in on itself and dropped over the side of the bridge before Ashok could get to it.

"Are you all right?" Ashok called to Vedoran. They were over twenty feet apart on the bridge.

Vedoran jerked a nod. "This isn't done," he said. "It'll come back for another pass."

Judging by his expression, Ashok knew retreat wasn't an option for Vedoran either. He held his chain, thinking.

"Can you hold my weight?" he said finally, coming forward.

Vedoran looked him over. Ashok knew what he saw: an underfed body, wiry muscle, and bone. But he was tall, and the tension would be incredible.

"I can," Vedoran said. "Do you trust me?"

Ashok smiled and shook his head.

Vedoran held out a hand. "Do it," he said.

Ashok threw the chain.

The cloaker unfolded beneath them, caught an updraft, and flew straight at Vedoran. When he saw it coming, Ashok sprinted across the bridge, closed the distance between himself and Vedoran, and jumped over the side just before he would have plowed into the shadar-kai.

His momentum carried him headfirst over the cloaker's body, out of reach of its bony claws. He held the other end of the chain in both hands as the inertia pulled him down.

The cloaker, its attention fixed on Ashok's plummeting form, didn't notice the chain unfurling above it.

Ashok angled his body, trying to turn his fall into a swing to lessen the impact. It didn't help. When the chain jerked taut, the jarring pain traveled up his arms and into his shoulders. He heard the crack as his left shoulder dislocated, and felt the brilliant explosion of agony. He ground his teeth, absorbed the pain, and concentrated on his grip. Above him, Vedoran grunted, his boots skidding across stone. But he'd been right—he was strong enough to hold Ashok.

The cloaker was not so fortunate. Barbed spikes descended, tore flesh, and trapped the struggling monster against the bridge with the chain. Vedoran pulled his end toward himself, and together with Ashok's weight, the barbs cut the cloaker in half.

Two pieces of ichor-dripping mass fell past where Ashok hung. They landed on an invisible platform fifteen feet below: the second bridge.

Ashok looked up at Vedoran. Color suffused the shadar-kai's powder gray skin. His black eyes glimmered like wet onyx.

"Well done," Ashok said.

Vedoran nodded. "You as well," he replied. He looked past Ashok, down to the second bridge. "Are you ready for me to let go?"

Ashok glanced down at the thin strip of bridge below him, invisible but for the cloaker corpse marking how far the drop truly was. The curved stone tusks were everywhere, waiting to impale him if he fell too far to either side of the bridge. Excitement bloomed anew, working right off the fire from the battle.

"I'm ready," he said.

Ashok dangled from a thread, a thought between life and death, yet he'd never felt more connected to the world. He was aware of everything: the wind pulling him back and forth, the city breathing around him. All of it yanked into focus as if outlined in crystal. He felt everything, yet there was no pain. Even the roaring fire in his shoulder seemed dim compared to what he experienced in that breath.

Vedoran let go. The air left Ashok's lungs, and for the shortest space, he hung in midair. The chain sang, metal against metal. Ashok fell, his eyes closed, trusting the slender thread to hold him.

CHAPTER
SEVEN

TRAINING FOR ASHOK, VEDORAN, AND THE OTHER RECRUITS, BEGAN shortly after the first bell of the day—the Monril bell, Ashok learned. He remembered Cree had said Ikemmu marked six intervals of the day with the bells. He learned them quickly: Monril, Diteen, Trimmer, Tet, Pendron, and Exeden. Sleep, for the shadar-kai, was accomplished in six groups in the time between bells. When Ashok rolled off his cot he felt awake and on edge—he'd rested enough to stay alert, but his muscles had had no chance to become lethargic.

Morningfeast was served in an open, communal hall at the mid-level of the barracks by a team of young humans. Sweat glistened off their pale skin as they ladled a sweet stew into bowls for the lines of shadar-kai that came through the hall. Ashok was still fascinated by the skin of the other races—light or dark, they virtually glowed.

"Ready for some play?" Cree asked Ashok as he was leaving the hall. Cree and Chanoch were practically vibrating as they exited the tower with a cluster of other shadar-kai men and women, all in a similar state of agitation.

They walked out into the training yard and immediately formed up into lines as they had the previous day. Ashok took up a position in the back row next to Skagi and Cree. Vedoran stood two rows ahead of them.

A shadar-kai Ashok didn't recognize stood in the shadow of the tower next to a weapon rack of spears. When the recruits stood in their lines, he stepped forward. A pair of tattoos in the shape of serpents traced the muscles up each of his long arms.

"I am Jamet," the shadar-kai said, addressing them. His voice was a soft rasp, as if his throat had been ravaged by thirst. "I am your teacher. I have not the tongue for speeches as the Watching Blade does, but mark me well: what I lack in voice I more than make up for with these." He took a spear from the rack and held it crosswise above his head. "The spear, the sword, the club," he continued. "They will be your arms, your nerves—every part of you will defer to their guidance in battle, save one." He tapped his temple. "Fight with your head," he said. His hand slid down to cover his chest, his heart. "This belongs to Tempus. He will take care of the rest."

Jamet walked up and down the lines of men and women, pausing every so often to scrutinize the recruits. On his last pass, he stopped in front of Ashok. He picked up a bit of Ashok's chain dangling from his belt. Ashok followed his movements but made no reaction.

"Those of you who come to us bearing your own weapons"— Jamet pitched his voice to carry to the rest of the recruits—"prepare to unlearn everything you've learned up to this point. I'm going to show you new ways of fighting." He held a length of chain up in front of Ashok. "These links are loose, rusted," he said. "They need to be repaired."

Ashok didn't disagree. "I have no talent for the forge," he replied.

"That too you will learn," Jamet said. He added, "But you would do better to choose a different weapon."

"Why?" Ashok asked suspiciously.

"This weapon," Jamet said, feeding the links through his hands, "doesn't distinguish friend from foe. It will sting your allies in battle."

"And my enemies," Ashok said.

Jamet grunted. "How will you avoid striking them in close quarters?" he said, nodding to Cree and Skagi.

"I've never had to consider allies in my fighting," Ashok said.

"You're a solitary?"

"I didn't say that."

"What do you say?" Jamet said, pressing Ashok, his tone mocking. "You don't care whether you kill friend or foe in battle?"

Ashok realized, nearly too late, that he was being led. "I meant only that it's impossible to distinguish friend from foe," he said levelly.

"So it is," Jamet said. He let the chain fall to Ashok's side. "But that was your old life. This city is different."

Jamet moved on, back to the front lines. "Remember Uwan's words," he said. "Your first duty is to Ikemmu, and your second"—he glanced pointedly at Ashok—"is to your allies who help defend it. Fail them, and you fail this city. There is no higher crime."

He replaced the spear in the weapons rack. "I'm done with speeches," he said. "Training begins *now*."

At that instant, the Diteen bell tolled. Jamet divided the shadar-kai into teams of sparring partners. Ashok found himself grouped with Skagi, Cree, Chanoch, and Vedoran. Jamet instructed them to choose the weapon they knew from the myriad weapon racks, or to choose the weapon they most wanted to learn. Ashok kept his chain. He noticed Cree and Skagi held onto their own weapons, as did Vedoran.

Chanoch selected a greatsword from the rack. It wasn't as finely honed or as impressive as Uwan's weapon, Ashok thought, but to see Chanoch's face he knew that hardly mattered. Uwan had taken him over completely. He would wield the sword of his leader.

"Spar with me?" he asked Ashok, all eagerness and energy.

"Careful, Chanoch," Vedoran said, throwing Ashok a knowing smile. "This one isn't a newborn."

The training yard had been roped off into squares. Ashok tested his footing, but the surface was good. He wouldn't slip.

Chanoch stood before him, his sword held two-handed. Ashok unhooked his chain and let one end fall to the ground.

"Aren't you afraid I'll cut it in half?" Chanoch asked, a half-smile twisting his features.

"No," Ashok said. He snapped his arm out from his side. The chain whipped up like an awakened snake. It clipped Chanoch on the jaw before Ashok jerked it back.

Instinctively, Chanoch fell into a crouch, his lips pulled back in a snarl. He tensed for a charge, but Ashok read the move as if Chanoch had spoken his intentions aloud. He snapped the chain again, and that time Chanoch felt the bite at his sword hand. He flinched but to his credit did not drop his weapon.

"Come ahead," Ashok said, unable to stop the taunt from rising to his lips as his blood pumped. He knew it wasn't fair. Chanoch was too young. Too easy.

Chanoch charged across the yard, the greatsword thrust viciously before him.

It was a good move, Ashok acknowledged. But Chanoch was not as fast as Cree, not fast enough to take him by surprise. And the greatsword hadn't the reach to make up for Chanoch's lack of speed.

Ashok spun out of the way, using the force of the maneuver to bring the chain around swinging. It cut the air with a whistle, nearly taking off Chanoch's head. The young one ducked to avoid the blow, which drove him almost to his knees.

Ashok brought his boot down, stamping on Chanoch's blade and forcing it into the ground. Ashok not only had the superior height, but with his weight bearing down on the sword, Chanoch couldn't get any leverage to free his weapon.

Chanoch realized it too, and skittered back before Ashok could get in any close-range attacks. He gained his feet and stood before Ashok, weaponless but defiant.

It's over, Ashok thought. I could take him with the chain or cut him with his own sword. The urge to finish the fight and put his enemy down was as natural to Ashok as breathing. He felt the surge in his blood and the need to satisfy it. He stood again on the Span, in the breath between life and death. But the life at stake was not his own. Not an enemy's. Not his brother's.

In that breath, Ashok made his decision. Instead of forcing his need into his weapon, he drew it inward. He took a breath to steady his body and channeled all the violence into a different focus. Deliberately lowering his arms to his sides, he did not move to strike. His body trembled with the effort of maintaining control, but he reveled in his success.

"Concede," Ashok said to Chanoch. "You're disarmed."

"Not yet," Chanoch said.

Ashok heard chuckles from the side of the field. "Give it up, won't you," Cree called out. "We want our turn. We're getting restless."

"And pained from the sight of Ashok taking you apart," Skagi added, snickering.

Chanoch's face reddened. The blood swelling just under the surface of his skin gave his face a sickly appearance. "Not yet," he said stubbornly.

Then he did something Ashok truly wasn't expecting. Weaponless, he came at Ashok with his bare hands.

Ashok jerked the chain up defensively, but his reaction was slow—all his focus had been on restraining himself from attacking. The young one was too close. He would peel the skin from Chanoch's face if he completed the motion with the chain. But Chanoch was still coming at him, with fury in his eyes.

Every instinct in Ashok's body roared that he should defend himself. He would be killed if he didn't. His muscles trembled, but something, an impulse almost separate from his body, made him release the chain and absorb the impact as Chanoch hit him.

They went down in a cloud of dirt. Through the grit in his eyes, Ashok managed to get his hands around Chanoch's throat. He felt the shadar-kai's blood pulsing erratically through his veins. Of course he knew such excitement well. Ashok had felt it himself, just moments before. It was more than survival; it was the need for the kill. Feeling it, so close, Ashok found himself unable to control his own instinct for self-preservation. He let it come and squeezed, trying to break Chanoch's windpipe.

Choking, Chanoch rolled them, slamming Ashok's tender shoulder into the ground. Ashok gave an involuntary, strangled cry as his arm went dead. He'd fixed the dislocation himself; he hadn't sought Tempus's healers, and he was paying the price. He reached for Chanoch's face with his good hand, but the young one batted it aside.

Then suddenly, Chanoch eased back. Blinking through the pain and the dirt, Ashok tried to sit up. He saw Chanoch groping to free the dagger at his belt. Ashok remembered his own dagger, but instead of going for it, he brought his knees up and kicked. His feet connected with Chanoch's midsection. The breath whooshed out of the young man, and he fell back, his head hitting the ground with an audible crack.

Ashok scrambled to his feet, panting, waiting for the next attack, his blood pounding and his old instincts raging. He grabbed his discarded chain and wound the links around his knuckles. He wouldn't make the same mistake twice. The next time he charged, the young one was dead.

But Chanoch didn't attack again. He sat up, touching the back of his head. His fingers came away bloody. The feral excitement had left his eyes, banished by the blow to his head.

Ashok's awareness was not so affected. He was overcome with the need to finish what he'd started. The desire to kill sang in his blood. He took a step forward. An involuntary growl ripped from his throat, but Chanoch didn't hear and didn't recognize the danger.

Suddenly, Vedoran stood beside Ashok. He'd come from nowhere. Ashok snarled and struck out with his chain-wrapped fist. The punch passed right through Vedoran's insubstantial face and threw Ashok off balance. He righted himself, and when he looked again, Vedoran had come out of his wraith form. He gripped Ashok's upper arm firmly.

"It's over," he said.

And it was. Across the yard, the brothers were helping Chanoch to his feet and examining his head. They were talking and laughing as if nothing out of the ordinary had happened. Only Vedoran had seen Ashok's loss of control.

Ashok closed his eyes to try to clear his head. He was dizzy with the release of tension and didn't speak for several breaths.

Finally, he looked up at Vedoran and nodded. Vedoran released him.

"My thanks," Ashok said quietly.

Vedoran shrugged. "The battle was already over," he said. "The young one should never have pressed his attack. You would have been justified teaching him to know his limits."

"I would have killed him," Ashok replied.

Vedoran said nothing.

Ashok put his chain back on his belt. He noticed for the first time that the back of his hand was covered in blood. The chain spikes had dug deep furrows into the skin around his knuckles. His inner struggle had eclipsed the pain and the fire in his shoulder.

Jamet walked across the yard toward them. He stopped to examine Chanoch, then moved on to Ashok.

"Well fought," he said as he examined Ashok's shoulder and the hand wounds. "You're done for today. Go to the temple and receive Tempus's blessing."

"I'm fine," Ashok said.

"You're no use to me with a dead arm," Jamet said briskly. He pointed to Vedoran and Skagi. "You two take their places," he said.

Vedoran nodded to Ashok and went to spar with Skagi while Cree and Chanoch looked on.

Left alone, Ashok moved off and wandered the training yard for a time, watching the other sparring matches. The shadar-kai fought well and were far more disciplined than most he'd seen—and they were only warriors in training, the lowest rank in the hierarchy.

Ashok's arm throbbed, reminding him where he was supposed to be. He turned and walked off the training yard before Jamet saw that he'd lingered.

He passed beyond the iron fence and came to a startling realization. It was the first time he'd been alone since he'd been captured. The shadar-kai in the training yard were absorbed in sparring, Cree and Skagi hadn't noticed or hadn't cared when he'd left, and Jamet hadn't sent anyone with him to the temple.

Ashok's thoughts hadn't turned to escape since his adventure with the nightmare. After that first attempt, he knew they would be watching him closely, so he'd focused on learning all he could about Ikemmu and trying to divine what Uwan wanted from him. But his captors' attention had waned, he thought. How could he take advantage of the lapse?

Ashok walked slowly, crossing the markets, which were just as bustling as they had been the previous day. He saw Gaina, hawking his colorful clothing, and gave the human a wide berth.

The circuitous route took him down a quieter avenue of shops. The buildings here were older, showing only light fire damage, so Ashok could see shadows of their former beauty.

Many of the roofs had been tall and conical—a field of spherical stone to match the imposing towers. But the shapes had become tumbling and crooked. There were no doors on the older structures, only archways outlined in brick.

Ashok passed close enough to one of the shops to see strange carvings embedded in the bricks. He hesitated, tracing a finger in one that was roughly shaped like a bird. Latent heat brushed his fingertips, and a slight electrical shock. He took his hand away, surprised.

"Are you lost, friend?" a voice called.

Ashok looked down to see a diminutive woman step from the shop. She had bright hair stacked in thick braids on top of her head. Her angular face made her blue and white and black eyes look enormous, but they were friendly and curious as they met his.

"Come in," she beckoned him, when Ashok didn't reply. She spoke the shadar-kai tongue as well as if she'd been born one of the race.

Curious, Ashok followed her into the shop, which was dimly lit by candles in sconces scattered about the room. Tables covered in red and black cloths filled the floor space, and on them were racks of bottles and quills, stacks of blank parchment, wax, and seals. Ashok smelled the scent of thick ink deeply sunk into the place.

"Sit down," the woman said, guiding him with a hand at the back of his thigh to a human-fitted chair near the counter. She didn't seem the least intimidated by his size. "I would have invited you in sooner, but I must admit I was surprised to see you standing out there," she said.

"Why?" Ashok asked.

The woman looked at him strangely. The corners of her eyes crinkled in amusement. "It's just I don't get many shadar-kai visitors here," she said. "My clients are mostly human, dwarf, or halfling, like me."

Ashok picked up one of the blank parchment sheets. "What is it you do here?" he asked.

"Messages," the woman said. "We transcribe them, and a courier delivers them. The shadar-kai don't often communicate beyond the city." She added quickly, "That's not to say I'm denying you, not at all. If you need to send a message . . ."

Ashok shook his head. "I saw the runes on your doorway," he replied. "I was curious."

"Ah, yes," the woman said, smiling. "I've had visitors come to study them, seeking to learn Ikemmu's history." She gave him a quizzical look. "Are you interested in such things?"

"I don't know," Ashok said. He traced a fingertip across the smooth parchment stacked on the counter.

"Stop, stop!" the woman cried, uttering a startled oath in a language he didn't recognize. She took his hand in her small one. The blood had almost dried, but the cuts on his knuckles were ugly and inflamed. "You've hurt yourself," she said.

Ashok had acknowledged the continuing sting, but he hadn't noticed the blood streaks soaking through the parchment sheets. "Forgive me," he said.

She waved a hand. "It's nothing," she said. "Excuse me." She went through another archway to an adjoining room off the shop. When she returned, she held a roll of bandages.

Ashok reached down to take them from her, but she unrolled the strips herself and wound them over his knuckles. She tied a knot beneath his fingers.

"Done," she said.

"My thanks," Ashok said, flexing his fingers around the bandages, making sure he could still maneuver a chain. With regret, he watched the woman remove the blood-soaked parchment sheets and put them behind the counter.

Suddenly, he remembered the soiled bandages with his blood marks on them. He could feel them; they hadn't been lost in his escape attempt.

"What do you want for it?" he said.

The woman was rolling up the extra bandages. "What did you say?" she asked.

"The parchment," Ashok said. "Will you trade for the parchment, quill, and ink—including what was damaged?" He spoke without thinking. He had nothing to trade her.

The woman looked at him with the same curious expression she'd used earlier. "Are you new to Ikemmu?" she asked.

He worked his jaw. It was so easy for them to see he was an outsider. "Yes," he replied.

"Ah, I thought so," the woman said as she held out her small hand for him to clasp. "In that case, welcome. My name is Darnae. May I know you?"

"Ashok," Ashok said. He took the small hand in three of his fingers, marveling at her softness, like a child but with hard calluses where the quill had worn her skin.

"Well, Ashok," Darnae said, smiling. "You may select whatever of my wares you wish. You owe me no coin."

"Why not?" he asked, on his guard again.

"You're in training, yes?" she replied. "You came to fight?"

To fight. That was true enough. "Yes," he said.

"Ikemmu provides for its soldiers," Darnae explained. "Whatever their needs, we fulfill them. A small price, most of us feel, for the security we enjoy in the city, and the opportunity to trade with so many other races, so many worlds."

Ashok nodded, but he was remembering the confrontation

between Skagi and Gaina. "I have heard . . . the shadar-kai here can't do certain things for themselves," he said.

"Yes," Darnae agreed. "But not for lack of skill," she added quickly, looking uncomfortable. "We understand that, as warriors, your first concern is defending Ikemmu. In a trade city such as this . . . How do I say it? There are many races here with a variety of needs. And there is daily drudgery, mundane tasks created when so many choose to live side by side. These things the shadar-kai were not made to do. You would fade. So the other races fill those roles." She picked up a stack of parchment sheets, a bottle of ink, and a quill. She started to slide them into a brown leather case, but Ashok waved her off.

"There's no need," he said. "I'll carry them."

"As you wish," she replied, handing him the items. "Do you know how to use them?" she asked tentatively.

"I know enough," Ashok said. "How did the other races come to trade here?"

"Ikemmu is uniquely situated in the Shadowdark," Darnae said. "We are at a crossroads between the planes. The shadar-kai protect the passage and allow outlanders to establish permanent businesses within the city. Few enclaves are so fortunate, so Ikemmu has grown and prospered."

Ashok nodded, thinking how his own enclave would never open itself up to outsiders.

"My thanks," he said. He stood and walked to the archway. Darnae stayed behind the counter, watching him. He paused between the candlelight and the shadows. "Has anyone ever found out what the markings mean?" he said, reaching out to skim the air over the runes. He felt the hovering electrical charge, just out of reach.

"No," Darnae said. "But they all agree something terrible happened here, long ago."

CHAPTER EIGHT

Ashok took Darnae's parchment and found an abandoned stone building near the outskirts of the market. He could hear the babble of voices in the distance, but no one came near the half-collapsed structure. The roof had sagged, forcing him to stoop when he went inside. He found a darkened corner with enough light filtering through the gaps in the stone to allow him to see clearly.

He laid the parchment out on the ground, un-stoppered the ink bottle, and took the quill awkwardly in his hand.

It would have been easier to write with his fingers, but Ashok didn't want the stains to betray him. He worked slowly, and he ruined several of the parchment sheets; but Darnae had been generous with her gift. By the fifth sheet, he'd managed a rough sketch of the four towers, the bridges and lower city, and the wall. He copied the number of guards he'd seen on the wall from the soiled bandages to the parchment, and added notes on placement written in his own almost unintelligible shorthand.

He made other notes and observances on how often the bells tolled and their names. He listed the ranks of shadar-kai soldiers and wrote a complete physical description of Uwan.

They maintain a constant physical and magical presence on the wall, he wrote. *No knowing if the towers themselves are magically protected, but it makes sense that they would be, to protect the tall structures from siege equipment and anything that might come through their outer portal.*

He paused in his writing, wondering what his father would make of the information. His sire would never be able to mount an offensive against such a force, Ashok thought, but maybe the presence, the mere threat . . . .

It might be enough to draw the enclave's attention away from its infighting, at least for a time. A threat from without could cause them to band together and emerge from hiding. There would be no more useless waste.

Ashok waited for the ink to dry and tucked the parchment in the pouch inside his armor. He hid the quill and ink among the ruins for use later. He left the building, picked out Tower Makthar in the distance, and started walking roughly in that direction. He did not want Skagi, Jamet and the others to know he had been wandering alone. Let them think he was content to train with the other recruits. If they thought he was tamed, it would draw their attention away from him.

When he got past Tower Pyton, the stone buildings thinned out into empty dirt streets choked with stone debris. Near the base of the canyon wall, Ashok glimpsed another fence made of iron, like the one encircling Tower Athanon, but higher. A handful of low stone buildings squatted nearby. Thin black smoke rose from two of them.

Beyond the buildings, Ashok saw a yawning cave mouth set into the canyon wall. He slowed his pace. He smelled fire, metal, and animal fur all wrapped up in a stinging reek that made his eyes water. Cautiously, he approached the iron fence, his hands gripping the bars.

Then he heard it.

Faintly, so it only sent a shiver of apprehension up his spine, then gradually the sound—a hollow, terrible scream—drew closer. Ashok waited, watching the cave mouth with a kind of giddy dread.

When the nightmare appeared like a blazing torch at the mouth of the cave, Ashok caught his breath.

A shadar-kai woman brought it out, its face covered by a hood and secured with chains so it couldn't bite her. She'd wrapped a stiff cloth around her head and ears to dull the scream, but Ashok could see that it still affected her. She took sluggish steps, stumbled often, and jerked the nightmare's head each time the scream rang out until it finally fell quiet.

They reached the fence, which contained an open pasture of sorts, with dead, singed grass all around. The woman opened a gate, removed the nightmare's hood, and released the chain to let the beast run in relative freedom around the paddock.

As soon as it was clear of the woman, the nightmare immediately charged the fence, slamming its body against the iron. Ashok felt the bars rattle under his hands.

When it was clear the fence wasn't going to give in that spot, the nightmare cantered back and charged again, searching for a weakness in the fence it could exploit. Its headlong rush brought it only a few feet away from where Ashok stood, close enough that he could smell the burning hair scent of the nightmare's mane. Its steamy breath heated the air.

"Well met, again," Ashok murmured. "You're no happier here than you were in the cage, are you?"

The nightmare saw him and snorted, its red eyes so dark they were almost black. It strode up to where Ashok stood and slammed its head into the bars in front of his face.

Ashok leaped back, the nightmare's bloody breath in his mouth, the burnt hair scent all around him. The change in the air temperature was a palpable thing. He began to sweat, as if he were standing in the middle of a bonfire.

"I think he likes you," said a teasing voice from across the paddock.

Ashok met the gaze of the shadar-kai woman. "He's beautiful," Ashok said.

The woman shook her head. "He won't be tamed, no matter what Uwan wants," she said. "He tries to kill anyone who comes near him, and when someone does get close enough . . . Well, there are the dreams."

Ashok approached the fence again. The nightmare backed away and regarded him with his steely crimson gaze. Unable to dislodge him from the fence, the beast blew a steamy, impatient breath and pranced in place, threatening with his burning body.

Ashok smiled grimly. "You don't scare me," he said.

The female shadar-kai came to stand beside Ashok. "I'm Olra," she said, offering him her hand.

Ashok clasped it briefly. "Where did they capture him?" he asked.

"Out on the plains," Olra said. "He'd been in a fight with something bigger than him—got cut up bad enough that the caravan was able to get him in a cage while he was unconscious. Otherwise they'd never have been able to take him. He's too wild, even for his kind."

Ashok looked at the nightmare, the eyes burning with red hatred. He understood the feeling.

"What did you mean when you said 'there are the dreams'?" Ashok asked.

"The nightmare sends them," Olra said. "It's the scream that does it. Works into your mind somehow and roots out what you're most afraid of. After a few days, even a shadar-kai can't stand the horror." She nodded to the nightmare. "He makes them think they're fading."

"He knows it too," Ashok said. "Look at him."

The nightmare paced back and forth before the fence. Flame roared down his mane and fetlocks, scarring the ground an oily black as the beast took one stride after another across the paddock. He marks his territory and dares anyone to invade, Ashok thought.

"Are you all right?" Olra asked abruptly. She was looking at how Ashok's arm dangled at an awkward angle.

"I was on my way to Tower Makthar for healing," Ashok said. Taking one last look at the magnificent beast, Ashok stepped away from the fence.

Olra was looking at him curiously. Looking at her face, Ashok realized how heavily scarred she was.

Puckered flesh from burns, and a web-work of claw slashes decorated her collarbone. The marks were not self-inflicted, that much was evident. Her left cheek looked like it had been bitten and healed slightly off-center, giving her face an asymmetrical appearance.

"You're the one everyone's talking about," Olra said. "Uwan's ghost."

"A ghost?" Ashok said. "Why do they call me that?"

"Because no one knows who you are or where you came from. You came to us a prisoner, yet you walk among us as if you were an ally. But no one questions it," Olra said. "If Uwan has a reason for you being here, that's enough."

"You trust your leader that much?" Ashok said. "What if he's wrong?"

"Uwan is never wrong," Olra said.

The simple confidence in her voice kept Ashok from uttering the retort he wanted to. He changed the subject. "Will you break the nightmare yourself?" he asked.

"I'll try," she said.

"More scars," Ashok murmured.

"These?" Olra said as she held up her hands, which were covered with slowly healing blisters. "All were earned for Ikemmu," she said, with pride in her voice. "The beasts we train will either defend the city, or we'll sell them to the other races, which brings us coin. There is honor in both. There are also these." She bared her left arm for Ashok. From shoulder to wrist, the beasts of the Shadowfell stared back at Ashok in tattoos. Shadow hounds and ravens, nightmares and serpents—one picture blended into the next.

"Are these the creatures you've broken?" Ashok asked.

Olra nodded. "They're all a part of me. I own them, and they own me," she said, indicating her scars.

Ashok nodded. He could think of nothing to say.

"You'd better go on, get your shoulder looked at," Olra said. She walked away from him along the fence, her hand trailing against the bars. The nightmare measured her progress, but he didn't attack the fence again.

"Aren't you afraid of him?" Ashok called after her. "Afraid of fading?"

Olra stopped and turned to look at him. "Of course," she said. "I had a predecessor, head of the Camborrs, just like I am now. How do you suppose he died?"

Behind the fence, the nightmare breathed and stamped the ground black.

Ashok went to the temple to accept Tempus's healing, but he couldn't shake the image of the nightmare from his thoughts. Maybe he'd been doomed from the moment he heard the beast's scream, for when he'd been healed, Ashok found himself walking back to the Camborr pen. He spent time watching all the creatures as they were brought out: the shadow hounds, the jaguars, the serpents—any beast the caravan could capture.

But the nightmare was a creature apart from them all.

Ashok stood at the fence while Olra put the horse—it wasn't right to call him that, Ashok thought, the name was demeaning—through his paces from a distance with a long whip. She never actually struck the creature; she couldn't, unless her whip was iron-tipped. The flimsy leather end would burn to cinders if it got too near the nightmare's flaring mane.

"It's not going well," Olra said when she saw Ashok. "No one's going to be able to ride him. He sets fire to the ground whenever anyone comes near him, so we peck at him from behind the fence. It's all we can do."

The nightmare reared, biting at the whip that snapped near his face. Olra tried to jerk it free, but the nightmare yanked it out of her hands. Cursing, Olra backed away as the beast came at the fence and banged against the bars.

Olra dusted off her hands and went to stand beside Ashok. "He enjoys it," she said, "knowing he's the one in control. It's all sport for him."

Ashok shook his head. "It only makes the imprisonment bearable," he said.

Olra blew out a sigh. "Well, whatever it is, it's going to get him killed," she said.

"What?" Ashok said. It came out sharper than he'd intended.

"What else would I do?" Olra said disgustedly. "The shadar-kai can't use him, because of the nightmares. His screams would throw them off balance in a battle. I told you he was too wild, even for his kind. That's what I'll tell Uwan too."

"Sell him," Ashok said. "He must be valuable in coin."

"Oh, he is," Olra said. "Trained, he'd bring in a heap of coin. But wild as he is now, it would take just the right mix of wealth and crazy in a buyer to take him on, and I can't wager on that person striding up out of thin air. Meanwhile I'm losing time trying to wrangle the beast, time that could be spent training the shadow hounds or the panthers. Them I can work."

"Set him free, then," Ashok said. He clenched the fence bars in agitation. "Take him up to the plain and release him. It's a waste to kill him."

Olra shook her head. "I can't risk any of the Camborrs on that kind of mission. If something went wrong, I'd never be able to justify the loss of life to Uwan."

"Yes, because Uwan protects his people," Ashok said bitterly. "Except those he enslaves for no reason."

He pressed his forehead against the iron bars. When would he outlive his novelty to the shadar-kai leader? Ashok wondered.

He stared at the nightmare for a long time, then he turned to Olra. "Let me break him," he said.

Olra scoffed. "You're out of your head," she said. "Warriors in training don't come inside my fence. You'll be eaten alive."

"And you'll have lost nothing," Ashok said. "You said yourself I'm not a Camborr, so my death wouldn't matter to your work. But if I did make progress with the beast, then you'd be able to sell him for a great profit. Ikemmu would benefit from that coin—isn't that what you want?"

"It's not that easy," Olra said. "You may be an outsider, but Uwan values you. I can't do anything without speaking to him first."

"Then speak to him," Ashok said. "I'll train your beast."

CHAPTER NINE

Ashok's first tenday in Ikemmu passed quickly, filled with hours of endless training and sparring, first with his own weapons and then others of Jamet's choosing. At the end of any given day Ashok's muscles were so thoroughly worked he could barely lift his arms. He fell into his bed, but he'd hardly closed his eyes when it seemed they were open again at the tolling of the Monril bell, and the whole process began anew. The teacher was tireless with his students, and the recruits were eager to learn.

His second tenday passed more slowly, as Ashok found himself with a bit more time to himself. He spent much of that in his abandoned building in the trade district, copying to parchment as much as he could remember about the city's defenses and any weaknesses he noticed during his training sessions. By the end of the second tenday, he knew the names of many of the Guardians and their functions.

Some of them were teachers, like Jamet, but there were others he never saw in the training yard. They kept close counsel with Uwan, on the rare occasions Ashok saw the leader outside Tower Athanon. Once, he asked Skagi about it.

"They're planning the next raid," Skagi explained, as if it were obvious.

"I thought a caravan just left the city," Ashok said. "Is there more than one that goes into the Shadowfell?"

Skagi shook his head. "This party's going in the opposite direction, into the Underdark maybe—the details are kept quiet. The wealthiest traders coin the expeditions, and in return they profit from whatever goods are brought back and sold. But every raid is done with military support, a mix of sellswords and Tempus's warriors."

"The Underdark?" Ashok said. That was not a place in the Shadowfell, but in the mirror world. Still a place of caverns and tunnels deep underground, but not one that followed the ways of this plane.

Ashok stared at Skagi, and the shadar-kai laughed. "It's true we haven't trusted you with all our secrets," he said. "In fact, you've only seen about half of them." For some reason, that struck Skagi as intensely amusing. He was still chuckling when Ashok walked away in disgust, having been unable to pry any further information from him.

By the end of a month, Ashok had recorded as much information as he was going to get without arousing suspicions with his questions, though in truth he wondered if such a thing was possible. Cree, Skagi, and Chanoch, any shadar-kai he came in contact with was more than willing to share what they knew about life in Ikemmu. They accepted him without question, because they trusted Uwan. If their leader decreed it, there must be a purpose for Ashok's presence in the city.

Ashok had yet to find out what that purpose was, and the mystery was driving him mad. He hadn't spoken to Uwan since the day he'd attempted to escape. And every day since, though he'd thought of various ways to distract his captors, to use their trust to his advantage, Ashok found a reason not to try to escape the city. He told himself at first that it was because he hadn't collected enough intelligence.

His father would demand nothing less than a complete report on the city and its defenses.

When he'd exhausted all possible sources of information, Ashok decided it would be best to take as much training as Uwan offered. He'd been strong before, but he could feel himself changing every day he spent in the city.

The constant, controlled sparring; the fact that he ingested regular meals of fresh, spiced meat; and so much stimulation that Ashok never felt the need to put the dagger to his flesh, made his body stronger than it had ever been.

There was also the nightmare.

A month had passed, and he'd heard nothing from Olra or Uwan with regard to the beast. He walked to the Camborr pens every day, but he never saw the nightmare out in the open again.

Then one day he saw Olra standing near the fence. She motioned him over, but she didn't look happy.

"Uwan gave permission for you to be trained as a Camborr," she said without greeting him, "with training the nightmare specifically in mind."

Ashok felt his heart pounding in his chest, but the look on Olra's face tempered his excitement. "You don't want me here," Ashok said. The unwillingness was plain on her face. Did she resent that Uwan thought Ashok might succeed where she had failed? he wondered.

"You like him too much," Olra said, "the nightmare. That feeling might turn into trust. If that happens, he'll kill you the first chance he gets. It'll be a waste, and I don't like waste."

"Neither do I," Ashok said quietly.

So it wasn't resentment for taking her place, but something entirely different. Ashok thought they might be able to work together.

"I'll want to go into the paddock," he said. "Immediately."

Olra was quiet for a moment, her scarred face pensive. "One condition," she said.

"What is it?" Ashok asked.

"Bring your companions," she said. "You'll need people to be there, in case something goes wrong."

Ashok hesitated. "I don't know if I can," he said.

He'd never asked Skagi or the others for anything like a favor. Had he asked his brothers in the enclave for such support, he would have been laughed at. He wasn't sure how the shadar-kai would respond.

Olra shook her head, her forehead creased in exasperation. "You two"—she nodded at the nightmare—"are as hard-headed as they come. Those are my terms," she said, and turned to walk back to the cave where the pens were. "Find a way."

At the Tet bell, Ashok climbed the tower stairs to Eveningfeast. Cree stopped him before he picked up a bowl for his stew.

"Come with me," Cree said, his black eyes sparkling with barely contained excitement. "There's better fare to be had tonight. We're celebrating." He flashed Ashok a grin and moved off without a sound.

Curious, Ashok followed the shadar-kai down the stairs and outside, where Skagi, Chanoch, and Vedoran were waiting.

"Well done, brother," Skagi said. He lounged against the tower, twirling his falchion. "Did he put up a fight?"

"Brutal," Cree said. "I had to set him in his place."

Chanoch snorted. "You've lost, let's see," he said, pretending to stroke his chin, "four sparring matches with Ashok this tenday. Is that right, Vedoran?"

"It is," Vedoran said gravely. "And you lost five such against him, little one."

Skagi bellowed with laughter. "Then we go to celebrate Ashok's great victory." He slapped Ashok on the back. "You're a Camborr now."

"How did you know?" Ashok asked. He hadn't told anyone about his conversation with Olra earlier that day.

"You think it's a secret when any of us go up in rank?" Chanoch said, staring at him incredulously. "Ask Skagi about his tattoos."

Skagi traced the field of tattoos layered across his flank. "Got these the day I entered Tempus's service," he said. "Cost me everything I'd earned doing hard labor in the city, but it was worth every coin. Folk in the trade districts mark me now. They say, 'There walks Skagi, warrior of Ikemmu.' Someday it will be Skagi, Sworn of Uwan."

The absolute conviction in his voice left Ashok with little doubt that Skagi would be successful in his quest. The others nodded in agreement, nursing their own dreams behind their eyes. Only Vedoran seemed subdued.

"You need your own tattoo to mark this day," Cree said. "You're a Camborr; you need ink on your skin to show it."

"I say give him flames, since he's going into the fire with that nightmare," Skagi said. "Or maybe the shadow hounds?" He grinned at Ashok.

Ashok looked down at himself. His skin was bland and colorless next to the complex patterns of the tattoos on the others. But he didn't understand why they would want to celebrate his accomplishment.

"When one of you goes up in rank," Ashok said, "the others will be left behind. You're competing for the same honors." They should be trying to assassinate him in order to take his place, he thought, not congratulating him on his success.

"Whether we succeed or fail depends on our own efforts," Chanoch said. By the rapture in his eyes, it sounded like he was repeating something he'd heard Uwan say. "It's our own fault if we're unworthy."

"And when we are rewarded for our service"—Skagi threw an arm around Ashok's shoulder and towed him in the direction of Tower Hevalor—"we drink."

The tavern was impressive. It occupied three open levels midway up Tower Hevalor and saw mostly shadar-kai patrons, Ashok noticed. There were no signs marking its name, and whenever Ashok heard anyone refer to it, they called it simply Hevalor Tavern.

The tavern's stone walls were lit with enchanted blue torchlight, and the cloths covering the tables were black. The dark colors created the illusion of privacy in a room with no corners.

There was a circular bar on each level, but no food to be had. How could there be, Ashok thought, when the room was filled to capacity with kegs and bottles of more varieties of drink than he would have thought existed in the world.

Cree went to the bar for drinks while Ashok and the others sought a table on the third level. When they were seated, Ashok took the opportunity to examine his new tattoo. Green-inked flames encircled his right forearm from elbow to wrist. The fire appeared surprisingly fluid and gave the illusion that in the right light the flames might dance like a true blaze. The inker, a human female with a shop in the open market, had done an impressive job.

Ashok liked the design, but he still thought the others were being premature by insisting he mark his status as a Camborr-in-training. He'd done nothing to break the nightmare yet, and it might be that the flame tattoo would end up decorating his corpse if he failed.

Music drifted down to them from a small dais on the third level. Distracted from his thoughts, Ashok looked up and saw the only non-shadar-kai patron in the room. He recognized Darnae at once. She was playing some kind of instrument, her small voice curled around a song in a language Ashok didn't recognize. It must have been her native tongue, he thought.

Ashok had heard music, sometimes, carried by the wind through the caves of his enclave. He had never known where it came from. Those caves were strange entities that collected sounds from miles across the plains, or perhaps from the world that mirrored the Shadowfell.

But he'd never heard music like Darnae's, so close and warm and somehow personal. The mournful strains of the song filled the darkened room and made Ashok's chest ache with unexplainable emotion. Was there a spell in the words, to make him react this way? he wondered.

Skagi snapped his fingers in front of Ashok's face. "We can't be losing you already, you've tasted no drink!" he said.

Vedoran handed Ashok a tankard of something that smelled like almonds. "Start with that," he said. "If you prove yourself worthy, we'll move you up to something finer."

Ashok found it hard to draw his mind away from the song. He sniffed his drink and risked a swallow. He wrinkled his nose in disgust.

"Too sweet," he said.

"I told you he wouldn't like the zzar," Vedoran said.

"He's a pup, doesn't know what he likes," Skagi said, reaching across the table. He took Ashok's drink and poured the contents into his own tankard, which was already half empty. "Share your brew with him then, if you can pry your fingers away."

Vedoran handed Ashok a goblet of red liquid. Ashok sniffed.

The aroma was sharper, not sweet at all. He took a drink and felt all the moisture leave his tongue. He coughed.

"Doesn't like that one much either," Chanoch observed, but Ashok shook his head.

"No, I like it," he said. He sipped again to confirm his first impression. "What is it?"

"A Cormyrian wine," Vedoran said. "Highly acidic. Tatigan brings a few bottles in for the tavern twice a year."

"Charges a pretty price for it too," Skagi added.

"Who is Tatigan?" Ashok asked.

"He's a merchant. Human, like most of them, but he deals in rarer goods," Skagi said. "Exotic wines, but weapons too, and poisons. Whatever you need, he can find it. Rumor is the Watching Blade himself buys from Tatigan."

"You'll know him when you see him," Cree said. "He wears spectacles with green lenses in them. He says it's because he doesn't like the colors here."

"He's a strange one," Skagi agreed. He touched his tankard to Ashok's goblet. "Drink. Vedoran can get himself another."

"My thanks," Vedoran said sarcastically. Ashok tried to hand him his goblet back, but he waved it aside. "Finish it," he said. "It's a welcome change to find someone who doesn't enjoy piss and almonds."

Cree and Chanoch laughed. Skagi made a rude gesture but laughed as well. Vedoran headed to the bar.

When he'd gone, Chanoch elbowed Skagi. "You're holding your temper," he said. "I'm surprised you didn't set him down for that."

"That's because he knows Vedoran would be the one putting him on the floor," Cree said, snickering.

Skagi choked on his zzar. "Put me on the floor, eh? It's not too late to turn on *you*, brother," he said.

"If you can catch me," Cree said.

Skagi opened his mouth to retort, but then his face fell. "Got a point," he said. "You are too godsdamn fast for your own good."

"Vedoran's a fine warrior," Cree said, addressing Chanoch. "I've seen Uwan watching him. If he'd only take the oath, swear faith to Tempus, I think he'd be a Guardian by now."

"Why doesn't he take it?" Ashok asked.

"Won't say," Skagi replied, shrugging. "Ask me, he's just being stubborn. He's a warrior—of course he should follow the war god. What else is there to think about?"

Ashok swirled the wine in his goblet. "Maybe he doesn't see the warrior god as you do."

Chanoch scoffed. "Uwan follows Him," he said. "That's all I need to hear. Tempus's will, and Uwan's, be done."

Cree groaned. "By the Blade, Chanoch," he said. "Do you ever tire of rutting at Uwan's leg like a pup?"

Skagi choked on his zzar again. He bellowed with laughter.

Chanoch looked affronted. "You don't feel the same loyalty?" he said.

"We do. But we're more graceful about it," Cree said. He took a long swallow of his own zzar.

Vedoran returned to the table then, and the conversation subsided. Ashok listened to Darnae's song. She was playing something livelier now—a tune she wasn't as skilled with, Ashok noted. He felt the rhythm falter at times, but the tune was still beautiful, and she played as if her private enjoyment of the music was more than enough for her.

She hit another sour note—loud enough to make Ashok glance up at the dais. A crash and the sound of glass breaking followed.

"Godsdamn, shut it up!" came a voice from below them on the second level.

A shadar-kai with wild black eyes snatched another glass from the bar and hurled it up at Darnae. The glass shattered against the dais, spraying shards across her stage.

Darnae abandoned her instrument and backed against the wall, shielding her face with her hands.

Ashok stood up.

A human man standing behind the bar reached out to lay a hand across the wild shadar-kai's wrist before he could grab another glass. "Easy, now. You've had too much of the fruit," he said. The calming gesture poorly masked the anger in the human's expression. "Leave it alone, friend."

"Tell it . . . stop its screechin' then," yelled the shadar-kai. He jerked his wrist out of the human's grip. "And don' you touch me."

"Where you going?" Skagi called after Ashok, but he was already on the stairs.

The rest of the bar patrons had gone quiet watching the scene. Ashok saw the uncertainty in their eyes. They didn't know which side to support, he thought. The barkeep was not one of their people, but the shadar-kai was clearly out of control. Ashok could see the wildness swimming in his eyes, and he knew what the fruit was.

It grew in the dark caves in purplish clusters near the underground rivers. Some of his own enclave mixed the juice into drinks or ate the fruits whole for the giddiness they induced. The lightheaded feeling was the closest many of them could come to relaxing their minds. Physically, the drug sped up the heartbeat, and taking too much could cause reflexes and nerves to become ragged, as he was seeing in the wild shadar-kai.

He walked up to the bar, leaned against it, and motioned to the human with his empty goblet.

"More wine," he said. "The Cormyrian."

The silence was loud in the room. The human stared at him, his mouth agape, and didn't move. Next to Ashok, the wild shadar-kai wore a similar expression, but it quickly shifted to irritation.

"I was 'ere 'fore you, friend," he said. He swatted at Ashok as if to push him out of the way.

Ashok grabbed the shadar-kai's wrist and held the man's arm extended in the air. With his other hand he calmly slid his wine goblet across the bar. He didn't look at the shadar-kai; he never took his eyes off the barkeep. "You do have the Cormyrian?" he asked.

The human nodded, glancing between the two men uncertainly. The wild one struggled in Ashok's grip, his teeth clenched like a furious animal; but his mind was too sluggish to do more than pull ineffectually at the hand that held him captive.

"Then I'd like some more, please," Ashok said, his tone conversational.

The barkeep pivoted, took a bottle off the floor behind him, and uncorked it. He poured the red liquid into Ashok's goblet. The aroma wafting from the bottle made the hairs on Ashok's neck stand up. The wine's scent conjured the same inexplicable sensations the music had.

He took a sip, aware of his captive growing more and more agitated. His gray face had turned red with rage and humiliation. He clawed at Ashok's fingers with his free hand, but the fruit had dulled his strength, and Ashok barely felt the stings. The wine held all his attention.

"This is indescribable," he told the barkeep. He spoke carefully, aware of the rest of the tavern listening. Darnae came down the stairs in small, hesitant steps, watching him. "I never knew . . . there was so much more," he said. "It's not like wielding a blade or taking pain from a dagger cut, but it's similar enough, isn't it?"

The barkeep just stared at him.

"Yes," Ashok continued, talking mostly to himself. "By itself, the wine would do nothing. But taken together . . . this city . . . All of it keeps you sane."

Ashok's heart pounded. His body hummed with the tension of exquisite restraint, the feeling starting in his chest and funneling out to each of his limbs. The hand that held the struggling shadar-kai could have crushed the man's wrist, but Ashok held the pressure in check. He wasn't fighting himself anymore, only enjoying the sensation of control, the suspended time between inaction and action. His body was on fire and yet serene at the same time.

Carefully, he put down the goblet and released the man's arm. The shadar-kai stumbled back from the bar. He blinked in surprise, as if he couldn't believe he was free, then his face twisted in rage, and he went for the sword at his belt.

Ashok moved quickly. He crouched, swept the man's legs out from under him and pulled the sword from his scabbard, disarming the warrior before his back hit the floor. He tossed the weapon to Skagi, who was standing at the bottom of the stairs with Cree, Chanoch, and Vedoran.

Skagi looked like he was trying not to smile. "I've called the Guardians," he said. "They should be here in a breath or two. Aren't you glad we decided to celebrate?"

Ashok picked up his wine. "Definitely," he said.

Vedoran left Hevalor while his companions were still immersed in their celebrations, giving the excuse that he needed to have his blade worked on by the forge masters before the next training session.

When he was outside the tower, he stopped and probed his right flank with his fingertips. Fire licked his ribs. Vedoran savored the painful breath as his chest rose and fell, but he knew the feeling couldn't last. At least two of his ribs were broken, possibly more. He'd suspected the injury after a particularly hard training session two days before, but he'd done nothing about it, on the chance the bones were merely cracked. He wished he had known better. If he didn't seek out healing before his next training session, he might start bleeding inside.

Vedoran had had few occasions to seek out the clerics, but when he did he went deep into the trade district market, to a small, well-kept building with a green-painted door. Carved into the stone above the door was the symbol of Beshaba, the lady of misfortune.

Vedoran knocked on the door, then pushed his way inside to a dark, herb-scented chamber. There were three beds arranged along one wall, a fire pit in the corner, and an altar to Beshaba opposite the door.

A curtained doorway near the altar led to an inner room, and from that room Vedoran heard the sound of prayer. When he closed the door behind himself, the chanting ceased, and he heard footsteps.

A shadar-kai cleric pulled back the curtain and came into the room. He wore Beshaba's vestments and had thin black hair and a scar that half-closed his left eye. There were three such clerics that shared the small temple, but the scarred one tended to Vedoran most often when he came. His name was Traedis.

"Greetings, Vedoran," the cleric said. "Are you in need of Beshaba's blessing?"

"I have flesh that needs mending," Vedoran said gruffly. "Beshaba can give her blessing or not, it makes no difference to me."

The cleric smiled. "You never change, Vedoran," he said. "I believe the Lady enjoys this trait in you. Please sit down."

When Vedoran was seated, the cleric probed his wounds. "You were right to come to me," he said. "These blows are serious. You must be facing a mighty opponent in your training sessions."

Vedoran scowled. "Ashok is not so mighty," he answered. "He's undisciplined. He fights every sparring match as if he's going to be killed. But his control improves daily."

"And a good thing for you that it does," Traedis said. He closed his eyes and murmured a prayer. By the time he had finished speaking, Vedoran's wounds were healed.

"My thanks," Vedoran said. He left a handful of coins on the bed as an offering and rose to leave.

"You say this warrior's name is Ashok?" Traedis asked. "I've heard his name around the city. There are whispers that he is The Watching Blade's pet."

Vedoran shrugged. "If he is, it's nothing to me," he replied.

"Isn't it?" Traedis said. "From what I've heard, Ashok and Vedoran have much in common. They are both great warriors, though neither one worships Tempus."

Vedoran stared at the cleric. "And what interest could that hold for anyone?" he said.

"Oh, you'd be surprised," Traedis said, his voice deceptively casual. "I make it a point to know who in this city follows the warrior god, and who chooses not to be swept along by Uwan's will."

"I see," Vedoran said carefully. "But those individuals . . . their numbers can't be large, can they? It's no secret that Uwan's way is the way to power and prominence in Ikemmu. Most choose to follow his path."

The cleric shook his head. "There are more of us than you think, Vedoran," he said. Many believe that Uwan has led the shadar-kai according to his—and Tempus's—whims for too long. Perhaps you and this Ashok should think about your place in this city and your future."

Vedoran stood with his hand on the door latch. "You speak persuasively," he said. "But I have a secure place in Ikemmu. I'm not ready to trade that for the word of one Beshaban cleric." He opened the door and stepped through.

"Come and see me again, Vedoran, when you have need," Traedis called after him. Vedoran detected amusement in the cleric's voice. "That day might come sooner than you think."

CHAPTER
TEN

THE FOLLOWING DAY Ashok spoke to Skagi and Vedoran after their training session ended. Cree and Chanoch were off sparring with some of the other shadar-kai. After those first two tendays, Jamet had widened their pool of fighting partners to give them experience battling different types of weapons and fighting styles.

Skagi grinned when Ashok told them Olra's conditions for training the nightmare. "As if we'd miss that spectacle," he said. "Of course I want to be there when the beast plants you in the dirt. I'll tell the others." He moved off.

"The Tet bell," Ashok called after him.

Vedoran hadn't spoken, though that was no surprise. The shadar-kai rarely spoke in mixed company, Ashok found, unless it was to trade barbs or jests. He regarded Ashok in a considering silence.

"What is it?" Ashok asked, finally growing impatient.

"I must congratulate you," Vedoran said.

"For what?"

"You are a Camborr now, or soon will be. I didn't quite believe it before, but there can be no doubt."

"I was never truly a warrior in training," Ashok said. "One can't move up to a rank when he started with none."

"Even so," Vedoran said, "Uwan favors you with a great honor."

"You mean a great honor for a prisoner," Ashok said.

"More than that," Vedoran said. "You refuse to wear Tempus's mark. You reject Ikemmu's god, yet you've earned the city's favor."

Though he hadn't agreed to Ashok's request, Vedoran started walking in the direction of the Camborr pens and outbuildings. Ashok followed, considering the shadar-kai's words.

"Does it give you hope?" he asked.

Vedoran glanced at him sidelong. "What do you mean?" he asked.

Ashok chose his words carefully. "Hope that someone of Vedoran's prowess might hold military rank one day, under the banner of whatever god he chooses," he said.

"Or no god at all?" Vedoran said.

"Or no god at all," Ashok replied.

Over their shoulders, the canyon wall cast long shadows. The wind blew cold against Ashok's face.

"I have worked my sword for the merchant lords these past six years," Vedoran said. His voice betrayed no emotion, but his black eyes smoldered. "I began with nothing. I had no place but a guard's standing in front of a store of food crates. But I worked my sword."

"Now you have the ear of the lord himself," Ashok said.

"Lord Karthen has rewarded me well for my service," Vedoran agreed. "But the path I've followed, the line behind me, ends at the same place, the same store of food. What is that worth, after all?"

"Everyone in Ikemmu must eat," Ashok said.

"Yes," Vedoran said bitterly. "Every animal must take from the trough."

Ashok thought of Gaina, and his uncomfortable truth of the shadar-kai race. Darnae had said the same thing, though far more diplomatically. Some tasks were not meant for the shadar-kai.

What they considered lesser professions were filled by the other races—the dark ones, the humans, the dwarves, and the halflings like Darnae.

Shadar-kai like Skagi, Cree, and Chanoch can nourish their pride on their military service, Ashok thought. What of Vedoran's pride, no lesser a force and too long diminished by his rank as a Blite?

"You could leave," Ashok said, "take your services to another enclave. You could go far."

"I was born here," Vedoran said. "It's my city. It belongs to me as much as it belongs to Tempus."

He looked at Ashok, and the burning was still there, but mingled with it was a curiosity that softened him and made him voice his next words with trepidation.

"I look at you," Vedoran said, "and see the last place I should look to find hope. Yet I do. Perhaps with you, things will be different."

They had reached the paddock. The wide field was empty, and Olra was nowhere in sight. Ashok knew she was preparing to bring the nightmare out. The only time they could force a lead on him was when he was in his cage, deep in the caverns, where his deathly screams wouldn't touch the nearby buildings.

For in the Camborr compound the forge masters also worked, the Guardians who created all Ikemmu's weapons for its warriors and its trade. There at least, was a craft the shadar-kai could engage in. They worked the dangerous fires, day and night, forging the tools of battle. Ashok had learned to recognize the black smoke that drifted up in a constant plume from the forges. Olra came out of the cavern first, leading the nightmare with his face chained and hooded. Beside her walked a contingent of guards with spears. She nodded at them to spread out along the fence.

"Are you prepared for this?" Vedoran asked, as Olra released the nightmare into the paddock. The beast immediately began to run in ever-widening circles, striking sparks off the rocky ground, stamping his black marks into the cave grass.

"Worried your great hope might get his brains dashed out under a flaming hoof?" Ashok asked in a light tone.

"Why is it so important to you that he be broken?" Vedoran asked. "I'd have thought . . . you of all the rest would want him to stay as he is."

Ashok met Vedoran's shrewd gaze. "Did I ever say I intended to break him?" he said.

"Then what are you planning?" Vedoran asked.

But Ashok just shook his head. "You're right," he said. "I do want him to stay the way he is. So I hope he and I can come to an understanding. Though I admit, he is the last place I should look to find hope." Smiling crookedly, Ashok checked his armor and weapons, then pulled himself up and swung a leg over the iron fence. "If he tears me apart," he called down, "you'll know I was wrong."

He landed in a crouch. The dry, scorched grass crackled under his boots. His heart rate had already picked up, but he worked to even his accelerated breathing. He fought to show his respect for the red-eyed menace bucking wildly across the paddock, so the beast would not misinterpret the relish in Ashok's eyes.

Olra caught sight of Ashok standing on the wrong side of the fence. Her eyes widened in furious horror.

"That wasn't our agreement, fool!" she shouted at him.

"Don't stop him now, I beg you," came Skagi's voice. "The fun's just beginning."

Skagi, Chanoch, and Cree walked side by side toward the fence from the direction of the training yard. Vedoran joined them, and together they spread out and climbed the fence at various points, forming a protective perimeter around Ashok. The guards filled in around them.

The nightmare stilled when he saw Ashok inside the fence. Ashok watched his cunning eyes and saw them register that something was different. Somehow, the beast knew what was coming.

A quiver ran down the nightmare's body as it regarded Ashok from a distance. He didn't charge, as Ashok had expected him to do. Instead he regarded the shadar-kai calmly, pacing back and forth thirty feet in front of him. There was almost no fire burning up the beast's mane, only the intermittent flashes of gold nested in the flowing black hair.

Ashok stood with his arms loose at his sides. Slowly, he removed the chain at his belt.

"What'd you do to your spikes?" Chanoch called out, and the nightmare froze, hissing a steamy breath that hung on the cold air like a phantom.

Ashok turned a brief, fierce glare on Chanoch, and the young one obediently fell quiet. He unwrapped the chain and let the spikes loop upon the ground. The sharp points he'd wrapped in a protective coating of leather—stiff, but not fire resistant—into an iron whip, except he had no intention of striking the beast unless it was absolutely necessary.

But the nightmare couldn't know that. As soon as he saw Ashok loop the end of the chain across his knuckles, he backed off, rearing high in the air, his flaming fetlocks streaking yellow afterimages across Ashok's vision.

Ashok slid a step forward, refusing to show any sign of intimidation.

The nightmare snorted a breath and charged, his scream echoing across the paddock and beyond, into the city.

Ashok dived to the side. He felt the wall of heat graze his body as the nightmare barreled past, but it was the scream that tore into his concentration and shredded all his carefully composed plans.

In the open space, the sound echoed off the canyon wall and came back magnified a dozen times. Skagi, Cree, Chanoch, and Vedoran all wavered on the fence, but they held, balancing with their legs and clamping their free hands over their ears until the sound became bearable.

Ashok didn't have that luxury. As soon as the nightmare could, it skidded to a stop and turned its huge body, charging again. Ashok leaped to his feet and whipped the chain over his head in a wide arc. He brought the weapon down in front of his body to strike the ground, over and over, warning the nightmare off.

"My ground," Ashok cried, and his voice was loud and disjointed in the wake of the awful scream. "Yield!"

But the nightmare kept coming, heedless of its own safety. It was going to run Ashok down.

Ashok knew it was a critical test. If he gave way, the nightmare would always be in control. No matter what he tried, the beast would know that in the end, Ashok would be the one to yield.

So Ashok swung the chain and forced himself to stand while the flaming death charged him, eating up the ground between them in mere breaths. The scream rang out again, and crimson eyes were all Ashok could see.

It happened so fast, Ashok hardly had time to register the outcome.

The nightmare changed its course a fraction and charged past him. Ashok felt the heat again, so close that his eyes watered. He felt the burn in his nostrils. But he was still standing. The nightmare charged past him and screamed in terrible fury.

The nightmare ended its failed challenge by ramming its head into the fence inches from where Cree perched. The shadar-kai was forced to jump down to safety, and Ashok caught the faint scent of singed hair where the nightmare's flames had kissed him.

The beast's mane was fully ablaze, with flames that glowed blue at the roots. The nightmare gave off a horrible scent of burning flesh, though Ashok knew he was unharmed by the fire that came from within. The stench of burning was for the benefit of its prey, a warning to any who would dare attack him.

"You won't burn me," Ashok said, "not when I'm on your back."

"You won't ride him without a saddle," Olra hollered across the field. "Don't even try it."

"She's right," Cree said. "The wizards have a means: a saddle enchanted to protect you from the fire."

"I'll get it," Olra said.

"No," said Ashok, shaking his head. "It's not fair to him. He should have his chance at me."

Olra cursed, loudly enough for Ashok to hear across the field. "I knew this would happen," she said. She motioned to one of her guards, who handed her a longbow and a full quiver. She perched on the fence and nocked an arrow, training it on the nightmare.

Ashok glared at her. "You won't use that," he said, "unless I give the word."

"Careful," Vedoran warned from Ashok's other side.

Ashok set his chin stubbornly. "This is my fight," he said.

"This is my ground, fledgling," Olra said. She raised the bow. "You do as I tell you."

Fury burned in Ashok's chest. He stripped his dagger from its sheath before he thought and threw it across the field. It passed over the nightmare's head and clanged loudly off the iron fence next to Olra.

The Camborr flinched; the arrow wavered, and she jumped down so she wouldn't fall. When she'd regained her balance, the look she cast Ashok was one of pure rage.

Behind Ashok, Vedoran sighed. "That was a mistake," he said.

"I'm aware of it," Ashok said through gritted teeth. But he couldn't take it back.

"Take him out of there," Olra said to her guards. "If he resists, put a spear in his gut. I'll get the nightmare."

"Wait," Ashok said as the guards approached the fence. If they disturbed the field, it was all over. He looked at Olra, but was aware all the time of the nightmare standing strangely quiet, as if he too were waiting to see how the tableau played out. "I apologize for my disrespect," Ashok said. The words came to his lips as if dredged from deep water. "But I'm here now, and"—he glanced at the nightmare, forcing himself to meet that red, inscrutable gaze—"I'm not leaving. We have to compromise."

"He's right," Vedoran said. "Even if he is a fool."

Good-natured laughter came from Skagi and the rest, and even Olra's black gaze softened a bit. Ashok felt a strange prickling along his skin, a feeling like the others were in the struggle with him. They wanted success for Ashok as much as he himself did. It was the sense of community again, of trust that he couldn't fathom.

This is how it could have been with them, Ashok thought. Lakesh . . . My brothers.

No. That kind of distraction truly would get him killed. Ashok clamped down on the treacherous thoughts and the echoes of the past, and focused on the nightmare.

"You're in my thoughts, aren't you?" he whispered. "You and I will dance now, but we'll dance again tonight, on your field." Ashok hoped he was ready.

Slowly, with the chain dragging loosely, non-threateningly at his side, Ashok took two steps toward the nightmare. The beast flicked his tail. Sparks showered the ground. They flared and singed the grass before going out.

Ashok took another step forward, without hesitation. He kept walking until he was almost close enough to touch the nightmare's thick black chest. The reek of burning flesh clung to the beast like a shroud. It dipped its head, releasing a cloud of steam that Ashok did touch, his fingers caressing the phantom heat. He blew a breath of his own into the nightmare's face, letting him take in his scent. He stood still while the nightmare's nostrils flared, and the beast tossed his head, whether in apathy or disgust Ashok couldn't say.

More breaths passed, and Ashok stretched out a hand tentatively. The nightmare snapped at him, its wicked teeth sinking into Ashok's flesh. Ashok tore his hand away, but that only made the wound worse.

Ashok immediately backed off, clutching his hand, which had a large chunk of flesh torn out of the heel. Blood spattered the ground.

"Are you all right?" Chanoch called out to him.

Ashok could see the warriors were tense, their bodies half hanging over the fence, prepared to strike. But the nightmare seemed in no danger of charging or lashing out again. It stood as sedately as before, and Ashok thought he read a smug expression in the beast's eyes.

"I'm fine," he assured them. He smiled darkly at the nightmare. "You were just greeting me, weren't you?"

The nightmare snorted. Ashok tore a bit of his sleeve and wrapped it quickly around his hand to staunch the bleeding. The wound would need to be tended, that was certain, but he wasn't surrendering the field.

He stalked forward, boldly entering the nightmare's space, and put his entire body within striking distance of those teeth and deadly hooves. He reached his bloodied hand out again.

As before, the nightmare struck, faster than Ashok's eyes could track. But he'd been expecting the snap, and instead of recoiling he jerked his other hand up—the hand that held the chain.

In a swift motion he encircled the beast's neck twice with the chain, the leather-covered spikes snarling with mane and flesh in a rough lasso. Ashok dropped to his knees to try to avoid the gnashing teeth, but the nightmare caught his shoulder, ripping apart the bone scales of his breastplate.

Ashok fell forward against the beast's legs and instantly felt the fetlocks burning him. The flames surged up around him as if he'd sat in a campfire. He would burn alive if he didn't move.

Throwing himself backward, Ashok rolled to put out the flames that had sprung up along his cloak and shirt. The nightmare, to Ashok's relief, did not pursue him, but bucked and jumped, his four legs leaving the ground. He tossed his head madly, trying to dislodge the wicked chain.

Flame roared from the beast's mane, consuming the metal. The leather burned away to blackened scraps, exposing the sharp spikes. The barbs dug into the nightmare's flesh, and the beast let out another scream of pure rage and frustration.

"The fire won't get you what you want," Ashok said. He lunged and grabbed the dangling end of the chain. A mistake.

The nightmare reared and yanked Ashok up to his toes. Ashok tried to dig in, but his palms were slick with sweat from the fire. The chain slipped out of his hands.

Free, the nightmare barreled forward, knocking Ashok to the ground with a blow from his chest. The chain swung above Ashok's head. He grabbed for the end, but the nightmare pulled it out of reach. The beast reared up again to strike at Ashok with his hooves.

Ashok rolled away over the hard ground. His world spun, but he kept his body moving until it fetched up against an obstruction.

He looked up to see Skagi gazing down at him in amusement.

For a breath, Ashok was confused. The shadar-kai was on the wrong side of the fence. Then he looked around and saw that the others had entered the paddock.

The nightmare, pursuing Ashok, came up short when he saw the other shadar-kai had closed in. The beast snuffed a breath and turned a defensive circle, still dragging Ashok's chain.

"He turned you crispy yet?" Skagi asked.

Ashok coughed. His chest burned where the nightmare had struck him. "Not yet," he replied.

Skagi helped him to his feet. "Maybe that's enough for one day," he said seriously. "You don't have to break him on your first try."

Ashok watched the chain snag and drag through the dead grass. Skagi was right. He was still trying to establish dominance, something he'd told Vedoran he would not do.

He walked forward, weaponless, aware of his companions looking on in trepidation. He motioned them back.

For a third time, he approached within striking range of the hooves and teeth. He held out his hands, one bloodied, the other creased with blisters and scratches from trying to chain the beast. He stared the nightmare in the eyes.

"Your choice," he murmured. "We'll fight, and one of us will die, if that's what you want. But maybe I have something more to offer you."

At first the nightmare stood frozen, his tail swishing back and forth in time with the chain around his neck. The beast's flaming mane glowed brightly.

Suddenly the beast lunged. He came toward Ashok.

And Ashok stood perfectly still.

He was prepared to dodge at the last possible moment, but the nightmare stopped his charge before he could run Ashok down. The crimson eyes were so close. Ashok smelled his own blood on the nightmare's breath. He waited for the scream, but silence reigned in the paddock.

"That's it," Ashok whispered. The nightmare blew steam on his face. He shivered. "You're interested in me now, aren't you?" Ashok asked.

The nightmare jerked his head back, the chain swinging, but the fire ceased to flare from the beast's mane. The flames softened and died out, leaving black strands. The beast pranced in place, agitated, but Ashok had expected nothing less. He would never be fully tamed.

Ashok reached up and took hold of his chain. The nightmare threw his head from side to side, but Ashok ignored the fury and untangled the spikes and ruined leather from the beast's mane. The hair strands were still hot.

Then it was done. The chain fell to the ground, but Ashok kept his hands at the nightmare's neck, stroking his flesh in small circles. His scent went into each stroke. Ashok spent long breaths running his hands up and down the nightmare's neck before he moved on to its flank.

The creature was dense and so tall—fifteen hands at least, Ashok surmised. His muscles were a wonder. A beast like that had no need for fire, when with one kick he could cave in a man's chest.

Ashok ran his hands under the nightmare's mane. The heat radiating there was intense. He pulled his hands back, half expecting them to be black, but they weren't. His skin was red and slick with sweat.

"You're calm now," Ashok said, and threaded the mane through the fingers of his left hand. "But what will you think when I do this?"

He hoisted himself up and swung a leg over the nightmare's body.

All around the paddock came audible gasps from the watching

shadar-kai. Ashok didn't look at them, refused to reassure them. Let them think he was crazy.

Beneath him, the nightmare quivered, every muscle in the beast's body resisting the thing that dared to sit on his back. Ashok knew exactly what the beast felt, struggling against his nature, fighting to maintain control. He reached out to stroke the nightmare's neck, exposing his chest to the hot mane.

"No reins," Ashok said. "No chains. You can burn me anytime you want. You still have a choice."

Ashok knew the beast didn't understand his words, but he thought the nightmare could read his intentions.

Across the paddock, Skagi whistled. "I'd never have believed it if I hadn't seen it with my own eyes," he said in bemused admiration. "Assuming it doesn't burn you to ashes, you may have made a new friend."

Ashok allowed himself a smile. Chanoch and Cree applauded, whooping with excited laughter. Vedoran's expression remained neutral. Ashok knew only half his attention was on the spectacle in the paddock. The other half considered the greater implications of where Ashok sat, of his place as a Camborr.

Suddenly, amid the noise, the nightmare came to life. Ashok gripped handfuls of mane when the beast reared up, pawing the air with fire licking his hooves. He came down hard, throwing Ashok forward against his neck.

"Hold!" Ashok cried as the shadar-kai moved in. The nightmare charged, and Olra's guards broke the protective ring around Ashok. The beast took the gap and ran for the fence, veered aside at the last breath, and galloped in a wide circle around the paddock.

Ashok held on, half-blinded by the wall of heat rising around him. The nightmare's fetlocks and tail were fully ablaze. His mane flared pale orange but did not ignite. Ashok could see the blue roots outlining the nightmare's spine. He was holding back. Ashok couldn't imagine the restraint it took for the nightmare not to burn his rider alive.

The faces of the watching shadar-kai blurred together as they ran, and Ashok—sweating, fevered, close to burning—almost didn't see the other figure that stood watching from outside the fence.

Uwan regarded him from a distance, his face unreadable. But as Ashok rode past, the Watching Blade raised his hand to his chest in salute.

Euphoric, Ashok raised his own hand in answer.

"He can't be trusted with this mission," Natan said.

Uwan and Natan stood in the empty training yard, waiting for Ashok and the rest of the recruits. The cleric's face looked dangerously thin in the half-light. It reminded Uwan how little Natan had done except pray in the last month. He ate only what he needed to survive, slept in vision-shrouded dreams, and rarely ventured outside except to come to Athanon to report to him.

"There's no questioning Ashok's skill," Uwan said. "He could best many of the Guardians in open combat, though Jamet still has reservations about his control."

"You sound as if you're proud of him," said Natan.

"I'm proud of them all," Uwan said. The footprints of the recruits had torn up the ground. They'd sparred amid the distant nightmare screams, never breaking. Warriors, all. Yes, he was proud of them.

"Yet Ashok isn't one of ours," Natan reminded him.

"He has acquitted himself well this past month. And he tamed the nightmare," Uwan said. "I wouldn't have thought it possible, but the two of them, riding in that paddock, they looked right together."

"Once he's outside the city, he's beyond our control," Natan said. "We can't stop him, if he chooses to betray us."

"That's when Tempus takes over," Uwan said. "He will guide Ashok in our stead."

Natan looked at him. "My Lord, Tempus has already warned us of an imminent threat to our city that *will* involve Ashok in some form. Now he sends me a vision—" Natan's voice broke.

Uwan put a hand on the cleric's shoulder. "I know, my friend," he said. "He's showing us the way to find her. We're very close now."

"I saw the vast bog," Natan said. "Fire burned a path through the swamp and pointed the way. I saw her face, my Lord. She *is* alive."

"I never doubted it," Uwan said. "We will bring them all home, Natan. I promise you."

"But if you send Ashok . . . If something should go wrong—"

"He will not be alone," Uwan assured him. "I will surround Ashok with his companions. They are all fine warriors, and I believe they will bind Ashok's heart to Ikemmu."

"Forgive me for doubting, my Lord, but you risk much with this plan," Natan said.

Uwan saw the worry and fear etched on the cleric's gaunt face. He squeezed Natan's shoulder. "Be strong," Uwan said. "It won't be long now."

CHAPTER
ELEVEN

Ashok didn't hear the Monril bell. He was buried in the dream.

His back was to the cold cave wall, his chain snapping across the fire to warn his brother away. Lakesh had fallen after taking a blow to the face from Ashok's chain. He hadn't gotten up yet.

Somewhere in the distance, Ashok heard a scream like a mad horse. He shivered despite the heat of the fire. Where had he heard that sound before?

Another shadow moved in the tunnel mouth, and Ashok tensed, his lips curling in a feral snarl. He clutched an arm against his chest. It was wet with his blood and raw from the sword slash Lakesh had given him.

Was it another brother come to challenge him?

"No," Ashok growled. "No more."

His father stepped around the fire, his boots crunching gravel. He held a torch and a bucket of water, which he poured onto the flames.

Smoke erupted in the confined space. Ashok's eyes watered. "What are you doing?" he demanded. Half blind, he couldn't tell if Lakesh was preparing another attack. Why would his father interfere?

"No fires so deep in the caves. You know the rules," his father said. He was an imposing figure, with a mane of dirty red hair and beast hide armor. Thick, ropey scars covered his arms and legs. He was the most physically dominant figure in their enclave, but not the most cunning. The cunning had gone to his sons, seven of them.

Once there had been nine.

They'd all been got on different mothers in the enclave, but those were either gone or with other men. The shadar-kai existed as rogues, or in enclaves like wolves, but they did not have that animal's notion of a pack when it came to mating or raising offspring.

Shadar-kai mated for stimulation first and to produce young second. Offspring were divided up between sire and dam as they saw fit and raised until they could fend for themselves and contribute to the enclave.

"Get out of here," Ashok said to his father, his chain held crosswise in front of him. It was a flimsy defense against his father's brute strength.

"Stand at ease," his father said with narrowed eyes. "Lakesh is dead."

"What?" said Ashok. He came around the ruined fire and saw that his father spoke the truth. Lakesh lay on his back, his throat slashed open by Ashok's chain. The blood looked black against his brother's gray skin.

"Well done," his father said gravely.

"I didn't challenge him," Ashok said. Mechanically, he gathered his chain—the spikes still stained with his brother's lifeblood—and put it back on his belt. His dagger was somewhere on the ground; he would find it later. "He came to me," Ashok said.

"Lakesh underestimated you," his father said. "The others won't."

"But they will come for me," Ashok said. He could still hear the harsh scream echoing in the caves. The sound was coming closer. "What will happen when there are none of us left?" he asked. "Who will defend the enclave?"

"The strongest will find a way to survive," his father said, unconcerned. "They will dominate the weak."

"Such a waste," Ashok said. "All of it."

"It's the only way we keep power," his father replied.

"What benefit to Lakesh?" Ashok asked, his voice rising. "He put food in my mouth when I was a babe. I remember that time. Now you're pitting us all against each other. *You* make us weak."

His father moved fast. His big hand encased Ashok's throat and drove him back against the cave wall.

"Choose your words well, my son," he said, bending his face close to Ashok's.

Ashok choked. The screaming was so loud he could barely hear his father's voice. "Don't do this," he cried.

"Don't do this?" his father said, his face twisting. With shoulders shaking, he bellowed with uncontrolled laughter that mingled with the scream. "What makes you think we have a choice, child?"

His father was still speaking, his lips moving and his eyes alight with unholy glee as he choked his son. But Ashok could no longer hear the words. When his father spoke, all he could hear was the screaming.

Ashok awoke sitting up, his back pressed against the wall. His first clues that he wasn't in the cave anymore were the smooth stone and the warmth. He looked around the room and saw the empty beds, the discarded clothing. Even the air smelled different. Torches burned on the walls, but the smoke filtered out through gaps in the stone above his head.

He was alone in the room. Ashok listened for the Monril bell but heard nothing except the echo of the nightmare's scream in his ears. He'd missed the waking call. The other shadar-kai must already be at morningfeast.

Someone would be coming to look for him soon. Ashok sat up, swung his legs over the side of the bed, and ran trembling hands through his hair.

You expected it, Ashok chided himself. You shouldn't have let it hit you so hard.

Olra had told him the nightmare would exploit his fears. Planting the dreams was the beast's greatest power, more terrifying than being burned alive by his fire.

But Ashok had expected to dream about losing his soul.

It was every shadar-kai's worst fear. The shadar-kai welcomed death in battle, for the alternative was to fade, their souls lost to the shadows, doomed to wander a nameless void. To be so alone, all life and feeling denied—Ashok shuddered at the thought of such nothingness.

Ashok had expected to dream of that void, yet he'd dreamed of his father and brothers. Those weren't nightmares, they were memories. Yet they couldn't harm him in Ikemmu's vast stone towers. In Ikemmu he was a different person, safe from the past and a life he barely recognized as belonging to him.

Ashok dressed, armed himself, and went down to the training yard. The shadar-kai were still assembling into lines. No one had missed him yet.

He took his place next to Skagi, Cree, and Chanoch. They nodded to him.

"Interesting dreams?" Cree asked.

Ashok started. The rest of them were eyeing him. "What do you mean?" he said.

"You were talking in your sleep," Skagi replied. He stretched, cracking his knuckles. "I pity your enemy, I truly do."

Ashok thought he was jesting, but Skagi looked serious. "It was nothing," he said.

"It was the nightmare," Chanoch said. "We knew it would happen."

"It was one dream," Ashok said. "I'm still going to work with the beast."

"Soon as your punishment is finished," Skagi said, and that time they all chuckled. "How long is Olra making you stay back here, eh?"

"Until she thinks she can trust me," Ashok said. He worked his chain between his hands, snapping the spikes taut in frustration. "It's a game, nothing more."

"She'll come around," Skagi said. "She's just upset you have such good aim with a dagger."

Ashok shook his head. Vedoran had been right. He'd been stupid and careless to lose his temper. And he was banished to training with the recruits until Olra said otherwise.

Jamet strode down the lines, an unnatural lightness to his step. "Pair off," he said. "Sparring first, and then, if you do exceptionally well, we will have some sport. Our Lord, the Watching Blade, wants to see how you're progressing in your training. Are you ready to show him the warriors you've become?"

A fierce cry went up among the recruits. Ashok turned to ask Skagi to spar, but the brothers had already paired off.

"I've got a few insults to repay you for, little one," Skagi said as they moved to one of the roped off areas. He tapped his shaved head. "I forget nothing."

"Was that a hollow sound I heard?" Cree said, and ducked when Skagi grabbed for his ear.

Ashok started to look for someone else and saw Chanoch eyeing him hopefully.

"I've gotten better since our last matches," Chanoch reminded him. He rocked back on his heels, all energy. "I may be a challenge to you now."

Ashok wanted to say, "Or I may make a corpse of you," if he forgot himself, as he had that first time they'd sparred. But he didn't think that would happen. His skills had also improved since that day.

"Ashok," said a voice from behind him.

Ashok recognized it at once, as did the others in the training yard. Dozens of heads bowed instantly. Ashok was too surprised to make a move.

Uwan motioned the rest of the recruits to continue as they were. He looked Ashok up and down. "Still in one piece I see," he said. "The nightmare hasn't gotten the best of you?"

"No," Ashok said.

"Are you certain?" Uwan said. "The nightmare's powers affect the mind in ways we can't comprehend."

"I'm fine," Ashok said tightly.

"I see," Uwan said, smiling. "Well, then." He grasped the hilt of his greatsword and drew it from its scabbard. "Would you care to spar with me?"

Ashok heard the gasps issue from the other shadar-kai. Jamet even looked surprised, though he tried to conceal it.

"Well, recruit?" Jamet said. "Lord Uwan asked you a question. What do you say to his challenge?"

Cautious, Ashok raised his chain and inclined his head to Uwan. "I accept," he said.

"The rest of you mind your own partners," Jamet said when several of the shadar-kai made as if to gather around the combatants.

They faced off near the iron fence. The shadow of Tower Athanon hung over Uwan's left shoulder. Ashok let his chain hang loosely in an arc at knee-level. Uwan held his greatsword in a two-handed grip.

"Are you prepared?" Uwan asked him.

Ashok nodded.

Uwan came forward. Ashok, acting by reflex rather than plan, snapped the chain up to greet him, one end cutting the air as the nightmare's teeth had grazed Ashok.

Uwan dodged, but he didn't flinch or give ground. He came forward again with his greatsword, and again Ashok struck out.

"You have a fine reach with that weapon," Uwan said.

Ashok said nothing. He would not let himself be distracted.

"What if you were fighting a siege battle and the attackers broke through the wall?" Uwan continued as he lunged, and Ashok dodged rather than try to bring the chain up for a defense. "How would you use the chain to defend when a thousand of your comrades stood around you?"

Jamet had asked him a similar question. "I've never had to fight a siege," Ashok said, and snapped the chain taut in time to parry an overhand strike from the greatsword. The weight of the weapon was astonishing. Ashok's grip slipped on the wooden chain handles, but he held them until Uwan broke off the attack.

Ashok swung the chain as Uwan raised his blade again, and struck a glancing blow off the leader's shoulder. Metal rang loudly against Uwan's armor, but there was no exposed skin to strike. Ashok's chain fell harmlessly to the ground.

"You're not used to fighting heavily armored opponents either," Uwan said. "You've only fought those with little or none. Perhaps you should try wielding a blade."

"So I can defend Ikemmu?" Ashok said, dodging another swing and finding himself with his back to the fence. He sent the chain out, closer to Uwan's face. Unhelmed, the leader's skin was flushed with the battle, his hair wet with sweat. He'd been in training already that day, Ashok thought, but he hadn't lost a step. The leader seemed to have a boundless supply of energy.

"Everyone needs a reason to fight, Ashok, and comrades to stand with him," Uwan said. Metal screeched on metal as Uwan's blade ground against Ashok's chain spikes. "Else you'll end up alone on the plain, pursued by the hounds."

"It's as good a death as any," Ashok said.

Uwan hesitated, his sword tangled with Ashok's chain. "You truly believe that?" he asked. "You believe that if attacked, Skagi, Cree, and the rest would not stand with you in defense of your life?"

Ashok didn't answer, but an image of the shadar-kai surrounding the paddock while he challenged the nightmare flashed in his mind. On its heels came an image of Lakesh's slashed throat. Ashok stumbled but managed to free his chain and held it one-handed. With the other he drew his dagger.

"You fight impersonally," Uwan said. "That's your mistake. You push the enemy away, and that's fine, it'll keep you alive. But you leave no room for allies."

"Because the ally might plant his own weapon in my back," Ashok said. He couldn't get the image of Lakesh's dead eyes out of his head. He wished Uwan would stop talking, but the leader persisted.

"Not in Ikemmu," Uwan said. "Here your allies would die for you." He came in tight at Ashok's right side. Ashok tried to parry with the dagger, but the greatsword was too much for the weapon. It broke through Ashok's guard and took a slice at his breastplate. A handful of bone splintered, and Ashok felt the blade open his skin.

They broke apart, and Ashok reached up to feel the wound. His hands came away soaked in blood. "You have me," he said.

"You still stand," Uwan pointed out.

"Not on a battlefield, I wouldn't," Ashok said. "The challenge goes to you."

He gathered up his chain and left the field. The other partners were sparring heatedly, probably hoping to impress their leader, Ashok thought.

He wadded up his sleeve and pressed it to the chest wound. It wasn't deep enough to need healing, but it bled liberally. His shirt stuck to his chest, and the copper scent mixed with the smoke smell drifting over from the forges made his head swim.

Lakesh's blood had been all over his chamber. He'd smelled it constantly, even when he slept . . .

"On your knees at last!" called a voice.

Ashok glanced over to see Cree and Skagi nearing the end of their duel. Skagi had disarmed his brother. Cree tried to evade Skagi's reach, but he stumbled. Skagi raised his falchion.

Blood scent in his nose, and the smell of smoke so close. Suddenly, Ashok was back in the cave, his brother stalking toward him with a sword in his hand. He stared across the training yard and saw him, Lakesh, a falchion in his hands, going for Cree's throat.

"No!" The scream ripped out of Ashok. He ran, his feet pounding the ground as he tore across the yard. "Don't!"

His brother turned to look at him, confusion in his eyes. Ashok slapped the blade out of his hands and tackled him. Lakesh cursed and fought back, his hands pushing at Ashok's chest and shoulders. Ashok straddled and held him down with a hand pressed against his jaw, his fingers digging into Lakesh's cheeks.

"You won't kill him," Ashok growled.

Lakesh slapped him across the face, getting dirt in his eyes. "Get off me!" he yelled. "Are you godsdamn crazy?"

Ashok's vision swam. He wiped the dirt away with his other hand and saw Skagi lying beneath him. Ashok's fingernails had gouged red lines into his gray face.

Stunned, Ashok's arms went slack. Skagi shoved him off, and he landed on his back on the ground. Ashok looked at the bloody dirt caked under his fingernails, and his breath started to come fast. He couldn't control it. The training yard started to spin.

Above him, he heard voices, faintly, as if they echoed from the bridges far up the canyon wall.

"What happened? Who's hurt?" they said.

He thought he heard Jamet's voice, but he couldn't be sure. He heard the wind echoing through the cave, and he could still smell the fire, though his father had put it out long before . . .

"He came out of nowhere; he was like an animal," said Skagi, as furious as Ashok had ever heard him. "I thought he was going to kill me."

Ashok couldn't blame the warrior. Blindsiding him like that—he was worse than Chanoch.

Then he heard Uwan's voice.

"All right, everyone get back," he said. "Jamet, take your recruits inside the tower. Cree, take your brother and see to his face." A pause. "Vedoran, help me with him."

Blurred shapes leaned over Ashok with their hands outstretched.

Come with us, brother, the phantoms said. *We're going to throw the dice.*

CHAPTER
TWELVE

WHEN ASHOK AWOKE, HE WAS IN THE CAVE. THE SCAR FROM HIS campfire blackened the floor, along with Lakesh's blood. He reached up to feel the wound in his chest, the wound Uwan had given him, but it wasn't there. His flesh was unmarked.

"A dream?" he said aloud, his voice groggy with sleep. Slowly, Ashok sat up and rubbed his eyes. The cave was still there. He smelled the lingering smoke and blood. His weapons were on his belt, and he could hear the sounds of the enclave stirring for the new day.

Everything was as it should be.

Gods, please no, Ashok thought. Ikemmu—his deepest desires given form—all of it couldn't have been just a dream.

He heard footsteps coming down the tunnel. Ashok's father came into the chamber, his red hair wild and dust-covered.

"You've been out on the plain," Ashok said.

His father grunted. "Yes, while you were safe abed," he replied.

"Hardly safe," Ashok said.

"Lakesh. Yes," his father said, waving a hand and dismissing Ashok's brother. "We have more important things to worry about now. I've been scouting. There's a party approaching the caves a few miles out. We don't know how many there are or what they are, but it's clear they're headed this way. They know we're here."

Ashok stood and faced his father. "What do you want me to do?" he asked.

"You've heard the pack calling," his father said, "when we sleep, and the caves are quiet?"

"The shadow hounds?" Ashok said. "Yes. They've moved their hunting grounds closer to the cave. We'll have to deal with them some day."

His father nodded. "That day is today," he said. "I don't want us hemmed in with a shadow hound pack to the north while enemies approach from the south. Take two of your brothers with you and get rid of the hounds. I'll handle the threat from the south."

As his father turned to leave, Ashok said, "I'd rather go alone."

That brought a rumbling laugh from deep in his father's chest. "If you want to kill yourself, go ahead," he said. "I have other sons."

When he was gone, Ashok looked at the fire and blood stains on the floor and thought of the city of towers, already fading from his waking memory. If he concentrated, he could taste the Cormyrian wine, dry and smoky on his tongue, and smell the forge fires. He felt something clutch his chest, and he closed his eyes against the ache.

When he opened them, he was standing on the Shadowfell plain. A hound struck him in the chest, its teeth gnashing, and found the tender flesh of his throat.

"No!"

Ashok sat up in his bed, screaming and clawing at his throat. A dark shape and a weight held him at the shoulders. He punched out with loosely clenched fists, rolled off the bed, and pinned the hound to the floor.

"Cease, Ashok, cease! It's Vedoran."

Ashok's eyes adjusted to the dimness, and suddenly he could see everything. He was lying on the floor next to his bed with his hand across Vedoran's throat. Vedoran held up his hands, showing that he had no weapon. He regarded Ashok calmly.

"Do you know me?" he asked.

Slowly, Ashok nodded. He sat up and took his hand away from Vedoran's throat. The shadar-kai sat up gracefully, his arms still raised, making no sudden movements.

"Is this a dream?" Ashok asked. He looked around, but the tower room was empty. Skagi, Cree, and Chanoch were not there.

"Uwan thought it would be best if there were as few people here as possible, in case you had another nightmare," Vedoran said. "I volunteered to stay with you—"

"Is this a dream?" Ashok demanded again, cutting him off.

"If I say no, it proves nothing," Vedoran said reasonably. "That's the power of the nightmare. You don't know what's real and what isn't."

Ashok laughed faintly and put his head in his hands. They were clammy and trembling. "So I'm damned?" he said.

"No," Vedoran said. "You're awake, and that's a very good sign. You've been in a fevered sleep for a day. Most who have worked with the nightmare don't last that long."

"Olra's old master," Ashok said. "He lost his soul."

"You don't appear to be in danger of that," Vedoran observed. "But your mind is another concern."

"Why did you stay?" Ashok said, looking up. "I could have killed you."

Amusement flickered across Vedoran's face. "Not likely," he replied.

"I didn't realize . . ." Ashok said, raising himself up and sitting on the edge of his bed. "He's stronger than I thought, the nightmare."

"After this it will get easier, I think," Vedoran said. "You've come through the worst and know what to expect. If you still intend to train the beast."

"Yes," Ashok said. He looked at his hands, the blood still crusting the edges of his nails. "Skagi?" he said.

"More embarrassed than hurt," Vedoran assured him. "He was angrier at you for knocking him down in front of all the recruits. You took him completely by surprise. I'm sure he'll want to pay you back in kind, someday."

Ashok nodded. "I deserve that and more," he said.

Vedoran stood up and straightened his armor. His black hair had come loose from its horsetail, making him look even larger as he stood over Ashok.

"What did you see in your dreams?" he asked. When Ashok hesitated, he added, "If you don't wish to speak of it—"

"They weren't dreams," Ashok said. He saw his father, the hounds, Lakesh's corpse. "They're memories."

Vedoran nodded. "Of the time before you came to Ikemmu."

"Yes." Lost in thought, Ashok wasn't sure how much time passed, but when he looked up, Vedoran was still standing there, watching him. His eyes were impossible to read.

"What is it?" Vedoran said.

"Why do you not worship Tempus?" Ashok asked.

Briefly surprised, Vedoran recovered and sat cross-legged on the floor next to Ashok's bed. His scabbard scraped the stone. He unbuckled his sword belt and set the weapon on the floor next to him.

"I feel," Vedoran said, hesitating, "like I don't want to be controlled. My father served Netheril, and then he escaped it, for the reasons many shadar-kai did—because he didn't want to be a servant to a controlling empire ruled by a dark goddess. Ikemmu is not Netheril, but if he were alive, my father would see it in the shadows of these towers. Should we have come so far, only to have our choices limited now? To have our future decided by clerics who whisper an invisible god's words in Uwan's ear?"

Ashok saw the burning was back in Vedoran's gaze. With his fists clenched in his lap, the sellsword radiated such anger, a controlled fury that threatened to consume him from the inside out. Ashok didn't know how he could stand it.

"But this city," Ashok said. "It's different from any place I've ever known. I've seen places that were numb to the gods' influence. Maybe the shadar-kai weren't meant to walk unguided. Maybe we need some hand to keep us from wasting ourselves."

"Are you thinking of taking the oath? Of embracing Tempus?" Vedoran said. His voice was neutral, but Ashok read his stunned expression. Ashok was hardly less affected himself.

What would it mean if he swore loyalty to Tempus? Would Uwan and the others truly accept him as one of their own? The implications of what he considered roiled inside Ashok. His father and brothers, they would all be dead to him, as he was to them. His old life and everything he had been would be washed away. Then could he finally escape those caves, the memories of blood and fire?

Vedoran waited, tense beside him. Ashok chose his words carefully, sensing that for Vedoran, more rested on his answer than idle conversation.

"I think," he said, "that I need to learn more about this god, so I know what I'm swearing my life for."

"All that you need to know of Tempus rests in Uwan," Vedoran said bitterly. "You see how the recruits look at him, the worship in their eyes. Now you're becoming one of them."

"I've decided nothing," Ashok said.

Vedoran nodded, but Ashok saw the anger and—worse—disappointment in his eyes. "I shouldn't be surprised," Vedoran said. "Whatever memories you battled in your sleep, Ikemmu must seem a paradise by comparison. But beware, Ashok, of putting your faith in this city and in Uwan. You may come to regret it."

CHAPTER
THIRTEEN

VEDORAN LEFT HIM TO REGAIN HIS STRENGTH, AND WHEN ASHOK awoke again, he didn't remember dreaming. Nor did he know the day; he heard no bells tolling, and the room was empty.

Ashok sat up. There were fresh clothes lying at the foot of his bed. He checked his armor to make certain the parchment sheets hadn't been found. As he was donning the bone scales, there came a tentative knock at his door.

"Come in," he said, his voice still rough from sleep.

A dark one entered the room with a trencher of bread and meat and a cup of water. He handed Ashok the food.

Ashok thanked the creature and bit into a chunk of bread. The bland crust tasted amazing. He couldn't remember when he'd eaten last. He scooped up the pink meat and juices with his crust and ate it all while the dark one waited.

The little humanoid shifted from foot to foot, his right hand clutching the knuckles of his left. He was a bit shorter than Darnae, but he walked in a stooped manner, his shoulders, arms, and knees curling inward toward his stomach. His eyes were dark and watery in a pudgy face.

When Ashok had finished the food, the dark one said in a low voice, "Lord Uwan instructs me to give you a message."

"What is it?" Ashok asked.

"I'm to say that if you're feeling up to the task, you should come to Lord Uwan's chamber. For a *private* meeting."

The food settled heavily in Ashok's stomach. "I'll come now," he replied. "Do you know what it's about?"

The dark one's expression turned sly. "I wasn't to say," he said.

"But you do know," said Ashok.

The creature's eyes gleamed wickedly. "Perhaps," he replied.

Ashok thought of pressing the point, then decided against it. He already knew what the meeting was about—of course he did. He was being summoned to answer for his actions in the training yard. Better he hear it from Uwan himself instead of the creature.

The dark one led Ashok out, and they climbed the winding steps. The walk seemed to take forever. When at last they stood before Uwan's door, the dark one left Ashok. He knocked on the door and immediately heard Uwan's voice beckoning him inside.

Ashok saw the painting first, the beautiful cityscape above the long rectangular table. He was surprised to see most of the chairs at the table filled, and even more shocked to see the occupants.

Uwan sat at the head, of course, but Vedoran, Chanoch, Cree, and Skagi all occupied places down the table. At Uwan's right hand sat Natan. There was an empty chair next to the cleric that Vedoran, seated on the other side of him, pulled out and indicated for Ashok.

"The time has come for you to decide your future, Ashok," Uwan said. "Sit down. We have much to discuss."

***

Uwan leaned forward and clasped his hands together on the table top. In the middle of the table, spread out, was a map of the Shadowfell plain. Ashok recognized the Aloran Tor and several other landmarks. By their locations, he could tell his own enclave was about a six day journey to the north.

"I've summoned you here," Uwan said, glancing at Ashok and his companions, "because you've all proven yourselves to be exceptional warriors. I've watched you train, seen your strengths, your weaknesses and your faith.

"I have a journey that should you undertake it will require all of your efforts working in concert. I am not ordering you to complete this task. Every shadar-kai in this room who volunteers for this mission will do so of his own free will." Uwan glanced meaningfully at Ashok. "Will you consider the mission I propose?"

"Yes, Lord Uwan," Chanoch said at once, and Skagi and Cree were quick to add their assent.

"I will consider it," Vedoran said.

Ashok looked at Uwan. He had not expected such a proposal at all. He felt off balance, as if everyone in the room knew more than he did. A journey outside Ikemmu? He'd not been outside the city's walls since the day he'd tried to escape.

"Will you consider this mission, Ashok?" Uwan repeated, when the silence stretched.

"Yes," Ashok said uncertainly. He didn't know what to think.

"Thank you," Uwan said. He addressed Natan. "Will you tell them, my friend?"

The cleric nodded and cleared his throat. "Thank you for agreeing to hear Uwan's request," he said. "My own tale is a simple one. I am a servant of Tempus, and I have been blessed with the gift of Sight. The warrior god has chosen to grant me visions of what will come to pass in Ikemmu's future."

He paused. Ashok felt Vedoran stiffen beside him. He stared down at the table, his black gaze boring holes in the map.

"Several nights ago, Natan received such a vision," Uwan said. "Tempus showed him that Negala has returned to the plain."

"The bog witch?" Skagi said. "Close to Ikemmu?"

Uwan shook his head. "Many miles distant," he replied. "The city is in no immediate danger."

"Who is Negala?" Chanoch asked.

"That's right, you're probably too young to know her," Skagi said, which made Chanoch's face flush with embarrassment. "She's a hag, a creature twisted by the shadows."

"She's like the nightmare, in human form," Ashok said quietly. He remembered his father telling him a tale of encountering the witch. Her bog was merely an illusion, a part of her mind she could alter at will.

Uwan looked at him sharply. "You know Negala?" he said.

"No," Ashok said. "But I know what she is. She moves her swamp around the Shadowfell according to her whim. She's an annoyance, nothing more."

"Bog may be an annoyance, but you can still die in it," Skagi said.

"Agreed," Uwan said. "She must not be underestimated, as this mission will take you straight across her domain."

"Why?" Vedoran spoke up.

"Shall I tell them?" Uwan said, speaking to Natan.

The cleric shook his head. "If you please, my Lord, I'll do it," he said. Natan leaned back in his chair, and the lines on his face made him look ancient, though Ashok guessed he couldn't be much older than himself.

"A little over a month ago," Natan said, "a decision was made that instead of dispatching an entire caravan to search the Shadowfell for beasts to capture and train, it was more feasible to send out a smaller scouting force to search for hunting grounds, watering holes, anyplace the shadow beasts might be likely to gather. Such a force could range farther than a caravan and be able to return to the city faster with its intelligence.

"We sent out a band of ten shadar-kai," Natan said. "Our best scouts. One of them was my sister, Ilvani. Their party disappeared. They never returned to the city."

Natan paused as if to gather himself. Uwan continued in his stead. "We dispatched patrols to search, but their trails went cold. No bodies were ever found. I believe, and Tempus has confirmed it in Natan's vision, that some or all of the party are still alive. They were taken prisoner."

"You believe Negala has them?" Vedoran asked.

"No," Natan said. "I saw the hag's lands in my vision, but Tempus pointed me beyond them. Somewhere on the other side of the bog is where we will find our people."

"We've had wizards watching with farseeing spells, waiting to see any sign of Negala's bog," Uwan said. "Patrols have been ranging far out from the city, and a few days ago, they saw the bog had appeared."

"Where?" Skagi asked.

"Five or six days journey north," Uwan said, indicating the map. "We don't know how large Negala's domain is—it could be a stone's throw or miles of treacherous land. Your mission, then, is twofold: go to the surface and cross Negala's domain in safety, and once on the other side, find the missing party and return them to Ikemmu."

Uwan fell silent, waiting for their response. Gradually, Ashok heard Chanoch, Skagi, Cree, and Vedoran accept the mission one by one, but Ashok didn't speak. He was staring at the map, comparing the landmarks in his mind with the journey north to Negala's bog.

The Aloran Tor. But he'd been running from the hounds long before he'd stopped in the mountain's shadow. They'd chased him away from the enclave and his father's confrontation with the party that had been approaching the caves.

Hemmed in from both sides. The hounds . . . and Ikemmu's scouts.

"Ashok," said Uwan.

Dazed, Ashok looked up. The leader regarded him half in expectation, half in hope.

"Natan hasn't told you the rest of his vision," Uwan said. "Perhaps that will influence your decision. Natan?"

"Yes," Natan said. Ashok thought he spoke with reluctance. "Before you came to the city, Ashok, Tempus showed me a vision of your face. I knew you, before you came here."

"I don't understand," Ashok said. But he was beginning to, and it frightened him more than anything ever had.

Uwan said, "Tempus foretold your coming, Ashok. We believe He sent you to us to find our people. He's chosen you to aid us."

"But I am not his servant," Ashok said, aware of Vedoran's tense posture beside him. He could feel the heat of the shadar-kai's gaze.

"It doesn't matter," Uwan said. "Tempus has chosen to work through you. Will you answer His call?"

The silence in the chamber was unendurable as everyone waited for Ashok to form an answer. How could they expect so much, when Ashok couldn't find a coherent thought?

For a moment, Ashok wondered if he was still locked in a strange and terrible dream and just didn't know it. They were asking him to seek out and rescue a party of shadar-kai that had likely been attacked and slaughtered by his father, his brothers and other warriors who'd once fought beside Ashok.

His enclave relied on secrecy to protect their domain. They didn't take prisoners. Yet Natan insisted that some or all of them were still alive, so something must have changed in Ashok's absence.

But if he told them the truth, if he revealed that he'd led shadow hounds away from his enclave so its warriors could more easily capture and kill Ikemmu's citizens . . . he was as good as dead.

All those thoughts converged in his mind, and Ashok felt lost. The silence dragged on. They were all staring at him, he could feel it.

Finally, he couldn't stand it any longer. "May we speak in private?" he asked Uwan.

The leader must have seen the desperation in Ashok's eyes. He nodded at once. "Of course," he said. "Would the rest of you excuse us, with my thanks?"

Chairs scraped back as Natan and Ashok's companions left the table. Vedoran was the last to leave. He got up stiffly and headed for the door.

"Vedoran," Uwan called to him.

"Yes, my Lord?" Vedoran answered. His tone came off unmistakably cold, though Uwan didn't appear to notice.

"You will lead the party," Uwan said.

"My Lord?" Vedoran replied.

Ashok raised his head. Vedoran's face was like a mask that had cracked at the edges. He'd never seen the shadar-kai look so shocked.

"You're an exceptional warrior," Uwan said. "The others are skilled, but they lack your discipline and grace. I trust you to guide them on this journey."

Vedoran bowed at the waist. "I will, my Lord. My thanks," he said fervently.

When he'd gone, Uwan put his palms flat against the tabletop. He studied Ashok's face. Ashok couldn't imagine what he read there, but after a breath, Uwan smiled slightly.

"Are you afraid?" he asked.

Ashok swallowed. The emotions he was experiencing were unlike anything he'd ever dealt with before. His heart beat an unsteady rhythm in his chest. He was in no danger of fading, yet he felt as if he was. That was the best way he could describe his fear. "Yes," he said.

"Good," Uwan answered. "It's humbling, and it should be, to see the gods at work in our lives."

"How do you know I'm Tempus's agent?" Ashok asked. "I told you I've never followed the warrior god. What if Natan is wrong?"

"He's never been wrong before," Uwan said.

"I tried to kill one of your people," Ashok said. "You have no reason to trust me."

"Don't I?" Uwan said. He stood, restless, and began pacing the room. He stopped before the portrait of the city. "I've been the Watching Blade in Ikemmu for twenty years. During that time, I've executed countless warriors for crimes against our people. Disobey orders, endanger the lives of your fellow shadar-kai, betray our people—these are the highest crimes in Ikemmu. Discipline is paramount to the survival of this city, to say nothing of our race. The shadar-kai are built for self-destruction. It is how we were made, but it doesn't have to be who we are."

"It's the only way I know," Ashok said.

"I don't believe that," Uwan said. "When you ran across that field and attacked Skagi, what was in your mind?"

Ashok remembered Lakesh's face, the blade in his hand. Another brother dead.

"I thought he was going to kill Cree," Ashok said.

"And you were trying to prevent that, at the cost of your own life," Uwan said. "What higher service could you render to Ikemmu than to give your life for one of its warriors?"

Ashok didn't know what to say. He wanted to tell Uwan the truth, to unburden himself of the awful knowledge of the leader's misplaced faith. But he couldn't bring himself to speak. He remembered what it was like, waking up in the dark cave with his father, when he'd thought that Ikemmu was only a dream—a hope conjured by his desperate imagination.

The enclave was his nightmare. He couldn't go back to it. There was only one thing he could do.

"I accept your mission," he said. His voice became stronger with his conviction. "Whatever it takes, I'll find your missing people."

He couldn't meet Uwan's gaze. He felt the leader's hands come down on his shoulders and squeeze.

"Thank you," Uwan said. "Tempus guide and go with you."

Tempus guide me? Ashok thought bitterly. Tempus had known who he was all along. Ashok might be able to deceive Uwan and the rest, but the god was sending the perfect person to rescue the missing party, the person who knew the enemy's strengths and weaknesses best.

Uwan released him, and Ashok started for the door.

"One more thing," Uwan called after him. "I think you should take the nightmare with you. He would be a presence to be reckoned with, should you encounter trouble along your journey."

"Is that wise?" Ashok said. The last time he'd ridden the beast, he'd thought he was in control, yet the nightmare had ridden his mind into near madness.

"The fire will burn a path through the witch's domain," Uwan said. When Ashok only stared at him, Uwan laughed. "Never mind," he said. "Go and join your companions."

Ashok nodded and left the chamber.

When he stepped out into the hall, he found Vedoran and the others waiting for him. Natan was not among them. For a breath, nobody spoke.

"Well, chosen of Tempus?" Vedoran said. Ashok heard the edge beneath the words. "Are you with us or not?"

"I'm with you," Ashok said.

"Excellent," Chanoch said, and grinned.

"Told you," Cree said, nudging his brother, but Skagi was stone-faced, his deformed lip curled in disgust. He said nothing.

Tempus's clerics had healed the marks on his face.. There were no scars, but Skagi obviously hadn't forgotten their last encounter.

Ashok inclined his head to the warrior. "I apologize for my actions," he said. "I was arrogant in dealing with the nightmare. I thought it couldn't affect me. I was wrong."

He held out his hand. After a long breath, Skagi clasped Ashok's forearm. His menacing gaze softened.

Suddenly, Skagi's grip tightened. He pulled Ashok forward a step and punched him in the face with his free hand.

Ashok stumbled. Skagi released him so he could stem the flow of blood gushing from his broken nose. Ashok raised his arm to ward off the next blow, but Skagi was grinning, his hands on his hips. His expression looked cheerful.

"Forgiven," he said.

Despite everything, Ashok felt himself laughing, along with the others. He looked at Vedoran. "Do we have a plan?" he asked. He spat blood on the stone floor.

"We won't speak of it here," Vedoran said. "Meet downstairs, in our chamber."

Ashok nodded. The brothers and Chanoch went down, but Vedoran lingered.

"It isn't what you think," Ashok said when the others were out of hearing.

"Doesn't matter," Vedoran said. "All that matters is what he thinks." He nodded to Uwan's door. "The hope I had when I looked at you—"

"Was misplaced," Ashok agreed. "You should have been looking to yourself. Now Vedoran has his chance. Uwan has made you leader. Prove yourself worthy, without Tempus's aid."

"So I will," Vedoran said.

He started to move past Ashok but paused when Ashok said,

"What about Natan? Do you believe his visions?"

"With that cleric and his sister, I don't know what to believe," Vedoran said. "What I know is that those two—their lineage at least—is valued in Ikemmu."

"Why?" Ashok asked.

"Their family was here when Ikemmu was founded," Vedoran said. "They were the first shadar-kai to inhabit the city."

"I see," said Ashok. So brother and sister were a piece of the shadar-kai's history in Ikemmu, he thought. If possible, it added even more weight to their mission. It would be a blow to the city to lose one of its links to the past.

"You should know this," Vedoran said. He looked Ashok in the eyes. "No matter what Natan's visions say, I don't believe it is Tempus who will save Ilvani and the others. *We*, the shadar-kai, will dictate success or failure. The gods have no part in this mission. Do you understand?"

"I do," Ashok said. "I would have it no other way."

The next several days were a blur of training and preparation for the journey north. Vedoran seized his leadership role with ferocity, making Ashok and the others train during all their free time, with no rest but for the time they ate or slept. He allowed Ashok time to train with the nightmare when he learned of Uwan's concession with regards to the beast, but he kept a wary eye on Ashok the entire time, to make sure the beast didn't get the best of him again.

But the nightmare, for his part, must have sensed that something was about to happen, for the beast obliged Ashok's commands without a fight, and though Ashok continued to dream of the caves, his brothers, and his father, the visions did not follow him into his waking hours. He was able to separate his past from his current reality.

Not for long, Ashok thought. Soon his past would come to claim him. He refused to think about what he would have to do when that time came, and concentrated instead on preparing himself physically for what lay ahead.

On the day before they were to depart, Uwan, against Vedoran's wishes perhaps, gave them all leave to have the day to themselves to do whatever they wished. Ashok went to see Darnae. He wasn't sure why he did it. He hadn't seen the halfling since the night at the tavern.

When he stepped into her shop, Darnae was standing at the top of a high stool, brushing cobwebs off the ceiling with a damp cloth.

"There's a face to wilt a lesser man—or a shadar-kai," she said with a grin. "I didn't know if I would see you again."

Ashok lingered in the doorway, leaning against the frame. "I came to see . . . how you are?" he asked uncertainly.

"Very well—practicing hard for my next performance at Hevalor. There's a reason I'm only a messenger," she said, and winked at him.

"To me it sounded like a dream," Ashok said earnestly. "I've never heard music like that before."

"You should hear the truly great bards sing," Darnae said. She flicked a strand of spider silk off her sleeve. "Or hear the elves when they perform in the native tongue. You would weep."

"I came to tell you that I'm leaving," Ashok said. "But I hope . . . I think I'll be back, in a tenday, or a little more."

Darnae nodded as if she wasn't surprised. "Since we met, I've heard folk talk about you in the trade districts," she said, "and not just because of what happened at the tavern. You have my thanks for that—I should have mentioned it before."

"You don't have to thank me," Ashok said.

"But I did, and it's done," Darnae said. She draped the cloth over her shoulder and sat on the top of the stool, which put her almost at eye-level with Ashok. "I haven't heard where you're going and why, but folk who whisper about you say you're a messenger from Tempus."

Ashok shook his head. "Don't believe the things you hear," he said.

"So you're not?" Darnae asked, looking speculative. "But you are something different, aren't you?"

"Why do you say that?" Ashok asked.

Darnae swung her short legs back and forth, curling them beneath the stool rung. Her feet were bare, and bore a fine coating of dirt. "No one else in that tavern would have done what you did," she said. "They wouldn't have considered it. Not because they're cruel or heartless, but the hierarchy is well established here."

"They see you as beneath them," Ashok said.

Darnae nodded. She worked the rag in her hands. "It isn't easy for them to have to rely so much on the labor and trade of other races," she said. "They are proud of their accomplishments as warriors and of the grip they have upon their souls. But the truth is they slip, sometimes—you've seen it for yourself. They are not always as in control as they would like others to think."

"You speak bluntly," Ashok said. "You weren't like this the last time I came here."

"You're right," Darnae said. "I have to keep up polite appearances for the sake of my business. But as I said, something about you seems different. It makes me feel as if I can speak, that you will understand and not be threatened by the truth."

"I do understand," Ashok said, waiting while Darnae climbed down the stool. "I should go."

"I wish you a fair journey, Ashok," Darnae said. "Come to see me again, when you return."

"Are you saying that for appearance's sake?" Ashok asked.

Darnae smiled at him. "What do you think?" she replied.

Ashok smiled back, a tentative expression. "I think I will look forward to seeing you," he said.

Ashok went back to the tower and lay down to rest before the Exeden bell. He felt himself drifting on the edges of sleep when he heard the sound.

Ashok opened his eyes in the darkness and listened. He heard nothing, and thought he must have imagined it, but when he reached automatically for the weapons at his belt, his hand grazed the wall, and he felt the vibration through the stone.

Sitting up, Ashok put his ear to the tower wall. Low, rhythmic beats, so deep that they passed through the stone into his skin.

He pulled on his boots and left the tower room. Down the stairs the beats got louder, until they shook the dust off the walls. Ashok could see it drifting in the air. There were voices too, a host of men and women shouting in time to the beats.

Ashok threw open the tower door and strode out into the training yard. What he saw stopped the breath in his chest and sent a wave of fear and awe through his soul.

Hundreds of shadar-kai had gathered in the yard. Ashok recognized warriors in training, Guardians, all ranks of the military including Neimal, and the other Sworn. Their feet pounded the ground in a dance even as their voices rose to the shadows above. It was not a song they sang; there were no words, only shouts of triumph and pain as over and over they lifted their legs and drove their feet into the ground in a punishing rhythm that echoed throughout the city.

Among them, humans and dwarves carried bundles of wood, flint, and steel. They arranged the wood in three large circles in the yard and lit fires from them.

At first the small golden blazes were lost amid all the dancing gray bodies, but then Neimal swept forward in her gray and black robes. She climbed into the back of a wagon near the iron fence so she could see over the crowd. She opened her arms and uttered words that were lost over the rush of shadar-kai cheers. Her lips moved, the crowd's shouts built into a roar, and Ashok felt the heat rising in the air as the flames climbed and turned from orange to brilliant white.

Everywhere there was light. It was painful to look at, but it drove back the shadows in a way Ashok had never seen light do in the dismal Shadowfell.

The other races skittered back from the fire circles, but the shadar-kai formed their own rings around the blazes. Ashok stepped into the yard. The shadar-kai's stomping feet and shouts invaded his mind, and Ashok found himself joining the crowd. The shadar-kai enfolded him—strangers he'd never seen before that night—until he could not tell his own body from the others.

The crowd moved in a slow circle, and Ashok found himself swept along with them. His feet joined the rhythmic pounding. Every stamp against the ground was a roar and sent a shudder of pain through his bones. As one, they could crack the earth, split it open, and expose another world, or so it felt to Ashok.

Fire surged before Ashok's eyes, and his face became slick with sweat. He tried to pull back from the circles, but the crowd guided him inexorably forward, closer to the enchanted flames. There were hands on his shoulders, his hands were on other shoulders, and suddenly they were all running forward, one body, one mind, and jumping.

They passed through the flames and landed in the heart of the fire rings. Ashok could hear the triumphant cries from the other circles and see shadar-kai shadows dancing in the light. The men and women within his own circle bounded up and threw their heads back, screaming to the world above. Their clothing fire-blackened, the shadar-kai shed their garments and continued to dance naked, their feet always pounding the ground.

Ashok felt hands draw him up and into the dance. Bodies pressed together, slick with sweat, the heat unbearable but vital. They were in the heart of a forge.

Ashok let the shadar-kai pull his shirt over his head, strip away his armor until he was completely naked. The fire surged. Ashok shouted and danced with his people. They could be burned to ash, their skin seared off their bodies, but he'd never felt so utterly whole. He wasn't being torn apart or cut to shreds with a blade.

He was Ashok. No: he was shadar-kai.

When the flames burned low enough, they leaped over the fire and collapsed upon each other, screaming, laughing like wild children.

Ashok fell on his back and closed his eyes. He could hold no thoughts in his head, had no room for doubts or pain or fear. There were too many of them. His flesh touched that of another, and another, with nothing to distinguish him from the whole. No one could see him; nothing could hurt him. For all his arrogance, he'd never been stronger than he was there, at that breath in time.

He could see the others shouting to each other, kissing, dancing. He sat up, wanting to take it all in, to remember this feeling always.

A hand touched his shoulder. He turned to see Chanoch kneeling on the grass, naked, his eyes shining with tears.

"I came to tell you," Chanoch said. Ashok could barely hear him. "I wanted you to see." The young one's voice broke. He pitched forward on his hands, exposing his back to Ashok. "I've been given the mark. Praise Tempus!"

Ashok saw the black blade, the symbol of Tempus tattooed down Chanoch's spine. His surrounding skin was deep red and raw from the work, but Chanoch's body quivered with rapture.

Praise be, Ashok wanted to say, but he stopped before the words reached his lips. He touched Chanoch's shoulder instead. He could hear the young one weeping.

Skagi and Cree found them sometime later. They were similarly adorned with the black swords, and though they did not weep as Chanoch had, both brothers wore the rapture on their faces. Ashok could feel the power radiating from them, the wholeness.

Ashok caught his breath. All around him, he saw the black tattoos, the warriors in training who had taken their oaths, the final steps that would bind them completely into service of Ikemmu and their leader. The swords were everywhere, yet Ashok's skin bore no mark except the flames of the nightmare. He stood out from the rest, a pale blemish among the joyous celebration. No one spoke of it. They accepted him as one of their own, but suddenly, Ashok felt cold. The fire couldn't touch him. He was a creature apart.

He turned, looking for an open space, a place to breathe and escape the press of bodies, the reek of sweat and dirt. Stumbling, he made it to the shadows of the tower. He fell on his knees and vomited. Pressing his face against a patch of cool ground, he breathed in and out.

Footsteps sounded behind him, barely discernible above the noise of the celebration. Perhaps he heard them because he knew, before he looked up, who would be watching him.

Vedoran stood armed and fully clothed, which made Ashok feel horribly exposed. He stepped forward, his movements graceful, and handed Ashok a bundle that included his bone scale armor and the weapons he'd thoughtlessly discarded during the dance.

Ashok wiped his mouth, took the clothing, and with a nod of thanks began to dress himself. When he'd finished, he turned to face Vedoran, who watched the celebration dispassionately.

"They form the circles on the eve of every long journey undertaken by the shadar-kai," Vedoran said before Ashok could speak. "The ritual will last until the Monril bell, long after those making the journey have gone to rest."

"An offering to Tempus?" Ashok said. "To ensure a successful mission?"

"A prayer for success, perhaps," Vedoran said. "But mostly it's a method of girding the soul for what lies ahead. We'll be traveling on the open plain for many days before we reach the bog. Unless we encounter other dangers—and I pray we do—we'll have no one but each other and the wind for company. The inactivity of a long march . . ."

"We risk losing ourselves," Ashok said. He remembered well his own solitary days on the Shadowfell. He'd sought danger for the same reason.

"The other races, especially the merchants who are used to long, monotonous caravan runs, mock us for creating such ceremony for what they consider an insignificant distance," Vedoran said. He dipped his head, his lips quirking in some private amusement. "Your halfling friend would say as much."

"How do you know Darnae?" Ashok said, his eyes narrowing. "Have you been following me?"

Vedoran shrugged. "I've been curious about you since we first met. I've wondered why you hide yourself away in ruined buildings and scribble on parchment, why you went after that shadar-kai in the tavern," he said. "At first I thought you confronted him for amusement, but then I began to think it was something more."

"Are you satisfied now?" Ashok said tersely.

Vedoran met Ashok's eyes. They held each other's gazes for a long breath. Neither spoke. Finally, Vedoran smiled again and went back to watching the shadar-kai dance.

Ashok started to walk away, but Vedoran grabbed his shoulder. Ashok resisted the urge to throw off his hand and merely turned to glare at the graceful warrior.

"Always remember exactly what you are and what you are not," Vedoran said. "Otherwise, that's where you'll be left." He nodded at the vomit-stained ground. "Weak and begging for guidance that will never come."

Ashok reached up and calmly removed Vedoran's hand from his shoulder. "May the gods, any and all, grant us success on this journey," he said. "And may Vedoran lead us safely home again."

Vedoran nodded. "Sleep well, Ashok," he said. "Sleep dreamlessly."

When Vedoran left Ashok he went to the trade district, to the small temple with the green-painted door. Traedis did not look surprised to see him.

"He's lost to you," the cleric said when Vedoran had finished telling him of Ashok. "Like so many others before him, he will take Tempus and Uwan into his heart. You must think of yourself now, Vedoran."

"Uwan put me in charge of the mission," Vedoran said. "There is still the possibility that I will be rewarded—"

"With what—more coin for the sellsword?" the cleric challenged. "Are you so blind that you truly think Uwan will give you power and esteem you above Ashok, who he believes is sent by the warrior god Himself! You must look beyond Tempus, Vedoran. There are other gods in Ikemmu."

"And where do your gods live, Traedis," Vedoran said. "In small temples or secret hideaways? Where is the glory in that?"

"Then help us," Traedis said. "Join us, and as our numbers swell we will become a force that Uwan can't afford to ignore. We can change things, Vedoran."

In his heart, Vedoran knew Traedis spoke wisely. Uwan and Ashok were in each other's thrall, and Tempus had a stranglehold on the city. But he would not deny his mission, not if it meant he could prove that he was just as capable—no, more so—as Tempus's faithful. His pride demanded that he show Uwan and the rest that he could succeed without visions and whispers from Tempus to guide his hand.

"We will see," Vedoran said. "If I return from this mission, and all goes as you say, then we will surely speak again."

CHAPTER FOURTEEN

Six days later, Ashok, Vedoran, Skagi, Cree, and Chanoch sat with their backs to a cluster of stunted kindling trees, which he'd learned were called Dark Needles by Ikemmu's shadar-kai. Similarly, they had found no good use for the spiny trees but the fire.

The Dark Needles were covered in a fine film of white dust. When Ashok had passed through the portal outside the city gates and tasted the open air of the Shadowfell for the first time in a month, he'd thought it deliciously sweet. But for four days now, a dust storm had been ravaging the plain. When Chanoch had first sighted the roiling clouds bearing down on them from the west, they had tried to outrun the storm. When it had overtaken them at last, it had been an exhilarating moment for all. Ashok had reveled in the dust searing his skin, feeling alone in the sudden darkness, yet a part of the storm.

They had pressed on, traveling until they could see no landmarks and risked becoming hopelessly lost in the painful fog. The shelter they'd found under the kindling trees was paltry at best. White dust covered Ashok's entire body. He could feel the grit in his mouth, his ears, and buried in the roots of his hair. Their food was soaked in dust, as well as their clothing and bed things. No fire could withstand the fierce wind, so their fingers were numb with cold, and their minds were slowly following.

For the fourth time that day Ashok drew his dagger from its sheath and laid it against his bare flesh. He wanted so badly to press down, to feel something other than the dust scratching his skin.

Vedoran had forbid them to cut themselves. They were weak enough, he said, from having to ration gritty water and eat stale biscuits instead of the fresh meat they'd planned on hunting. But Vedoran couldn't see his companions in the dust storm. The only impressions they had of each other were the occasional bits of conversation shouted over the wind. At all other times, they were silent, waiting and praying for the storm to pass.

Ashok laid the dagger against his arm and contemplated the pain. Sometimes, it was enough just to imagine the sensation rather than to actually experience it. His imagination could make up a lot of ground, if he willed it.

But in the end, the whicker and snort from over his left shoulder stopped him. The nightmare, his reins tied to the kindling tree, was no more able to move around in the storm than they. The dust had dulled his mane to a faint blue glow, and his red eyes were the only thing clearly visible in the unnatural darkness.

Ashok would not cut himself. He would not make himself any weaker than he already was while he held the nightmare's lead. Neimal had placed a compulsion on the beast to calm him, but Ashok knew such magic would only have a superficial effect on the nightmare's nature.

The only reason he had not tried to win his freedom was a feeling Ashok had. He couldn't explain it, but they were connected somehow, the nightmare and he, ever since the night the beast had first sent him dreams. The nightmare read his intentions, if not Ashok's thoughts. The journey was important. The beast knew he would finally have the chance to kill and feast.

He felt one of the others nudge his arm and tensed. Cree was suddenly at his ear, shouting.

"We need to speak!" Cree yelled.

Cree pulled him forward, and Ashok saw the silhouettes of the others converging. Cree threw a blanket over their heads to block out some of the dust and wind. He heard the scrape of a sunrod against the ground, and bright light filled the confined space. Vedoran cupped and dimmed the glow with his palm.

They were five ghosts in the muted light. They'd improvised masks to cover their mouths and noses, but it hardly helped.

"We have to move on," Skagi said. Ashok could see how the light carved deep hollows into the brothers' faces. They fidgeted and plucked at the flapping edges of the blanket to hold it in place.

"We can't risk moving now," Vedoran said. "We stay here until the storm passes."

"How long will that be?" Cree demanded. "We'll lose a tenday if this keeps up."

"Then we lose a tenday," Vedoran said.

"That's fine with us," Skagi said. "And you can explain it to Uwan when we bring back the corpses of his missing people."

"If we blunder off course in the storm we lose just as much time," Ashok said.

"This isn't a discussion," Vedoran said, a warning in his black eyes. "We stay here and wait out the storm. Anyone who disagrees can keep his thoughts to himself."

Beneath the dust, Skagi's face reddened, but Cree laid a restraining hand on his arm before he could retort. The tension in the small space threatened to explode.

Behind them, the nightmare snorted and neighed. Distracted, Skagi looked at Ashok. "What's wrong with the beast?" he said.

"It's choking on dust," Cree joked. But Ashok was listening. He held up a hand.

"Do you hear that?" he said.

"Hear what?" Vedoran said. "There's nothing but the damn wind."

Ashok waited, and eventually the sound came again: a deep rumble underlying the piercing wind. "It's thunder," he said. "The nightmare smells the rain. This storm's about to be swallowed."

Vedoran raised his mask and pulled out from their makeshift tent. He returned a breath later. "Ashok's right," he said. "I can smell it too. Put this blanket away," he told Cree. "Be ready to move out."

The thunder grew louder. They huddled under the shelter of the kindling trees, Ashok holding the nightmare's reins. Lightning flashed, and for the first time in days, they had a view across the plain.

"Did you see that?" Chanoch cried.

"What was it?" Skagi shouted.

At that instant, a jagged bolt split the sky and poured into the trunk of the kindling tree. The electric charge threw all five of them to the ground, and the nightmare reared and fell on his side, screaming.

The rain came then, a driving torrent that turned the dust on their bodies to a pasty white mud. When Ashok could see past the lightning blindness and muck, the dust had cleared, revealing a path before them, and in the distance, a rising black mass. Shadows writhed at its edges, and the lightning seemed to spear from its heart.

"There," Chanoch cried. "What is that?"

Ashok dipped his head back and caught the rain in his mouth. The water burned his throat. He spat on the ground.

"It's the witch," he said, wiping his mouth in disgust. "These storms are hers. She must have seen us coming."

Lightning savaged the tree again, and the warriors scattered. Ashok grabbed the nightmare's reins and heaved himself onto the beast's back. He leaned forward so he could whisper in his ear.

"We need your flame," he said. "Show the witch you aren't afraid."

The nightmare screamed into the darkness and fire raced up his mane. Ashok sat back from the heat. The nightmare whipped his tail and shot sparks into the air. The fire burned off the dust and the wet, sending steam clouds toward the sky. The beast paced forward and screamed again as if in challenge.

Vedoran and the others gathered close to the nightmare's flanks. Lightning continued to play across the open plain before them, but the beast strained against the reins, eager to run into the storm.

"Let it go," Vedoran instructed Ashok. "We march," he told the others. "Stay close to the beast."

Ashok eased his grip on the reins, and the nightmare obligingly sprang forward, his long strides forcing the other shadar-kai to run to keep pace. They moved toward the shadow mass.

"Come! Come and give us a kiss, witch!" Skagi cried out and raised his falchion to the sky.

"Tempus!" Chanoch yelled, his arms thrown wide.

Ashok could hear the others shrieking in wild abandon as they ran alongside the flames. Vedoran held his hand out to graze the fire and tilted his head back to let the burning rain kiss his cheeks. Laughter rumbled from his chest, and the skin stretched taut across his face like a mask.

They passed a cluster of boulders and the remnants of a streambed. A lightning bolt struck the rocks, exploding stone. Ashok felt the stings as the tiny shards embedded in his flesh. He felt the nightmare's body quiver, but the beast didn't break stride.

Ashok's eyes burned from the heat and the pain. He kept his legs tight around the nightmare's flanks, half-expecting to be blown off by the lightning. He tried to see ahead of them in the rain, but instead of growing closer, the shadows appeared to be moving away.

Ashok wrapped the iron-shod reins around his knuckles and

pulled. The nightmare screeched a protest and bucked his hindquarters in the air. Thrown forward, Ashok found his hands suddenly in the middle of a fire.

Cursing, he pulled back and almost lost his balance. Cree reached up to steady him. Ashok nodded his thanks and yanked on the reins.

The nightmare reared again, but he slowed, and the rest of the shadar-kai realized something was amiss.

"What is it?" Vedoran demanded.

"It's a trick," Ashok said. "She wants us to think the shadows are her bog. Likely she'll lead us off a cliff before she'll show us the way into her domain. In this storm, we wouldn't know any better until it was too late."

Vedoran squinted into the darkness at the roiling shadows and the lightning all around. His jaw tightened. "You're right," he said. "Turn around."

Ashok wheeled the nightmare and dug in with his thighs. The beast broke into a halting run, and the shadar-kai hurried to follow.

A deafening roar of thunder rolled across the plain. The nightmare screamed in answer, and so the shadar-kai screamed too and brandished their weapons as they charged away from the black storm. The rain pelted them, burned their skin, and slowed their steps in the mud.

The witch doesn't realize what she's done, Ashok thought as he listened to his pounding heart. She should never have stopped the dust storm. After their long journey, his soul was awake at last. The stone shards in his leg and the blisters on his hands were proof that he was still alive. They would come through the storm.

"Fly!" Ashok cried, and reached out to grasp the flames. "Fly and let us all burn!"

They emerged from the storm breathless and bleeding, on the verge of a vast swamp. The rain had stopped, and the air had a dense, saturated feeling. The bog itself seemed a quiet haven in the middle of the open plain, a paradise after the violent storms. There were only the faint sounds of bird and animal life penetrating the thick canopy of leaves, moss, and undergrowth.

Ashok slid off the nightmare's back and took a breath to steady himself on his feet. The others were taking stock of their surroundings. Skagi rubbed the bark of one of the trees. It came off wet in his hand, and the smell of decay filled the air. "Looks pretty on top, but underneath everything's dying," he said. "We'll find nothing to eat in there."

"Assume everything is an illusion," Vedoran said. He crouched to examine Ashok's leg. "This needs to be seen to," he said.

Ashok looked down at his leg and for the first time was able to see all the cuts, the half-melted shards embedded in his flesh. He bled from dozens of these small wounds, and where he didn't the skin was blackened from burns. His hands were raw and throbbing from where the nightmare had thrown him into the fire.

The beast stood quietly beside him, his attention fixed on the bog like an enemy he wanted nothing more than to devour. The nightmare's foul breath steamed the air, and he pawed the wet ground.

"Take this," Vedoran said, pressing a small vial into Ashok's hand. "We get two of these draughts apiece, no more."

Vedoran handed the rest of the vials out to those that needed them. Chanoch bled from a gash above his eye, and Skagi's green tattoos bore patches of black, but none of them were seriously wounded. Indeed all of them looked alive through the eyes in a way they hadn't during the dust storm. The tension that had built up over their long journey had vanished.

Skagi and Vedoran compared burns and jested at their size. Vedoran laughed easily and accepted Skagi's slap on the back when the shadar-kai accused him of running like a slug.

"Why did the storm stop?" Chanoch asked abruptly, stealing the good humor. "If she'd kept it up, she might have hacked us to pieces."

"No, she wouldn't have," Ashok said.

"Once we saw through her ploy, she knew we'd get here," Vedoran agreed. "She's prepared her next offensive. She's waiting for us now."

"Where does she get all this power?" Cree asked. He stood on a raised hillock a few feet away. "I can't see where the bog ends. It runs straight to the horizon."

"It's an illusion," Ashok said. "Just like the shadows we were chasing. The bog exists in her mind."

"Storms felt real enough," Skagi complained. "I've got dust all down my throat and my godsdamn ears are ringing from that thunder."

"Those storms were real," Vedoran said. "I think . . . the witch just heightened our perceptions of them, made us think they were more dangerous and lasted longer than they actually did." He looked at Ashok, who nodded agreement.

"So we have no idea how much true time has passed since we started our journey," Cree said.

"It doesn't matter," Vedoran said. "We've reached the bog, and our mission lies ahead of us. But we can't let the witch worm inside our minds again."

"I can lead with the nightmare," Ashok offered. "The creature clearly isn't afraid of the hag's magic."

Vedoran nodded. "Do it, but make sure you keep the beast from bolting," he said. If we get separated, the hag will be that much stronger taking us on one at a time. The rest of you, weapons out and on the march."

Cree jumped down from the hill, and the rest readied their blades. Ashok mounted the nightmare, whose mane once again shone a dull, heatless blue. He let the reins hang slack in his lap and unhooked his chain from his belt. Using his legs, he guided the nightmare into the bog.

The ground immediately turned spongy and slick. Mosquitoes and biting flies circled fetid pools of stagnant water. The air was so heavy that after a time Ashok's hair was plastered to his skull.

The nightmare's steps became sluggish and uneven, hampered by the sinking ground and the cloying heat. The beast flicked his tail often to combat the flies, and each time he did Ashok got slapped in the back with the stinging horsehair.

"Keep an eye out for predators," Vedoran said. "Don't fill your waterskins from any of the pools."

"Not if I was dying of thirst," Chanoch said, wrinkling his nose at the stench rising from the water. "Smells like corpse brine."

As the day wore on, they found drier ground, but apart from the occasional bird cry or rustle in the undergrowth, they encountered no other living things save the insects. Grass, which before had been sparse and water-logged, grew in abundance in that part of the bog, and soon the nightmare waded in it. The green and brown tendrils came up to Ashok's knees and the other warriors' chests.

Vedoran halted them. "Skagi, take point," he said, "and Chanoch with him. Cut us a path. I want to be able to see my feet. I'll watch our backs. Cree, stay close to Ashok."

They changed positions fluidly, without conversation, and soon the silence was filled with the sound of Skagi's falchion and Chanoch's greatsword scything the grass. Each time they sliced through the blades, the smell of rot grew worse, until Ashok put his mask up over his nose again.

Two hundred feet or so into the brush, the nightmare stopped dead. Ashok dug in with his knees, but the beast wouldn't move. His ears pressed flat against his head, and he snorted a breath. Ashok felt the tension all down the nightmare's body. Orange flame hovered at the roots of his mane.

"What's wrong?" Vedoran asked.

"I don't know," Ashok said. "He senses something."

"I hear it too," Cree said. "That's not your blade, brother?"

Skagi bobbed his weapon in the air to show it was not him who'd made the noise. Ashok heard it then too, and the rest of them tensed.

A scrape in the underbrush, moving fast and very low to the ground. Vedoran drew his sword and put his back to the nightmare. "Form up, make a circle now!" he cried.

They closed ranks around the nightmare. From his high vantage, Ashok tried to see what was swimming in the grass, but the disturbance moved too fast for him to track whether it was beast or man or hag.

Suddenly, there came an explosion of movement and cries ahead of them. The nightmare reared and screamed. A flock of ravens burst out of the underbrush—at least fifty of them—and swarmed the circle of shadar-kai.

"Stand fast!" Vedoran cried. He swung his blade overhand and took two of the birds out of the air.

Ashok grabbed the nightmare's reins, as much to steady himself as to calm the beast. He swung the chain in a protective arc and tangled one of the large ravens. He dragged the chain in and grabbed the struggling bird. It snapped at his fingers with its black beak.

The bird's feathers were like slippery wax. Ashok started to cast the vicious creature away, when suddenly its wings and body collapsed into a mass of feathers and bones. The body parts turned to writhing maggots in his hands.

Ashok cursed and hurled the vermin away. Skagi and Chanoch cut three more out of the air and got showered by the maggots. The rest of the birds flew away, until the raven cries were a distant echo.

"Everyone still got their eyes?" Skagi said.

"My eyes are safe, but not my appetite," Chanoch said as he brushed the maggots off his armor and stomped on them. "Filth! Everything smells like death."

"Calm down," Vedoran said sharply. "Work your blades up front. We're not stopping for a distraction. Ashok, move on."

"I'm trying," Ashok said. The nightmare still wouldn't move. With his head down, the beast stamped the ground with his fetlocks burning. The few strands of green grass around his feet curled up into black husks.

The rustling sound came again, that time from behind them. Vedoran sliced the grass with his blade. Ashok twisted to look, but there was nothing there. Vedoran took two steps forward, then two more and sliced again.

"Vedoran," Ashok said, "Don't stray too far—"

Then it came. A dark shape burst from the grass to Vedoran's right and completely enveloped the shadar-kai. Vedoran fell into the high grass and disappeared from view. A breath later, the grass crumpled in a line moving away from them, as if something were eating a path through it.

"Form a line behind me!" Ashok called out. He jerked the nightmare around by the reins and showed the beast his target. With an enemy in sight, the nightmare charged, burning up the ground with Skagi and the others running behind them.

The nightmare got close enough for Ashok to see Vedoran being dragged through the grass by a small humanoid figure. Green-skinned, with ragged strands of black hair plastered to her back, the hag blended with the undergrowth and moved with preternatural speed. She dragged Vedoran by his left lower leg, her talons encasing his boot and twisting until Vedoran cried out.

When she heard the nightmare's hoofbeats approaching, the hag spun and hissed up at Ashok, exposing her black teeth. Her eyes were a deep, burnt orange and full of hate.

Ashok released the nightmare and fell upon the hag with his chain outstretched.

The hag dropped Vedoran and reached up, grabbing Ashok's spiked weapon even as her body absorbed the impact of his. They rolled into the underbrush, Negala hissing, biting, and spitting black ichor in his face.

Ashok pushed back, and his chain dug into the hag's flesh. He wrapped it around her body once and tightened his grip. Her skin was like stone, but she still felt the pain. She shrieked in a voice that rang shrilly in Ashok's ears. The cry cut off abruptly, and Ashok felt a blaze of heat against his back.

He saw the hag's eyes widen. Quickly, Ashok rolled to the side as the nightmare reared up, his flaming hooves poised to come down and cave in the hag's skull.

The trees and the grass warped around them and turned white. Ashok heard briefly the howl of the Shadowfell wind and saw the open plain spread before him in all its colorless magnitude. Then the scene disappeared, the bog heat swelled around him, and the hag was no longer wrapped in his chain.

The spikes dripped blood, but Negala had disappeared. Ashok looked around frantically. She couldn't have escaped behind him; the others were closing the gap. In front of him Vedoran had his blade out, but he looked disoriented. He stood up and wavered on his feet.

"Did you see that?" Vedoran said.

Ashok nodded. "The illusion broke for a moment, when I cut her, and the nightmare had her cornered," he said.

"Was it a fatal wound?" Vedoran asked.

"I don't think so," Ashok said. "But it and the nightmare were enough to make her run."

"We need to get out of this grass," Vedoran said. The nightmare paced back and forth between them, snorting. The beast nudged Ashok's shoulder as if in accusation.

"Sorry," Ashok said, and reached up absently to touch the beast's forehead. "Next time, we'll have her."

He noticed Vedoran watching him. "Are you all right?" Ashok asked.

"Fine," Vedoran said. "My thanks."

Before Ashok could reply, the others ran up. Skagi looked furious.

"If you killed the godsdamned thing without us, I'll take your head right now," he said.

"She got away," Vedoran said. "Ashok and his beast nearly had her."

"We should keep moving," Ashok said. "Take advantage of the time while she nurses her wounds."

"Agreed," Vedoran said. "Same formation as before."

They fell into line, and Ashok mounted the nightmare. As they pressed on, the tall grass thinned, and the air gradually turned colder. Ashok's breath fogged, and he found himself holding his hands closer to the nightmare's warm body.

"She's trying to freeze us out now," Skagi said. "Ugly bitch," he added, pitching his voice louder.

"I don't think it's for us," Ashok said. "I think it's the nightmare she's attacking." He noticed the beast's stiff-legged movements. The cold dimmed the nightmare's fire and made his red eyes dull. The beast snorted and pranced, forcing the blood down his legs for warmth.

"The nightmare almost crushed her," Vedoran said. "Makes sense she'd want to return the favor."

"Sounds like she's not threatened by us at all," Skagi said, laughing. "She only fears the pony."

Ashok and Vedoran exchanged a glance. "I don't know whether to be comforted by that or not," Vedoran remarked.

"They are similar creatures," Ashok said. "They manipulate the mind."

Snow began to fall. The swampy pools iced over, and the sounds of the animals were gone. There was no pretense that it was a bog anymore. Soon they were all covered in a thick coating of freezing wet snow.

"I complained about the dust, but this is intolerable," Cree said, shaking out his wet hair.

The nightmare slowed his steps until he was barely keeping pace with the group. Breath wheezed in and out of the beast's chest.

Ashok leaned forward to whisper in his ear.

"You're not going to be felled by this," he scoffed. "By a small, ugly creature that howls and shrieks. You are fire. You will burn a path through this false wilderness and take us out the other side." He heard the echo of Uwan's words in his own. "Her flesh awaits you. Don't disappoint me now."

The nightmare snorted—a sound of amusement, Ashok imagined. The beast didn't need his encouragement.

The wind blew cold into Ashok's face, but suddenly his legs were burning, his skin slick with sweat. He looked down and saw the snow melting, running in rivers off the Nightmare's flanks.

Ashok didn't need further warning. He slid off the nightmare and backed the others a safe distance away.

"What's he doing?" Skagi asked.

"Sending a message," Ashok said, and before he'd finished speaking, the nightmare burst into flames.

The beast's mane, fetlocks, and tail were all ablaze, but the flames didn't stop there. They spread to consume the rest of the nightmare's body until the beast had transformed into a walking fireball. At his feet the snow melted and turned back to swampy water. The nightmare reared up and snorted gouts of flame into the frozen air.

"Godsdamn, will you look at that?" Chanoch said. "Did you know he could do that?"

Ashok shook his head. "I've never seen anything like it before."

"Hard to be cold with that striding beside you," Skagi said.

Negala must have thought so as well, for the snow stopped falling, and abruptly the white scene faded, the swamp disappeared, and the group found themselves standing on an open expanse of the Shadowfell. The wind plucked at their clothing and hair, carrying away the smells of rot.

Skagi looked around. "That's it, then?" he said, sounding disappointed. "She's giving up?"

"Don't question it," Vedoran said. "Let's move along while the beast is still aflame."

Ashok walked beside the nightmare. In the wake of the beast's footsteps, fire surged ten feet or more into the air. Heat from the flames beat against his face, but Ashok didn't care. He was fascinated by the orange and deep blue glows that played in waves across the nightmare's flesh.

"Your fire burns as your soul burns," Ashok said. "But right now, in this place, you are our light."

What would Tempus think of such a guide? Ashok wondered.

CHAPTER FIFTEEN

"ARE YOU SURE THAT'S THE PLACE?" CREE ASKED VEDORAN.

A narrow valley of jagged rock lay below them. At the bottom a silt stream cut a path to the east.

"It has to be," Vedoran said. "Uwan claimed we would find our destination on the other side of the bog. This valley is the only landmark for miles."

"Look," Ashok said, pointing at a spot several feet away from where they stood. "The rocks look like stairs. I think they've been shaped, and not by the weather."

They went to the spot, and Vedoran bent to examine the rock. "You're right," he said. "There's a path going down to the bottom." He glanced up at Ashok. "You have good eyes."

Ashok said nothing. Tension suffused his body, no matter how hard he tried to force himself to relax. But Vedoran's compliment seemed genuine. He didn't sound suspicious.

Vedoran took Chanoch, and the two of them went down the steps to scout the bottom of the valley while Ashok, Skagi, and Cree stayed with the nightmare and kept watch.

Ashok tried to look at the valley with fresh eyes, but he had been over every stone of the place since he was a child. He knew what Vedoran and Chanoch would find at the bottom, and as he marked their progress down the stone steps, he knew the instant they would see the entrance to his enclave.

He didn't know how much longer he would be able to hide his ignorance.

When the pair returned, Vedoran said, "We found it. On the opposite bank of the stream there's a cave entrance. It's hidden unless you climb down the valley."

They camped for a short rest, their last chance to sleep and prepare themselves before the second part of their mission commenced. Ashok stood apart from the others, waiting to begin his watch. His thoughts were eaten up with how to proceed.

By showing Vedoran the path to the caves, Ashok had betrayed his enclave. He would have their blood on his hands, unless he could convince Vedoran and the others to barter for the missing party members.

He dismissed the possibility almost as soon as it occurred to him. Even if by some grace of Tempus the captives were still alive, Vedoran would never bargain for his people's release. With so much to prove to Uwan, he would accept nothing less than an all-out annihilation of the captors. Similarly, Ashok's father would never agree to release his prisoners, nor would he allow a hostile force to know the location of his enclave.

No matter what Ashok did, in the end there were only two options: betray Ikemmu, or betray his father and the rest of his enclave.

"Ashok," called a voice.

Ashok turned. "Yes, Chanoch?"

The young one grinned and said, "Good hunting, eh?"

Ashok nodded stiffly. "Good hunting."

"Wake us before you become weary," Vedoran said. He lay down on the hard ground and propped his head on one arm. They were all asleep within breaths. As eager as they were for the challenge ahead, they wanted to be as fresh and alert as possible when the time came.

Ashok watched them all at rest, their faces slack. Sleep took the stress and wildness from their expressions, so that Ashok barely recognized them as the warriors he knew.

A memory surfaced, of the few journeys Ashok had undertaken to the Shadowfell with his father and brothers. There were no watches, no long marches across the open plain. They traveled only so far and did only so much as they could do without sleep. Sleep on the unguarded plain was as good as a death sentence, if you failed to hear the dagger coming for you in the dark.

Ashok stared down at the cave entrance. There was no movement, though he knew there were guards just inside the cave mouth. He would have to find a way to alert Vedoran to their presence, if his other companions didn't detect them.

Restless, he stood and paced the camp. He went to the nightmare, tied to a cluster of kindling trees a few feet away. The beast's hair appeared flat black now, with only a feathering of blue at the roots of his mane and tail. The heat had dulled enough that Ashok felt confident running his hand up and down the beast's neck.

They're all good, Ashok thought, Vedoran and the rest—warriors to equal any in the enclave. But his enclave had numbers in the caves. They knew where there was enough space to swing a sword, and where the passages narrowed so two shadar-kai couldn't walk abreast. There was a reason they'd survived in the valley so long.

The nightmare's ears twitched. He whickered and nudged Ashok with his body when he ceased the gentle rubbing.

"You've done your part," Ashok said, "and have my thanks. It's time for me to return the favor."

He untangled the reins from the needle branches. The nightmare lowered his head, and Ashok removed the bridle and bit. The metal was hot in his hands.

"Go," he said, slapping the beast on the rump. The nightmare whinnied in indignation and took off at a gallop across the plain. When the beast was almost out of sight, Ashok saw the flames burst from his mane. Streaks of fire cut the ground in the wake of his passage. Ashok watched until the flames disappeared.

He turned back to the camp. The others slept on, their dreams unfettered by the nightmare's influence.

Some time later, Ashok woke Skagi and took his place. The ground was still warm from the heat of his body. Ashok closed his eyes, but he didn't sleep.

He planned.

⛓

Natan woke in a sweat in his small chamber. His skin was hot as if flames had grazed him while he slept. Had he been dreaming, or was there vital portent he'd missed?

Cursing himself, Natan got up but went almost immediately to his knees by a small wooden altar, bearing only a candle and a dagger with a ruby set in the hilt. The weapon had been a gift, long before, from Ilvani. He touched the hilt and called for Tempus.

"Forgive me," he said aloud. "I was weary and slept. I shall not be weak again. Show me your will, I pray you."

Uwan had been the one to send him to his rest. Natan didn't fault his leader for it; Uwan only meant to help. He could see that Natan had been fasting and holding vigil. He'd done so almost since the day Ilvani had disappeared, and the exhaustion was starting to take its toll on his body.

What Uwan did not understand was that Natan cared nothing for his own health. Wherever Ilvani was Natan sensed she suffered far worse. He would not be well until she came home.

"Tempus," he prayed, and repeated his wish for the god to speak, to give him some sign that Ashok and the others walked the right path. Was the fire an ill omen or a promise of rebirth? "Tell me that this has all not been in vain."

"Is it wise, brother, to chatter so much at your god's mind that he forsakes all others for your entreaties? Isn't it selfish?"

Natan gasped and clutched his chest. He didn't dare look behind him for fear he might break at last, but the voice was so familiar and beloved he couldn't dismiss it as a phantom.

He shifted on his knees and saw her, sitting cross-legged in the corner of his chamber. It was such a familiar pose when she came to see him that Natan almost wept. She looked exactly as she had when she'd left, her pale skin and garnet hair—the red he'd hated on himself but that suited her so well.

"Ilvani," he said.

"You look terrible, brother," Ilvani said. She pretended to sniff the air. "Have you been bathing?"

He chuckled. "This is what I'm reduced to when you're not around to look after me," he said. He wanted to go to her, but he was terrified that if he moved she would vanish.

It wasn't truly Ilvani. Natan knew that, though he ached to admit it. It was prophecy, Tempus's visions given a voice and a face that wouldn't frighten or overwhelm a mortal. But Natan felt overwhelmed, and full of joy, hope. Surely Tempus would not be so cruel as to send him a vision of his sister if she were gone?

"You're watching the wrong things, brother," Ilvani said seriously. "You're too much on your knees and not enough in Ikemmu. You're missing it."

"I can't just sit by and not look for you," Natan said. "How can Tempus ask that of me?"

"You see the fire," Ilvani said, "but you have no idea how it shapes them. It may forge or destroy, save them or damn them. Why do you force them to choose one or the other?"

She sounded like the Ilvani that Natan remembered, the beloved sister with her mind in two worlds, though where or what the other was, no one knew. At times Natan thought it was a safe harbor for her mind, but at others it seemed a prison she'd created for herself.

He wondered if he should have told Ashok about his and Ilvani's unique heritage. It did not matter. The others would tell him, if they felt he needed to know.

"Ilvani, can you tell me where you are?" Natan asked. "There are shadar-kai warriors seeking you. Can you feel their presence?"

"Yes," she said. She stood up and walked past him.

"Wait!" Natan called as he jumped to his feet and went after her. She passed through the wall, a phantom. Natan fumbled with the door latch and ran out to the stairs.

She was already walking up the spiral, her long black cloak with its overlay of tiny chains clinking behind her. Natan followed her.

"Everything is turning," Ilvani said.

"What do you mean?" Natan said. He felt dizzy looking up at her while they turned on the stair. "What's turning?"

"Don't you feel it, brother?" Ilvani said, scoffing and fluttering her hands impatiently. "You should be feeling them, every one. They will change everything, and you won't stop to see it until it's too late. Then the fire will come."

"Ilvani!" Natan cried. "Tempus, what are you trying to tell me!"

Ilvani stopped so fast that Natan passed through her. He collapsed on the stairs, breathless, and looked up at her. The light shone through her flesh, and she was a specter with his sister's voice.

"He will bear the burden of Ikemmu," she said, and her voice reverberated off the walls, deep and angry. "The faithless will guide the faithful, but by then it may already be too late. You must look to your people."

She tipped her head back and spread her arms. White wings burst from her spine and spread out behind her. She brought them down, and in a rush of air that Natan felt on his face, she took flight.

The tower steps disappeared, and Natan found himself floating in a formless void. The specter-angel flew above him, and as he watched she was joined by other winged folk, circling in an endless vortex of wings and light.

Natan stood up and stretched his arms out. "Ilvani!" he cried. But he knew she was gone. He watched the angels cavort in the sky beneath a glowing sun. Natan felt the heat on his face, so warm he began to sweat.

The memory of his dream came back to him then in a rush, and Natan knew what had woken him. He looked up; the angels flew higher and higher, toward the golden sun.

"Stop!" he yelled, but his voice was very faint. It barely touched the vast sky. "Come back! Don't fly there!"

He screamed until his throat was raw, but it was all in vain. One by one the winged specters caught fire. The flames outlined their wings, and for a hopeless breath they were mighty phoenixes. Then the fire consumed them and turned their beautiful appendages to ash.

Bodies fell shrieking out of the sky. As they passed they reached for Natan, and he tried to grab onto them to stop their fall, but his hands passed through their flesh, and all he felt was the fire. His hands blistered, and he cried out in agony as they all perished before his eyes.

Natan awoke in his bed, sweating. He could still feel the fire on his skin. He stumbled out of bed, went to the altar, and turned to the corner where Ilvani had appeared. But he saw nothing, sensed nothing but an empty chamber.

Trembling and awash in horror from what he'd witnessed, Natan couldn't find the strength to pray. He went to his bed, took the blankets off, and piled them in the corner of the room. He lay down and felt the cold stone floor start to calm him and cool the sweat from his body. His heartbeat was frenzied in his chest.

"Tempus," he begged, "Tempus." Over and over he said his god's name. "Let that not be our fate. Let it not be. Let it not be."

He slept, a dreamless stupor, but he did not see Ilvani again, or the winged specters.

CHAPTER SIXTEEN

"Down the valley in single file," Vedoran told them as they prepared to leave. "Lean into the cliff wall if you lose your balance."

"The wind is strong, especially near the top," Chanoch said. "It almost plucked me off a couple of times."

"I'll take point, then Skagi and Cree, Ashok, and Chanoch watching our back," Vedoran said.

"We should use our masks," Ashok said. "The ones we made for the dust storm. If by some chance they do see us coming, they won't know who or what we are."

He looked to Vedoran for support. The shadar-kai considered then nodded. "Do it," he said.

Ashok tied the dust-covered cloth across the bridge of his nose and pulled his cloak hood up so that only his black eyes were visible. Unless he spoke, no one in his enclave would know him, and none of them were expecting to see a dead son returned to his home. Still, considering what lay ahead of him, the protection seemed as flimsy as parchment, and as they proceeded down the valley, Ashok felt horribly vulnerable.

Tempus sees you, if no one else does, Ashok thought bitterly. At any moment he expected the warrior god to reach down and expose him for the traitor he was.

The wind was indeed vicious, and more than once they had to stop and crouch low to the rock to keep from being plucked off. But the farther they descended, the easier the way became, until they touched down on the valley floor.

Ashok's heart pounded a dull, uneven rhythm against his ribs. The landmarks were so familiar. He knew exactly how far he was from his own chamber in the caves. Everything was the same; only Ashok had changed.

They weaved among rocks, keeping low and to the shadows as they crossed the stream and approached the cave entrance from the east. Ashok felt confident they wouldn't be spotted. The guards were looking for threats on the valley ridge. They didn't realize their domain had already been penetrated by enemies using their own stone staircase.

As they neared the mouth of the cave, Ashok carefully readied his chain. He kept the spikes taut so they made no sound. Vedoran drew his blade and motioned for Ashok to come join him at the front of the line. The others he motioned to stay a distance back.

Ashok came forward, and Vedoran whispered, "Stay at my back when we go in. Ten feet, no farther, until we see how many guards there are at the entrance."

Ashok nodded and waited, while Vedoran darted past him and into the cave. He came in behind and heard the surprised cries of two guards, quickly stifled when Vedoran grabbed one of them from behind and covered his mouth.

Ashok grabbed the other and clamped a hand over his lips. He recognized both guards. Those men had the watch during the enclave's sleeping time, and Ashok had often greeted them when he left on his journeys across the plain. They had been the last members of his enclave he'd seen before he left to hunt down the shadow hounds.

He dropped his chain and took out his dagger. Reversing the blade, Ashok struck the back of his guard's skull with the hilt. The shadar-kai went limp, and Ashok let him fall to the ground.

As he sheathed his blade, Ashok heard a sudden crack. He fumbled and dropped the dagger, but Vedoran didn't notice. He'd broken the neck of the other guard.

Vedoran went out and motioned for the others to join them inside the cave. He dragged his guard's corpse over to Ashok's unconscious one and dropped the body on top of him. Fortunately, he didn't pause long enough to see that Ashok's guard still breathed.

The passages ahead of them were lit by torches sparsely placed along the walls. They burned a low flame, casting just enough light to mimic the perpetual dusk of the Shadowfell. It was the gateway, the long walk in the dark.

Their greatest chance of failure lay in these twisting passages, Ashok thought. Initially, the tunnels were wide and tall enough for large groups to walk abreast, but the illusion of space soon faded. The deeper caves were designed to be like a maze, with so many dead-end passages and narrow halls that the uninitiated would quickly be lost and starve to death trying to find a way back to familiar territory.

Vedoran put them in line again, with himself and Ashok up front, Chanoch in the middle, and the brothers bringing up the rear. They proceeded down the long, wide passage, keeping close to the wall. Ashok could hear the echoing voices of his enclave drifting up from the deeper caves. Each time the voices came, Vedoran halted them to listen, but it was impossible to tell how close the voices were, and how many spoke. Ashok knew it must be driving Vedoran mad.

The fourth time they stopped to listen, Ashok put a hand on Vedoran's shoulder. The shadar-kai turned and raised an eyebrow.

"They make no sound of alarm," Ashok said. "For now, I believe we're undetected."

Vedoran nodded, but he was still unsettled. They marched on. The straight passage continued for a quarter mile into the rock before curving slightly to the west.

So it begins, Ashok thought, and watched the passage narrow drastically and split, offering tunnels in three different directions. Phantom voices babbled from all three.

"Which direction?" Chanoch whispered. "They all look the same."

"Cree, we need a map of these tunnels," Vedoran said quietly. Cree nodded and reached in his pouch for tools. To the rest of them, Vedoran said, "Take alive the next shadar-kai we encounter. We question them about our people, but if they make any move to sound an alarm, kill them."

Skagi and Chanoch nodded eagerly. Ashok looked at the split in the passages. "This way," he said, pointing to the left branch. "The voices seem to be louder coming from this tunnel."

"How can you be sure?" Vedoran asked.

Ashok shrugged, trying to appear casual. "I can't. But it comforts me to think we aren't choosing at random."

"True," Vedoran said, and the others laughed quietly. "Are you ready, Cree?" he asked.

Cree's deft hands sketched a chalk map on a piece of parchment. He folded it carefully and tucked it away. "Ready," he answered.

They took the left passage and had no choice but to walk single file down the narrow tunnel. The ground sloped downward at a gradual angle, and the air grew colder the deeper they descended into the earth.

Ashok judged they had another mile of tunnels to navigate before they got close to where they needed to be. The enclave had no formal dungeons—only graves had ever been needed to accommodate their enemies—so if the captives were alive, they would be in the food room, Ashok reasoned. It was a secure chamber with a dedicated guard, the place where live animals were caged for slaughter. Unfortunately for the rescue party, it was also snarled in the most heavily-trafficked areas of the enclave. It would be nearly impossible for them to get there undetected.

They reached another intersection, and Vedoran halted the group. Two passages forked left and right, joined by a hole halfway up the wall. The hole was large enough to accommodate a shadar-kai, but the tunnel was more a chute than a passage, with sheer walls on all sides.

"Any intuition about this one?" he asked Ashok.

Ashok stepped forward and pretended to examine the three tunnels. He stood beneath the hole in the wall and sniffed.

"This is a waste chute," he said, "which means there's at least one level of tunnels above this one, probably more."

"In other words, we're not dealing with a small band of shadar-kai hiding in a cave," Vedoran said. "This is a functional enclave that's been here for some time."

"I'd say at least ten years," Cree said. "The tunnels vary in size, and the clearing done in some of these passages was by living hands, not age."

"Are you sure?" Vedoran asked.

Cree nodded. "They've made themselves a fortress here," he said. "It's not as intimidating to look at as Neimal and her wall guards, but it's defensible. Depending on how much food they have stored here, they could live comfortably hidden for a year or more, if they had to."

"But that's good news," Chanoch said. His face split in a relieved grin.

Vedoran shot him a look of incredulous disgust. "How do you see it as such?" he demanded.

"Tempus knew a large force couldn't penetrate the caves," Chanoch said. "Uwan sent us, and Ashok, who saw the way into the valley. Don't you see? It's all come together. We've done right. Praise to Tempus and Uwan," he said, his voice echoing down the tunnels.

Vedoran's expression darkened. He stepped up until he was in Chanoch's face. "Tempus and Uwan be damned, and if you don't be silent, pup, you'll stay here with the corpses," he said. "Alert anyone to our presence, and I'll make you one of them."

Chanoch's jaw tightened. Ashok held his breath, waiting for the young one to utter the wrong words. If Chanoch lost control with Tempus's name on his lips, Ashok thought Vedoran might strike the young one down.

Chanoch put a hand on the hilt of his greatsword. A tense breath passed, but then, with a visible effort, Chanoch released his weapon and stepped back, yielding to Vedoran's authority.

"Choose a tunnel, Ashok. We're moving on," Vedoran said, but his gaze never left Chanoch. Skagi and Cree said nothing, but Ashok noticed their hands stayed close to their own weapons.

Ashok considered the passages. "Left," he said, after pretending to deliberate for a breath or two.

"I can't hear the voices anymore." Vedoran said. "Why left this time?"

Ashok grappled for an excuse. "This tunnel appears to stay wide for a greater distance," he improvised. "More room to fight, should it be necessary."

Vedoran examined both ways in silence. "I see no difference," he said. "We'll have to split up, check them both."

"Is that wise?" Ashok said sharply.

A mistake. Vedoran had already had his authority challenged once. "Am I leader of this expedition or is Ashok, chosen of Tempus?" he demanded.

Ashok bowed his head. "Respectfully, if we split up, we may become more easily lost," he said.

"Not if you're able to draw a decent map," Vedoran said. He lowered his voice so that only Ashok heard him. "You know how to chart an enemy's defenses, don't you? You made lovely pictures of Ikemmu when you first arrived. Don't you remember sitting alone in your little hut, where you thought no one could see?"

"You've been watching me closely," Ashok said, struggling to keep his voice even. "I'm surprised. You, who hate to be controlled, keeping such a stranglehold on someone else's freedom." He raised his voice so the others could hear. "You're right, Vedoran," he said. "Speed and efficiency are the best way. We need to split up."

Vedoran nodded. "I thought you'd see it that way. Skagi?"

"Yes, Vedoran?" Skagi said promptly.

"You'll go with Ashok down the left tunnel. Let him map the way. The rest of you come with me to the right. Meet back here with what we find."

Vedoran and the others moved off down the tunnel, and Ashok stood alone with Skagi. He clapped Ashok on the shoulder.

"Don't worry about it," he said. "Vedoran's wound himself into a frenzy to make this mission good."

"I'll be happy enough if he doesn't get us all killed," Ashok said.

CHAPTER
SEVENTEEN

Ashok and Skagi started down the tunnel, and after a distance encountered another intersection, then another beyond.

Skagi cursed. "Now what? We report back?" he said, sounding disappointed.

Ashok came to a silent decision. It was a risk, but if he didn't act now, either dissension in the ranks or his enclave would kill them all.

"Follow me," he said and took the tunnel to the right off the second intersection. He moved fast. Skagi had to trot to keep up with him.

"Where're we going?" Skagi said.

Ashok raised a hand for him to be silent. He listened for signs of anyone coming from the intersection behind them, but he heard nothing.

"Keep moving," he said, and continued on down a straight, narrow passage that would take them past the food preparation area. The animal pens were just beyond that.

"Godsdamnit, Ashok, you're going to get us lost with your guessing," Skagi whispered.

Ashok hesitated at the next intersection. Skagi was not a subtle warrior, by any means, but he wasn't stupid either. Sooner or later he would start to suspect that Ashok knew exactly where they were going.

Then, the answer came. It was carried on the wind.

"Do you smell that?" Ashok said.

Skagi sniffed the air. "Blood," he said.

"Someone's been fighting here recently," Ashok said. "Maybe the captives are striking back?"

Skagi grinned and drew his falchion. "Maybe they'd like some aid?" he said.

"We should expect guards," Ashok said, and Skagi nodded eagerly.

They moved ahead, and the smell of blood and rotting meat grew more intense as they passed the food preparation rooms. Ashok stopped at an intersection and risked a quick glance around the corner.

The door to the slaughter chamber was barred, as it never had been when they kept animals in there. Ashok's heart pounded. There was hope after all that the captives were still alive.

Two guards stood at the door. They carried a mace and an axe, and there were bloodstains on their armor. Ashok knew he wouldn't get away with simply knocking those guards out. He'd made his choice, and he had to live with it.

"Quick and silent," he whispered to Skagi.

Skagi nodded, and together they charged around the corner.

The guards saw them and were so shocked they froze with their weapons against their chests. Ashok whipped his chain around the neck of the one with the mace. He pulled it tight, choking off the guard's breath and severing the throat vein in one motion. The shadar-kai gargled on his own blood and slid down the wall.

Skagi hit the other guard in the flank with his blade, but the weapon passed through empty air. The guard teleported a few feet away and reappeared at the mouth of the passage where Skagi and Ashok had entered. She ran down the tunnel, her insubstantial form wavering in and out of the torchlight.

"I'll get her," Skagi said. "You get the captives out."

"Wait!" Ashok cried, but Skagi took off before Ashok could stop him.

Ashok went to the door and yanked up the bar sealing it shut. He listened for a breath and then opened it.

Inside the slaughter chamber, the stench was overpowering. Had his mask not blunted the smell, Ashok would have retched. Blood, waste, and an underlying air of decay filled the room.

From the doorway there was a short stair leading down into a roughly circular chamber. A second door on the opposite side of the room led to more guard areas as well as an underground river. Along the left-hand wall were dozens of thick-barred iron cages of various sizes, some stacked on top of each other. Within the smaller ones, coneys, foxes, and spindle-legged deer crouched, watching Ashok with large eyes. Ravens and crows let out deep-throated caws from the higher cages, and feathers fell in a black rain.

To Ashok's right, two iron bars were suspended lengthwise by chains from the ceiling. From those dangled blood-stained leather straps cinched tight enough to hold an animal's front and hindquarters. Beneath the bars someone had placed a long trough to catch the blood and organs as they were removed.

Two of the leather straps were not in use. They dangled free and were half-shredded as if from the claws of a struggling animal. The others were cinched tight around the wrists of a naked shadar-kai man.

There were no guards in the room. Ashok secured the door behind him and went cautiously down the stairs. He approached the captive but could already see the man was dead, and thanked the gods for that small mercy.

Ashok raised his hand to press the mask more fully against his face. The man's body dangled limply from the straps, his bare feet brushing the inside of the trough. His toes had been removed and lay in a pile of blood and urine at the bottom. His genitals had been cut off as well.

The man's flesh had been split from his navel to his breastbone. The shredded halves had been peeled back, exposing his insides to the air. Ashok did not spend time examining the crawling movement he could see from the open cavity.

The captive's face was shockingly peaceful, his head bent forward, his chin against his chest, his eyes closed. His shaved head bore several open wounds where it looked as if his captors had carved out the tattoos from his flesh. There was the rough imprint of a sword just above his left ear.

"Tempus take your servant. Give him rest." Ashok murmured the prayer without considering what he said. "He's suffered enough."

He heard a sound then from one of the cages. Ashok spun, his dagger ready in his hand, but there was no movement and no other sound, only the animals watching him from behind the bars.

He moved along the row of cages, releasing the catches to let the animals run free in the room. Ashok wasn't sure what possessed him to do it—the sounds the animals made could alert someone outside the room. But something in their eyes compelled him, or maybe it was just the sight of the dead shadar-kai. There was a flurry of wings and clumsy shuffling as the beasts, too long confined, tried to learn to walk again.

At the end of the row, in the largest cage, Ashok found the remaining Ikemmu captives.

He released the latch—the cage wasn't even locked—and stepped inside. The low top forced him to stoop, but he could still stand on his feet. Ashok clutched his dagger reflexively against his chest.

There were five of them left, counting the man outside. The naked corpse of a woman near the cage door had been mutilated in much the same way as the man had been. Her fingernails were split and broken, or worn down to the bloody quick where she'd fought the straps.

At the back of the cage, the bodies of a man and woman had been propped up in a half-sitting position, their arms and necks tied with chains looped around the cage bars. They sat with legs splayed and wore sweat-stained tunics but no breeches.

Ashok crouched to examine them. There were no visible signs of mutilation, until he saw the dried bloodstains between their legs.

Overcome at last, he staggered away on his knees until his back hit the cage wall. The force knocked the breath from his lungs. Ashok put his head between his knees and breathed through his mouth. The smell clung to his clothes, his hair. He would never be rid of this vileness.

When he'd gotten his breathing under control, Ashok thought he heard another sound. He looked up and stifled a cry.

The man had his eyes open and was looking at Ashok.

Ashok couldn't believe what he was seeing. He'd assumed they were all dead. How could any of them be alive in such a charnel house? They were so still that even the man, staring at him, looked like a corpse with a faint light in its eyes.

Another woman lay a few feet away on her side, her back to Ashok. He couldn't tell if she breathed. She'd wrapped her arms around the cage bars and pulled herself as close to the wall as possible.

Swallowing, Ashok went over to the man and began working the chains at his neck. The man's eyes tracked what Ashok was doing, but otherwise he remained completely motionless, with no expression on his face.

Ashok got the chain loose enough to slip over the man's head. Without the tension to support it, the man's head lolled forward.

Ashok caught it, and gently pushed the man back to rest against the bars. Then he went to work on his hands.

When Ashok had finished, he went to free the woman. As he worked the chain at her neck, he listened for a heartbeat, for breath. He heard nothing. She was gone.

Ashok laid his dagger aside and supported her weight as the chains fell free. He laid her body down on one side like the other woman. He wanted to give her some semblance of dignity. As he did that he spoke to the man.

"Can you walk?" he asked. "We don't have much time."

Ashok reached back for his dagger, but it wasn't where he'd left it. He looked up and saw the man holding the weapon in both hands. He was so weak he could barely raise the blade above chest level to brandish it. His hands trembled, but his expression remained detached. He might as well have been holding an apple for all he knew what to do with the weapon.

Ashok raised his hands. "I'm not going to hurt you," he said. "I'm from Ikemmu."

Nothing. Not a flicker of recognition.

"We were sent by Uwan—by Tempus—to rescue you," Ashok said. "Do you remember Uwan?"

"U-wan." The man's lips came together clumsily to form the word. His voice was a shredded whisper. Ashok could see faint bruises on his throat where he'd been choked.

"That's right," Ashok said. "Uwan wouldn't stop until he found you. I've come to bring you home."

"Home," said the man. He sighed and let the dagger rest in his lap, running his fingers over the hilt. "Tempus be praised."

"We don't have much time," Ashok said. "If you can walk, I need you to check your companion," he pointed to the other woman, "to see if she lives. I'll be right outside."

He was going to take the other body down and conceal it behind the trough so his companion wouldn't have to see it. He headed for the door of the cage, but stopped when he heard a strangled gurgle.

Ashok spun around. Horror washed through him.

The man fell back against the cage bars, his body twitching. He'd stabbed himself in the chest with Ashok's dagger. The hilt was held between his two hands, and an expression of utter peace suffused his features. His aim had been true. The life went out of the man's eyes as the blade penetrated and stopped his heart.

At that moment, the door at the top of the stairs opened, and Skagi entered the room. Ashok barely registered the warrior's presence. He was trapped in the cage, unable to look away from the dead man's peaceful countenance.

"Tempus be merciful!" Skagi said. He saw Ashok in the cage and ran over to him. "What happened here?" he demanded in a raw voice.

Ashok couldn't find the words. He just shook his head. He was looking to the other woman, but all the strength had gone out of his body. He didn't want to look, was terrified to see any more of the brutal work of his enclave.

"Ashok? Ashok!" Skagi said, shaking his arm.

Ashok slowly came back to himself. "Where are the others?" he asked.

"I don't know," Skagi said. "I killed the guard and came straight back. She had time to yell up and down the caves before I took her, so we can expect company soon."

"Go find the others," Ashok said. "Tell them . . . what you saw."

"What about you?"

"I'll be right behind you," Ashok said. "We'll have to clear a path out of here."

Skagi nodded and backed out of the cage. Ashok could see the relief on his face when he left the torture chamber.

Steeling himself, Ashok went to the other woman. He reached out to touch her shoulder, and several things happened at once.

The crows flying around the room cawed loudly, and the woman rolled onto her back in one violent motion. Her hands clawed at Ashok's face. She caught his cheek and raked with her blunt, ruined nails. Ashok felt the fire lines across his face and wet blood drip down his neck.

He hurled himself back, his hands up in defense, but the woman did not pursue him. Ashok retreated against the opposite wall of the cage and stayed there.

Facing him on her side, the woman brought her knees up against her chest and wrapped her arms around her legs. The bones of her skeleton shone clearly through her taut flesh. Ashok couldn't imagine when she'd last been fed. Blood-matted hair fell in uneven chunks across her face. She put her head down, as if trying to make her body as small as possible.

Ashok tried to get a look at her eyes, but he couldn't see through the curtain of her hair. Staying crouched he came toward her a step and stopped to gauge her reaction. She didn't move, only curled tighter into her protective ball.

"Ilvani?" Ashok said, with a knowledge he didn't at first comprehend. Then he saw it, in the shape of her face, an echo of Natan's countenance. Ilvani had survived, despite all the horrors she'd experienced.

She had survived. And if it killed him, Ashok would see her returned to Ikemmu.

Ashok pulled the mask down so Ilvani could see his face. He reached up and fumbled with the catch of his cloak. He pulled the garment off and took another crouching step forward. He spread the cloak out on the ground between them like a buffer, then he backed away until he was against the opposite bars again.

He waited, his hands between his knees, to see what she would do.

He could feel time slipping away, precious breaths they needed to get out of the caves before the enclave realized what was happening and sealed off all the escape routes, before they ran them all down and hung them from the straps over the slaughter trough.

His breath tight in his chest, Ashok forced himself to wait, patiently, to make no reaction when she stretched out one hand, scraping it across the floor until she could grasp a corner of the cloak with her fingers.

She pulled the garment toward herself, threading it through her hands as if through the eye of a needle. She covered her body and curled into herself, pulling the cloak over her head. Ashok's heart wrenched in his chest.

"Ilvani," he said brokenly, "can you hear me?"

He waited, not really expecting an answer. More breaths ticked by, and finally, no more than a whisper among the bird cries and animal stirrings, she answered.

"I hear."

"My name is—"

"Ashok," Ilvani said, cutting him off. Her voice was quiet, but strong. "I hear your name on the wind."

"You knew I was coming?" Ashok said.

Beneath his cloak, Ilvani moved, but she did not uncover herself. "The wind whispered your name," she said. "I tried to keep it, but they took all my boxes away." She sounded sad, her voice growing fainter as she spoke.

"That's all right," Ashok said. "I'm here now. I've come to take you out of here. Back to Ikemmu. Back to Natan."

Ilvani sighed. Ashok could see the cloak moving with her breath. "I remember him," she said. "I walked with him in dreams. So many beautiful, twisted faces. I told him not to be unhappy."

"You'll see him again," Ashok said. "But first, will you look at my face?"

Silence, and a tremor through the cloak. But a breath later, her hand emerged, long, delicate fingers curled into claws still stained with his blood. She pulled the cloak down so he could see her face.

"Who are you?" she asked, her eyes narrowed.

"I am Ashok," he said patiently. "I've come to take you back to Ikemmu, but we have to move quickly or we'll be trapped here. I know you don't want to be touched, but I need to know if you can walk. Will you try?"

She considered him in wary silence, but then she put her hand against the ground and pushed herself to a sitting position. With her other hand she held the cloak around her like a shield.

The crows cawed again in warning, and the other door to the chamber opened.

With his heart in his throat, Ashok looked up to see a single guard enter the room. He shut the door behind him and didn't immediately appear to notice Ashok. He was too busy watching the animals running free in the room.

"What's this?" he shouted. "Godsdamnit, Fridl, I told you to check the cages!"

He came into the room, swatting aside the crows and ravens circling the air. Ashok moved to the cage door so he wouldn't get himself trapped, and the guard noticed him at last. His eyes widened. He opened his mouth to speak, but no words came out.

Ashok's eyes took in the guard's clothes, stained with blood that was obviously not his own, and the locks of red hair tied with leather cord hanging from his belt. He looked at Ilvani, at her uneven, blood-stained hair, and a snarl ripped from his throat.

Ilvani shrank back against the bars of the cage. A wail rose in her throat, like an animal trying to claw free. She raised her hands in front of her face and began beating her head against the cage bars. The blunt sounds shivered through Ashok's body.

"Ilvani, stop!" he cried, but she kept on, until she slid down the bars, unconscious. A trickle of fresh blood filled her hairline and ran down her forehead.

The guard saw it all, but his gaze stayed riveted to Ashok's face. Unmasked, Ashok saw the recognition in his eyes. The guard knew him, and Ashok recognized the man in turn.

Reltnar was his name. He had close-cropped black hair and a fresh scar across the bridge of his nose. Ashok remembered he and Reltnar had prowled the Shadowfell together in their youth, when both were still learning how to fight for their place in the enclave. Not brothers, not blood, but companions at least.

"Ashok," Reltnar said. His voice gushed out in a relieved sigh. "I thought I'd seen a ghost, but . . . I thought you were dead. We all thought—"

"What's going on here?" Ashok said, cutting Reltnar off. His gaze lingered on the blood and scraps of hair Reltnar wore. "Explain this."

"That's right, you weren't here," Reltnar said. "We took these after you left to hunt the hounds. They put up a fight, and we had to kill half their group outright. We brought the rest back here to question them, but they wouldn't say where they were from or what they wanted."

"Ikemmu," Ashok said quietly.

"What?"

"They're from the city of Ikemmu," Ashok said. "It lies to the south. Did my father order this?" he asked.

Reltnar pursed his lips. "Your father was killed in the battle," he said. "One of your brothers too, but the rest are still here."

Ashok braced himself for the shock, but it didn't come. He felt nothing at the revelations. "Who ordered this?" he said.

Reltnar looked confused. "No one ordered it," he said. "After they wouldn't talk, we were just going to kill them, then a few of us"—his forehead scrunched up as if he were trying to remember—"we decided . . . we were getting restless, and the fighting, it wasn't helping anymore, so we came down here to fight the prisoners, only they were too weak. That's how it started."

Of a sudden, Ashok found himself remembering the wine he'd tasted that night in the Hevalor tavern.

It's not like wielding a blade or taking pain from a dagger cut, but it's similar enough . . .

"Listen, Ashok," Reltnar said, sounding anxious. "I came down here because . . ." He nodded at Ilvani's unconscious form.

Ashok's brought his chain up diagonally across his chest. "No," he said. "That's all over now."

"W—What?" Reltnar said, as if Ashok were jesting. "If you want a bit for yourself, I don't mind sharing."

He took a step forward, and Ashok sent one end of the chain flying. It clipped Reltnar on the ear and took off a chunk of flesh.

"Godsdamn you!" Reltnar said as he stumbled back and touched his bleeding ear. "What are you doing?"

"You want pleasure?" Ashok said. "Is that what this is to you? Did it make you feel alive, climbing into that cell with them weak and chained to the walls? You're a coward, Reltnar. You didn't stand on the edge between life and death, risking your own destruction at your enemy's hands. Look at them, Reltnar. You took their souls, and now you're feasting on the bones."

Reltnar's gaze hardened. "I don't care," he said, slapping his chest. "All the battles in the world won't do any good! You see this?"—he flicked his maimed ear, spraying blood.—"I feel *nothing.*" He came forward again.

"By the gods, Reltnar, I swear I won't give you another warning,"

Ashok said. "You may not feel the pain, but you can bleed, and you can die."

Reltnar's face crumpled. He held up his hands in supplication. "Why are you doing this? I told you I'd share, but don't take her away. I need this, Ashok. You don't know what it's been like. I stand guard in the caves and stare at dark walls. There's no sound but the godsdamn wind, and I can feel everything seeping out of me, a little every day. The only time it doesn't is when I'm with her."

"Not anymore," Ashok said. "We're leaving, Reltnar. The enclave is finished."

"Says you?" Reltnar said, barking an ugly laugh. "Did you think I was the only one using them? You already killed the other one. You're a walking corpse if you try to take her out of here by yourself."

"I didn't come alone," Ashok said.

The others were waiting for him. It was time to finish things.

No more hesitation. Not here.

"Stand aside!" Reltnar cried.

"No," Ashok said.

He watched the rage take over Reltnar's face. Ashok's former companion came at him stumbling in his fury and desperate need. Ashok dodged to one side, leaving the shadar-kai a path to the cage door. Reltnar went for it as soon as he saw the opening, like an animal chasing a piece of meat into a trap.

As he passed by, Ashok calmly pivoted and slipped his chain over Reltnar's head. The metal noose stopped Reltnar's forward movement, and his momentum drove the spikes into his neck.

Warm lifeblood spilled down Reltnar's chest, but he barely reacted, except to stiffen and raise his hands to grip the chain. A reflex, nothing more. Reltnar's fading attention was fixed upon Ilvani's unconscious form.

Ashok let Reltnar's body slide to the floor and wiped the blood off his chain with the shadar-kai's cloak. Listening, he heard faint shouts coming from the tunnels.

They'd discovered the dead guard, Ashok thought. Or worse, they'd found the others and were already cutting off their escape.

Ashok put his chain on his belt. He paused before the dead man at the back of the cage, but in the end he left his dagger protruding from the man's chest. He'd chosen his death, and Ashok would not violate his flesh any further.

Wrapping his cloak tightly around Ilvani's shoulders, Ashok picked up her unconscious body and made for the stairs.

The door opened before he got there, but Ashok saw it was Cree. He breathed a sigh of relief. The warrior's left arm was covered in blood, but from no wound of his own.

"You found them?" Cree said. He sounded out of breath.

"Ilvani is the only one still alive," Ashok said. "The others are . . ."

Cree put a hand on his shoulder. "Skagi told us," he said grimly. "We met up with him in the tunnel."

They ran as they talked, backtracking to the intersection where they'd all split up. Vedoran, Skagi, and Chanoch were waiting for them. Chanoch had a small wound at the corner of his mouth, but otherwise they were unmarked. Shouts echoed from all directions, but the cries were disorganized, and Ashok heard the metal clash of weapons, and the screams of wounded.

"You found them?" Vedoran said.

"Only Ilvani," Ashok said. "But Natan will be relieved."

"If we make it out of here," Vedoran said as he beckoned them all to keep moving up the passage.

Ashok, still holding Ilvani, ran up beside Vedoran. "What happened?" he said. "Did they raise the alarm?"

Vedoran shook his head. "We encountered a group in the tunnels, heavily armed," he said. "We thought they were a patrol, but then they were set upon by another, larger force. They decimated each other, and when they saw us—"

"We joined the fray," Chanoch said, his voice trembling with excitement. "We took them all."

"They're fighting each other," Vedoran said. "As near as we can tell, instead of realizing they'd been invaded, they thought they were betrayed from within."

Skagi hooted with laughter as they ran back through the tunnels the way they'd come. "Ikemmu!" he cried. "Tempus!"

A few more steps and they would be at the long tunnel and beyond that, freedom. They fell into close formation as the passage widened.

Ashok felt a stirring in his arms.

"Stop!" Ilvani cried. Suddenly awake and alert, she was struggling to free herself from his grip.

"It's all right," Ashok said. He set her down on her feet and grabbed her elbow when she swayed. "You're safe now."

She was smaller than Ashok had realized, just over five feet tall. And with her skeletal thinness, she was barely visible in the folds of his cloak.

"I need my satchel," Ilvani declared. "He has it."

"Who does?" Cree asked.

Ilvani didn't reply. Her eyes went vacant. Ashok could imagine her going back to that slaughter chamber in her mind, to Reltnar, and the locks of her hair he'd kept. It wasn't a thing anyone should have to remember. Ashok had a feeling he would be trying to banish it from his own mind for a long time.

"The guard who was watching the prisoners," Ashok said. "He must have had it. I left his corpse back in the room." He touched Ilvani's shoulder, drawing her back from the dark places in her mind. "Is it important?" he asked.

"It holds the winds," Ilvani told him soberly. "All the voices—they broke some of them, but not all . . ." Her voice failed. "Not all," she whispered.

Ashok was torn. The voices—the real voices—in the tunnels were growing louder. Scattered as they were, it was only a matter of time before the enclave pulled itself together enough to realize what had happened. All it would take was one look at the dead guard and the open cage door.

Ashok looked at Vedoran. "She doesn't know what she's saying," he said. "She's been through too much; it's hurt her mind."

"No it hasn't," Cree said. "She sounds almost normal."

"What?" Ashok said.

"She was like this before," Skagi said. "Weren't you, mad witch?"

But Ilvani wasn't paying attention. She got down on her knees and pressed her ear against the cavern floor. "We can go now," she said. "They won't know."

"We're not going back," Vedoran said. "With those intersections, we'll be hemmed in from all sides. You'll have to let it go, Ilvani."

Ilvani stood up slowly. She turned to stare at Vedoran, her empty gaze uncomprehending. Ashok felt the look like a knife twist in his gut. Vedoran didn't blink.

"Come on," Chanoch said, weaving his bloodstained blade in the air. "We can take whatever they have. Let's get the witch's satchel."

Vedoran caught Chanoch's wrist, stopping the display of waving steel in midair. "You heard me," he said in a low, dangerous voice. "We're leaving."

"Damn you," Chanoch said, wrenching his arm from Vedoran's grip. "Go on, then, you Blite coward. I'll do it myself."

For a breath it stunned them all. Ashok recovered first and cried, "Chanoch, no!" He lunged for the young one's arm, but his hand passed through empty air as Chanoch teleported down the tunnel.

By the time he reappeared, he was half out of sight around a bend in the tunnel.

Skagi cursed. "Now it's done, and we have to go," he said. "Ready, brother?"

Cree saluted with his blade. "Always," he replied.

Ashok noticed neither of them looked too disappointed. "Vedoran?" he said, looking to their leader, who stood frozen, his expression unreadable. "Vedoran?"

A muscle in Vedoran's jaw worked. He looked at Ashok. "Yes, let's go," he said.

They ran down the tunnel, Ashok behind Ilvani, all of them plunging back into the heart of the chaotic enclave. Ashok felt a swell of dread in his stomach. He pulled his mask up around his face and took up his chain.

At the first intersection they collided with a pair of shadar-kai, man and woman, who'd been running just as hard from another direction. When they saw the group, they skidded to a stop and stared for just a breath. That breath cost them their lives.

Vedoran came at them both, and with one stroke took off the man's arm at the elbow. The man shrieked as his mace and appendage hit the floor. Ashok saw him try to concentrate, to teleport to safety, but Vedoran came in hard, hacking at him relentlessly. Animal fury consumed his face, making Ashok shiver. He knew at whom that rage was directed.

Skagi and Cree dispatched the other guard before Vedoran was finished. Vedoran wiped blood from his eyes and mouth and motioned them on.

They hit the next intersection and heard running footsteps coming from the opposite direction. Cree trotted forward, setting his blades against the charge, but then Chanoch came into view in the dim torchlight. He was blood-spattered and vicious-looking with his blade leading the way. Wild glee shone in his eyes. He held up a dark green velvet bag tied with a black leather cord.

"Yours?" he said to Ilvani proudly.

The witch came forward and took the burden from his hands. She handled the bag as if she were cuddling a newborn, pressing the stained cloth against her cheek.

"I hear you," she said. "All the little ones." She looked up at Chanoch. "My thanks."

"We have to move," Ashok said.

"Go," Vedoran said. "Ashok, stay by Ilvani; the brothers will back you up. Chanoch and I will lead the way."

Chanoch moved to the front to join Vedoran. He didn't look at his leader.

They ran back through the tunnels the way they'd come, but Ashok could tell immediately that something was different. The voices had quieted. There was no longer the sound of reckless shouts and the screams of dying shadar-kai.

"They're mustering," Ashok said. He pointed to where the passage widened into the long tunnel. "Once we get to the last stretch, they'll have gathered. We're too late."

Vedoran kept on running, his gaze fixed on the distance ahead. "We're not stopping," he said. "Kill as you run."

"Kill as you run," Skagi agreed, and Cree and Chanoch's wild shouts echoed in the tunnel.

Ashok looked down at Ilvani, who ran unsteadily beside him. Her long confinement had taken all her strength. Ashok gripped her elbow when she stumbled, but she pulled away as soon as she'd righted herself.

"Don't," she said. Short and sharp. Ashok nodded.

The group hit the tunnel at a dead run, and there they were. Warriors had gathered to cut them off from the entrance. Ashok didn't see any of his brothers, but there were plenty of faces he knew.

"Keep going," Vedoran ordered, but he needn't have bothered. All of them knew what fate awaited them should they be captured.

Luck stayed with them, and they took the first group of shadar-kai by surprise. Vedoran and Chanoch cut through the lead two warriors with their blades and didn't break stride. Plunging into the next group, the brothers fanned out beside Ashok and Ilvani, protecting their flanks. Together the group was a rolling gauntlet, but the wide space was a blessing in more than one way.

Ashok whipped his chain above their heads and let it fly at the warriors that managed to teleport into the midst of the group. Instead of scattering them, the warriors appeared to stinging strikes from Ashok's chain. Over and over he sent out the spikes, and each time they returned to him bloody.

"Stay at my back!" Ashok cried to Ilvani. The witch moved behind him without looking at or acknowledging him. In fact she appeared oblivious to the battle, or to any fear of its failure. She clutched the green satchel against her chest and ran along with them, stumbling often, but always picking herself up.

They fought on. Ashok tried to gauge where they were in the long stretch, and when he realized they were not even halfway near the entrance his heart sank. No time to rest. The warriors who survived their initial pass were starting to fall in and attack from behind them, forcing Skagi and Cree to the back to protect Ilvani.

A shadow appeared in front of Ashok. He had just enough time to bring his chain up before the warrior solidified in front of him and attacked with a dagger in each hand. Ashok blocked the first dagger, but the second got through and found a slit in his armor. Still moving, Ashok didn't immediately feel the pain.

He raked his chain down the warrior's arm. The shadar-kai cried out and took a step back onto Chanoch's waiting blade. The warrior dropped to the ground, and Ashok stumbled over the body. Forgetting her protests, Ashok hauled Ilvani forward over the obstruction, and Skagi and Cree bunched up against them both. Vedoran and Chanoch didn't see this and kept running, creating a huge gap in their protective wall.

"Wait!" Cree yelled after them, but it was too late. Five shadar-kai teleported into the gap and split the group in two.

"Go left!" Skagi told his brother, and he angled right to cover the far ends of the tunnel. They each picked off a warrior and pressed forward, out of reach of Ashok's chain.

Ashok had no time to marvel at the brothers' skill or strategy. He took advantage of the open space to swing his chain in an arc, striking the ground in front of him to slow the charge of the three other oncoming warriors. Two men and a woman, they tried to dart in to form a circle around Ashok and Ilvani, but Ashok snarled behind his mask and snapped the chain at their legs, catching the woman in the thigh. A bright spot of blood welled up through her breeches.

"Get down," Ashok said, and Ilvani crouched and moved a safe distance away. Ashok calculated he only had a few breaths before more warriors closed in from behind them. By that time he hoped Skagi and Cree would be free to cover them again.

"Not hounds, but you'll stand in just as well," Ashok muttered under his breath. He remembered that day on the plain, crouching in the kindling tree. So long before, but the desperation that coursed in his blood was the same. He drew it in with each breath, fed on it, reminded himself over and over that he was alive.

He thought of the nightmare, of riding the beast through the paddock, blazing bright fire licking off his hooves and mane. The images were so clear in Ashok's mind—he held onto them all, grasped the end of his chain, and bore down on the three shadar-kai.

His body became a blur before his own eyes and those of his targets. The chain coiled around Ashok's body and then flew out like an extension of it. He barely guided the motion with his arm. A black, writhing aura snaked up the chain, settling among the spikes like lengths of silk. The chain ripped a long gash in the woman's side. Ashok yanked the weapon free and carried on to the next enemy. He moved too fast to assess what he left in his wake.

He caught one of the men in the neck. A hard leather collar only partially absorbed the blow. The spikes dug into the shadar-kai's ear and ripped it off, along with a sizable portion of the his cheek. The man screamed and clutched his face, losing his weapon in the process, but even that Ashok did not celebrate. His third target, the other man, was close enough for him to smell, but he had one stroke left in him, and he used it to rip open the man's thigh.

The black aura surged once, as if feeding, then it peeled away from the chain, and absorbed back into Ashok's own body.

Ashok turned to check on Ilvani and saw the witch crouched several feet away, watching him intently. She stood when he beckoned to her and followed him back to where Skagi and Cree were finishing off their opponents.

Ahead of them, things were much worse.

Vedoran and Chanoch were surrounded and bleeding liberally from multiple wounds. Vedoran's cheek had been sliced open. The flaps of skin and the shadar-kai's burning, unfocused gaze as he hacked at the line of enemies were ghastly to behold. Chanoch's hysterical cries to Tempus filled the tunnel.

Ashok shot a glance at the brothers and saw the fatigue in their faces. Their guards wavered; he knew they wouldn't be able to hold their weapons up much longer, let alone fight the lines of shadar-kai still before them.

He gazed up the tunnel. They'd passed more distance with the last surge than he'd thought. They were over halfway out.

So close. Ashok looked down at Ilvani to see if she realized how desperate the situation was. But she merely stared blankly ahead of them. The mob of shadar-kai could have been a swarm of insects for all she knew.

"You're a witch," Ashok said. "Do you have any magic that might aid us?"

Ilvani blinked and tucked her satchel close to her neck. She glared at Ashok. "Do you want to talk to them?" she said. "You think they have a care for what you say?"

Defeated, Ashok could only shake his head. Skagi and Cree had waded in to try to relieve Chanoch and Vedoran, but there was a long distance between them. It would be where they would make the last stand, Ashok thought. He had no dagger to give Ilvani to do away with herself, when the time came. Perhaps, if he wasn't cut down, he could do the deed himself.

Ashok put his body in front of the witch and prepared to wade into the fray. Up the tunnel, in the distance, a cry rang out. Not the warrior screams of the shadar-kai, or the death cries, but something much more horrifying, magnified a hundred times by the cave.

The sound caused the line of shadar-kai in front of them to fold. They went to their knees and clutched their ears against the sound, their faces twisted in agony. Never had they heard a sound such as that, a scream that would invade their deepest nightmares long after the cry had faded away.

Ashok had heard the sound before; he knew it intimately. And in its wake only he, Ilvani, and the rest of his group stood on their feet, too bewildered with exhaustion and pain to believe what had come to their aid.

The nightmare thundered up the tunnel, his large body filling the tall space. He burned everything in his path, and the warriors who did not recover themselves to jump out of the way were trampled under his flaming hooves.

The beast stopped several feet away from Ashok and tossed his head imperiously. He had tasted blood, Ashok thought, and gloried in it. As he watched, the nightmare turned and started a charge back up the tunnel.

"Go," Ashok cried, pulling Ilvani along, shoving Skagi and Chanoch and Vedoran until their trance was broken and they were all surging forward.

The warriors scrambled to get out of their way. Ashok cut down the few who tried to reach for them as they ran past. Breaths before, they'd been trapped behind a wall of death, and yet they were flying, following the rolling fire, until Ashok saw the brittle daylight of the open Shadowfell.

The nightmare dropped back as the enclave gathered itself to mount a pursuit. Ashok pushed his group toward the entrance. "Get out," he ordered, and fell back to join the nightmare.

"Where are you going?" Skagi cried.

"We'll cover your escape," Ashok said. "Don't stop until you get back up the valley."

The nightmare slowed enough for Ashok to leap on his back. Fire surged greedily along the beast's spine, but as before it did not reach Ashok's flesh. Together they rode up the tunnel, and Ashok let his chain swing free at any enemies who got in their way.

The warriors saw him coming and fell back, but Ashok ran them down, shouting, urging the beast forward. The only thought in Ashok's head was to let the nightmare taste blood, to let the fire burn a path through the enclave and burn all the images of the slaughter chamber from his mind. He let the nightmare run and let the beast within himself free, hacking a path until the tunnel became too narrow for them to continue.

The nightmare whickered and pawed the ground, as if he wanted to tear the walls apart. Ashok urged him back and around, and with the way clear of living things, they charged down the tunnel, the wind whipping the flames around Ashok's face. His eyes stung, but the tears were not caused by the flames. He sobbed and screamed as he rode, and the nightmare screamed with him, warning all enemies and friends away.

CHAPTER EIGHTEEN

THE CARVED STEPS UP THE VALLEY WALL WERE TOO STEEP FOR THE nightmare, but when they cleared the caves the beast seemed to know exactly where he was going. That was a fortunate thing, for Ashok was still gripped by the frenzy of the battle and could not tell the beast which way to turn.

They climbed a steep, rocky hill, and Ashok had to hold on to keep his seat. The bumps and jolts returned some sense to him, and with shaking hands he put his weapon away. Newly aware of the pain from the dagger slash and the blood coursing down his body, Ashok pulled the mask away from his face and wiped his soiled hands.

He slid off the nightmare's back when they reached the top of the valley. Weak, he stumbled and fell. His hands left bloody prints in the rocky soil from the deep gouges on his palms where he'd forgotten to hold the chain guard.

Looking down the valley, Ashok saw no movement at the cave entrance.

Not yet, but they would come.

He stood up. The nightmare waited silently nearby, his fire dulled but simmering beneath his flesh. Ashok felt the heat, the waiting. The beast wanted more of the battle.

"Let's go," he said but didn't mount the beast. He trotted alongside, and they traced the rim of the valley back to find the others.

Black dust hung in curtains on the air, obscuring Ashok's vision beyond a few dozen feet. Chanoch hailed him from a distance; he must have seen the nightmare's stunted fire. Ashok followed Chanoch's voice and saw them all huddled at the brink of a roiling darkness to the south. When he got close enough, Ashok recognized Negala's bog, and the dust storm enveloping the surrounding plain.

"She's cut us off," Vedoran said when Ashok joined them. "We can't circumvent the bog without trudging right into the dust storm."

Ashok surveyed the group. Skagi and Cree were in the best shape of all of them—their wounds were superficial, but Ashok could see the exhaustion dragging down their bodies. They would be no good in a fight against the hag. Vedoran and Chanoch were one step away from collapsing from their wounds, and Ashok knew he looked no better to their eyes.

The most alert among them were the nightmare and Ilvani, who sat some distance away, watching the bog and the surrounding dust storm. Wrapped in his cloak, she dipped her head and peered into her satchel, whispering something Ashok couldn't hear.

"Do we have any healing draughts left?" Ashok asked.

Vedoran shook his head. "It took all of them just to get us halfway up that tunnel. If that beast hadn't shown up . . ." He looked at the nightmare, then at Ashok, with a strange mixture of awe and wariness in his expression. "Why did he come?" he asked. "How did he even know where to find us?"

"I don't know," Ashok said. "The nightmare seeks out death. He craves flesh. Maybe he knew that following us was the only way to get both."

"It's more than that," Vedoran said. "That beast is connected to you. He knew to come for you."

And I was never more his master than I was today, in that place of death and carnage, Ashok thought. I fed him as no one else could. The shame rattled through him. More than ever Ashok could smell the blood clinging to him. He tried to shake it off. He needed to focus, to find a way to get them all through the storm.

"What are our choices?" Skagi asked, coming up to the pair. Cree and Chanoch stayed close to the nightmare, as though drawing strength from the beast's heat. He ignored their presence and whipped his tail impatiently.

"Fight through the bog or fight through the dust storm," Vedoran said grimly.

"What are our chances?" Skagi asked, a smile pulling at his crooked lip.

"We'll probably die in the dust storm or be killed by Negala when we get to the heart of the bog," Ashok said. "Given the choice, I'd rather die facing an enemy."

"My thoughts as well," Vedoran said.

They turned and were surprised to see Ilvani standing near them. None of them had heard her approach.

"The green is calling," she said matter-of-factly.

"The bog," Ashok said, nodding. "A hag lives there."

Ilvani looked at him as if he were a slow child. "It isn't real," she said.

"Real enough to kill us," Skagi said. "Come on, we're wasting time."

Ilvani's expression darkened. To appease her, Ashok tried to explain. "The witch created the bog in her mind and made it stretch across the plain."

"Really?" Ilvani said. She looked toward the bog, and a strange expression spread across her face. An indignant look, Ashok thought, but for the utter coldness of her eyes.

She reached into her satchel and removed a sphere of blown glass. Sealed inside was a piece of what Ashok thought looked like red silk. The fabric rippled in an impossible wind.

"What is that?" he asked, but Ilvani put her satchel on the ground and strode away from him, past the nightmare, toward the bog. "Stop!" he cried. But she didn't heed him.

He started to chase after her, but Vedoran grabbed his arm. The others hesitated as well.

"Wait," Vedoran said flatly.

"She'll be killed," Ashok said, struggling. But he was too wearied to break the warrior's grip. "What is that sphere?" he asked.

"If we're very lucky, there's magic in it," Vedoran said. "Be still now."

Ilvani took small, unhurried steps, Ashok's cloak dragging behind her like an oversized shadow. Her bare feet were purple with cold. She walked with one hand gripping the cloak closed, the other holding the sphere out in front of her.

Ten feet from the first twisted trees, she stopped.

"Come out Negala, witch of the fell bog," she called in a strong, clear voice. "Come to Ilvani, witch of Ikemmu."

The dust storm continued to rage at the fringes of the bog. Ashok and the others waited in frozen silence. None of them had the strength to be stunned at Ilvani's abrupt transformation. They could only stare. And hope.

Movement came from deep within the bog—a sudden, fast motion like a running deer. The trees peeled back under black shadows, and Negala the hag stood before Ilvani. Her hair curled in wet strands around her naked, withered body. She raised a spindly arm in greeting and smiled, exposing jagged teeth and an oily black tongue.

"You not called to Negala in long months, lesser one," the hag hissed. Her amber eyes gleamed with malicious interest. "You brought a token?"

"A trade," Ilvani said. "Your thoughts for mine."

The hag cackled, her green skin flushing, and pranced from foot to foot in amusement. "Come forward," she invited. "Gladly I show you my mind. How you frighten *me* in return?"

Ilvani stepped forward and held up the glass sphere between them. Eagerly the hag put her hands on the orb. They shut their eyes and fell into a trancelike concentration.

"Can she take that?" Cree whispered. "What if the hag takes over her mind? She could be lost in a storm just like us."

"No she won't be," Ashok said, understanding at last what Ilvani intended.

"How can you be sure?" Cree demanded.

Ashok didn't answer. He saw the hag's forehead scrunch up in consternation. Her body began to tremble. She jerked her head from side to side and spat, convulsions wracking her body.

Lightning tore across the sky, and the black winds raged. The dust blew in cutting streaks, digging into their wounds. Having no cloak, Ashok covered his face with his hands. Through his fingers, he saw the hag bite her tongue and let out a pathetic wail. Negala's head fell back, and black blood poured from her mouth.

Her arms fell from the sphere, and she faded back into the bog as the trees and brush reached out to absorb her. The green fell into itself and pulled back from the edge of the valley, consumed by the dust storm.

Ilvani stood amid the violence with her eyes closed. She put both hands on the sphere and raised it above her head. It glowed brilliant crimson and burst forth light in a blinding nimbus. The red arc rolled across the plain and slammed into the retreating bog. Fire enveloped the trees and burned them to ash. Deep within the illusory world, they heard the hag's scream.

Then it was over. The bog disappeared, and the clouds absorbed the storm. The black sky faded to gray, and the dust cleared. They had visibility for miles across the plain.

Ilvani lowered the dormant sphere to her side. She turned and started walking back to the group. She paused in front of the nightmare and reached up absently to stroke his neck. The beast whickered and leaned into the touch.

Struck dumb, none of them spoke for a breath. Then Skagi muttered, "Pity she couldn't have managed that feat in the tunnel."

"That wasn't magic," Ashok said quietly, watching Ilvani lean her head against the nightmare's neck.

"What was it, then?" Skagi said.

"Just what she said," Ashok told him. "She showed the hag her thoughts, her memories." He glanced at Cree. "She couldn't get lost in the storm, because she still lives in that cell."

Despite their exhaustion and still-bleeding wounds, Vedoran got the group up and moving to put as much distance as possible between themselves and the caves. After an hour with no sign of pursuit, Vedoran stopped at a copse of kindling trees. He leaned against one of them for support.

"We'll make camp here," he said.

"Will we be safe?" Chanoch asked.

Vedoran barely regarded him. "We'll be dead if we go much farther," he said.

Ashok agreed. "They're not coming," he said. "With any luck the hag moved the bog as we left her."

They made no fire but spent the time seeing to their wounds. Ilvani lay down on the ground with Ashok's cloak spread out around her and went to sleep.

Skagi snorted when he saw her. "Can't blame the witch for being sleepy, can you, after that show on the plain?" he said.

"You shouldn't be so surprised," Cree said. "She knows as much about magic as Neimal."

"I know it," Skagi said. "Her and Natan could rule Ikemmu, if they weren't odd in the head." Cree shot him a look, but Skagi just laughed. "Not like it's a secret," he said. "Even Uwan knows."

"Why is she like that?" Ashok asked. He watched Ilvani sleeping. "Did something happen to her?"

Skagi shrugged. "Nobody knows for sure, but most think it's because of the family," he said.

Ashok remembered Vedoran telling him that Natan and Ilvani's lineage was valuable to Ikemmu.

"They're all dead now," Cree spoke up, "not that there were many to begin with. Skagi's right—the story's well known. When the first shadar-kai came to Ikemmu, they didn't find the city deserted. There were two shadar-kai living in the ruins, a feral man and woman. The woman was heavy with child."

"Who were they?" Ashok said.

"No-names. They couldn't speak any language the shadar-kai knew," Cree said. "The man attacked the shadar-kai on sight and was killed. The woman died giving birth to a son."

"But the child lived," Skagi said. "Stories say he grew up half again as feral as his father, got a child on a woman before leaving the city for gods know where. Never saw him again, but the woman carried her burden and gave birth to twins."

"Natan and Ilvani," Ashok said, understanding. "The third generation."

"Raised by the mother in Ikemmu," Cree said. "She saw them grown before she died on a raid to the Underdark side. They weren't wild like their father and grandfather, but Ilvani obviously inherited some of their strangeness. Some say"—he hesitated—"you never know what to believe, but I suppose it's possible that those who lived in Ikemmu before the shadar-kai may have shared their city with Natan and Ilvani's grandparents. They may have witnessed whatever disaster befell the city."

"How could they have survived, when so many others didn't?" Ashok said.

"We don't know that all or any perished," Cree said. "If they were Tempus's servants, he could have spirited them away and protected the shadar-kai who remained. Either way, Ikemmu looks on Natan and Ilvani with great pride. They believe the twins are favored children of Tempus."

"Except Ilvani's as unpredictable as a dust storm, and after what she's been through it'll probably be worse," Skagi said.

Chanoch, who'd been listening quietly, said, "She'll be fine once we get her back to Ikemmu. We'll all be fine once we're home. What say you, Ashok?"

Ashok nodded absently. "Yes, home."

"Get some rest, all of you," Vedoran said from across the camp. "I'll take first watch and wake Skagi after."

The conversation broke up, and Ashok went to Vedoran.

"Are you sure you don't want me to take first watch?" Ashok said. "You look like death."

Vedoran shook his head. "I'll be fine," he said. "Sleep while you can." He glanced behind him to where the nightmare hovered at the edge of the camp. "Is the beast going to stay with us?"

"I don't know," Ashok said. "Right now, we're not strong enough to deny him, if that's what he wants."

Vedoran grunted. "Sleep then. Let him help stand the watch."

"Very well," Ashok said, taking a dust-covered blanket out of his pack and spreading it on the ground.

When he slept, he dreamt of fire.

Neimal, the Sworn of the wall, saw them coming first. Her farsight stretched many miles across the plain, and she recognized the five, the nightmare, and the witch.

Gasping, Neimal sent her thoughts soaring across the city and up to the summit of Tower Athanon, where they connected one by one with the other Sworn. Thus linked, her voice touched them all, and wherever they were, whatever business they conducted, all paused to heed her mind voice.

Together, they touched Uwan, their leader, and pressed for the Watching Blade's attention. After a breath, his answer came.

"What do you see?" he demanded of the witch on the wall.

"They've returned," Neimal told him.

Uwan felt her agitated state through the link. "Did they bring back the missing?" he asked.

"One," Neimal said. There was an ache in her mind voice of both pain and joy. "Ilvani comes home, but without her flock."

In his chamber deep within Tower Athanon, Uwan closed his eyes, and with Neimal's magic he reached for Natan.

"She's alive," he said.

Natan's answer came not in words, but as a swell of joy he'd never felt from the cleric before.

"Praise Tempus," Uwan said.

CHAPTER
NINETEEN

THE PORTAL OPENED FOR THEM WHILE THEY WERE STILL A QUARTER mile out. At that point the nightmare broke away from the group and galloped off across the plain. Ashok was not surprised, nor did he expect that would be the last time he saw the beast. They were connected, as Vedoran had observed.

Blood attracts blood, Ashok thought. When he lost himself to rage, the nightmare would be there, if only in his thoughts and dreams.

A crowd of shadar-kai had gathered by the time they crossed into the city, and the air trembled with celebration as the warriors surged forward to greet them.

"Ashok! Praise Tempus!"

"The emissary has returned!"

The crowd converged on them and splintered the party. People plucked at Ashok's clothing and hair and that of the others, slapping them on the back or simply chanting their names.

He heard his own loudest of all.

Stunned, Ashok let the crowd carry him along toward the towers. He sought Vedoran to ask if such a reception was normal for a victorious mission, but he could not find him in the crowd. The others were with him but scattered. Chanoch accepted the praise and greetings with pleasure, but Skagi and Cree looked as baffled as Ashok felt at the attention, and when he could get close enough to ask them about it, Cree shook his head.

"We celebrate at the return of a successful raiding party, but this"—he surveyed the wild crowd—"is something different."

"They're showering you with kisses though, aren't they?" Skagi said, nudging Ashok with his shoulder.

Cree looked around. "Where's Vedoran gone?" he asked.

"I don't know," Ashok said. "I lost him in the crowd." Ilvani was missing too. Ashok felt a surge of distress. He shoved through the crowd of men and women, but they only called his name louder. "We're all separated," he said.

"Ah well, enjoy it," Skagi said, clapping him on the back. "We wouldn't be here without you. Hail Ashok, warrior of Tempus!' he cried, and the crowd took up the chant.

Ashok found himself swept along to the gates of Tower Athanon, where another crowd waited with Uwan at its head.

The Watching Blade beckoned the crowd to let Ashok, Chanoch, and the brothers through. Bodies parted, and suddenly the four of them were standing before Uwan. Ashok bowed his head with the others.

"Where is Vedoran?" Uwan asked.

"We were separated at the gates," Ashok said, "from Ilvani as well, we—"

"She is being seen to by clerics of Tempus," Uwan interrupted. "Don't worry. You've brought her safely home. You could not have cared for her better, or pleased me more."

Ashok looked to Chanoch and the brothers, but they nodded that he should speak, so Ashok raised his eyes to Uwan's.

"The others in Ilvani's party we found murdered by another shadar-kai enclave," Ashok said. He told the story of their journey across the plain and the rescue. He left nothing out except Chanoch's defiance and confrontation with Vedoran. They were all alive and had returned safely. There was no reason to emphasize that conflict.

When it came to explaining the harrowing battle, he told of the nightmare's appearance and Ilvani's subsequent defeat of the hag. Neither Chanoch nor the brothers contradicted his story.

As he finished, the crowd erupted in cheers. Uwan let them go on for a time, then he gestured for Ashok and the others to follow him inside the tower.

They entered an antechamber on the first level. Neimal stood watch outside the door, leaving Uwan alone with Ashok and his companions.

"I asked Natan to join us," Uwan said, "but as you can imagine, he is quite anxious to look after his sister."

Ashok nodded, distracted by the continuous cheers and sounds of celebration filtering through the stone walls.

"You've heard your city," Uwan said to them all. "And Ikemmu has heard the tale of your mission. Natan's vision—Tempus's word—has been fulfilled." He looked at Ashok. "Ikemmu rejoices."

"You told the people about the vision?" Ashok said. He felt suddenly uncomfortable, caged, with the shouts beating against the walls.

"Yes," Uwan said. "The people have seen that Tempus is at work in their lives. He reserves a place for everyone"—he put a hand on Ashok's shoulder—"even those who believe they have none."

Ashok said nothing. The shadar-kai cheered for him, accepted him. They thought he was an emissary of Tempus. Ashok could feel himself sweating beneath his armor. He glanced at the brothers and Chanoch, expecting to see resentment. They had had as much a part in the mission's success as he. He would be dead without them. Why should the people not cheer them—the city's true sons?

Yet they cheered Ashok, messenger of Tempus, slayer of his own people. He was a hero and a traitor.

Cree and Skagi came to him, but instead of resentment there were only hearty grins and slaps on the back. Chanoch's reaction was the most disturbing of all. He stared at Ashok with an awe usually reserved for Uwan's presence. That he directed the feeling at Ashok was more than he could bear.

Ashok stepped back and stammered, "Vedoran should give you his report. His leadership was crucial to our success. We would all be dead without his guidance." He shot Chanoch a meaningful look meant to wipe the awestruck fervor off the young one's face.

It worked. Chanoch ducked his head and nodded, acknowledging Vedoran's contribution along with Skagi and Cree.

Uwan nodded. "Vedoran will be well rewarded for his service. In the meantime, I will let you all go for some much-needed rest. Visit Makthar and accept healing. We'll speak again soon," he said, looking at Ashok.

When Uwan had gone, Cree said, "That's done it all, hasn't it? You'll be accepted into the city for good. All that's left is for you to take Tempus's oath."

Ashok didn't know how to respond. His head was full of the crowd's noise. He couldn't think beyond the cheers.

Chanoch said, "You are taking the oath, aren't you?"

"Come on, Ashok, don't make the little one cry," Skagi said, and dodged a swipe from Chanoch. "Of course he will."

They all looked at him expectantly. In Ashok's mind, the images ran together: Ilvani's skeletal form huddled beneath his cloak; Reltnar's desperate, hungry gaze as he reached for her; the split-open bodies of the shadar-kai. And he heard the screams of his dying enclave as he trampled through the tunnels of his home carrying death's flaming banner.

By the time Vedoran waded through the crowd of shadar-kai, he was at the point of collapse from his wounds and exhaustion. Finally he reached the trade district, and Traedis's small temple to Beshaba loomed before him. The green door opened before he could knock.

"I saw you coming," Traedis said. "The whole city is afire with talk of your mission."

The cleric helped him to one of the cots and immediately began seeing to his wounds. Vedoran stared blankly at the altar to Beshaba while Traedis prayed over him.

"They chant his name," he said when the cleric had finished. "I can still hear them. They chant Ashok's name and Tempus's."

"Of course they do," Traedis said. "I told you this would happen, Vedoran." He took Vedoran by the shoulders, but the shadar-kai was lost in his own thoughts and didn't immediately acknowledge the cleric.

When he did look up, he saw Traedis's holy symbol wavering before his vision. The gods were everywhere, he thought. He couldn't escape them.

"Why do they follow him, Traedis?" Vedoran said. "Why do they love him so much?"

"Not all of us love Uwan and Tempus," Traedis said. "You are not alone, my friend. Come, unburden yourself. What happened on your mission?"

Lost in thought, Vedoran told the cleric everything. He left nothing out, including a suspicion he'd been nursing in his mind during their long journey back to the city. When he finished, Traedis's eyes were lit with triumph.

"This is more than I could have hoped for," he said. "Now we must plan."

When they had recovered from their mission, Ashok and his companions took up their training again as if nothing had changed. But there were subtle differences Ashok could not ignore.

His Camborr training resumed, for one. Olra came to fetch him without ceremony one day from the training yard. She said only, "Come," and jerked her head toward the forges and the pens.

There was no nightmare to train, and Ashok found himself missing the beast's presence without meaning to. But Olra started him working with the hounds and shadow panthers, the stalking beasts of the Shadowfell. They were no replacement for the nightmare, but they were deadly enough to satisfy him, Olra said.

Ashok worked by lantern in the caves where the animal pens were kept. Most of the time, he had only the beasts for company. The forge smoke hung heavily in the air, stinging his eyes, and the flickering light made them water, but Ashok never complained. He kept his mind focused obsessively on his work so that the deep tunnels only occasionally transformed into the blood-soaked passages of his enclave. He banished those images as soon as they intruded on his thoughts and accepted them as the price of solitude.

Anything to be away from the rest of the shadar-kai.

Ikemmu regarded him as more than one of their own. Strangers greeted him on the tower steps with warmth and deference. Ashok heard them whispering when he was not quite out of earshot. He hurried his steps to get away from their words. He didn't want to hear himself called Tempus's emissary.

A tenday passed, and Ashok had not spoken to Uwan again, nor had he seen any sign of Vedoran either at training or in the trade district.

He was surprised then one day to be summoned to Uwan's

private chamber, where he found not only the shadar-kai leader but Vedoran as well.

Ashok glanced at Vedoran as he entered the room and saw that the warrior's wounds had been healed, and there were no visible scars from the battle in the tunnels. Vedoran looked healthy and strong—a sharp contrast to the way he'd appeared outside Negala's bog. He met Ashok's gaze and nodded. Ashok returned the greeting, but there was no time to exchange words.

"Thank you for coming, Ashok," Uwan said. The light in his eyes, the enthusiasm he'd expressed a tenday before was absent from his demeanor today. His face was subdued, his tone business-like as he came around the long table to face Ashok and Vedoran.

"Vedoran has made his report," Uwan said, "and he's brought a disturbing accusation to my attention. This concerns your escape from the shadar-kai enclave. Do you know what I'm referring to?"

Ashok glanced at Vedoran, but the warrior's expression revealed nothing. He felt panic clawing the pit of his stomach. Did they know? Had Vedoran seen through Ashok's pretense in the caves and realized he'd known them as his own home?

If so, he was lost. Ashok bowed his head, and was preparing to confess, when Uwan spoke again.

"In your report, you failed to mention Chanoch's actions in the tunnels," Uwan said. "Vedoran claims that he defied orders, and in doing so endangered Ilvani and the rest of the group. Is this true?"

Ashok felt a dizzying mixture of profound relief and trepidation. His shameful secret was safe, but Vedoran had not forgotten Chanoch's insult.

He chose his words carefully. "It's true that there was a confrontation," he said. "Chanoch went back to retrieve an item that was obviously important to Ilvani. I do not believe he acted out of malice—"

Uwan held up a hand. "Did he or did he not disobey Vedoran's orders?" he pressed.

Ashok felt the weight of the leader's gaze. "There were many disagreements during the journey," he said. "The storm, the bog, the illusions . . . All of it took a toll on us."

"Answer yes or no," Uwan said flatly. "If the next words from your lips are any other words, you'll be disobeying *my* orders, and punishment will follow accordingly."

He spoke calmly, but Ashok heard the threat underlying the words. It was a side to Uwan he'd never seen before—a coldness as forceful as his words in the training yard.

That was the ruler of Ikemmu speaking, Ashok thought. The Watching Blade who had executed countless warriors for disobeying orders and endangering shadar-kai lives.

Desperately, Ashok looked to Vedoran, but the shadar-kai's face remained a neutral mask.

"Don't do this," he begged Vedoran.

"Damn you!" Uwan cried, slamming his fist down on the tabletop. He drew his greatsword and put the blade's edge against Ashok's throat. "Answer or die."

"No," Ashok said. "Chanoch didn't disobey any order."

Uwan's face went livid. The blade quivered at Ashok's throat. "Are you calling Vedoran a liar? If you are, the punishment will be the same for him, for bearing false witness against Chanoch. Consider your answer carefully, Ashok."

Ashok clenched his fists. He was trapped and damned, and Uwan knew it. He half-expected the leader to slit his throat, but he held the strike. Of course Ashok knew why. The chosen of Tempus, he thought bitterly. The gods preserve my life once again.

"Vedoran does not lie," Ashok said through gritted teeth. "Chanoch disobeyed orders. But I beg Lord Uwan's mercy. We would never have made it out of the caves without Chanoch's blade. He is a true warrior of Ikemmu and a devoted servant of Tempus."

Uwan lowered his sword and stepped back. "True words," he said. "Do you think I don't realize Chanoch's worth?"

"Then spare him," Ashok said. "Forgive him."

Uwan shook his head. "Chanoch knew his responsibility to himself and to his comrades, and he chose to ignore it. *My* responsibility is to uphold the laws of this city."

"By killing one of its protectors?" Ashok shouted. "Is that Tempus's word or Uwan's?"

Uwan's jaw tightened. Ashok thought he would raise his blade, but he did not. Deliberately, he sheathed the weapon. "Wait outside, Vedoran," he said.

Vedoran nodded and left the room. He did not look at Ashok.

When he'd gone, Uwan went to the table. He pulled out one of the large chairs. "Will you sit?" he asked Ashok.

Ashok shook his head. Uwan sighed and sank down in the chair himself. He let his elbows rest on his thighs and his shoulders hunch. It was the first time he'd ever shown a hint of weariness, but Ashok saw it, in the posture and in the dullness of his black eyes.

"Cree told me what you saw in the enclave's dungeons," Uwan said. "How you found Ilvani. That can't have been an easy sight."

"It wasn't," Ashok said tightly. He tried not to conjure the faces of the dead shadar-kai, but they came anyway, and he was conscious of the empty dagger sheath at his belt. His blade had been so much a part of him that he hadn't yet removed it.

"If I had seen that . . ." Uwan said. He cleared his throat. "A room like that would have driven me mad."

"So I was," Ashok said. And he'd reveled in the madness.

"That place where you found Ilvani—those were shadar-kai,

but they were not our people," Uwan said. "They'd lost themselves, driven mad by the lurking shadows."

"Such a thing," Ashok said slowly, "would never happen in Ikemmu."

"Not while I live," Uwan agreed fervently. "But you must understand . . . The line we walk . . . That thread is so delicate as to be terrifying, Ashok. We could become them so easily—without order, without discipline to govern our passions."

Ashok rubbed his bare wrist. "We cut ourselves, and when it's not enough we cut each other," he said.

"Yes," Uwan said. "Without laws to govern us, we would slay our rivals, then our allies. We would do unspeakable things, just to grab whatever bit of life we could. Our city, our community would destroy itself, just as the shadar-kai in the caves did."

"They could have allowed themselves to fade," Ashok said. "I would welcome my soul's flight before I became master of that slaughter room."

"Perhaps you would," Uwan said. "You're strong. But to give yourself up to nothingness—the shadar-kai are made to resist that fate with everything inside us. It's not so easy to give up your existence."

"No," Ashok said, remembering the misery, the near hysteria in Reltnar when he'd realized Ashok intended to take Ilvani—his lifeline—away. "But Chanoch is different. He made a mistake."

"He crossed that line," Uwan said. "We can't afford to forgive, Ashok. Our nature doesn't allow it."

"So that's it, then," Ashok said bitterly. "Tempus or the shadows? We're damned?"

"No. We are shadar-kai," Uwan said.

Vedoran was leaning against the wall when Ashok stepped outside Uwan's chamber. They looked at each other across the small span. Ashok tried to control his rage, his desire to hurl himself across the space and take Vedoran by the throat.

"None of the others spoke against Chanoch," Ashok said.

"I didn't expect they would," Vedoran replied. "Tempus's flock spoke as one."

"Uwan says you're to be rewarded handsomely for your service to the city," Ashok said. "Does it make you happy?"

"Do you know what the 'reward' for a sellsword's service is worth?" Vedoran said.

Ashok shook his head. "I don't care," he said, starting for the stairs.

Vedoran's voice carried after him. "Uwan instructed my master to fatten my purse for a month, to show his appreciation," he said. "That's what Vedoran's honor is worth: a handful of coin." His voice rose. "What else should a godless sellsword want in life but more coin to please him? He can never be Tempus's emissary."

"Cease!" Ashok cried. "That is nothing to me, and you know it. Will Chanoch's death satisfy your honor?"

"Chanoch is nothing to me," Vedoran said, mimicking Ashok with a sneer. "Do you think I give a thought as to how that dog sees me? No, this was for Uwan and his god. You and I are Blites, the other races are coin slaves, and Tempus's followers sit above us all in judgment and contempt. Fine, then. Let them look down from their high places. But by the gods, let Uwan be bound by the same laws that damn me. Let him see how his own faith will be the downfall of his city."

"What are you talking about?" Ashok said.

Vedoran laughed. "You've not lived in this city long enough, Ashok. Do you think there aren't others who feel as I do? Did you imagine Tempus was the only god in Ikemmu? There are others, and we're tired of being silenced."

"You once told me you didn't want to be controlled by the gods," Ashok said. "Forgive me, but this newfound empathy is unconvincing."

"Maybe," Vedoran said. "But you should think of your own position in this city and where your loyalties lie."

"I've sworn no oaths," Ashok said. "Nor will I swear any—to Tempus, or to the other gods."

"Then what will you do, Ashok? Return home?" Vedoran said. His shrewd gaze made Ashok go cold inside. "Do you have a home to go back to anymore?"

CHAPTER
TWENTY

Vedoran left Tower Athanon and weaved slowly through the trade district. He picked a random path and checked often to see if he was being followed. Not that he expected Ashok to try to come after him. He'd been too shocked when Vedoran had left him.

Smiling to himself, Vedoran cut across the stone remains of a cluster of dwellings and ducked inside a two-story building marked as a warehouse belonging to his master's trade consortium. It was not a warehouse, but his master often used the building in discreet business transactions and encouraged those closest to him to do the same.

Inside on the upper story, there was a room with no windows. A candle burned in a copper dish on the mantle of a boarded-up fireplace, and several chairs were arranged around the fireplace as if it were still a source of heat.

Traedis sat in one of the chairs. He looked up when Vedoran entered the room.

"You're late," he said.

"Forgive me," Vedoran said. "I was meeting with Uwan and Ashok."

Traedis's eyes narrowed. "And is it certain?"

"Yes," Vedoran said. "I confirmed it just now." The look in Ashok's eyes had told him all he needed to know. "Ashok's was the enclave that slaughtered Ilvani's scouting party. He knew the trail and those tunnels far too well for it to have been otherwise."

"Amazing," the cleric said, shaking his head. "Why did no one else have your insight? There were others with you in the caves."

"All of whom believed they were following a vision sent by Tempus," Vedoran said. "But if you take the god out of the mission, it was easy to see who was truly leading us."

"Yet he helped you," Traedis said. "Ashok betrayed his own people. Why?"

"Because he wanted a better life," Vedoran said quietly, "an existence that wasn't shameful to him. I could have given that life to him. But he chose Uwan instead."

That part burned inside Vedoran almost more than anything else. He'd asked Ashok to consider his loyalties, but in his heart he knew Ashok had already chosen.

"Your life has been touched by many misfortunes," Traedis said, drawing Vedoran out of his memories. "But this will be a new beginning for Ikemmu and for Vedoran."

Vedoran nodded. "There is still an obstacle," he said.

"Natan," the cleric said. "Yes, I'd thought of that."

"His visions are disturbingly accurate," Vedoran said. "He could uncover our plans before we carry them out."

"If that's true, have you considered that Natan may already know Ashok's true identity?" Traedis said.

"If he did, he would have told Uwan long before now," Vedoran said.

"Not necessarily," the cleric said. "Not if it meant he could have his sister returned to him safely. We can't know what knowledge he has of Ashok."

"I'll speak to him," Vedoran said, "find out what visions he's received. Then I'll decide how to proceed."

"Wait," Traedis said when Vedoran moved to the stairs. "I will not see you again until the thing has been set in motion. You must swear the oath before you go, and accept protection."

Vedoran felt a wave of involuntary disgust. "You want me to swear faith to Beshaba. I've told you—"

The cleric laughed. "I don't need your faith, Vedoran, for what we intend," he said. "Only the appearance of it. When Tempus's false emissary is exposed, the shadar-kai will need a rallying point. You will play that role."

"In Beshaba's name," Vedoran said.

"Yes." Traedis shrugged. "Power shifts, and you will have the recognition you want. Things will be different. We will not abuse the city in Beshaba's name, as Uwan has done with the warrior god."

The cleric smiled. Inwardly, Vedoran laughed at the futility of it all. First it was Tempus, then Beshaba, and in the future whatever god won out in the struggle for Ikemmu. Whatever happened, the gods would always have a collar around the shadar-kai.

But at least there, at that moment, Vedoran would choose the god.

CHAPTER
TWENTY-ONE

ALL THE WARRIORS OF IKEMMU GATHERED AT THE BASE OF TOWER Makthar to watch Chanoch receive his sentence.

Ashok stood with Skagi and Cree at the front of the crowd. They gazed up at the tower summit, where four obsidian spikes rose like a crown. Purple lightning played between the spikes and arced up to scatter the shadows of the cavern ceiling.

Four figures stood at the top of the tower among the stone spikes and arcane light. Uwan led the way, with Chanoch standing behind him flanked by two guards. Chanoch had been stripped to the waist. His hair blew wildly in the wind, but Ashok could see nothing of his face.

"Why are they having this ceremony?" Ashok said. "We already know the outcome."

"Tower Makthar is also the tower of Judgment," Cree said, his manner subdued. There were deep shadows under his eyes. As far as Ashok knew, he hadn't slept in days. Cree had known Chanoch best and would feel the loss more than any of them.

"Twenty years ago, when the second ruler of Ikemmu died, Uwan stood up there and accepted the trial to take his place," Skagi said. "You stand among the spikes, and if the lightning doesn't strike you dead, you're deemed worthy to rule. Clean. Simple."

"But who makes the judgments?" Ashok asked.

"The gods," Skagi said, but he sounded uncertain. "According to the first shadar-kai who came to the city, the tower was used for that purpose by those who held the city last."

"Tempus's angels," Ashok said, remembering the carvings on the tower, the single eye gazing down from Tower Athanon that saw all of Ikemmu. "Or something else."

"Uwan's preparing to speak," Cree said, looking up at the tower.

"Will the lightning kill Chanoch?" Ashok asked.

Skagi shook his head and spat. "No, he'll be banished to the caves, to the chambers above where they keep the animals," he said. "They'll chain him to a wall in the dark and wait for him to fade."

"What?" Ashok said, recoiling. "He'll go mad."

Cree shook his head. "They call it a quiet death. It's not painful," he said faintly, "or so I've heard."

"Send him to the shadows," Ashok said, horrified. "What of his soul?"

Skagi shot Ashok a warning look as Cree flinched. "He's a strong one, and his faith in Tempus has never wavered," Skagi said. He put a hand on Cree's shoulder and shook him. "The warrior god will take him home, eh brother?"

"That He will," Cree said, but Ashok heard no conviction in the words.

"Godsdamn Vedoran for his vile tongue," Skagi murmured. His expression was grave as he watched the proceedings at the top of the tower.

Uwan was addressing the crowd, but Ashok didn't want to listen to the words. He didn't want to hear Tempus's name shouted above the wind. He turned and left the yard, heading for Tower Pyton and Hevalor. He needed to be away, and there was only one person's company he thought he could stand.

It was late when Ashok arrived at Darnae's shop. He half-expected her to be gone to her rest. He knew the humans and other races kept a different routine from the rest of the city. It seemed they required more rest than two shadar-kai put together, and they savored the tranquility that came with sleep in a way Ashok could not comprehend.

The other races did not bear the burden of rest and calm potentially turning into a battle against the shadows, Ashok thought. He knew that, yet he felt a powerful, gnawing envy when he considered Darnae in that light, and he thought he understood a little better the enmity the shadar-kai bore for the other races.

The candles were lit as usual when he entered, but Ashok was surprised to find that Darnae was not alone in the shop. A human man sat at her counter with a glass of wine in one hand and a quill tucked in the other. The quill he held over a sheet of parchment while Darnae looked on from the other side of the counter. Neither of them noticed his entrance.

"That's an interesting list you've got this time, Tatigan," Darnae said.

The name rang familiar to Ashok. Then he remembered. Skagi and Cree had mentioned the exotic goods merchant, the one responsible for bringing the Cormyrian wine to Ikemmu. Tatigan, the merchant who wore spectacles with green lenses. Ashok saw them, glinting darkly in the candlelight. They obscured the human's eyes.

Tatigan had a finely trimmed black beard with streaks of gray running through it. His hands as they moved over the parchment were graceful, steady.

"You have company, Darnae," Tatigan said without glancing up from his writing. He spoke in a clipped, lightly accented voice. "You should pay better attention."

Darnae looked up, and her eyes lit up with pleasure. "Well, and you're right, Tatigan, I've no manners at all. Come, look up from your list and meet my friend Ashok."

"Ashok?" Tatigan said. He raised his quill and looked at Ashok with interest. "I'm hearing that name spoken all over the city. Does it belong to you?"

Uncomfortable, Ashok nodded. He hadn't wanted such attention. "I'm sorry to disturb you," he said to Darnae. "I'll come back another time."

"Nonsense," Darnae said. She came forward and reached for his arm. He put his hands at his sides so she could grasp one and pull him over to the counter. "I haven't seen you since you returned from your journey," she said. "Are you well?"

"Yes," he replied. He hoped she wouldn't ask him for stories about where he'd gone or what he'd done on that journey. He didn't want to lie to her, but he could never tell her about riding the nightmare down the tunnel, about the trampled bodies in his wake. He could never tell her any of that. "Are *you* well, Darnae?" he said.

"Oh, yes," she replied. "Tatigan, Ashok is the one I was telling you about—that night at Hevalor. You remember?"

"Hmm," Tatigan said, seeming to want to go back to his list. "I do remember. You and the rest of Ikemmu are all in an uproar over this one. Uproar, especially when it involves a war god, is rarely a good thing for business."

"Tatigan," Darnae said. "Be polite."

"Very well," Tatigan said. "Darnae called you a hero, Ashok. Now the city calls you Tempus's emissary." He lowered his spectacles so he could look at Ashok over the gold rims. "Tell me, which is it?"

"Neither," Ashok said.

"Then be welcome," Tatigan replied. "Darnae, get him a drink while I finish this list. Then we'll talk."

Darnae poured them wine in small cups and seated Ashok next to Tatigan at the counter. She closed up the shop, lit a few more candles, and rejoined them.

The light made it warm inside the shop, and the wine felt good going down Ashok's throat. He allowed himself to relax a little in Darnae's and Tatigan's company. He even told them, haltingly, about Chanoch and his sentencing. He hadn't intended to, but once the wine was inside him he couldn't stop himself from telling the story.

Darnae patted his arm. "I'm sorry for your friend," she said. "Many shadar-kai revere Uwan like a father, and he has always dealt fairly with the other races. But his law is rigid."

"It wasn't always like that," Tatigan said. "Uwan's predecessor—"

"Oh, speak not of him, Tatigan," Darnae said scoldingly. "He was as inflexible in his rule as Uwan, and he had far less compassion."

"Kelreck is whom we speak of," Tatigan said for Ashok's benefit. "Second ruler of Ikemmu. He was assassinated by a mad cleric of Shar, the night goddess. It was believed he acted on his own, but there were rumors that Netheril was trying to plant agents in the city and had planned the assassination for years."

"Why?" Ashok asked.

Tatigan sipped his wine. "The city had begun to grow," he said. "Survival in shadar-kai enclaves is one thing; prosperity is quite another. Other races were building a presence in the city. Nothing like it is today, but enough for Netheril to grow concerned. I suspect we haven't seen the last of their concern either."

"The stronger Ikemmu gets," Darnae said, "the more likely it is that more of Netheril's shadar-kai might wish to defect to the city, start their own lives in service to no master."

"No master except Tempus," Tatigan said. "Kelreck's assassination had more effect than anyone wants to admit."

"After Kelreck died and Uwan ascended to ruler, things began to change," Darnae explained. "It started subtly enough—tattoos and carvings on the walls. But then, as Ikemmu swelled in population and grew stronger, Uwan declared it was a sign that the city was favored by the warrior god and marked for greatness. He decreed that only Tempus's followers could serve in Ikemmu's military. There was no room for Shar or any other god but the warrior god."

"The assassination—is that why Uwan is so intent on Tempus being the only religion?" Ashok said. "Because he wants to keep Shar out of Ikemmu?"

"If it were only that, I'd wish him well," Tatigan said. "Uwan is a shadar-kai of deep faith. But the day he met the cleric, Natan, was not a good day for Ikemmu."

"The cleric's visions have given Uwan what he believes are clear directives," Darnae said. "As long as he has Natan by his side, he believes he's being guided directly by Tempus."

"Perhaps he is," Tatigan said, "but unrest is growing among the other religions. Uwan doesn't see this."

"And I'm making it worse," Ashok said. Vedoran's bitterness, the people's fervor . . . Everything was building to a fever pitch, and Ashok feared something was about to snap. "I should leave the city."

"Don't do that," Darnae said. "If you left, you would be missed, by your companions and by me. Tempus must have something in mind for you to serve this city."

"Do you have faith in the warrior god, Darnae?" Ashok asked.

Darnae laughed. "I'm a messenger and sometimes I'm a singer," she said. "These things do not make an army—a poet, perhaps, but not an army. But I see you, Ashok, and I have faith in you."

"You don't know everything about me," Ashok said.

"No, she doesn't," Tatigan agreed. He blew on his spectacle

lenses and wiped them on his shirt sleeve. "But you can hardly blame her for that. In the span of time, you shadar-kai are such a young race," he said, "and so much time spent under Netheril's influence. Now that enough of you have broken with the empire, you're all scrambling around, trying to survive. You have no time to learn about yourselves."

"What is there for us to learn?" Ashok said. "We are shadow. We know where we come from, and we know what fate awaits us if we fade."

"Yes, and that knowledge lessens whatever life you might make for yourselves in between," Tatigan said. "She's a singer"—he gestured at Darnae—"but there are no poets among the shadar-kai, no artists, no craftsmen who take such pride in their work as to elevate it to the definition of their race."

"You're not being fair, Tatigan," Darnae said, chiding the merchant. "I know that the shadar-kai forge masters are considered great artists, masters of their craft. What can you say to that?"

Tatigan shook his head. "A small progression," he replied. "To forge weapons of death in fires that can easily take an eye or a hand . . . There can be great art in savagery, I grant you, but I was speaking of poets—singers, not battle drums. A battle hymn is different from a love poem."

"Maybe we're not capable of poetry," Ashok said.

Tatigan leaned back in his chair. "Not yet, perhaps," he said. "You have no rich history to preserve in song or story. But if Ikemmu survives, your race might one day be capable of great works."

"And if we're not?" asked Ashok.

"You preserved Darnae's song," Tatigan said. "You must have seen some value in it. And anyway, she's already declared you her hero, so how can you argue?"

"You see?" Darnae said. She grinned and poured more wine.

Ashok drank, and listened while they talked, and for the first time in his life he felt peace without fear. In Darnae's shop, on the edge of an uncertain fate, he could be himself without fear of losing himself. He only wished the feeling could last.

CHAPTER
TWENTY-TWO

When Ashok returned to Tower Athanon he intended only to rest a short while and head out again to try to visit Chanoch in the dungeons. He needed to see the young warrior, to make sure that he wasn't suffering, and to confirm the feelings stirring in him after his conversation with Tatigan and Darnae.

Despite the halfling's faith and Uwan's, Ashok knew his presence in Ikemmu was a detriment to the city. If Vedoran was right, and unrest was brewing among the other religions, Ashok needed to leave before it exploded into an all out conflict.

A dark one waited outside Ashok's room. He recognized it as the same one who'd brought him food after his nightmares.

"A message for you, come from Makthar," the dark one said. "The cleric Natan wishes your company. If you cannot speak to him at Makthar, he will be glad to come here."

Ashok sighed. "Tell him I'll come to Makthar at once," he said.

Natan received him in what Ashok thought must be the main chapel room for followers of Tempus. There were no benches, and the room was dimly lit by candles. The sword of Tempus was carved into the wall, as large and as ominous-looking as the day Ashok had first awoken in Ikemmu.

He'd woken up in a new world and emerged from that world a

different being—except that he had no idea where he truly belonged. He could not go home, and he could not stay in Ikemmu under the shadow of that sword.

Natan came across the room to greet him. Ashok had expected the cleric to look well given that his sister's safety was assured, but if anything, Natan appeared even more haggard than he'd been the last time Ashok had seen him.

A creeping fear stole over him, and Ashok blurted out, before Natan could utter any pleasantries, "What's happened? Is she all right?"

Natan looked briefly taken aback, then his face softened, and he clasped Ashok's arm. "I knew it was right to come to you," he said. "Tempus forgive me—I had my doubts about you before, but no longer."

"Tell me she's well," Ashok said.

"Physically, she is well," Natan said. "In other respects, she suffers, as I'm sure you're aware."

"Yes," Ashok said. "Has she spoken of her ordeal?"

"No," Natan said, and a look of frustration crossed his face. "She has not spoken to me. She will not see me."

"Give her time," Ashok said. "The memories of her prison cell . . ." He wasn't sure how much to say. It wasn't his place, if Ilvani wouldn't speak of it. "I was there, and what I saw won't soon fade from my mind. For Ilvani, the agony is a thousand times worse."

Natan put a hand over his eyes. "I know," he said. "But that is just what aches. She is my sister. We are very different—*she* is different, as I'm sure you also know—but we could always talk to each other. When her speech didn't make sense to anyone, *I* understood her." His voice hardened. "Yet now I'm helpless. She won't let me help her. She has sealed herself in her chamber and won't admit anyone.

I cannot"—his voice shook—"sit idle, as I have done for a month and more, while she suffers."

Ashok stayed silent while Natan unburdened himself. When the cleric finished, he looked a hundred years old. Ashok realized then that not one but two shadar-kai had emerged from that slaughter room, and both had been deeply scarred by their experience.

"Perhaps," Ashok said cautiously, "if only for now, you shouldn't think of Ilvani as your sister."

"What?" Natan looked stricken. "How else could I see her?"

"The person I took out of that cage is not the same person you knew here in Ikemmu," Ashok said. Natan flinched, but Ashok didn't spare him. "Ilvani suffered and was made to watch her companions be tortured to death in the most hideous ways imaginable. You and I cannot comprehend what she had to do to endure, what she had to give up of herself. Whoever she is now, she is not the sister you knew. You have to stop treating her as if she were."

Natan was silent. The words hurt, but Ashok could see him considering them. He nodded, reluctantly, after a time, and looked up at the sword on the wall.

"Why did He give her this burden?" he asked. "What they did to her . . . it was not an honorable death in battle; it was a death of the mind and spirit. Why did Tempus not give her the strength to defeat her enemies?"

"This wasn't Tempus's doing," Ashok said. "Mortals did this. The gods—what do they care to preserve or ruin one life? What are we to them, truly? I would be afraid if the gods took such an interest in me, for good or for evil."

Natan looked at him in confusion. "You don't want a god to act on your behalf, as Tempus has done?"

Ashok shook his head. "I don't know that he's acted for my

benefit," he said. "But if he has, I question why he took such an interest in a single life. There are bigger concerns in the world."

"But what if a single life can change the fates of many?" Natan said, and Ashok saw some of the fire rekindled in his gaze. "Wouldn't that be worth a god's attention?"

"I don't have that in me," Ashok said. "You think too highly of me. Uwan thinks too highly of me."

"Perhaps," Natan said. "But you changed my sister's fate. That's enough to place you in my highest esteem, for the rest of my life." He smiled faintly. "And now I'm here, asking you to help me again."

"What do you want me to do?" Ashok said wearily.

"Speak to Ilvani for me," Natan said.

Ashok sighed. "I don't believe she would welcome that," he said.

"I think you're wrong," Natan said. "You've made me see that she is in a terrible, dark place, a place where she doesn't recognize herself, let alone the ones who care about her. Knowing that, I think of all the beings in the world, the only one she will speak to is the one who knows what it feels like in the dark. You are that person."

"If she says no," Ashok warned, "that'll be the end of it. I won't press her."

"I understand," Natan said. "Will you go to her now?"

Ashok shook his head. "No," he said. "There's something I need to do first."

Natan started to argue but seemed to think better of it. "Chanoch," he said.

Ashok nodded. He started to turn away, then abruptly he said, "Do you believe in forgiveness?" He kept the bitterness from his voice, but it was a struggle.

Natan smiled sadly, as if he saw every bit of Ashok's internal struggle. "I do," he said. "But the rule of this city is not mine. We put our lives in Uwan's hands and must trust his judgment."

"And Tempus's?" Ashok asked.

"Yes," said Natan.

"Because Tempus would never choose someone unworthy to serve Ikemmu," Ashok said.

"Never," Natan said. His faith restored, he put his hand on his chest and bowed his head to the sword on the wall.

When he raised his head a breath later, Ashok was on his way to the door.

"I'll speak to Ilvani soon," Ashok promised, and left before Natan could say anything more.

The walk from Tower Makthar to the forges and pens was not a long one, but as Ashok entered the caves the Tet bell tolled. He'd been out of Athanon during his rest time and beyond. Olra would be missing him for his Camborr training.

Strange how in the short amount of time he'd spent in Ikemmu, he'd come to think of the day to day activities as routine, as if they and his companionship with Skagi, Cree, and the others had always been a part of his life.

He would miss them when he left.

He walked past the pens with their howling beasts and the cawing crows and ravens, and headed up the passage to the dungeons. The deeper he went into the caves, the more sound became muffled, until the animal cries died completely, and he could no longer smell the forge smoke.

His breath fogged the air, and the torches along the walls became sparse. Ashok was about to turn around, thinking he'd gone the wrong way, when he saw a pair of guards up ahead of him in the passage. They flanked a wooden door with bars at head level.

Ashok nodded to both of them. "I've come to see Chanoch," he said.

The guards exchanged a glance. "No one's to see prisoners sentenced to solitary," one said.

Ashok remembered when he'd stood on the edge of the Span with Vedoran, how he'd been able to get the guard to leave because the man was unsure of his place in the hierarchy.

"Do you know who I am?" he said imperiously.

The guard on his left murmured, "The emissary of Tempus."

Ashok suppressed a shudder at the reverence in his voice. "Uwan has given me leave to speak with the prisoner, who is still a warrior of Ikemmu and a devoted servant of Tempus," he said, narrowing his eyes. "Let me pass."

The guards exchanged another uncertain glance, but then they stepped aside, and one of them unlocked the door and gestured Ashok through.

A single candle burned in the small room, which was taken up by three smaller cells—glorified boxes, Ashok thought. Chanoch was in the farthest cell, chained to the wall. His face was covered with a black hood so he couldn't see to teleport. The other cells were empty.

Chanoch raised his head at Ashok's approach and tried to shift against the chains. "Since when do you speak in Tempus's name?" he asked. Ashok heard the wry amusement in the young one's voice.

"Are you offended?" he asked, with a good humor he didn't feel.

"No, but Tempus will be," Chanoch said. "I'll speak to Him on your behalf. We'll preserve your soul, whether you like it or not."

"It's your soul I'm worried about right now," Ashok said quietly. He pressed his back against the cage bars and slid to the floor, unwilling to speak to the black hood. He could feel the shadows already waiting in the dark. "It's so quiet," he said. "There's nothing to hear in this place but echoes."

"Time enough to listen to your own thoughts," Chanoch said. He sounded tired. "You shouldn't be afraid for me."

"It isn't fair," Ashok said.

"I brought this fate on myself," Chanoch argued. "Lord Uwan, he knows—"

"Don't . . . speak to me of Uwan," Ashok said. The anger rose in him, threatening to become something ugly. "The leader you idolized sentenced you to die alone in the dark."

"Not alone," Chanoch said. "Uwan came here twice in the last day to sit with me, so that I wouldn't be afraid."

"Gods," Ashok exclaimed, putting his head in his hands. "It's a waste, all of it. It should be me."

"No," Chanoch said firmly. "You're going to serve Ikemmu."

"I'm not staying, Chanoch. As soon as"—*As soon as you die*—"when I can, I'm leaving the city."

That stopped him. Ashok could imagine the look of horror on Chanoch's face. "Where will you go?" the young shadar-kai asked, shaken.

"Does it matter? There will be another emissary, another servant of Tempus. Have faith," Ashok said blithely.

"We're not speaking of Tempus," Chanoch said. "I thought . . . you'd found a place here. I hoped you'd found companions."

"I did," Ashok said. "But that's over now. You're here, I don't know where Skagi and Cree are, and Vedoran . . ."

That was over too. Vedoran knew, or at least suspected, Ashok's involvement with the enemy enclave. Whether he would reveal what he knew remained to be seen, but it was yet one more reason for Ashok to leave. He did not fear Ikemmu's punishment so much as he feared seeing the faces of his companions when he was exposed as a betrayer and a murderer of his own people. To have their faith in him disappointed was more than Ashok could bear.

And Ilvani . . .

For her to know his part in her capture . . . No, let him leave having done one good thing for Ikemmu and its shadar-kai. Though he despised what was happening to Chanoch, he would not trade his short time in Ikemmu for the life he'd been living.

"Chanoch," he said.

Silence.

"Chanoch," Ashok said urgently.

"I'm here," Chanoch said. His voice was faint. He coughed and said again, his voice stronger, "I'm here. It's just I'm so tired, Ashok. I've never felt so weary before."

Ashok swallowed. "It's all right," he said. "You don't have to talk. I'll come back to see you again tomorrow, if you want. So you won't be alone."

"I'd like that," Chanoch said sleepily.

Ashok pressed his forehead against the bars, letting the cold metal numb him. They didn't speak anymore, and eventually, for the first time in days, Ashok slept.

CHAPTER
TWENTY-THREE

He returned the following day after his training session with Olra, who didn't question his absence the day before. Ashok thought word must have reached Uwan of his visit to Chanoch as the guards didn't question him again. And so every day after his training, he went into the caves and back to the cell where Chanoch waited. The young one was strong, but every day he grew a little weaker.

They talked of many things during those visits. Ashok asked about Ikemmu and Chanoch's journey to the city. Like Ashok, he'd been born on the Shadowfell plain, the child of a small enclave. His mother had been killed by a childless woman who'd tried to take Chanoch as her own, but Chanoch had run away rather than be claimed as another's son.

A patrol found him wandering the plain, half-starved, bleeding, and feral. They brought him to Ikemmu and tried to foster him with several shadar-kai, but he'd attacked them all. In the end a cleric at Makthar had taken him in, and that's when he had found Tempus. The cleric arranged for him to join the military and swear the oath to Tempus.

"You were going to become a cleric yourself?" Ashok asked.

"I think so, yes. It wasn't an easy decision. I love the fighting. There are times I can't sit still. But my mentor said that my prayers in battle would level the enemy. He knew that I would fight for my city and my god."

"What happened to him?" Ashok asked. "Your mentor?"

"I'll see him soon," Chanoch said.

Days passed, and on the tenth, Chanoch barely greeted him. Ashok sat in his customary spot with his back to the bars and listened to Chanoch's faint breathing.

"I'm going to see Ilvani today," he said. "Natan asked me to speak to her. He's worried that she's not recovering from her ordeal."

He got no reply from the cell. Ashok turned to look at the hooded figure.

"Chanoch," he said, but his voice came out in a haggard whisper. "Chanoch," he said, louder.

Chanoch's head came up a fraction. Shadows seemed to bleed from his skin. The heralds of death and decay, Ashok thought. He'd heard the humans speak of their bodies feeding the earth when they died. Chanoch's flesh would feed the Shadowfell.

Ashok reached through the bars and through the shadows to remove Chanoch's hood.

Blinking in the sudden light, Chanoch looked at him through half-closed eyes. He opened his mouth to speak, but only a hiss of air escaped. Chanoch's lips moved, but his words were gone. He had no voice.

Ashok gripped the bars helplessly. "I don't . . . Say it again, Chanoch," he said roughly. "I can't hear you."

Chanoch stopped speaking. He nodded, smiled at Ashok, then turned his head to the side. He was looking at something in the corner of the cell. Ashok followed his gaze, but he saw nothing, only the shadows.

"Chanoch, look at me," he said desperately. "You're still here. You're alive. Don't give in, Chanoch." He yanked the bars, rattling them. The sound echoed in the dark, but Chanoch's attention remained on the nothingness in the corner.

Panting, Ashok reached through the bars again, trying to grasp Chanoch's arm. He felt the warrior's cold skin and recoiled. "No!" he cried.

But his pleas meant nothing. Chanoch couldn't hear them. The light had gone out of his eyes. He was dead.

Ashok sank to his knees before the cage, shivering in a sudden chill. The only sound was his own harsh breathing.

He'd never seen it happen before. Members of his enclave had succumbed to the shadow often, especially in recent years, when the darkness of the caves clung to them like wraiths. But they'd always been alone. Ashok had never seen the quiet death, but that's exactly what it was. Chanoch had faded away without fanfare or pain. Peaceful, yet horrifying.

Ashok got to his feet and stumbled from the room. He tried to say something to the guards, but he couldn't stop and found himself running through the caves. He pelted through the dark until he broke free and smelled the forge smoke. Gasping, Ashok breathed in the hot scent, but his heart wouldn't stop racing. He couldn't stop. If he stopped, he would think, and the shadows would be waiting.

He crossed the trade district and climbed the steps of Tower Pyton. He came out on the lower Span. The wind roared, tossing his cloak and hair. The canyon wall hovered darkly over his left shoulder.

Ashok walked across the bridge with his eyes on the ground below. Other shadar-kai walked in front and back of him. Below, the outdoor markets bustled with activity. The moving lights and color mesmerized him.

Ashok stopped in the middle of the bridge and stood at its edge. He swayed from side to side. His heart felt as if it would explode in his chest. His breath came ragged, and his eyes watered in the wind.

Behind him, a voice said, "Are you all right?"

Ashok looked up and was surprised to see a human staring at him. He didn't recognize the man, but he was looking at Ashok in concern.

"I thought . . . only shadar-kai walked here," he said to the man.

The man shook his head. "I walk the Span every day," he said.

"Aren't you afraid?" asked Ashok.

"Of course," the man replied. "That's why I do it—gives me a little bit of a thrill. Are you crossing?" the man asked.

Slowly, Ashok nodded. His trance broken, he found the spell of panic and terror had passed. Feeling weak, he turned and walked toward Hevalor with the human trailing behind him.

He went down the stairs and headed for Tower Athanon. Within, he asked one of the guards where Ilvani's quarters were.

He climbed the stairs nearly to the top of the tower and knocked on the second door to his left. There was no response.

Ashok raised his hand to knock again, but he stopped with his knuckles brushing the wood. He sat down in front of Ilvani's door and stretched his legs out in front of him. His boots were scuffed and stained with mud and old blood. He leaned against the door and waited.

Outside, the Pendron bell sounded. Ashok closed his eyes and immediately an image of Chanoch's chained body came into his mind. He opened his eyes and stared straight ahead until his breathing quieted.

After a while, his back started to ache, and his legs cramped from sitting. Ashok stood and walked back and forth around the tower. He considered going outside to one of the archways but dismissed it. The hypnotic effect of the height was not what he needed. What he needed was calm. What he wanted was to jump off the tower and let the wind rush past him. He didn't care where he landed.

Behind him, he heard a door open. Ashok turned and saw Ilvani looking at him. She stepped back into her room and left the door standing wide. On the strength of that invitation, Ashok followed her inside.

Her room was torn apart. Trunks containing clothing, books, and parchment writings were upended and scattered all over the floor. Her bed was covered with twisted blankets, their edges torn and flecked with blood. A ladder leaning against the far wall led up to a small sitting ledge.

Ilvani perched on the ledge, her legs swinging free above the ladder. Behind her, a crescent-shaped window looked out over the city.

Ashok picked a careful path across the room and stopped in front of the ladder. He climbed up slowly, waiting for her to tell him no, but she only watched him. When he reached the top, she scooted as far back against the wall as she could.

Ilvani wore a dress of crimson velvet. Its collar came up almost to her chin and pressed flush against her skin, emphasizing her unhealthy slenderness. She spread her skirt over her knees to make a lap and brought her green bag from a corner near the window.

Ashok settled himself opposite her and looked out the window. The view was breathtaking. He could see the training yard, the towers, and the rest of the city spread below them like a dark storm.

"You have the entire city here," Ashok said. "You can almost touch it." He looked at Ilvani, but she was absorbed in arranging the bag. "Did you paint the picture of Ikemmu that hangs in Uwan's chamber?"

"Yes," she said. Her voice sounded like she'd been sleeping. "He took it before I had them all in."

"Who took it? Uwan?" Ashok said.

She nodded. "He's always taking things before they're ready," she said. Her thin fingers worked the string on the bag. She tossed the cord aside and without warning turned the bag upside down, dumping its contents all over the ledge between them.

Her glass orb, the one with the red silk, rolled across the ledge along with others like it, clear and bottle green and flat black. Ashok put out a hand so they wouldn't roll away. There were other things too—all containers, Ashok noticed. Miniature chests with tiny locks and gold catches; plain wooden boxes, their warped lids tied with string; layers of cloth wrapped tightly and knotted.

"What is all this?" Ashok asked.

Ilvani counted each of the containers out loud. "One impressive feast," she said, pointing to a coin-sized silver box. "Two shiny baubles in my ears; three swords blocking the way." She touched a fragile bit of parchment folded to look like a box. "Four interlocking braids; five shadow hounds." And on and on—twenty boxes of nonsense that she counted as if her life depended upon finding them all.

"What does it mean?" Ashok said when she'd finished.

"They're all trapped in here," she said. "Every wind, every soul. I keep them here. Whether they like it or not."

Ashok picked up one of the strange boxes. The wooden lid came loose. He looked inside.

"Empty," he said. He picked up a clear glass sphere. "They're all empty."

"Of course," Ilvani said. She held up the wooden box. "Uwan," she said.

"Uwan gave that to you?"

"It is Uwan," Ilvani said. She stuck a finger beneath the lid. "The first time he showed me this room. Said it was all mine." Her clean hair was pale red in color, but she'd made no attempt to even out the chopped strands.

Ashok held up the clear glass sphere. "Are they your memories, Ilvani?" he asked.

"Every wind, every soul," she said, and laughed. "A lot to take in—I have to put them somewhere. Out of sight, so they don't crowd everything." She pressed the heel of her hand against her temple. "Not enough room."

"No, I suppose not," Ashok said. "Which one is your brother, Ilvani?"

"What?" she said, looking at him as if noticing his presence for the first time. "Natan? He's not here," she said.

"Which box did you put him in?" Ashok said.

She smiled. On her face it was a painful expression. "He doesn't fit," she said. "I could never fit him into any box."

"He misses you," Ashok said. "He hasn't seen you since . . . Well, it's been a long time."

"Exactly," Ilvani said in a brusque tone. "One day too many. He wouldn't recognize me."

"I think you're wrong," Ashok said. "I don't think it matters how much time has passed. Natan will know you when he sees you."

"How do you say that?" Ilvani asked. "You're just putting words together because they look pretty. You don't really want to see them."

"You're right." Ashok sighed. "I don't want to talk at all."

"That's why I let you in," Ilvani said, sounding as if he'd betrayed her. She picked at the frayed hem of her dress. "I felt a spirit leave while I slept. Then I heard you crying."

Ashok's body tensed. "How did you know about that?" he said.

"You can take anything out of the wind," she said, "and put it in a box."

"I don't know what that means," Ashok said. "I don't want to talk about this."

"Too late," she said. "You came in here and everything spilled off your face and cluttered the room."

Ashok groped for a distraction, anything among the boxes to tempt her. His gaze strayed to the view out the window. "I didn't know there were any windows shaped like this in the tower," he said. He hadn't known there were any windows at all, none that had glass.

"It's the eye," Ilvani said. She leaned forward, surprising him by putting a skeletal finger against his cheek. She traced a crescent around his eye. "The eye of Ikemmu," she said.

Ashok remembered the eye at the top of Tower Athanon, the one that seemed to absorb the entire city with its gaze. "You mean it's an illusion?" he said. "The eye is really a window?" He thought about it and laughed without meaning to.

"What's funny?" Ilvani said. "I didn't know there were such words."

"It's just . . . I thought it was Uwan who watched everything from up here," Ashok said. "He's the Watching Blade, he could see the whole city. But it's you who was looking all along."

There was at least one artist in Ikemmu, Ashok thought.

"I see the city, and I see them," Ilvani said. "The ones with wings. I see them in the sky when it's dark."

"The winged folk—the pictures carved on the tower," Ashok said. "Are they angels?"

"No," Ilvani said. "The feathers burst from their backs and they pull themselves up and up. Their arms are free for other things, but they can't escape the fire."

"What happened to them?" asked Ashok.

"They all fell out of the sky," Ilvani said. She cupped her hands then spread her fingers and let something imaginary fall between the cracks.

"I see," Ashok said. "Thank you for telling me."

They didn't speak for a long time, and Ashok thought she was restless for him to leave. He moved to the ladder and climbed down while she stared out the window. He thought he would be out the door before she noticed him again, but her voice carried after him.

"You'll see the Veil soon," she said.

He lingered in the doorway, but her face was hard to see with the light from the window behind it. "Will I?" he said.

"There are more doorways than towers," she said. "Maybe some escaped. Maybe not all burned. But the Veil . . . I'll come with you, when you go." She turned away from him and lay down on her side facing the window.

Ashok left her to watch the city.

CHAPTER
TWENTY-FOUR

That night Ashok slept in the burned-out building where he'd first drawn his maps of the city. He hadn't intended to, but as he'd stood outside the door of the room he'd shared with Chanoch, he realized he didn't want to go in and see it vacant.

He slept little and woke often from strange dreams he couldn't quite remember. Finally, he got up and walked the torn pathways around the trade district, avoiding people wherever possible.

Ashok knew he should be preparing to leave the city. Chanoch was gone, and he'd fulfilled his promise to Natan. There was no longer anything keeping him in Ikemmu. Yet he couldn't make himself leave. He craved solitude, but he couldn't stomach the thought of walking the Shadowfell plain alone.

Truly, father would laugh to see how pathetic I've become, Ashok thought. Weak and indecisive.

After three days of little rest and listless wandering around the city, Ashok returned to the training yard and saw Cree and Skagi talking to Jamet. When they saw him, they immediately excused themselves and came quickly over.

"Where have you been?" Skagi demanded. "Uwan's had us looking everywhere for you. He almost gave up on the mission."

"What mission?" Ashok said.

"The four of us—Vedoran's meeting us later today—are to escort Tatigan through the Underdark," Skagi explained.

"Tatigan?" Ashok said. He hadn't seen the merchant since they'd spoken in Darnae's shop.

"That's not all," Cree said. "You're going to lead us."

"Me?" Ashok said. "What about Vedoran?"

Skagi shook his head. "Uwan says it's going to be you this time," he said. "Fitting punishment, I say, for what that Blite bastard did to Chanoch. What do you think, eh?"

Ashok didn't know what to say. He'd come to see Skagi and Cree ostensibly to say goodbye, yet in the next breath he found himself asking, "When do we leave?"

"Last bell," Cree said. "Vedoran said if we found you he'd get Tatigan and meet us and Ilvani at the Veil."

"Ilvani?" Ashok said, shocked. "What does she have to do with this?"

Cree glanced at his brother. They both looked uneasy. "We were as surprised as you," Cree said. "But Uwan thinks—see, Ilvani used to go on raids, and scouting missions of course. But ever since we got back . . ."

"Uwan thinks she needs to get back to her old duties, that it'll do her good," Skagi said.

Ashok shook his head. "He's wrong." he said. Again. Wrong about so much.

Cree shrugged. "It's not for us to decide," he said. "She's meeting us, and we're to escort Tatigan."

Something Cree had said suddenly registered in Ashok's brain, and he said, "What's the Veil?"

You'll see the Veil soon, Ilvani had said.

Skagi chuckled. "I've been waiting to show it to you," he said. "It's our way to the other side." He motioned to Cree and started walking.

"Come on. We'll get some provisions together." His lip curled into a mischievous smile. "Then you'll see it with your own eyes."

It took longer than they expected to gather the necessary gear and provisions, even though Skagi assured Ashok that the journey through the Underdark and back would take only a day.

The brothers guided him north of the trade district to a well-worn, deserted road that led straight to the canyon wall. Ashok remembered the road, but he'd ignored it when he had made his maps of the city, thinking it was a dead end. They passed beneath the Spans, and Ashok heard the waterfall in the distance behind Makthar.

The shadows on the deserted road were deeper, and as Ashok's vision adjusted to the lower light conditions, he saw a raised stone arch set into the canyon wall ahead of them. Four guards stood at either leg of the arch, and the keystone bore the carved sword of Tempus, its blade pointed down toward the ground. It was exactly like the portal arch outside the city gate. Ilvani stood beneath the sword, her back to them. She was staring at the wall. None of the guards paid her any attention.

"Well met, Grecen," Cree called out to one of the guards. "Any sign of our merchant friend?"

The guard shook his head. "Not yet," he replied.

"Vedoran's missing too," Ashok said. He went up to Ilvani. "Are you all right?" he asked.

She turned to him and bowed her head in greeting. "I told you I would be here," she said.

"How did you know?" Ashok asked.

She tapped her temple with a fingernail. "Too many questions. Not enough space for them all," she said.

"Fair enough," Ashok said. "But are you certain you're up to this?"

Weariness crossed her face. "Uwan," she said simply.

"Uwan," Ashok said, understanding. "He's always taking things before they're ready."

"Yes," she replied.

"Well met, Tatigan," Skagi called out, and Ashok turned to see the merchant coming toward them.

He had his green spectacles on and a large sack on a strap over his shoulder. "I've a lot of coin this time, Skagi," Tatigan said. "You'll have to walk extra slowly."

Skagi snorted. "Prepare to be left behind, old man," he said.

"And who's this going to accompany us?" Tatigan asked, peering over his spectacles at Ashok. "Tempus's emissary, is it?" He winked at Ashok.

"We're waiting for one more," Ashok said. "Then we should be ready to leave. Not"—he looked at Skagi—"that I fully understand where we're going."

Skagi grinned. "Be patient," he said.

Cree and Skagi went over to converse with the guards, and Ilvani drifted back to the arch. Ashok stood with Tatigan. Neither spoke for a time.

"I saw Darnae early this morning," Tatigan said. "She asked after you, said she hadn't seen you in days. Where have you been keeping yourself?"

"As far away as possible," Ashok said. "I'm not good company these days."

"She's afraid you're going to leave," Tatigan said.

Ashok sighed. "She's perceptive," he said. "I won't go anywhere without giving her word."

"That's good to know," replied the merchant.

"There's Vedoran," Skagi said grimly, pointing up the road.

Ashok turned to look and saw Vedoran coming quickly toward them. His normally graceful stride was broken. He dragged his boots and nearly stumbled twice before he got to them. Skagi laughed derisively.

"Have you been in Tatigan's wine, Vedoran?" he said. "No wonder you're late."

"I'm fine," Vedoran said tersely. He walked past Skagi to greet Tatigan. "I apologize for my lateness," he said. "We can leave anytime you're ready." He glanced briefly at Ashok. "Lead on," he said.

Ashok noticed Vedoran's hands shaking. He'd steadied his walk, but it was an effort, Ashok thought. As the group gathered together, Ashok walked past Vedoran, but smelled no strong drink on his breath. His hair was slightly askew from its tail, and his skin was paler than normal, but in all other respects he seemed in control of himself.

Skagi called him to the front of the group, and Ashok had no more time to wonder about Vedoran's condition.

"Time to lead us through the Veil," Skagi said and nodded to the arch.

Ashok looked at the bare canyon wall. He glanced at Skagi and the rest, but they were waiting on him. Even Vedoran accepted his new role as leader without comment or conflict. Ashok found that a jest indeed, since he had no idea where he was going.

"But I go," he murmured to himself, and stepped forward until his nose was almost touching the stone. He smelled earth and something faintly electric, like contained lightning, and underneath them both dampness. He closed his eyes and took the last step forward.

His body passed through the wall, and Ashok felt a breath of wind blow his hair back, like the air currents between doors. The electricity hummed along his skin and then was gone. The air turned to damp, and there was a smell of moss everywhere.

Ashok opened his eyes, looked around, and was engulfed by a sudden vertigo that made him stumble back a step.

Hands on his shoulders steadied him, and Ashok looked back to see Ilvani behind him. She had to reach above her head to touch his shoulders.

"What is this?" Ashok asked her. "I don't understand."

"You passed through the Veil," Ilvani said. "Everything here is real, even if your eyes say no. The eyes always say no, but they lie."

Ashok tried to get his breath, but his senses were still awry. The city before him was obviously Ikemmu, except that everything was wrong.

Before him there were the four towers whose summits nearly brushed the top of the cavern—the trade districts and Makthar with its thundering waterfall, and Athanon with its fence. But the towers on the far side of the Veil were smaller than those on the other, with fewer of the archways for teleportation.

The people Ashok saw coming and going from the trade districts were almost all human, dwarven, or one of the other races. He saw one shadar-kai for every two dozen other races. The trade district was much larger and more built up on that side of the city as well. The buildings were newer, constructed in the last ten years, Ashok thought. Much of the debris that cluttered the roadways on the other side of the Veil was missing.

"Two faces for one city," Ashok said.

Tatigan stepped through the Veil with the others. Ashok hadn't realized that he and Ilvani had been the only ones to cross for several breaths.

Skagi said, "Surprised?"

"I had no idea," Ashok said. He nearly laughed aloud at his feeble plans when he'd first arrived in Ikemmu, of his enclave ever having a chance to attack the city. "How many people live here?" he asked.

"Roughly eight thousand souls," Tatigan said before anyone else could answer. "But that's not counting the traders and planewalkers that come through here every day. Most of them only ever see this side of the city."

"Where is this side of the city?" Ashok said. "Are we below where we were before?"

Tatigan chuckled. "Prepare to be dizzy, lad," he said. "We're in *exactly* the same spot we were before. We haven't gone anywhere at all."

"I don't understand," Ashok said.

"We're in the Underdark," Tatigan said. "Specifically, this place is known as the Ramparts of Night. We crossed from the shadow world to the thing that cast the shadow. Right now we're below the world of Faerûn, my home."

Cree laughed. "Tatigan has made a study of Ikemmu's geography," he said. "He'll go on for days if you let him."

"Someone has to chronicle the marvels you take for granted," Tatigan said. "Your city exists in two worlds simultaneously, and you don't think that's something to respect?"

Skagi shrugged. "Means we can be attacked on two fronts. That's why only certain people get to cross to the Shadowfell side," he explained to Ashok. "Only permanent residents get to go there."

"They trade comfort for security," Tatigan said. "The other races have worked hard to restore the Underdark side of the city, but the Shadowfell side is the point of refuge in the event of an invasion."

"And this?" Ashok said, nodding to the bustling market. "This is the true trade district?"

"Where all the coin is made," Tatigan said. "You can smell it in the air."

"We're wasting time," Vedoran said, speaking up. He'd been so quiet Ashok was startled to hear his voice. "Tatigan, if you please."

"I do please," Tatigan said, sniffing. He fell into step beside Ashok. "I'm writing a memoir about the city. There is a path that we'll take up to the surface and then you'll tell me, you who have never seen the colored world like this"—he poked his green lenses—"if this city is not a wonder. I wager you won't be able to say it."

"I wouldn't make the wager," Ashok said as they started off into the mirror city. He glanced at Ilvani. "The wonders in this city are limitless."

CHAPTER
TWENTY-FIVE

THE TRIP THROUGH THE CITY WAS AGONY FOR VEDORAN. HE crawled the walls of his mind, seeking peace, but there was nothing except the memory of the last day and how it had gone so horribly wrong.

I will not see you again until the thing has been set in motion, the Beshaban cleric had warned him. Had he known what that meant?

Vedoran had gone to see Natan at Makthar. The cleric had been willing and, Vedoran thought, eager to speak to him about the successful mission and his sister.

They stood in the main chapel, and Natan dismissed the guard so they could speak in private.

"I'm glad you've given me this opportunity to thank you for your role in my sister's rescue," Natan said. "Your leadership brought your party back safely. Uwan and I both recognize your potential to serve this city. We won't forget what you have done."

Vedoran clasped his hands behind his back and said formally, "Thank you for your words, and my thanks in turn to Lord Uwan. But I'm well aware that the gratitude of Ikemmu extends only so far. You need not pretend otherwise."

Natan's face clouded. "No pretense, I assure you," he said. I'm aware that you place your faith in yourself, Vedoran, and not in the gods, but you may not always feel this way. Surely, you can keep yourself open to the destiny Tempus may have planned for you. You can't deny that He is at work here in our lives."

"I recognize that He is at work in some lives," Vedoran said. He walked up a set of steps leading to the altar and Tempus's sword carved into the wall. The candles on the altar were warm on his face.

"You mean Ashok?" Natan said as he joined him and sat on the steps. His informality made Vedoran uncomfortable, though he could not say why. Perhaps it was because he'd expected Natan to condemn him with the righteous love of Tempus. But the cleric looked, if anything, extraordinarily weary, aged beyond his years. He was too weak to lecture anyone overmuch on faith, Vedoran thought. Uwan is the strength of the pair.

"You and Uwan have chosen Ashok as Tempus's emissary," Vedoran said. "A stranger, with no connection to this city and no love for its people. How can you trust such a person to carry your god's message?"

"Because Tempus spoke to me," Natan said. "My vision was proved true. Ashok is no longer a stranger."

"But you remember the way he was when he first arrived in Ikemmu, don't you? Dangerous, half-crazed? We were among shadar-kai like that in the caves where we rescued your sister," Vedoran said. He reached up and caught a tongue of hot wax dripping down one of the long candlesticks. He wiped it across the altar. "They made your sister rut in the dirt with them like an animal."

Vedoran heard Natan's sharp intake of breath. He turned to look at the cleric and shamefully enjoyed seeing his serenity shattered. Tears filled Natan's eyes, and he put a hand against the stone floor to steady himself.

"I didn't see her there in that cage," Vedoran went on. He stepped back from the altar, offered a mocking bow to the sword on the wall, and came to sit beside Natan, who was trying to compose himself. "Ashok did, and I've never seen a hardened warrior look the way he did when he came out of that place. If your sister were to take her own life because of it, I would not condemn her."

"Why?" Natan said breathlessly. He put a hand over his face, as if he were in physical pain.

"I don't know why," Vedoran said. "Maybe they required a stronger hand to lead them. Maybe shadar-kai can't live in dark holes without some madness seeping in with the shadows. If you really want to explore the motives, why don't you ask Ashok?"

"What do you mean?" Natan said. Confusion and wary fear swam in his eyes. "Why ask him?"

"You sense it, don't you?" Vedoran said. He felt a mixture of pity and disgust for the small cleric cowering before him. Why had he ever feared the servants of Tempus? Even in the chapel they had no power over Vedoran. "That small doubt buried in your mind."

"No, not anymore," Natan said. He shook his head vehemently. "Uwan believes in him, and so do I."

"But it was terribly convenient how Ashok led us straight to where Ilvani was being held," Vedoran said. Natan tried to turn away from him, but Vedoran moved closer; his presence shrank the cleric further. "As much as I would love to take credit for my leadership," his voice dripped spite, "it was Ashok who got us in and out of that place alive, and he accomplished it because he'd been in that enclave before. I'll wager he was born there."

"It makes no sense," Natan said. He looked up at the altar and to the sword. "If they were his people, why did he not betray you to them? Why did he help Ilvani?"

"For the same reason he's still here among us," Vedoran said. "He's fallen under Ikemmu's spell. He thinks this is a better life."

"It is," Natan said. He touched his chest and his voice came stronger. "It is better. Ashok must have seen the path of destruction his people were set upon. He chose a different path. For that he should be commended."

"In any other city, perhaps he would be," Vedoran said. He savored the next breath as he prepared to deliver the final blow. "But Ikemmu—Uwan—cannot forgive traitors."

"Ashok is not a traitor," Natan said. "You said it yourself. He brought you all out of that place alive."

"He did, but previous to that act, he planned to betray the city to his own enclave. I have proof of this," he said before Natan could refute it. "I intend to present my accusation to Uwan."

He waited for Natan's reaction, but the cleric said nothing. He stared blankly at the sword on the wall as if waiting for it to offer an answer. Finally, he said, "Why are you doing this? I thought Ashok was your friend."

"That doesn't negate the law of this city," Vedoran said. "The law created by your beloved leader will condemn Ashok to death."

Natan shook his head. "He is Tempus's emissary. The god will forgive. He has a purpose in mind for Ashok."

Vedoran felt the rage boiling up inside him, but at the same time he felt a strange detachment, as if he were merely a spectator at the scene instead of a participant. He leaned forward and felt the skin of Natan's throat beneath his fingers.

The cleric's eyes widened, but Vedoran tightened his grip so Natan couldn't speak. He didn't want to hear any more of the hypocrite's words.

"Uwan does not forgive," he said in a quiet, spitting voice against Natan's ear. "Chanoch was executed at my word. Ashok will not be elevated for his actions while Chanoch died for them. I will see this city destroyed before that happens."

Natan's body had begun to twitch. His legs slapped against the stairs like a fish trying to get off the land. Vedoran, watching the scene from a distance, thought that Natan probably wasn't able to hear himself raving, not with blood and fear roaring in his ears.

It was over soon after that, and Vedoran slowly drifted back to himself. When he could recognize his surroundings again, he saw that Natan's body lay on the stairs. His neck was mangled, his hand outstretched toward the altar. The sword of Tempus cast a band of shadow across his face.

For a long breath the horror didn't sink into Vedoran's mind. He felt only the breathless satisfaction that comes from muscles held too long without release. He'd been holding back for years, and finally all the rage, pain, and injustice had come roaring out of him. With the violence in him spent, he felt light-headed, free.

And with the freedom to think rationally came the recognition of all that he had just lost.

As the group strode up the long tunnel toward the surface world of Faerûn, Vedoran found himself in the most unlikely position imaginable. He was walking up a tunnel, with nothing ahead of him but darkness, and he had only faith left to him that they would reach their destination at the end of it. On the other side of the Veil, he'd been forced to place his faith in a cleric of Beshaba, goddess of all the misfortunes in the world.

"Go," Traedis had told him, after Vedoran had hidden Natan's body and contacted the cleric to tell him what had happened. "Leave the city and carry out the plan. I will make certain Natan's body is discovered at the appropriate time. Your crimes will become Ashok's. You've sworn the oath to Beshaba. I will protect you."

He'd sworn the oath, and whether it was a trick of the cleric's magic or his own mind trapping him, Vedoran felt the presence of the gods around him, directing him to a fate that was no longer of his own choosing.

"Rest here," Ashok called out from the front of the group.

Vedoran could see that they were near their destination. He didn't know why Ashok had stopped until he saw Ilvani swaying on her feet and breathing heavily. A stab of hatred for Uwan went through him. Ilvani was in no condition to undertake this journey. She would return to Ikemmu weaker than she'd ever been to find her brother murdered.

I will make amends for your loss, he promised her silently. He couldn't undo his instant of madness, but he could give her justice for the violations she'd suffered.

You'll have one of the animals before you, helpless, and you can punish him however you choose, Vedoran thought. No one will begrudge you taking back that control. It was a more fitting death for Ashok than fading away into shadow.

Tatigan was speaking to Ashok, probably about the city, Vedoran thought. Ashok's attention was focused more on Ilvani and her comfort. She ignored them all.

"Ashok," Vedoran said. He moved to the front of the group to join Ashok and Tatigan. "I suggest we scout ahead, you and I, to make sure the passage up to the surface is clear. It's a customary action we take to prevent us walking into an ambush."

"Once we're at the surface, I'll join a caravan a mile west and take it back to civilization," Tatigan said. "In a month or more, I'll come back, once I've filled all the orders I've taken in Ikemmu." He patted a pocket in his vest.

Ashok nodded at Vedoran. "The rest of you stay here," he said. "Cree, keep watch behind us."

They started up the tunnel together. Vedoran was struck, suddenly, by the familiarity of the two of them together. Warriors of almost equal skill, they had complemented each other well. Vedoran felt that Ashok understood him better than any shadar-kai he'd ever known. If it had not been for the cold set of Ashok's face, and his silence, such a scout would have been routine for the two of them, perhaps for years as they fought together.

It was Tempus that had come between them, Vedoran thought with renewed bitterness. Tempus and Uwan.

They reached a bend where a rock slide had caved in a portion of the passage. There was enough room for the group to pass the obstruction and little more to contend with than rocky terrain, but Vedoran hesitated and Ashok stopped too.

"Was this here the last time you came through?" Ashok asked.

"No," Vedoran said. As he spoke he saw movement in a crevice near the top of the slide. Ashok saw it too and motioned Vedoran back.

They didn't speak until they'd retreated several steps back down the tunnel, out of sight of the fallen rocks.

"Did you see it?" Ashok said.

Vedoran nodded. "Spider," he said. "Hound-sized or larger. It was hard to tell how far the crevice went back."

"Probably made itself a good ambush spot after the rockslide," Ashok said.

"We should deal with it now," Vedoran said.

"Why not bring the others up?" Ashok said. "Between the four of us, we should be able to dispatch it with little effort."

"So can you and I," Vedoran pointed out. "And with minimal stress put upon Ilvani. If she feels pressured to use her magic in defense of the group, it could weaken her further."

"You're right," Ashok said. He took out his chain. "We'll deal with it now."

"Wait here," Vedoran said. A plan had begun to form in his mind. "I'll draw it out, and you can finish it from afar."

"Be careful," Ashok said. "If it jumps, you won't have much time to react."

"Don't worry. It won't touch me," Vedoran said.

They moved cautiously back up the tunnel, watching the crevice for movement. After several breaths they saw hairy brown legs feather gracefully across the stone. Pebbles knocked loose by the movement tumbled down the slide with the faintest of sounds. The legs drew back out of sight.

"Go," Ashok said.

Vedoran darted up the tunnel, keeping his body as far away from the crevice as possible. He was almost past the slide when the spider popped out. As Ashok had predicted, it was a deathjump spider, a creature with an incredible ability to leap on its prey from a distance.

Watching the spider prepare its attack, Vedoran caught his foot against one of the loose stones. He uttered a cry and went down hard on his knees, exposing his back to the spider.

Like a dream, everything fell into place. Vedoran heard Ashok's chain whistling as it flew through the air. The spider leaped for Vedoran, and at the last possible breath Vedoran spun and put his hands up to block the bite attack he knew was coming.

Ashok's chain got to the spider first. The end stuck in the creature's abdomen and dragged it back several feet.

The spider immediately changed its attack course and leaped on Ashok, covering his torso with its body and knocking him to the ground. While Vedoran pretended to recover, the spider sank its mandibles into Ashok's shoulder.

Vedoran got to his feet and limped toward Ashok. He waited until the spider had delivered its poison before he drew his own sword and came at the creature from behind.

Ashok raked the chain across the spider's abdomen so he could push it off him and draw out the poisoned mandibles. He got his boot under the creature and levered it off him, just in time for Vedoran to put his blade through the spider's body.

Legs jerked and twitched as the spider tried to move, but Vedoran's sword held it in place like a pin until it died with Ashok's blood still dripping from its mouth.

Ashok cursed and sat up gingerly, wiping blood from his neck and chest. His wounds bled and oozed poison liberally. Vedoran saw Ashok's face crease in pain.

"You were right. We should have waited for the others," Vedoran said. He hooked the end of Ashok's chain with his boot toe and dragged it out of reach. Ashok heard the metal links clink against the stone and looked up at Vedoran.

"You were clumsier than usual," Ashok said. He tried to gain his feet, but Vedoran stepped close, into his space, and Ashok was too unsteady to rise without making himself helpless. "I always thought you were the picture of grace—a true, cold warrior."

"And you are the opposite," Vedoran said. "You fight with too much passion and too little regard for yourself."

"Is this where it ends then?" Ashok said. "You kill me for taking your place as leader?"

Vedoran laughed. "I gave you credit for being smarter than that," he said. "I told you: you and Chanoch are nothing to me. This is much bigger than both of you."

"Yes," Ashok said. "It's about the gods. Neither of us can control our fates."

"I can take the burden out of *your* hands, at least," Vedoran said. "It's time for the truth to come out. It's time for you to claim your heritage."

Ashok's mouth tightened. He held a hand over his bleeding wound. "Whatever you think of me, I didn't kidnap Ilvani, and I didn't have anything to do with her torture."

"I believe you," Vedoran said. "But you're planning to overthrow the city anyway, or so the evidence will show."

Ashok winced as the poison threaded through his blood. His face was flushed, though from pain or anger Vedoran couldn't say. "Is this going to give you what you want, Vedoran?" he asked.

"No," Vedoran said. "But ruining you is ruining Tempus, at least for Ikemmu. I'll have to settle for that."

Ashok surged up then and wrapped his arms around Vedoran's waist. Caught off guard, Vedoran stumbled and fell back over the spider corpse. Ashok got on top of him and reached for Vedoran's blade.

Grunting, Vedoran punched Ashok in the face with his left hand. The blow got Ashok in the jaw and broke his momentum. He grabbed Vedoran's tunic to steady himself. Vedoran swung his sword and clipped Ashok on the back of the head with the pommel.

Weakened already by his wounds and the poison, Ashok went limp on the ground next to the spider's corpse. Vedoran sat up and sheathed his weapon. He crouched next to Ashok and loosened the buckles of his armor. He removed the bone scale breastplate and searched inside until his fingers found a slit in the leather where a pouch was hidden.

He reached inside and pulled out several folded parchment sheets, blood-spattered but legible, written in Ashok's hand. Vedoran unfolded the maps and noted the detail Ashok had used in recording the city's defenses.

"You damned yourself from the beginning," Vedoran said.

Gravel crunched near the tunnel bend, and Vedoran looked up sharply.

Ilvani stood several feet away, watching him.

"What are you doing here?" Vedoran demanded. "You were supposed to stay with the others."

Ilvani walked forward and kneeled next to Ashok's prone body. She brushed the hair off his forehead and trailed her hand down to his neck to feel for a lifebeat. Her hand came up bloody, but she seemed satisfied. She wiped her hand on her skirt.

"He was attacked," she said. She looked up at Vedoran.

"A spider jumped out of the crevice up there," Vedoran said, pointing to the creature's hiding spot. "It poisoned Ashok."

"Poisoned him with a sword hilt," Ilvani said. She fixed a mocking, innocent expression on her face.

Vedoran worked his jaw. There were two courses open to him. If she'd only witnessed him rendering Ashok unconscious, there was nothing to worry about. But if she'd heard everything . . . .

There was one way to know, Vedoran thought. He wondered if Ilvani would rattle as easily as her brother had.

"You're right, I knocked Ashok unconscious," Vedoran said. "He was trying to run away—with this." He held out the bloody parchment sheets.

With a curious tilt to her head, like a child, Ilvani took the sheets and unfolded them. Vedoran went on, "This may be hard for you to hear, Ilvani, but I've discovered something shocking about Ashok. He's been deceiving us all this time."

"Everyone lies," Ilvani said. She examined the notes, and her brow furrowed. "He's not an artist. Why would he draw pictures?"

"So he could deliver the information to his enclave once he had escaped the city," Vedoran said. Ilvani looked even more confused. "Natan didn't tell you about that, did he? Ashok was captured by patrols outside of Ikemmu. He was a prisoner of the city while you were a prisoner in those caves."

"Two prisoners, two different prisons," Ilvani said. But she was listening, Vedoran thought. That was the important thing.

"Ashok was able to rescue you because he came from the same enclave that took your scouting party prisoner," Vedoran said. "I saw it myself—the way he knew the layout of the tunnels, where the guards would be—only I couldn't confirm it until now. Ilvani,

Ashok was responsible for what happened to you."

He waited for her reaction, but she only continued to stare at the parchment sheets in her hands. She didn't appear to have heard him, or the words weren't registering in her mind. She looked down at Ashok, but her gaze was turned inward.

"He looks peaceful," she said.

"Even the guilty can seem at peace," Vedoran said. "Ilvani, I'm sorry to have to tell you all this. I didn't want to."

"Uwan," Ilvani said. "Natan. Ask them."

"They were deceived as well," Vedoran replied.

Ilvani's face scrunched up, but there were no tears. She looked as if she might break apart instead. She brought her hands up in claws to cover her face.

Vedoran took a step toward her, but she backed up and screeched, "No! Ask them. Ask them, and they'll tell me, and then it can be but not before. Before it's just words, and you're putting them together so they'll sound pretty." She looked at him with an expression very close to hatred in her eyes. "Why do you all do that?"

"We'll make this right," Vedoran said. "I'll present the evidence to Uwan, and Ashok will be dealt with, I promise you."

Ilvani looked at the parchment in her hands and said a series of words Vedoran didn't understand. The parchment floated up from her palm, hung in the air for a breath, and vanished.

Vedoran caught his breath. "What did you do with them?" he cried.

"Safe," Ilvani said. "They're safe in the Ashok box until needed." She looked at him, a hard set to her face. "Time to go," she said.

A woman made of stone, Vedoran thought. He realized he wouldn't get her to change her mind. He briefly cursed the loss of the evidence, but perhaps it was meant to be.

Who better to make the case before Uwan, than the woman whose life Ashok's people had ruined?

CHAPTER
TWENTY-SIX

ASHOK AWOKE TO A DULL THROB AT THE BACK OF HIS SKULL. HE was on his feet, blind, and breathing hot air. It didn't take him long to assume the rest.

He was in a cell, chained deep in the caves behind the forges. Maybe it was Chanoch's cell. He couldn't tell for the hood covering his face. There were no sounds; the room was absolute silence and cold.

In a flash of morbid humor, Ashok remembered the cleric's words to him, when he'd first woken in Ikemmu.

Perhaps someday you'll see how we treat our prisoners. Prophecies abounded in Ikemmu.

You have no one to blame but yourself, Ashok thought. You should have left the city when you had the chance. But you didn't really want to escape, did you? Ever since he'd ridden out of that cave and left the slaughtered members of his enclave behind, he'd been looking for punishment in place of absolution. He'd betrayed his own people, and he'd betrayed Ikemmu by not confessing the truth.

Ashok only hoped, before it was all over, that he would be given the opportunity for that confession. If they left him alone in the dark, forgotten, he would fade away and still bear the shame.

No. It wouldn't happen. Uwan would come. Ashok knew the leader would be there in the dark, at some moment. He hadn't left Chanoch alone.

Ashok closed his eyes and tried to sleep, but he was aware of the lingering ache in his shoulder. His hands were numb from being held above his head. A tingling sensation ran down his arms. And he was cold, so cold all over, except where his breath was trapped inside the hood.

They were none of them sensations that he cared to think about. All were associated with a lack of feeling, a frozen state from which he couldn't emerge. Ashok stomped his feet hard just to feel the shock go up his legs. He twisted his body from side to side as best he could, trying to coax some feeling back into his limbs, but the chains were suspended so tightly he had trouble drawing a full breath.

He tried to remember the journey back to Ikemmu, but his mind was choked with fog. There were snatches, bits of conversation where his name had featured prominently, but he couldn't remember the words. He hoped Tatigan had reached the surface and his caravan safely, and he enjoyed the brief regret that he would never see what the world of Faerûn looked like. He imagined that it would be a place full of people like Tatigan and Darnae, and that gave him comfort.

Some time passed, and perhaps he slept, but more likely Ashok thought he drifted in and out of stupor. Once a guard came into his cell with a bucket and helped him to relieve himself. Ashok was faintly grateful for not having to soil himself, but the guard never removed the hood, and Ashok felt it was one of the most humiliating experiences of his life.

The next time the door opened, Ashok didn't detect the heavy tread of the guards, but a single set of footsteps. They stopped in front of his cell. Whomever it was, Ashok could hear their slow indrawn breaths, and feel the contemplative silence with which the stranger regarded him.

"Well met, Uwan," Ashok said.

"The guards tell me you've been restless," Uwan said. "That's a good sign. If you'd been subdued, we'd have had to move you somewhere else. We won't risk you fading."

"So I haven't been condemned yet?" Ashok said. He turned his head to follow Uwan's pacing outside his cell, though it was a futile gesture to try to see through the hood.

"Not yet," Uwan said. His tone told Ashok that it was a foregone conclusion. "The evidence is being gathered."

"By Vedoran," Ashok said.

"Yes," Uwan replied, and he stopped pacing. Ashok heard his hands moving over the bars. He could picture the leader deciding how much he wanted to say.

"Ask your questions," Ashok said. He'd been waiting for the moment, and felt a profound relief that the time had finally arrived. "I've nothing left to hide."

"Is it true?" Uwan said. "Did you kidnap Ilvani?"

"No," Ashok said. "Not directly. My father ordered the attack on the scouting party. I was sent out of the city to track down a pack of shadow hounds that had been harrying us. Between them and Ilvani's party, we were surrounded."

"A wise tactical decision," Uwan said. "Your father is a shrewd leader."

"My father was a butcher," Ashok said. There was no passion in his words, but they were no less true for the lack of feeling. "He sacrificed my brothers to each other and to the rivalry within the enclave. We had a heavily fortified position in those caves; we didn't have the constant threat of attack, and we launched no offensives against other enclaves."

"So without any enemies to fight, your own people became the threat," Uwan said.

"We fought amongst ourselves, took any excuse to stave off the shadows," Ashok said. "When I came to this city and saw the arms you displayed, I thought, what an impossible challenge, to launch an attack against your forces."

"You'd found exactly what you needed to pull your enclave together and focus its attention on a new enemy," Uwan said.

"And maybe I could stop slaughtering my brothers," Ashok said. "Yes, that was the goal."

"Why didn't you go through with the plan?" Uwan asked. "Vedoran and the others . . . You had them all together on your home soil. Why didn't you give them up?"

Ashok sighed. His entire body was numb, and he was weary from speaking while only drawing half breaths. He needed pain, something intense to focus his thoughts. He hadn't felt so desperate in a long time. "I know what you want me to say," he said. "You want me to say that it was Tempus's will. It wasn't."

"Then why?" Uwan said, and for the first time anger broke through his carefully restrained tone.

"Because I had never known trust, or what it meant to fight with comrades who would defend me to the death, until I came here," Ashok cried. "I didn't want to lose that, so I attacked my own people. I used the nightmare to slaughter them." He'd done no better than Reltnar. He'd acted out of the same desperate need to feel alive.

"You rescued Ilvani," Uwan said. He seemed to be speaking to himself. "But that isn't enough for the Beshabans. They want you executed, so they can prove the fallibility of Tempus."

"By Ikemmu's law, I should be executed," Ashok said.

"We await the evidence," Uwan replied.

"I've offered my confession," said Ashok.

"Enough!" Uwan cried. Something metal—his sword perhaps—slammed against the cell bars and rang loudly in the quiet chamber. "I've heard nothing."

"You can't deny what you know," Ashok said. "It betrays everything you believe. You'll go mad."

"Not for this," Uwan declared. "You had a choice, and you made it. You chose the way of Ikemmu."

"You may forgive me," Ashok said. "But the shadar-kai cannot afford to forgive."

Uwan laughed bitterly. "Is that why you do this? To taunt me with my own words? You'd throw your life away to prove that I was wrong about Chanoch?"

"You're wrong about many things," Ashok said. "Chanoch was one casualty. Vedoran was another. You've done him and others like him a great wrong."

"And now I'm paying for it," Uwan said. He sighed. "I know. Tempus aid me, I know that I've brought this upon myself. He tried to warn me. My god tried to tell me what you would mean to this city, but I didn't understand. Now it's too late." He was silent for a breath then said, "Natan is dead."

Ashok had thought he had no emotion left in him, but when he heard that he sagged against the chains.

"It will destroy her," Ashok said.

"It may already have," Uwan said bleakly. "She disappeared as soon as she returned to Ikemmu, when they brought you back in chains."

"What happened?" Ashok said.

"Natan was murdered in the chapel," Uwan said. "We discovered his body hidden in an antechamber soon after you left the city with Tatigan. Vedoran claims you are responsible. He accuses you of killing Natan when he had a vision of your treachery. He says that you planned to escape to the surface."

"I didn't kill him," Ashok said.

"I thought not," Uwan said as he began to pace again. "But the damage is done."

Ashok closed his eyes. He wished he could sleep. He'd never desired oblivion more. "So it was all for nothing," he said. The one good thing he'd tried to do in getting Ilvani out of that nightmare place, all undone.

"You'll spend one more night here," Uwan said. "Tomorrow at the Monril bell you'll be taken to the top of Tower Makthar, and Vedoran and the Beshabans will present their evidence against you. They've rallied a large number of supporters to their cause, more than I thought possible. However I rule, it will divide the city. But if I judge you guilty, you'll be brought back here to await your death by the shadows."

He started to walk away. Ashok called after him, "You can't ignore the evidence. If you act according to your emotions, you'll lose the peoples' faith. Then the Beshabans will be able to act, with the full support of the discontent shadar-kai."

Ashok heard Uwan stop at the door. He knocked on it for the guards to let him out. "You've a tactical mind equal to your father's," he said. "I say this as a compliment, though I know it gives you little comfort."

The door closed, and Ashok was alone in the dark again.

CHAPTER
TWENTY-SEVEN

ASHOK SLEPT IN FITS, DREAMING OF HOUNDS AND RUNNING ACROSS the Shadowfell plains. His muscles woke him screaming with cramps. He broke out in a cold sweat until the pain and tightness subsided. Invigorated, he could not sleep again for a long time.

When he hovered again at the threshold of peace, he heard the door to the chamber open, and soft footfalls came toward his cell. It was not the guards, nor Uwan's purposeful stride. It was much lighter, faster, like an animal avoiding prey.

He waited for the creature to identify itself by sound or smell. Maybe one of the hounds had escaped from its pen and come looking for a meal. Ashok was not afraid. He'd been chained in the dark too long. His heart beat sluggishly, and he could not bring himself to turn his head when the creature approached the bars.

"Wake, little toad," said a familiar voice, one that made Ashok jerk his head around, though he couldn't see her face.

"Ilvani?" he said. Hope may have made him delirious. "Is that you?"

The witch whispered a word, and Ashok heard his cell door swing open. Her footsteps approached, and Ashok felt her small fingers touch his chest.

"Where have you been?" Ashok said. "Uwan . . . Everyone's been looking for you."

"It speaks," Ilvani said. Her palm grew warm, penetrating the deep cold that had spread over Ashok's body. Hotter and hotter, her hand began to burn him. "It should know when to be silent."

Her other hand touched his face. She pulled the hood off him. Ashok blinked at the sudden light. When he could focus again, he saw that Ilvani looked paler and thinner than ever. Her face was streaked with dirt. Her hand where she touched his chest glowed gold and scorched his flesh.

Ashok writhed in pain. He was alive again, but he pushed aside that feeling and forced himself to breathe, to speak through the pain. "Are you all right?" he asked. "What happened to you?"

"I've made a box," Ilvani said. "A box for Ashok. To keep all his lies safe. Do you know what's in that box?"

Ashok could smell his own flesh burning. He tried not to gag when he answered. "The maps . . . the notes. I did lie to all of you. I—"

"It admits what it did wrong," Ilvani said, in a tone of mocking surprise. "But I'm still going to put your ashes in the box. You'll stand in for all the others."

"You mean your companions. The ones who didn't come home," Ashok said. He gritted his teeth as she moved her hand, crept it up toward his neck. "I'm sorry for what was done to you and your people. If I could have stopped it, I would have."

"Would your lies have stopped it?" Ilvani demanded. "Would your pictures? You were going to kill us, just like you killed them."

"No," Ashok said. "Your companions—I swear they didn't die by my hand."

"Swear on your flesh!" Ilvani screamed, and she ground her hand against his chest. Ashok cried out in agony, but he didn't try to pull away. He leaned into her touch, endured the pain, and waited until he'd composed himself enough to speak again.

"I was . . . a different person . . . when I wrote those things," Ashok said. "I didn't know you and Uwan, Skagi, or Cree. I never knew a city like this existed. I wanted it to be . . . my home. So I lied. I tried to bury my past, but it didn't work." The searing in his chest made it impossible to concentrate. "I never meant harm . . . to you."

Abruptly, Ilvani removed her hand. The intense heat disappeared, but his chest burned with every breath he drew.

"What was Natan?" she said in a cold, dead voice. "He was the only one left. No boxes, no bad memories. You told me I should see him."

"I wanted you to," Ashok said. "Ilvani, I'm so sorry, but I didn't kill him. I swear on my soul."

"You put him in a box," Ilvani said. Her body trembled. Ashok thought she hadn't been so close to breaking even when she'd been in her cell in the slaughter room. "I told you he wouldn't fit, but you made it happen."

"No," Ashok said. She took a step back, but he strained toward her. He wished he could break the chains, but he had no strength; he couldn't focus his mind to teleport.

Ilvani raised a hand as if to stave him off. Her palm continued to glow, filled with magic. Ashok bent his head so his forehead touched her fingers. He felt the burning heat, power barely contained.

"Do it," he said. "Finish it."

She caught her breath, but she didn't lower her hand. "Why?" she said, her eyes narrowed with suspicion. "You're trying to store more lies."

"No," Ashok said. "But if it'll ease your suffering, then do it, Ilvani, kill me. Do it for both of us."

"You don't mean it," she said.

"I don't want you to put yourself in a box," Ashok said.

She slapped him. His cheek burned and went numb. His eyes watering, he tried to lean into the heat, but she backed away.

"You're false!" she cried, pacing before him like a starved, half-crazed cat. "You'll die when I say."

"Do what you have to do," Ashok said.

She sprang forward and raked her nails across his chest, shredding flesh. Ashok's body convulsed. He groaned as the fire lines bled, and the wetness ran down his torso.

"Fight back!" Ilvani screamed. She grabbed his hair and jerked his head to one side. She laid her burning fingers against his neck. Ashok couldn't find the breath to scream and sagged against the chains.

"Not yet," Ilvani said. "The darkness can't have you yet. I'm not done taking your ashes."

Ashok's head lolled to the side. He bit his lip and tasted blood. He tried to speak, but his throat burned. His entire body was on fire.

"What did you say?" Ilvani asked, stepping closer. Her fingers hovered before his eyes. Ashok watched the glowing points and waited for her to blind him. "Speak," she commanded.

Ashok's body begged for the release of unconsciousness. He tried to follow her voice out of the long, dark tunnel. "I said . . . Take them all. All the ashes. I want . . ."

"What?" Ilvani said. "Say it."

Ashok closed his eyes. "Forgiveness," he said. The darkness surged in to take him.

Ilvani stared at Ashok's mutilated body. He was not dead, but the pain had made him sleep. In a rare flash of pragmatism she recognized that she would need to summon healing, or Ashok would not live to face his trial.

Is that what she wanted? With clarity came confusion, fear. What had she done? Punished a murderer. Confronted the deceiver with his lies. Judged the guilty.

"Is it guilty?" she said, but of course Ashok couldn't answer her. She had only the answers he'd given her earlier to judge.

He'd denied nothing, except killing Natan and her companions. At the thought of her brother, Ilvani went away for a while, into a fugue place where she could be safe. In that place there were no thoughts or pain. She'd discovered the small world within her mind while she'd been imprisoned.

When she came back to herself, she was walking up the tower stairs to her quarters in Tower Athanon.

How long had she been away? She didn't know, and she didn't know what had become of Ashok. Had she told the healers to see to him?

She reached in her satchel and took out the evidence she'd taken from Vedoran. When she got to her quarters she locked her door, lit a candle, and carried it up the ladder to the window seat. By the faint light she read the evidence again. If she didn't read certain books or papers often, the words tended to rearrange themselves so she could no longer understand them. She had to keep watch over the pages carefully so they didn't try to trick her.

She read the notes and looked at the maps again. Would they be infected by Ashok's lies? Would they try to tell her a tale of innocence, when she knew Ashok to be guilty?

His eyes had tried to tell her the same tale. Ilvani remembered the pain in them, not from the wounds she'd inflicted, but from the thought of *her* suffering.

Ilvani clenched the pages in her hands. Deceiver. He wants you to pity him.

"That's not true," came a voice.

Ilvani started. She looked wildly around the room, but there was no one else there, only the long shadows staring at her from the corners of the room. They always stared at her, but she ignored them as usual.

It must have been her own voice speaking. She just hadn't recognized it.

She folded the maps and held them in her hands. Nothing had changed. Ashok's guilt was written in his own hand. All that remained was for her to take the evidence to Uwan. She should do it now while everything was clear.

"He was ready to die for you," came the voice.

"Stop it!" Ilvani said, covering her ears with her hands. She knew that voice, and it wasn't hers. It was the voice of dead hopes, of the person she used to be.

"Please look at me, sister. There is not much time."

Ilvani choked on a sob. She forced her hands down to her sides and turned unwillingly to look at her brother.

He stood at the foot of the ladder, looking up at her with a smile. The pose, the affection was so familiar she felt she was being ripped in two.

"It's not real," she said. She found herself using that phrase a great deal when she was alone. When Natan was around, he used it for her.

"I've seen you many times this way," Natan said. His skin looked healthy, and he'd put on weight. He'd always been beautiful, her brother, even when he'd stopped taking care of himself so he could talk to Tempus. She'd always resented the god for taking her brother away from her.

"You're in the box," Ilvani said. "I saw them put you in and cover you up. They buried you with swords. I wanted to bury you with silk."

"You know me best," Natan said. "Sister, you must set him free."

"He's a liar," Ilvani replied. He deceives beyond death, she thought. How powerful was Ashok?

"He told you the truth," Natan said. "And you know it, else I would not be here."

"You think you're putting the words together in my mind for me, but you're not," Ilvani said. "It's a trick." She scooted back against the window and wrapped her arms around herself. "I know what he did."

"He rescued you from something worse than death," Natan said. "In doing so, he betrayed his own people. He will never forgive himself for that, just like you will never forgive yourself for what happened to you in that cage. You'll both hate and condemn yourselves until you destroy yourselves."

"You don't know," Ilvani said. "You don't know either of us."

"I know you, sister," Natan said gently. "More now than I ever have. I see your mind, and I know what it's like to live inside you. You must forgive him. If you don't, everything that has happened will be for nothing."

Ilvani clutched the parchment sheets against her chest. Her eyes strayed to the candle beside her. Its wavering flame held her gaze as Natan's words held her in thrall.

"No!" she said. She shook her head to break the spell. "He killed you. No forgiveness for that."

Her brother sighed, an exasperated expression Ilvani knew well. It almost made her smile through her pain. "You were always the stubborn one," he said. "Look inside yourself, sister. You know the truth. He's been trying to tell you, but you're blocking him."

"I'm not," Ilvani said hotly. She crawled to the ladder and shook a rung. "He's never liked me. Not my fault."

"Now you're being absurd," Natan said. "He knows what you

endured in that cage. He holds you in the highest honor. You are stronger than you know, Ilvani. He thinks you are a wonder, and so do I."

Ilvani laid her forehead against the ladder. Tears ran down her cheeks and neck. "I don't want you . . . to see me," she sobbed.

"You are beautiful," Natan said, "powerful and wise beyond the limits of your mind. No one can take that away from you. Open your heart, Ilvani, and it will show you the truth. I will always be here when you need me."

The ladder moved beneath her. Ilvani looked up, wild with hope that her brother had come up to embrace her, to make everything all right again.

There was no one there.

Sobbing, Ilvani crawled back to the window. She took up the evidence against Ashok and held the sheets over the candle. The parchment darkened and curled. Orange flame licked up the sides, consuming ink and surface so fast Ilvani had to drop and stamp them out with a cup she'd left by the window. The ashes flew up into her face.

She gathered them and the unintelligible scraps that remained and put them in one of the empty boxes in her satchel. When she closed the lid, the lock slid into place without her touching it.

"Ashok box," she said. "Has all the ashes. Are you happy, brother?"

She flung out a hand. The window glass shattered, and the shards dug into her hand. She bent over the box, sobbing anew.

Too late. She'd done it—given her brother's murderer his freedom. What a worthless, worthless sister, an ugly failure.

"I won't forgive you," she cried, and wiped her hand across her face, streaking tears and blood. "Won't . . . won't."

The box snapped open.

Ilvani stared at it. The locks were magical. They only answered to her. She reached for the lid, but it wouldn't move. She tried with both hands, but it wouldn't shut. Grunting, she put her full weight against the hinges. Nothing.

She looked inside the box. The ashes were gone. Instead, she saw something that shouldn't have been there.

Within the box, she saw Tempus's chapel. Two tiny figures moved around in the scene like dolls. She recognized Natan sitting on the steps, and she thought it was Ashok next to him, but when she looked closer she realized it was Vedoran.

The tiny dolls were speaking, but she couldn't hear what they were saying. Natan looked upset, not at all as he'd appeared in her room. Ilvani wondered what the cause was, and hoped it wasn't herself.

What she saw next nearly made her throw the box out the broken window.

Vedoran leaned toward Natan and put his hands around her brother's throat. He squeezed, and Natan's eyes widened in panic.

"No!" she cried. She clutched the box, shook it, as if she could make the tiny Vedoran doll let her brother go. But the figures kept on and ignored her shouts and pleas and thrashing. She watched her brother die—at Vedoran's hands.

Natan's body fell across the steps. Vedoran looked as stunned as Ilvani felt. He staggered away from the body, and the scene blurred. When it came back into focus, there were other dolls present, though she didn't know them. They removed Natan's body, and when one turned to speak to Vedoran she saw the symbol of Beshaba at their breasts.

"All the misfortunes in the world belong to me," Ilvani said. She thought it might have been the words to a song she'd once heard, but there were so few songs in Ikemmu that weren't battle hymns, she couldn't be sure.

She closed the box lid and listened to the wind whistle through the broken glass shards. She knew who had sent the vision. "Thank you, Tempus," she said, "for putting the truth in the boxes." She added, "But stay out of them now. I can do it myself."

CHAPTER
TWENTY-EIGHT

Ashok awoke to the guards chaining his hands behind him. He was blind again, and weak as a newborn, but the searing pain in his chest and neck was gone.

"Ilvani?" he said. He could barely hear his own voice.

"He's fading," one of the guards murmured, as if Ashok wasn't present. "Good thing we're moving him now, or there'd be nothing left for the trial."

The guards each grabbed one of his shoulders and led Ashok forward. It took him a few steps to be sure of his footing. His feet felt large and numb inside his boots.

"Ilvani," he repeated. "Where is she?"

"She's been gone a while," one of the guards said. "Left you in pretty bad shape. She called a healer for you."

"Mad witch," the other guard said under his breath.

"Where are we going?" Ashok asked. They were leading him out of the tunnels. The air grew warmer; Ashok could smell the forge smoke. Back to the world of the living, if only for a little while.

"We're to take you to the top of Tower Makthar for judgment," the guard said. "It looks like the whole city has turned out to see what will become of you."

Ashok could tell when they reached the mouth of the tunnel. Crowd noise swelled and filled his ears with a mixture of cheers, jeers, and speculative murmuring. On the issue of his guilt, Ikemmu seemed equally divided.

"Part the way!" the guards shouted. "By order of Uwan, stand back!"

Their pace slowed almost to a halt. Ashok felt the heat of bodies pressing close. The voices grew louder and louder, and Ashok found himself thinking of the nightmare being paraded through Ikemmu in a cage.

Something hard hit Ashok in the shoulder. Numb pain shot up his arm, and one of the guards shouted, "The next one to throw a punch or a stone will be on his knees before Lord Uwan! Do you all hear?"

The other guard kept Ashok moving forward. More hands touched Ashok, but with gentleness.

"Tempus bless you!"

"We believe."

"Free the emissary!"

Ashok tried to pull away, but he couldn't escape the hands. He stumbled, fell, and was dragged up again to the march that would never end.

Finally, the guards stopped. A fist pounded on a door, which opened on creaking hinges.

"Inside," a familiar voice said. "Give him a rest before you take him to the stairs."

"Weak as a babe," another voice said, and Ashok's heart lifted. "Did I not teach you anything?"

"Cree," Ashok said. "Skagi."

The hood came off, and Ashok found himself being guided to a bench against the wall by the brothers.

"Uwan ordered he be hooded at all times," Ashok's guard said. "I won't take responsibility."

Cree snorted. "We'll take it, if it comforts you, but look at him. He's not got the strength to walk on his own, much less teleport out of here."

"Your heads," the guard said, and they left the tower.

When they were alone, Skagi sat down next to Ashok and leaned against the wall. "Well, you know how to attract the most attention, I'll give you that," he said.

Cree put a waterskin in front of Ashok's mouth. He tipped it up and let him drink deeply. Ashok had never tasted anything so sweet and cold. He started to feel stronger, and his head was beginning to clear.

"How long has it been?" he said.

"Since they put you in the dark? Three days," Skagi said. "We thought you'd be in better shape than you are. Uwan thought so too. He was pretty upset when he saw you."

"Uwan was in my cell?" Ashok said. He had no memory of the leader being with him since he'd made his confession. "What happened to Ilvani?"

"She's waiting for us at the top," Cree said.

On hearing that, Ashok stood. "Let's go," he said.

"We can take some time," Cree said. "Uwan told us to be certain you were strong enough to make it to the top."

"It doesn't matter," Ashok said. "We all know what the outcome will be. Let's get it over with."

Reluctantly, Skagi and Cree fell into step beside him, and they started the climb. Ashok had never been bothered before by the height or the hundreds of steps that wound up the towers, but that time he felt each burning step as he pulled himself slowly up the risers. Looking down made it worse as it forced him to count each step. He tried looking up, but the effect was so dizzying he had to stop and clear his head. Cree and Skagi steadied him, and they went on.

After walking in silence for a time, Ashok said, "Why did you come?"

"Uwan asked us," Cree said. "He wanted you to see some friendly faces."

"Is that true?" Ashok said. He caught himself holding his breath, hoping. "Is that what you are?"

Skagi sighed. "We were unfriendly for a while—would have been a lot easier if you'd told us what you knew in those caves."

"I know," Ashok said. "It was selfish, and it almost got us killed."

Cree nodded, acknowledging the words. Skagi said, "But when we talked about it—understand, I don't intend to admit this more than once—we realized you were the only reason we made it out of there alive. You picked your side, and that's good enough for us."

"We aren't the only ones who feel that way," Cree said. "Most of the military feels you should receive clemency, but then there are the Beshabans and the few Sharrans that have come out of their holes to protest that you should be executed. Vedoran stands with the Beshabans now, and shouts loudest. But there's been"—Ashok thought Cree sounded smug—"a development nobody expected."

"What is it?" Ashok asked.

"No time; we're here," Skagi said. He looked at Ashok warily. "If I leave the hood off, will you promise to behave? I'd hate to have to chase you outside the walls again."

Ashok smiled briefly at the memory. "I've got nothing to run from anymore."

At the tower summit, the wind howled as Ashok had never heard it before. He had to bend into the wind to move forward. Lightning from Tower Makthar's spikes played above their heads and struck the stone spikes in irregular intervals. The air was charged and smelled of fire. The shadows seemed close and black like hovering demons.

Across the tower from them stood several figures, including Uwan and Ilvani beside him. Ashok had to look twice before he recognized the witch.

She was dressed in a simple, long-sleeved black dress, and her hair was tied tightly at the back of her head. She wore a long black cloak with an overlay of silver chains, and at her belt she wore her green satchel. Her hand kept straying to it as if for comfort. She glanced at him and quickly looked away.

Uwan wore a neutral expression as Ashok, Skagi and Cree came across the tower to stand before him. He had his greatsword in his hands, its point downward between his spread feet. Next to him, but clearly apart, stood Vedoran and a group of male and female shadar-kai. Ashok didn't know them, but he saw the holy symbols they wore.

Beshaba and Shar—goddesses of misfortune and night. To my left stands oblivion, Ashok thought, and to my right salvation. He stepped away from Cree and Skagi and approached both groups.

Below them, the crowd noise swelled to a rumbling thunder. A storm created by the shadar-kai was about to burst.

Uwan spoke, and his voice was magically deepened, amplified to carry across the city. "I call upon you, shadar-kai of Ikemmu, to hear evidence against Ashok, a shadar-kai who is accused of treason and willful deceit of the city of Ikemmu and its citizens. I call upon Vedoran to stand as accuser and to present evidence for his claim. Step forward, Vedoran."

Vedoran came forward, and the contingent of clerics followed close behind him. He approached Uwan, and Ashok could see that something was definitely amiss. Vedoran looked agitated, more so than Ashok had ever seen him. When Chanoch had disobeyed orders, he hadn't looked so undone. Vedoran turned a black glare on Ilvani as he approached, but the witch stared through him as if he were made of smoke.

"My Lord Uwan," Vedoran said, and his voice too was amplified to carry. Ashok could see it took all his willpower to spit the words of respect for the whole city to hear. "I regret to say that I am unable to produce evidence against Ashok."

Uwan looked grave. "You bring a serious accusation to bear against your fellow shadar-kai. I trust you would not waste our time with pretenses?"

"I would not, my Lord," Vedoran said. He stared at Ilvani with pure hatred, so intense that Ashok and Uwan each took a step forward. Skagi came forward and put a hand on Ashok's shoulder to hold him back.

"The evidence which I intended to present to you has been lost," Vedoran continued, "taken, though I have no proof of that claim either, save my word."

"Your word the city once held good," Uwan said, "but now it is called into question. The claims you make are substantial, yet they go unsupported. Based on the lack of evidence, what judgment can I hand down?"

Cheers and anger came from the crowd, and Vedoran didn't immediately answer. Behind him, one of the Beshabans, a man, stepped forward.

"My Lord Uwan, if I may?" he said.

Uwan nodded. "Speak, Traedis, servant of Beshaba," he said.

"The evidence, or lack thereof, has been rendered moot by the accused's own confession. From his lips you heard the story of his deception in the caves where our people were being tortured and butchered. You heard him say that he planned to give vital information about the defenses of this city to his enclave. He has confessed to all the crimes of which he stands accused. Nothing remains but sentencing."

"We hear you, Traedis of Beshaba," Uwan said. "Yet I would put forth the following to dispute your argument. You claim Ashok betrayed Ikemmu, yet I have here"—he reached inside his cloak and pulled out several sheets of parchment with scrawled writing in various hands—"written testimony vouching for Ashok's character, testimony offered without coercion by no less than three shadar-kai in good standing with this city; one human merchant, Tatigan, who is known to all; and a halfling, Darnae, a prominent lady of business in the trade district. What say you to their words? They speak in praise of Ashok's character."

Ashok felt a swell of warmth, the first hint he'd had that there was something still alive inside him. He couldn't read what was written on the parchment, but seeing the ink Darnae and the rest had spent in his defense bolstered him as nothing else had.

"My Lord," Traedis said, and he sounded amused, "I could produce twenty, fifty such accounts for and against the accused, simply by sifting my hand through the crowd below. The opinion of the people does not prove guilt or innocence."

"You're right," Uwan said, "it does not. But these accounts are not the only testimonials I offer. You were wrong about one of your statements before, Traedis. You said that Ashok confessed to all the crimes of which he was accused."

"That is so," Traedis said.

"I submit that the accused did not confess to the murder of Natan, servant of Tempus," Uwan said. He looked at Ashok and addressed him for the first time. "Is this correct?"

"It is," Ashok said. "I didn't murder Natan." He looked at Ilvani as he said it, but she ignored him. She was a wax doll, only half present for the proceedings.

"Very well," Uwan said. "Ikemmu has heard from Vedoran, and Traedis of Beshaba, and from the accused himself. There is one among us who has yet to speak." Uwan turned to Ilvani, and the neutral mask he wore cracked just enough to show his uncertainty. He was not sure what was going to happen next, Ashok thought. None of them were. The collective at the top of the tower held its breath as Ilvani stepped to the fore.

CHAPTER
TWENTY-NINE

ILVANI CLOSED HER EYES, AND WHEN SHE OPENED THEM IT WAS AS
if she'd drifted back down into her body from some other place she'd
been. She gazed at all of them in turn, even Ashok. But when she
spoke, her eyes were on the crowd.

"I address the shadar-kai of Ikemmu," she said, in a voice that
magically enhanced made her seem like an immense entity occupying
a tiny, fragile body. "I come to offer my testimony in defense of
Ashok, and to bring you the vision Tempus has shown me. He has
come to me with the truth."

The crowd fell into a hush at her pronouncement, but the
Beshabans and the Sharrans erupted in protest at once. Vedoran
looked stunned. His gaze went back and forth between Ashok and
Ilvani, as if there were some private conspiracy between them that
he could root out. Once again, Ilvani ignored him completely.

"My Lord," Traedis said, and made an impatient gesture for his
companions to be silent. "I must protest. With all respect to Natan's
memory, his visions were never presented as evidence in the trials
of citizens. What credence can we give to—you'll forgive me, my
Lord—a madwoman?"

"You are not forgiven, Traedis, for addressing a servant of Tempus
with such disrespect," Uwan said. His hand tightened on his sword

hilt. "But I will address your concerns. Natan's visions were often used to guide this city in matters of trade and war, and in turn the city prospered. You voiced no objection at those times. Ilvani is sister to Natan. They are of the same blood and share Tempus's favor."

"I mean no disrespect," said Traedis. He was growing impatient, Ashok thought, eager to have the argument dismissed before the situation slipped out of his control. "I meant only to say that perhaps Tempus's vision may become clouded when filtered through her mind. She is blessed of Tempus and this city—I do not deny it. But she is not unaffected by the rigors of the world. They have damaged her mind. You know I speak the truth."

"Granted," Uwan said. His eyes were still dangerous. "But we shall hear the vision, and let all who witness be the judge of its merits."

Ilvani had been waiting all that time, patient and serene, until the two men finished their confrontation. She continued speaking as if nothing had happened.

"Tempus showed me my brother, Natan, conversing with the shadar-kai who would be his murderer," Ilvani said. Her voice wavered, and the calm façade almost slipped. She swallowed and went on. "They spoke as comrades. Natan trusted this shadar-kai and was betrayed. Vedoran"—she pointed an accusing finger at the sellsword, and Ashok thought he saw black energy crackling at her fingers—"killed my brother. So says Tempus, and so say I."

The crowd below, stunned silent by Ilvani's revelation, waited for the Beshabans to respond. Traedis bowed his head respectfully to Ilvani. She made no response.

"Your accusation is heard," Traedis said, "but my objection to its use as evidence stands. The only indisputable proof we have that a crime was committed is Ashok's confession. My Lord, we must act upon it, or you make a mockery of justice in Ikemmu." Traedis's voice rose, and the crowd rose with him in mixed tumult.

Uwan held up his hands and said, "Ikemmu speaks, and you are heard. I will pass my judgment and you, Traedis of Beshaba, will declare its merit."

Traedis bowed, and the rest of the Beshabans and Sharrans murmured their assent. Ashok faced Uwan while Skagi and Cree stood behind him.

The leader of Ikemmu approached, and when he spoke to Ashok the words came without magic, so that only Ashok and his companions heard them.

"I was wrong," Uwan said. "I have wronged you and this city, and on your shoulders rest the weight of those mistakes." He looked Ashok in the eyes. "But you are stronger than you know. Tempus believes you can bear this burden, and so do I. I believe in you."

He turned to the crowd, and his voice rose again in judgment. "On the weight of Ashok's confession we condemn him to the shadows."

The crowd exploded. Some of their reaction was excited applause, but there was also a strong uproar of disapproval.

Traedis smiled in satisfaction and said, "You are wise, my Lord Uwan."

Uwan looked at the cleric and the rest of the Beshabans. He spoke over the crowd. "There will be a provision to the sentence."

Traedis's smile froze on his face. Vedoran seethed in quiet rage, though only Ashok was paying attention to him.

"We will hear the provision," Traedis said neutrally.

"In light of Ashok's service to Ikemmu, we offer him this one chance to redeem himself and earn the city's forgiveness," Uwan said. He glanced meaningfully at Ashok. "When Chanoch was sentenced to the shadows, ten days elapsed before Tempus claimed him. I give this fate to Ashok. If, after ten days, Tempus has not claimed his soul, Ashok will be forgiven by the gods and by this city. He will be set free."

Traedis considered for a breath, then stepped back to confer with the other clerics. Several of them glanced at Ashok, their gazes accusing.

"Look at them. They're laying odds on how long you'll last," Skagi muttered.

"The way I feel right now, even I wouldn't bet on me," Ashok said.

Vedoran went to speak to Traedis. Ashok couldn't understand what was said, but Vedoran gestured angrily with his hands, and his expression got blacker with each passing breath. Finally he stalked off by himself, and Traedis turned to address Uwan again.

"We agree to your terms, Lord Uwan," Traedis said. Amid the ensuing roar of the crowd, he added, in a voice that did not magically carry from the tower, "You take a grave risk, my Lord. If the accused does not survive the ten days, it will send a powerful message that Tempus's might in Ikemmu is not infallible. If His emissary falls, who might be next?"

Beside him, Ashok felt Skagi and Cree stiffen. Cree went for his katar, but Uwan barked, "Peace. This is a seat of judgment. No violence will touch this place." He glared at Traedis. "You have your terms. Go and take your brethren. The sentence will begin at once."

One by one, the Beshabans and Sharrans went down. Vedoran went to Traedis, and it was clear the two were arguing again as they left.

Ilvani went to the edge of the tower and looked down. Uwan went to stand beside her. Skagi and Cree led Ashok away.

When they got to the bottom of the tower, Ashok's guards were waiting to escort him, but Skagi waved them off. "We'll take him," he said.

Outside Makthar, the crowd had mostly dispersed—helped along, Ashok thought, by the presence of dozens of ranking warriors of Ikemmu's military. Ashok was grateful for their presence. He didn't know if he had the strength to walk through that crowd again, engulfed by such measures of adoration and hate.

The walk back to the deep tunnels was a sluggish march. Skagi and Cree were subdued; Ashok knew they were drawing out the journey as much as possible, giving him a chance to work his muscles and gain a hold on the world. He would need it.

They passed the Camborr training grounds and the paddock where the nightmare had scorched the earth and where Ashok had first learned to ride the magnificent beast. He wondered where the nightmare was now, and if it had found a new master, one more bloodthirsty than he.

Olra passed by them on her way out of the tunnels. She said nothing, but her eyes met Ashok's, and she nodded. Her arm brushed his and then she was gone.

They stopped at the cave entrance, and Ashok turned for what he thought could be his last look at the city of towers.

The city appeared before him as it had in the portrait Ilvani had painted. The watching eye stared down at the city, and the carved, winged humanoids cavorted on the outside of the towers. Below them, the shadar-kai and the other races went back to their daily business in the city they'd adopted from their winged watchers.

Whether they were Tempus's angels or the last pictures of a dead race, Ashok would never know. But he could feel their presence. He thought that must be legacy enough.

"I'm ready," he told the brothers, and walked with them into the dark.

The guards at the door chained Ashok in his cell and put the hood back over his face. Skagi and Cree had refused those duties, but they stayed with him after the guards left. Ashok heard Skagi scuffing his boots against the floor restlessly. Cree was his normal, utterly silent self, but Ashok felt the weight of his concern.

"I'll be all right," Ashok told them.

" 'Course you will," Skagi said. "We ever say you wouldn't be?"

"He was right, you know," Cree said. "What Uwan told you—remember it. You'll be the one to determine your fate."

"Uwan said it's up to Tempus," Ashok said.

"I don't think so," Cree said. "Not this time. You live by your own will, or you'll give yourself to the shadows." He touched Ashok's shoulder. "But the gods be with you anyway, my friend."

Skagi coughed and patted his arm awkwardly. "Be well," he said.

Then they were gone, and Ashok settled into the darkness for a long, silent vigil.

CHAPTER
THIRTY

VEDORAN STOOD IN THE HALF-RUIN OF THE OLD HOUSE AND TRIED to keep from killing Traedis where he stood.

"You betrayed me," he said. "Ashok lives."

"Not for long," Traedis said. "My brethren are confident that he will not survive the ordeal. Uwan has too much faith in Tempus and in Ashok. Ashok will fade, and it will be but the first of many blows we strike against Tempus and Uwan. Be patient, Vedoran, and you will have the satisfaction you crave."

"You don't know Ashok," Vedoran said. "If there is a way, even the slightest hope—"

"There is none," Traedis said, growing agitated. "I am a servant of Beshaba and I know the face of hopelessness. You've won your battle against Ashok. His guilt and shame eat at him, and the shadows will do the rest of the work. You must trust me."

"That was my mistake," Vedoran said. He turned to leave. "You won't see me again."

Ashok passed the rest of the day and the next in darkness and silence. He awoke on the third day, but it may as well have been the fifth. He was numb again and had no sense of himself beyond the breath moving his chest. The blood had drained from his arms, and his legs wouldn't move no matter how much he tried to shift his position.

Once, wakeful, he bit his lip. He needed to taste the blood in his mouth, to feel something. He found an already festering wound. The pain and infection shuddered through his body, and Ashok wondered how many times he'd woken with the idea as if it were new. He sweated fever, and chills wracked his body. But that wasn't the worst of it.

The worst came when he began dreaming.

He stood chained in his cell, blind, yet somehow he could see. His father and brothers walked through the wall and stood in the corner of the cell.

Ashok stared at them. Shadows swirled around them and grew faces and emaciated hands that plucked at their arms and legs. They ignored them and stared back at Ashok. Whispering to each other, they pointed at him.

Ashok couldn't understand what they were saying, but he saw the condemnation on their gaunt, dead faces. He strained toward them and was shocked when the chains fell away from his arms. The shadows swallowed the cage bars and the cave until Ashok walked in a void toward his family, who continued to talk to each other as if he wasn't there.

"Why have you come here?" Ashok demanded. "Speak!"

His father stepped apart from the rest and took some of the living shadows with him. They scurried around his feet and laid their heads against his boots. Ashok tried not to look at them and their ratlike movements.

"We've been waiting for you," his father said.

"For a long time," said his brother Lakesh, stepping forward with shadows caressing his hair.

"You're dead," Ashok said. "There's nothing left for you here."

"You're still here," his father said. "We have no other link, no other amusements, and no god calls us from the void."

"You have to go," Ashok said. He backed away, but the void was limitless, black, and swirling. It was madness to watch it, for above and below him the faces swelled out of the shadows and reached for him.

"Where else can we go?" Reltnar said as he stepped out of the shadows to join Ashok's brothers. "What place would have us?"

"You're in my mind," Ashok said. "You're not welcome here."

His father laughed. "How do you know this is your place?" he said. "How can you know you haven't crossed over to our domain, the nothingness after sleep?"

Ashok recoiled. Was it over then? Had he already lost his soul to the shadows? "Father," he said, "you, all of you didn't fade. You were killed."

"You killed us," Reltnar said, and a shadow skull nuzzled against his neck. He batted it away like a fly. "No god calls us home."

"No one wants us anymore," Lakesh said, "so we'll stay with you."

"No," Ashok said. He looked down and saw the shadow figures swimming up toward him through the void. They reached for his boots, and he danced away from them. He smelled foul breath and in the distance heard the constant Shadowfell wind. "I don't belong here," he said.

"You were always going to end up here," his father said in a mock-soothing voice. "Didn't you ever think of that?"

"I . . ." Out of the corner of his eye, Ashok saw a figure dressed in black striding through the void. The shadow was just as small and emaciated as the rest, yet it stood apart from its brethren. Silver light outlined its body, and when it came near Ashok saw the other shadows shy away from the light and the waves of heat emanating from its body.

"What is it, son?" his father asked.

"I saw something," Ashok said. He looked again, but the figure was too far off for clarity. "We're still in the Shadowfell," he said. "I can hear the wind. But I've never seen this place before."

"This is the veil between one life and the next," Reltnar said. "You can't see beyond it."

"Then who are these?" Ashok said, swiping at the shadows that were clinging to his clothes and hair.

He searched for the figure in black, and found it still walking toward him, though it might have been a mile or a century distant. But its course was set to intercept them, and it walked patiently, unhurried by shadows. Ashok felt the urge to go to meet the figure, but he did not want to be cast off like one of the ghastly shadows.

"They are waiting here," his father said. He put his hand through one of the shadow skulls and shook until the thing dissolved into smoke. "No god calls them home."

Ashok saw a vision of himself as a grasping shadow—thin, lifeless and pathetic. He wished he could see himself. He held up his hands, but they appeared normal. The pain in his lip felt real.

"Give it time," his brothers said, their voices mingling. "You haven't been here long enough."

Ashok felt hysteria creeping in with the shadows. They were all over him, and he couldn't take a breath that was not foul. Dead things and cold hands all over his skin—he cried out, and his father and brothers mockingly cried out with him. His own voice was lost in the chorus and laughter.

"Damn you," he told his father, and allowed the hatred to course through him. "If you'd listened to me, none of this would have happened. You might be alive. Our enclave might have flourished."

"To what purpose?" Reltnar said. "Didn't we survive? Didn't we live by our own will, as you have done?"

"It's not enough," Ashok said, but they couldn't hear him over their own laughter. "Damn you all, it wasn't enough. All you cared about was yourselves."

Suddenly, the laughter stopped. Into the ensuing silence walked the figure in black with its tail of silver light. It walked into the space between Ashok and his family. His father and brothers stared in awe.

Ashok recognized the figure then, and a wave of profound relief washed over him. The figure turned and walked to his side, away from his father and brothers, and cleared the shadows that clung to Ashok.

"Ilvani," he said.

The witch smiled. "I told you I'd come with you when you went to the Veil," she said.

CHAPTER
THIRTY-ONE

Ilvani waved the shadows away from Ashok, and he could breathe again.

"You shouldn't pay them so much attention," she said. "They'll stay if you do."

Ashok looked at his family, but his father and brothers had been rendered mute by Ilvani's sudden appearance. They stared at her as if she were a beacon they were afraid to touch.

"This is the end, isn't it?" Ashok said. "I'm going to the shadows. My soul will be gone."

"This is the unknown," Ilvani said. "Domain of fear. Will I die bravely? Will my god find me among the shadows? Will I lose my soul? That's where you are now. You've always been here, all your life. Why should you be afraid of it now that it has a face?"

"Is this the fate of all shadar-kai?" Ashok said.

"This is their fate," Ilvani said, pointing without looking at Reltnar and Ashok's family, who cowered from her. "Are you with them, or didn't you make another choice?"

"I tried to," Ashok said. "But it all went wrong."

"Are you certain?" Ilvani said.

"I deceived the companions I trusted," Ashok said. "I slaughtered the only family I ever knew."

"So your punishment is to exist here with them in the void," Ilvani said. "No matter that Ikemmu forgives you, or the gods, because there is no forgiveness in Ashok for himself."

"Yes. I exist here because I deserve to be here," Ashok said.

"You have always existed here," Ilvani said, "in fear. Now you have an excuse to stay."

"I'm not afraid," Ashok said. "I accept my fate."

Ilvani reached up and touched his cheek. "You are selfish. You lay down to fade while others fight for you."

Ashok felt the warmth of her hand, and a vision of Uwan flashed into his mind.

You are stronger than you know. Tempus believes you can bear this burden, and so do I.

Skagi's face came next, and Cree's. Olra in the training yard. Chanoch in his cell.

The gods be with you, my friend.

He blinked the vision away and saw Ilvani again with the court of shadows behind her. "Do their words mean nothing?" she said.

Ashok swallowed his grief. He felt the weight of their acceptance of him, and for the first time he felt warmed by more than Ilvani's presence. "What of you?" Ashok said. "I was ready to give my life to make it better for you."

"I am not who you think I am," Ilvani said. "But if you decide to leave this place, you will see what you need to see."

Ashok closed his eyes. "I don't want to be here anymore," he said. "Please . . ."

Pain swamped him then, so much at once that he thought he would explode from it. He gasped and opened his eyes.

He was back in his cell, unchained and unhooded, lying on the cold floor. He tried to move, but his joints were so cramped that every muscle in his body screamed.

Fighting to stay conscious, Ashok pushed himself up on his elbows. He saw, on the floor in front of him, a small object. He picked it up and saw that it was a small box made of velvet-covered wood. He recognized it as one of Ilvani's many containers she'd spilled out of her bag that day he'd gone to see her.

The lock was open. He raised the lid and saw within a pile of ashes. He scooped them out with a finger. A few of the blackened scraps had unburned edges, scraps of parchment. He recognized his own writing on them, the evidence Vedoran had taken from him while he was unconscious.

"Ashok box," Ashok said. "Full of ashes." He closed the lid and held the box in his hands.

"I wondered what she'd done with them," said a voice that Ashok knew well. He looked up and saw Vedoran standing outside his cell.

"Are you real?" Ashok said. It was the first thought that came to his mind.

Vedoran laughed without humor. "I can see why you'd ask that. No one thought you'd survive the tenday, but I told them you were strong."

"Has it been that long?" Ashok said.

"You wouldn't have felt the passage of time, after a while," Vedoran said. "You still look faint, like you're not truly present in the world. I wonder if that will make you easier or harder to kill."

"Is that why you've come?" Ashok said. He didn't feel surprise or betrayal, only a sense of pervading calm that grew stronger by the breath. He'd survived the worst of it. He wasn't afraid. There were no shadows here.

Vedoran unlocked the door to his cell and tossed the keys aside. There was blood on them. "We won't be disturbed," he said.

"You know I'm too weak to fight you," Ashok said. He was too weary even to stand before Vedoran.

"I told you, if I kill you, I kill Tempus," Vedoran said. "It doesn't matter what Ikemmu thinks anymore." He drew his sword and came forward, his movements methodical, with none of the grace Ashok had once seen in him. That was all gone. He positioned his blade for a strike that would take off Ashok's head.

"Vedoran!"

Ashok and Vedoran both jumped at the shout. Vedoran turned, giving Ashok a view of Uwan standing in the dungeon doorway, the bodies of the guards at his feet.

"What have you done, Vedoran?" Uwan cried.

"I have become everything I was made to be," Vedoran said. "A Blite on Ikemmu."

Uwan stared at him in disbelief. "This bloodshed is not you," he said. "The Beshabans have poisoned your mind, taken away your honor."

Vedoran laughed. "No, my Lord," he said. "My mind was a foul place before the Beshabans found it. I have you to thank for that. When I kill your emissary"—he swept a hand at Ashok—"you will have no one but yourself to blame."

Uwan drew his sword, but he did not enter the cell. There was no room to fight there, and Vedoran was dangerous in close combat. Ashok remembered his skill in the tunnels when he'd been hounded by enemies from all sides.

"I didn't think Vedoran would allow himself to be ruled by envy," Uwan said. He paced outside the cage bars.

"You think that's what this is?" Vedoran said. He took a step away from Ashok. He'd not fully grasped Uwan's bait, but he was distracted.

Ashok tried to get up. He made it to his knees and fell hard on the stone floor. He cursed his weakness, but his faint voice was drowned out by Vedoran's laughter.

"Stay still, little one," Vedoran taunted him. "I'll come back for you soon." He turned his attention to Uwan. "Did you ever see the vistas of the empire, Uwan?"

"Netheril has no place here," Uwan said. He backed up to let Vedoran exit the cell and took up a defensive stance.

"Now who speaks with envy in his voice?" Vedoran said as he struck his sword off Uwan's. But the leader did not flinch. "Isn't that what you would create here—an empire of your own, with shrines to Tempus in every hall?"

"We can't forsake the gods entirely, Vedoran," Uwan said. "The shadar-kai need guidance."

"Tempus's guidance, and everyone else be damned," Vedoran said. "That was the law you made, and that is the law that will break you as it broke Natan."

He surged forward, and steel rang off steel. Uwan absorbed Vedoran's slash off the edge of his blade, and the bitter shriek hurt Ashok's ears. Uwan countered with a low thrust aimed to hamstring Vedoran. Ashok knew the blow would never land, and he marveled anew at Vedoran's speed as he leaped back, pushed himself off the wall, and came into the fray again.

Ashok dragged himself to his cell door and used the bars to lever himself up. He had to put weight on his feet and get the blood moving through his dead limbs. Pain shot up his arms as he strained to climb the bars. He finally got his feet under him and let his weight drop. The pain was excruciating. He gripped the bars and shook.

The pain—he hadn't inflicted so much on himself in over a month, but his body remembered what it was, and his mind cleared of every thought but staying on his feet. He would endure the pain, use it, and then go after Vedoran.

Outside the cell, Uwan's fight continued. The leader had worked Vedoran around into a corner. With his back to the wall, Vedoran teleported in a blur of shadows that flew around Uwan and coalesced behind him into a wraithlike image of Vedoran.

Uwan turned and thrust automatically. The weapon was an extension of his instincts, and when it passed through Vedoran's shadowy form, Uwan lost his balance. Fortunately, in his incorporeal form, Vedoran couldn't take physical advantage of the misstep. He laughed at Uwan instead.

"You wanted to end this quickly," Vedoran said. "I can see it in your movements. But this isn't that kind of fight. You've forgotten I didn't start out training with your military. I was trained by the sellswords of Pyton. We don't fight with fever in our minds."

"True," Uwan said. He eased back to catch his breath. "But I've seen the fighters of Pyton and Hevalor. They fight with grace, but it's a soulless dance. That's what holds you back from being a truly great warrior, Vedoran. You don't fight for anything but your own survival."

"Survival isn't enough," Ashok said. Speaking was a chore, but he could feel his quivering muscles beginning to balance him again. He didn't dare let go of the bars yet, but he was gaining strength.

Ashok caught Uwan looking at him, assessing his condition. He gave the leader a quick shake of his head, a warning to keep his head in the fight.

Vedoran's shadows fled, his body solidified, and Uwan waded back into the fight as if it had never ceased. They drove each other round and round, into corners, trapping blades, and just when it seemed one would take the other, someone would teleport to escape death.

Ashok couldn't count how many times they repeated the duel cycle, nor did he know how long they could maintain their pace. Both showed signs of fatigue. Uwan's hair stuck to his face in soaking ropes, and Vedoran's breath came fast and loud in the quiet chamber.

"Would it make any difference, Vedoran, if I told you I was wrong?" Uwan said when he'd taken on his own wraith shape for a brief respite. "I wronged you and the other warriors who do not stand for Tempus. If you would let me, I would make amends."

Necrotic energy sizzled in the air around him. So much shadar-kai magic in one place seemed to draw the energy of the Shadowfell to them.

Ashok thought of the living shadows pulling at his body and shuddered. He flexed his muscles and released the bars, testing himself. The room tilted and spun. He grabbed the bars before he fell, ramming his palm against the metal in frustration.

Meanwhile, Vedoran regarded Uwan in amusement. "You don't have Natan to whisper in your ear anymore. If I'd have known his death would bring about such clarity, I'd have killed him long ago."

Uwan shook his head, refusing to take the bait. "It was never Natan. He wouldn't punish anyone for not sharing his beliefs. *I* made the choice, because I thought it was best for Ikemmu to be united, and what better banner of strength could we have to stand under? I thought the rest of the city would see it my way eventually."

"Netheril thought much the same," Vedoran said.

"Yes," Uwan said. "But you always make your choices with the best intentions. You tell yourself you won't let it end that way, not this time. Isn't that what you told yourself, Vedoran, when you swore your oath to Beshaba?"

"But your crime was worse," Ashok said. When Vedoran glared at him, he said, "You had no faith to give them, only the show of it. It isn't too late. You can retain your honor."

As he spoke, Uwan became corporeal. Vedoran didn't see it, and Uwan raised his sword. He came in sharply at the left before Vedoran could get up a defense. The leader put his blade at Vedoran's throat, but he held the strike.

"Yield," Uwan said. "Do as Ashok says: keep your honor, redeem yourself."

"In Tempus's eyes?" Vedoran spat. "Work your blade, Uwan. Your god will never save me."

"Not Tempus," Ashok said. He met Uwan's eyes over the raised steel. "Earn forgiveness from Natan, from yourself."

"From Uwan," Vedoran said.

Uwan shook his head. "There's no need—"

The words ended in a choked gurgle. Uwan stumbled back and dropped his sword. It clattered on the stone amid Ashok's cries of fury.

Vedoran released the hilt of the dagger he'd been holding, the blade now buried in Uwan's chest. The leader grasped the hilt and pulled the blade free before he collapsed on the ground.

"Now you can forgive me," Vedoran said as he kicked Uwan's greatsword across the room and turned to face Ashok. "You're next," he said.

"You bastard," Ashok said. "You worthless, twisted creature." He released the bars. His muscles trembled, but now it was pure rage, a longing for the release that came with killing. Vedoran had done more to invigorate him, to call back the nightmare's master, than he would ever know.

Ashok stepped to the door of the cell. He had no weapon, no armor, just the visceral rage to guide him. Vedoran raised his sword to keep him at a distance, but he looked pleased.

"Almost," he said. "What you need is . . . ah." He went to Uwan and retrieved his bloody dagger from the leader's slack fingers. He tossed it to Ashok, who caught it without thinking, letting the blood smear his palm. "Now we're ready."

"You shouldn't be so smug," Ashok said. He fell into a crouch. "I've killed brothers with blades smaller than this."

"They were weak, just like you," Vedoran said.

He came at Ashok hard and fast with an overhand strike that couldn't be blocked. Ashok dodged, but his reflexes hadn't nearly recovered enough to keep pace with his emotions. He over-compensated and fell on his stomach. Vedoran's sword hissed through the air. Ashok gritted his teeth and teleported. Vedoran's blade rang off the stone floor with another deafening shriek.

Ashok reappeared inside his cell. He stayed in the far corner in his wraith form—the same place where he'd seen his father and brothers and their emaciated shadows, though he tried not to dwell on these thoughts. He thought instead of how to turn the fight to his advantage. That was the first step.

He stayed inside the cell, forcing Vedoran to come to him. The close quarters favored his dagger heavily, and Vedoran couldn't make him dance quite so much with so little room to maneuver.

"Where is the warrior who stood on the Span with me?" Ashok asked. He could feel corporeality seeping back into his limbs, but the question burned at him through the bloodlust. "Where is that shadar-kai who guided me through the nightmares?"

"We're still on that bridge," Vedoran said. "We're still falling. But it's almost over now." He slashed at Ashok's wraith body. The blade passed through his chest but caught his arm as it became flesh and laid it open.

Ashok grunted and clutched the wound. Blood soaked his fingers, but he didn't have time to determine how deep the sword had penetrated, because Vedoran had seen the blood too. He reversed his swing. Ashok blocked feebly with the dagger and tried to twist out of the way.

Vedoran's blade grazed his collarbone. Ashok felt the hot line where it cut him to the shoulder.

No choice. Ashok teleported again, but it took all his strength and concentration. He didn't think he'd be able to attempt the escape again until he'd rested, and Vedoran was already crowding him, forcing him to move in his incorporeal form to find a better position.

"You're tiring quickly," Vedoran said. "Why are you fighting so hard? You know you won't win. If Uwan could fall to me, you don't stand a chance in your current state."

"Uwan trusted you," Ashok said. "That was his mistake. I won't underestimate you or what you're capable of. Not anymore."

"I'm doing you a service," Vedoran said, "killing you now while you're still full of hope. This city does that to you, gives you hope. But even if you survive, they will never accept you fully. You heard the crowd at your trial. Half of them want you dead. Would they embrace you if you came out of these tunnels? Better to die here and never know that disappointment."

"Is that what grieves you the most, Vedoran?" said Ashok, gathering himself for the last exchange of blows. "All the people who have disappointed you? Uwan, the city, the gods . . ."

"You," Vedoran said. He gripped his sword and put it through Ashok's phantom chest, swirling it around his heart. "You disappointed me more than all the others. I would have been more than a brother. You were supposed to be with me."

"I was," Ashok said, "but this is bigger than you or I. Ikemmu is about more than survival. There are things worth protecting here. The city isn't perfect, but there's a future in it. There was no such haven in those caves where I prowled and killed."

His words came faster as his body faded back into the world. When he could hear his boots scrape on stone, Ashok went on the offensive. He dived in under Vedoran's guard and nicked his cheek, a light blow to get the graceful warrior backpedaling.

Vedoran teleported away over Ashok's sudden burst of energy, but he didn't speak, and as soon as he became solid they went at the fight again. Ashok ducked a sharp slash from Vedoran's blade, but he stumbled and fell prone with his dagger arm trapped beneath him. Vedoran came after him. Ashok grabbed his leg and twisted, bringing the warrior down beside him.

Ashok heard Vedoran's sword clatter on the ground. He rolled as Vedoran went for his throat and dug the dagger into Vedoran's shoulder. Pain spasmed across Vedoran's face, but he got his hands inside Ashok's guard and around his throat.

Choking, Ashok tried to pull his dagger out of Vedoran's flesh, but it was wedged against bone, and his strength was rapidly waning. He couldn't draw breath. The room started to spin, and Vedoran, through it all, looked half-crazed, his eyes bulging with triumph as he pressed Ashok's flailing body down and choked the life out of him.

Fading. Ashok felt himself become unmoored from his body, except he was aware of everything. The necrotic energy swirling in the room solidified into reaching shadows, and there was the void again before him, where his father and brothers waited. He wouldn't look at them, Ashok thought. He looked beyond them into the unknown and tried not to be afraid of what waited there.

Ashok glimpsed it then, behind the rest, the form rising up to fill his vision. It no longer wore Ilvani's face, but it cut through the shadows straight to Ashok's heart.

Through his dimming consciousness, Ashok reached up and wrenched the dagger free from Vedoran's shoulder. Vedoran cried out and loosened his grip. Ashok sucked in a desperate breath of air and brought the blade down nearly parallel between them. Driven by a strength Ashok had thought long gone, the blade disappeared into Vedoran's chest and pierced his heart.

Ashok felt Vedoran's whole body stiffen. He flailed, and Ashok caught his hands, holding them as the life drained from the graceful warrior. The breath eased out of Vedoran's chest slowly, and the crazed look left his eyes. He focused for an instant on Ashok's face and tried to speak.

"Say it again," Ashok said, his voice ragged from being strangled. "I couldn't hear."

"Forgive . . ." Vedoran coughed, and there was blood on his lips. "Forgive . . . yourself. Even . . . if I can't."

Ashok clasped the warrior fiercely to his breast. Vedoran drew his last breath, and Ashok felt the body in his arms go limp.

"You're in the shadows now, my friend," he whispered. He hoped that somehow, Vedoran's soul would find its way out of the void. From there he faced a journey beyond mortal knowledge. But the cares of Ashok's world could not touch him.

Ashok gently laid Vedoran's body on the ground. Light-headed with pain and grief, he crawled to Uwan's side and turned the leader's body to face him. He put his head against Uwan's chest and listened for some sign of life. The sign came with the leader's voice.

"You did well," Uwan said. His vacant eyes stared past Ashok at the invisible world full of shadows.

"Don't do this," Ashok said. "I can get healers here before your next breath. Uwan!" he cried when the leader's head lolled.

Uwan licked his lips and coughed. "I saw Him, just now. I saw Him, but He wasn't looking for me. He was watching you. You fought so well . . . You saw His pride, didn't you?"

"I don't know what I saw," Ashok said. "I'm not ready to accept—"

"So . . . stubborn," Uwan said. His lips curved in a weak smile. "Always thinking your life means nothing . . . to the gods. Every life is important."

"Prove it, then," Ashok said. "Live, and prove me wrong."

"I . . . will try."

"Don't look at the shadows," Ashok said. He stood and ran out of the dungeon, following the scent of the forge fires to the light and Tower Makthar. He prayed, to any and all gods listening, that he would make it in time.

CHAPTER
THIRTY-TWO

FOUR DAYS LATER, ASHOK STOOD ON THE TOPMOST SPAN BETWEEN Pyton and Hevalor, his cloak snapping in the wind. He watched the shadar-kai dance in the fire circles over a hundred feet below.

They were preparing a raid on a drow settlement in the Underdark. The Veil between the two parts of the city had been enspelled with golden glows to add to the ferocity of the fire. There were torches all along the wall, and the shadar-kai guarding it were over two hundred strong, or so Skagi and Cree had told him.

Uwan watched the proceedings with his Sworn from the base of Tower Athanon. The leader looked up toward the Span a couple of times, as if searching for Ashok, but Ashok stood behind one of the stone tusks, well hidden in the shadows.

Uwan looked remarkably well for having been near death a handful of days before. Ashok noticed that he did not make any speeches to incite the warriors that night. It was not the time.

Beshaba's clerics had accepted Ashok's pardon by Uwan, but their work to publicly discredit Tempus had met with enough success that people's emotions were still raw. Ashok had no doubt that the clerics of the other gods continued to spread dissent quietly. Uwan meant the raid to help unite the shadar-kai against a common enemy, but they would not soon forget what had transpired over the last month.

Nor should they, Ashok thought. They didn't need to see Tempus's emissary—if that was to be his curse—among them. When the celebration reached its peak, he would quietly slip out of the city. Until then, he waited and watched the fires.

Ashok turned when he heard footsteps coming from the Pyton side of the Span. Ilvani walked with her hands clasped behind her and her head tipped back as if she were enjoying the breeze. She didn't mind her steps at all, but her stride never faltered.

"Aren't you afraid of falling?" he said when she reached him.

She shrugged. "There are more important things to be afraid of," she said.

"Did Uwan send you?" Ashok said.

"I'm made messenger," Ilvani said, with no little disdain, "to ask irrelevant questions. There are more important questions."

"I'm sorry," Ashok said. "I thought putting some distance between me and the leader of the city would be a good idea, especially now."

Ilvani put her hands on her hips. "You have a box you don't want," she said accusingly. "What are you going to do with it?"

Ashok considered. "What do *you* do, when life gives you a box you don't want?"

"Lock it away," Ilvani said. "It's only fair, to survive."

"I have to leave," Ashok said, "because I want Ikemmu to survive."

Ilvani glanced down at the fire circles. She didn't look happy, but her moods changed so quickly it was hard to tell what she was truly feeling. "Not the best way," she said.

"But sometimes necessary."

"Uwan says to give you a message," Ilvani said. "Guardian, if you want it—equal to Skagi and Cree, equal to all who shared your training."

Ashok sighed. "Are we back to that again? After everything?"

Ilvani gestured impatiently. "Don't talk," she said. "He's ready. You're ready. Do you understand?"

"Ready for what?" Ashok said. He could find nothing lucid in the words.

"Uwan always takes things before they're ready," Ilvani said. She stared hard at Ashok. "Not this time."

"You mean, he'll accept my service without the oath to Tempus?" Ashok said. He could hardly imagine that was what she meant, but the witch nodded.

"The prophecy is fulfilled," she said, in a tone of finality.

Ashok was stunned. "But . . . Is Uwan certain? I take no allegiances. I'll make no secret of where I stand—loyalty and service only to Ikemmu."

"He was the one to say it," Ilvani said. "He found the words on his own. They mean something."

Ashok nodded, but he felt lost. "I don't know what to do with this box," he admitted.

Ilvani made a small sound. Ashok, thinking it was laughter, looked up at her, but the woman's face was composed. Whatever emotion she'd betrayed was well hidden.

"What should I do?" he asked her.

"How can I know that?" she said. "I have too many boxes of my own."

"You're right. Thank you," Ashok said. "Thank you for coming to tell me."

Ilvani nodded. She closed her eyes as the wind lifted her hair. She drew in a long breath and let it out. "Feels good," she said.

"What?" Ashok said.

"To see the beginning of something," she replied. "I've seen the end many times."

They stood in silence, until Ashok heard voices down the

bridge from where Ilvani had come.

The witch blew out a frustrated sigh. "I told them to wait. Dogs in heat, they wait for no sign."

Ashok looked and saw Skagi with his brother behind him. He raised a hand to greet them. "I'm fortunate in my companions," he said.

"May you always remember it," Ilvani said quietly, "and keep them safe." She turned and walked briskly back across the bridge without a farewell. When she reached Skagi and Cree she scowled at them and veered out of their path. She stepped off the bridge and walked on air toward Tower Pyton. With her hands clasped behind her back, she walked above the city and never looked down.

"Thank you," Ashok whispered, "for going through the Veil with me."

The brothers were approaching. Ashok could tell them that he was staying. He'd earned the rank of Guardian; Uwan would recognize it before all of Ikemmu. And if the leader held to his word, it would pave the way for the other sellswords and those who did not follow Tempus to join the military, if that was their wish.

Ashok didn't believe in prophecy. Though it was a start, Uwan's declaration would not heal the city's wounds, and it had been Vedoran more than anyone who'd convinced the leader of his error in judgment.

But Ashok couldn't deny the figure he'd seen in the shadows when he'd been near death. It had looked at him, and in that breath Ashok had known he wasn't alone. Something—whether Tempus or a power he could not comprehend—watched the shadar-kai from the shadows with compassion. Maybe that force would be enough to help his race survive.

Maybe someday there would be poets, and grand stories of the shadar-kai that would be passed down through the centuries.

Carrying that hope inside him, Ashok turned to greet Skagi and Cree.

RICHARD LEE BYERS

BROTHERHOOD OF THE GRIFFON

NOBODY DARED TO CROSS CHESSENTA . . .

BOOK I
THE CAPTIVE FLAME

BOOK II
WHISPER OF VENOM
FEBRUARY 2011

BOOK III
THE SPECTRAL BLAZE
FEBRUARY 2012

. . . WHEN THE RED DRAGON WAS KING.

"This is Thay as it's never been shown before . . . Dark, sinister, foreboding and downright disturbing!"
—Alaundo, Candlekeep.com on Richard Byers's *Unclean*

ALSO AVAILABLE AS E-BOOKS!

ABOUT THE AUTHOR

Jaleigh Johnson is the author of the FORGOTTEN
REALMS novels *The Howling Delve* and *Mistshore*. She
lives with her husband in the wilds of the Midwest,
where she enjoys reading, going to movies,
and mucking in the garden. You can visit her online
at www.jaleighjohnson.com.